HEAD WOUNDS

CHRIS KNOPF

HEAD WOUNDS

 RANDOM HOUSE CANADA

www.randomhouse.ca

Random House Canada and colophon are trademarks

Library and Archives Canada Cataloguing in Publication

Knopf, Chris
      Head wounds / Chris Knopf.

ISBN 978-0-307-35658-1

      I. Title.
PS3611.N66H42 2008   813'.6   C2008-900743-3

Text design: CS Richardson

Printed and bound in the United States of America

10 9 8 7 6 5 4 3 2 1

For Mary Elizabeth Farrell,
without whom
none of this would be possible

PART ONE

ONE

THE EVENING STARTED innocently enough, Amanda's outfit notwithstanding.

It was dinnertime at the big place on Main Street in
Southampton Village. Winter and early spring had been
colder than usual, until around April when it snapped out of
it and turned into July, at least for a week. The place had a
full wall of mahogany doors that opened to the street, so you
could feel like you were eating on the sidewalk and still be
within the confines of the restaurant. For the first time that
year they were swung open to catch the inaugural sea
breeze, rich with oxygen and hopeful expectations.

The warm weather had the row of tables next to the big
open doors in such demand they could have been traded on
the commodities market. This being Southampton, probably
half the guys in the place knew how to do that. All I knew
how to do was bring along Amanda, which usually guaranteed the most prominent table in the joint.

The other people there were locals like me who'd suffered the lousy weather with heads down and shoulders braced against the wind. Working people who knew they were forever living at the edge of possibility, with catastrophe and redemption within easy walking distance. The Friday night mood was celebratory and the noise agreeably deafening. The waitstaff was having a nice time managing the surging crowd, sustaining friendships and personal commitments while keeping up with orders for Campari and soda and crab-stuffed filet mignon.

We'd started out at the U-shaped bar. The bartender was a fresh hire, but I knew him from other gigs around the Village. I was helping him analyze the impressive range of vodkas his new employer kept behind the bar. This evolved into a blind taste test to determine the relative merits of the domestic product versus imports from Sweden, Poland and Russia.

Amanda had started out with her usual pinot noir, but was soon swept up in the competition. Being new to the game, it wasn't long before her critical judgment began to erode.

"Now I know why it's called a blind test," she said as I helped her into her seat at the table. "I'm half-blind already."

"It's all in the training."

Whoever made Amanda's dress had apparently forgotten to add the back, conserving even more material around the neck and hemline. I liked the way it looked, but I was more distracted by her green eyes and extravagant head of reddish brown hair.

"You must have a winner in mind," she said.

"A clear one."

We hadn't been out much lately. I'd been working long hours on a big house on the beach for most of the winter, but the end was in sight. More importantly, Frank Entwhistle had thrown a bonus on top of my week's pay to cover a string of ten-hour days. Amanda had also been busy with a pair of knockdowns she had going over on Jacob's Neck. So even if the weather hadn't decided to turn tropical, there was reason enough to act like the world was a convivial place.

The air flowing in from the sidewalk had lost a lot of the heat gained during the unseasonable day, but neither of us cared—our blood thickened to the viscosity of crude oil by months of outdoor labor. Amanda had always worked in an office before turning owner-builder, but she wasn't the type who hid out in the pickup truck with a clipboard and cell phone. More of an on-site operator, she was up and down ladders, schlepping material off trucks, sweeping up sawdust and tossing cut-offs into the dumpster.

She'd inherited Jacob's Neck on the Little Peconic Bay two years earlier—the whole peninsula—and most of the peninsula next door called Oak Point. In between was a lagoon, at the base of which was an abandoned factory owned by the company that owned all the property. Her father had owned the company, so that's how that happened.

One thing she didn't own was my cottage or the land under it, which was at the tip of Oak Point. But she did own the house next door where she'd been living since moving into the neighborhood. All the houses that came with her property had been built as rentals in the middle of the last century—single-story, asbestos-shingled and modestly appointed. It took almost a year for her to figure out what to do with it all. Property values in Southampton had been heading skyward for years, and showed no signs of abating. Especially waterfront. There had been plans once by other people to bulldoze the whole thing, reconfigure the lots and build 8,000-square-foot miniature mansions. There was even more demand for that sort of thing now, but Amanda had grown up in one of those rental homes.

"I'm already set for a lifetime," she'd told me. "Do I want to obliterate part of my past so I can be set for two or three more?"

Two of her places had become available for rehab when the renters moved out, giving her a chance to ease into the project. I helped her find a contractor and connected her with reliable surveyors and appraisers, but that was all either of us wanted me to do. We had enough to sort out without stirring money into the mix. Especially since she had a lot of it and I had enough to maybe cover expenses for the next two or three months. After you factored in the cost of a meal at the big restaurant on Main Street.

I was about to finish off my baked stuffed salmon when something over my shoulder made Amanda frown.

"What?" I asked her.

She looked back at me with a forced smiled.

"Nothing."

I turned around and looked at the crowd thickening around the U-shaped bar.

"Who?" I asked.

"Nobody," she said, but then the frown came back. She reached for her wine glass.

"Hell."

I turned around again and saw Robbie Milhouser walking toward us. It was kind of a rolling walk, the consequence of the weight he carried around his waist, which he almost got away with because the rest of him was also pretty big. He would have had an ex-football player's physique if he'd ever had the ambition to play football. Heavy arms, thick neck and large hands. Wide shoulders stuffed into a blue blazer a size too small. Just north of forty, he had dark brown hair, which he wore long and shaggy, as if still in pursuit of his unsuccessful college career. Somewhere buried inside his hand was a Scotch on the rocks.

"Check out Amanda Battiston," he said, approaching our table.

She sat back in her chair and looked up at him, pondering a response.

"Robbie," she said, in a voice you could use to make ice.

"Can you believe her?" he asked me.

"Most of the time," I said, truthfully.

"I drove by that job of yours over on Jacob's Neck," he said, as if that was a welcome event. "Good-looking lot."

"We're doing our best," she said.

"He working for you?" he asked her, pointing at me, then giving me the privilege of a glance. "I thought you were with Frankie."

"I am. But I wouldn't call him Frankie."

Robbie grinned at the thought of irritating Frank Entwhistle, whose quiet, levelheaded ways could fool you into thinking that would be a safe thing to do.

"Roy really fucked the duck, didn't he?" Robbie said to Amanda. She gave a stiff little jolt I could feel transmitted through the table.

Roy Battiston was Amanda's ex-husband. Roy, Robbie and Amanda all went to Southampton High School together, about twelve years after me. Roy had tried to take control of Amanda's inheritance before she even knew she had one, which was one reason he was now an ex. And also why the next place he'd graduate from was called Hungerford Correctional Facility.

"Let's pick this up where it got left off," he said to Amanda, dropping his bulky frame into the chair next to me. He had plenty of room, but somehow got one of his elbows half-stuck in my meal.

"I didn't think there was anything to leave off from," she said to him.

"Ah, come on. You know about my job over on Bay Edge Drive," he said.

"Is that where it is?" said Amanda, though she knew the place. We'd drive by it on the sand road that takes you over to my friend Paul Hodges's boat, and would occasionally stop in after the crew was gone to check on their progress. It was once a small bayfront cottage, like mine. The owners had bulldozed it and for some incomprehensible reason hired Robbie to build some warped approximation of a French château. From a part of France heavily influenced by the architectural vernacular of Staten Island. I showed Amanda how they were using the wrong substrate for a stucco exterior. Cheaper and easier to construct, but likely to fail in less than five years. Which I suppose would outlast some of Robbie's other failures.

"Well you gotta come over and see this crew I've got," Robbie said to her, undaunted. "These guys're keepers. People want me on those houses on the ocean, but I'd rather stay in North Sea."

He leaned further into the table, his elbow now nudging the edge of my plate toward my lap. I pulled it out of his way.

"I'll see," said Amanda. "I'm pretty busy."

"These guys're all from Up Island. Seen everything. Experienced. You can't get that from these local yahoos. You know what I mean?"

"Not really," said Amanda. "Why don't we ask my dinner date. A local yahoo if I'm not mistaken."

Robbie ignored me.

"You know we got to talk about this," said Robbie. "You got the work, I got the crews. Can I buy you a drink?"

He waved over a waiter, ignoring her attempt to refuse the offer.

"What is that, vodka?" he asked, pointing to her last test

subject, only half-consumed and now fully watered down by the melted ice. "Pretty hard core. Bring her another one," he said to the waiter, who looked at me curiously. I shook my head, so he left.

"Hey, Killjoy," said Robbie to me. "Who asked you?"

I used to work for Robbie's father when I was in high school. He managed a gas station for a while out on County Road 39. I didn't think much of the old man, but I barely remembered his son. Lately I'd seen Robbie around the Village driving a big white pickup with a chrome diamond-plate tool chest mounted in the bed. He'd sometimes insert himself into the easy banter that went on among the tradesmen at the deli or the counter at the lumberyard when we all lined up to order material or clear our tabs. Not my kind of thing, so I just kept my distance.

"I'm all set, Robbie," said Amanda.

"Thanks to Mr. Happy spoiling the fun," he said, looking at me with a smirk. "What're you, the father figure?"

Now that he was facing me I could smell the sugary stink of alcohol on his breath. He was at least half in the bag which, given his personality, could only make a bad situation worse. Amanda had grown up without her father. Robbie likely remembered that.

"Actually, Sam's my bodyguard," said Amanda.

Robbie snorted. "Whoa, scary," he added, turning his head back to Amanda and sliding his elbow in such a way that I couldn't stop it from dumping the remains of my baked stuffed salmon into my lap. Amanda watched me flick pieces of pink fish off my trousers while Robbie continued to press her about a potential partnership.

"You don't have to say anything now," he said, his voice lowered in a theatrical imitation of discretion, "just keep thinking about it. We could plan out half a dozen of those shacks at a time. I'll give you, like, a volume discount. You want to meet Patrick? He's one of my guys. He's right over there."

Before she could stop him, he yelled, "Yo, Patrick!" over the burble of restaurant conversation.

Patrick was a tall guy, taller than Robbie, and leaner and harder. He was wearing an expensive dress shirt without a tie, and blue jeans. His hands were thick and flecked with scratches and sores. His reddish blond hair was formed into tight natural waves, the kind you hardly need to comb.

"Hey, Patrick, this is Amanda Battiston. We're old buddies. She's the one doing those knockdowns on Jacob's Neck. I told you about her, didn't I? Owns the whole fuckin' peninsula."

Patrick stood between Robbie and Amanda and offered her his hand. She took it tentatively, looking over at me. Patrick followed her eyes.

"Oh, yeah, and this is Sam Aquinas," said Robbie. "Amanda's bodyguard, or so I'm told."

"Acquillo. Aquinas was the saint. No relation."

Patrick was still holding Amanda's hand. She tried to pull it back.

"Bodyguard? There's a gig I could do. Body like that, do it for free."

Amanda looked at me again. I half-stood, reached across the table in front of Robbie and got a grip on Patrick's forearm. It had a lot of tough meat on it, not unusual for a carpenter.

"Her name is Amanda Anselma," I told him. "Battiston's the ex-husband. You let go, then I let go."

Patrick looked unsure of what to do. I dug my thumb between the ribbons of muscle and ligament in his arm. A wince passed over his face and he nodded. He released his grip and I followed suit. Robbie leaned back to look at me, as if trying to get my face into focus.

"That was interesting," he said as I sat back in my chair.

"What do you say, boys?" I said. "Time to move along."

"You know this guy?" Patrick asked Robbie, rubbing his arm.

Robbie was still a massive and unyielding presence at our table. I had my plate back in front of me and used it to push his elbow out of the way. Amanda was looking out at the street through the open doors, as if hoping something would happen that would rescue us from the situation.

"We're waiting," she said, calmly.

Robbie muttered some sort of profanity.

"You know me, Amanda," he said to the back of her head. "For a long time. For a very long time. I'm serious about this. It's totally in both our mutual benefits."

She turned her head far enough to lock eyes with me. I shrugged.

"Your friends are waiting for you," I told him, nodding my head toward the bar. "Come on, give it up."

Robbie whipped back in my direction.

"Who the fuck are you? Who the fuck is he?" he asked Amanda.

One of the busboys in the place was a guy I'd known for a long time. He had a dark complexion and an accent, so he probably never felt totally at home in Southampton, but everyone liked him, including me. He had some unpronounceable name, so he had everybody call him Tommy. He must have heard Robbie start to raise his voice, because a second later he was there at the table, wiping his hands with a cloth napkin and asking us if everything was okay.

Nobody said anything for a second, then Patrick said, "We're fine, Sahib."

"Okay," said Amanda, tearing her gaze from the street-lit world outside the open doors. "That's it. Get lost."

Robbie still had this dopey look on his face, half sneer and half smile, and didn't look all that ready to leave. His boy Patrick was all business, staring at me.

I sighed.

"I think we're at that point," I said to them.

Robbie looked exasperated.

"Come on, Amanda," he said. "I'm just trying to get something going."

"Right," she said. "Get going."

I'd been in a lot of these situations when I was younger. In those days it usually didn't mean that much, until it did, and then it could mean life or death. I was fairly sure Robbie lacked the necessary wherewithal to take things beyond a lot of ridiculous talk, but I wasn't so sure about Patrick. He hadn't taken his eyes off me since I'd clamped down on his arm. I felt my chest tighten, though it wasn't my heart I was worried about.

It was my head. An ex-boxer's head that a doctor had told me had been whacked one too many times. I made a point of not asking him what that actually meant, assuming it was nothing but bad. But I knew my lifetime concussion allotment was all used up.

Robbie finally climbed out of his chair, using Patrick to steady himself.

"Okay," he said, "your fuckin' loss."

I kept my eyes on both of them until they were safely tucked back into the crowd hanging around the bar. In the process I noticed Tommy was still hovering nearby. We nodded at each other, then he went back to work.

"To quote Robbie Milhouser," said Amanda, "that was interesting."

When she took a sip of her vodka her hand was shaking.

"Sorry. I thought at first you were old pals."

"Not then, not now, not for all eternity," she said in a way that seemed more heartfelt than even the current situation warranted. My face must have betrayed that thought, because she quickly added, "And I don't want to talk about it."

It was the kind of thing I would say myself, so I was perfectly amenable to that. It just wasn't something I'd heard much out of Amanda.

With no chance of reconstructing the original mood, we sat there long enough to finish our drinks, then packed it in.

Given the off-season, there was plenty of parking space out on Main Street, even for my '67 Grand Prix. The yellow street-lamps sucked the color out of everything, but threw enough light to guide our way. Most of the storefronts were dark, except for the high-end fashion shops that styled their windows with strings of tiny clear bulbs and low-voltage spotlights. The air was dead still and silent but for a low rumble that could have been the ocean or simply road noise coming from Montauk Highway. Amanda walked next to me, but I sensed some distance, so I took her hand. That's why I felt her tense up before I saw Robbie and Patrick and one other guy come up to us on the sidewalk. Robbie looked a little unsteady on his feet, but the other guys were plenty steady. And big.

"We're gonna start calling you Vice-Grip, Aquinas," said Robbie. "Patrick said you put a bruise on his arm."

"Wasn't that bad," said Patrick for the benefit of the other guy, who thought it was funny.

"Acquillo," I said to Robbie. "But you can call me Sam, since you seem to have trouble with more than one syllable at a time."

They looked like they wanted us to stop and talk, but I kept moving. They followed. I hurried Amanda to the Grand

Prix, opened the door and shoved her inside before they caught up to us.

I left her there and moved back onto the sidewalk, away from the curb, where there was more room to maneuver. They approached in a loose formation, hands free and shoulders back. I was hoping even Robbie Milhouser wasn't stupid enough to start something physical right out on Main Street, though I wished I was wearing something grippier than a pair of penny loafers.

"Hey, Acquillo," said Robbie. "Fuck you. How many syllables is that?"

"Come on, Robbie, give it a rest. It's getting late. Everybody's had a lot to drink. Don't make it worse."

"Worse than what? All I want to do is talk a little business. Who the fuck're you, anyway? Amanda, please," he said, lurching toward the car. "It's me, Robbie. What the fuck."

I stepped in front of him.

"She doesn't want to talk to you. Pay attention to what people are trying to tell you."

"Yeah? What're you telling me?"

"Your boys need to get you home before you do something really stupid."

Robbie looked at first like he was considering my counsel. But then he surprised everybody by getting his big right arm in motion behind an approximation of a roundhouse punch. It took about a year to get there. All I had to do was lean back a little to watch his fist go by my head. His follow-up was thrown so artlessly it looked more like a parody of a drunken punch than the real thing.

Guys in this situation usually say things like, "Stand still and fight like a man," but Robbie was preoccupied with the basic requirements of balance and coordination. My concern was the two other guys, still hanging back, but probably feeling their adrenaline stirring, maybe thinking they ought to join the party. I couldn't wait for Robbie to just tire himself out, so on his third or fourth swing I caught the back of his arm with my right hand and used the left to grip the nape of his neck. Then, by simply adding to his forward momentum, I drove his head straight down into the front grille of a huge SUV parked next to the Grand Prix.

The resulting bang was loud enough to cover the sound of Amanda getting out of my car, so I didn't realize she was there until she touched my arm. Patrick and the other guy were bending over Robbie, who was still conscious, miraculously. He sat on the sidewalk holding his head. I tried to elbow Amanda behind me so I'd have enough airspace to get my fists into play if I had to.

"You motherfucker," said Patrick, standing up and coming toward me.

Fear surged inside of me. I didn't want this. I couldn't afford it.

"You don't want to do this," I told him.

"Oh, yes I do," he said, as he threw the first real live right hook of the evening.

I caught it on the elbow, which saved my face but almost broke my arm. I pivoted to the left to give me more room and draw the action away from Amanda. Patrick walked toward me, flat on his feet, fists held around the middle of his body. Amateur.

I let him get a little closer and stuck him in the nose. He reared back and grabbed his face, which is what amateurs always do, letting me step in and sink a right hook into his belly with everything I had.

"I call the police!" Tommy yelled from the door of the restaurant. The owner and one of the waiters pushed passed him and approached our little gathering. Patrick was doubled over, clutching his midsection. I held him up by his shirt and whispered in his ear.

"It'll only get worse," I said to him.

A flash of lights bounced off the store windows across the street, reflections from the Village police cruiser racing down Nugent Street, and then making a hard right onto Main Street. I let go of Patrick, who did his best to stand up straight. Amanda grabbed my bicep with two hands and pulled me back. The people from the restaurant were helping Robbie's other boy drag him to his feet. I could see a decent-sized egg already growing on his forehead.

The cop was a short, dark-haired woman named Judith Rensler. She wasn't much of a talker, but looked like she knew bullshit when she heard it, which is why she didn't believe Robbie's story about tripping on the curb. Since nobody was willing to contradict him she had to let it go at that.

Patrick just stared at me as he felt delicately around his nose. I ignored him, though I took note that he was still standing, not an easy thing given what I planted in his gut. It wasn't hard to know what the stare meant: next time was going to be different.

We drove in silence back to Oak Point. Amanda sat shrunk into herself, wedged into the corner defined by the back of the seat and the passenger side door.

When I tried to light a cigarette I discovered my hand wasn't steady enough to do the job. I had to reheat the Grand Prix's antique lighter and try again. I looked to see if Amanda was watching these exertions, but she was staring out the window.

"Just a jerk," I said to her.

"Worse than that."

There wasn't much of a moon, but the sliver cast enough light to reflect off the Little Peconic Bay, and the air was clear

enough to see the sparkle of the houses built along the opposite shore. When I pulled into our shared driveway she told
me she wanted to go right to bed.

"He's just a jerk," I repeated when she opened the door.
She shut it again, switching off the cabin light, so I couldn't
see her face.

She leaned over and kissed me, then got out of the car.

I watched her walk down her stretch of the drive and disappear into her house. I always liked to watch Amanda walk,
and despite it all that night was no exception.

Eddie Van Halen, the mutt who lived with me, was waiting
on my front stoop. He had a secret door to the house that led
through the basement hatch, but like me he preferred to stay
close to the weather, so I'd usually find him outside when I
came home. Either that or he faked it by running out the
hatch whenever he heard the Grand Prix coming up the street.

He honored me with a slow wave of his long feathered tail
and a look that said something glorious was awaiting us
inside the house.

In my case it was another Absolut on the rocks. For Eddie,
a Big Dog biscuit, which he waited to crunch on until I was
with him on the screened-in porch facing the Little Peconic
Bay. This was where we lived year-round with the help of a
woodstove and the big wooden storm windows my father
built as an energy-saving measure, or maybe as an act of self-
preservation against the screeching brine-soaked winds that
came off the bay throughout the winter months. Neither of
my parents ever used the porch in the cold weather, but I
found it impossible to be in the cottage without staring out
on the impatient, unpredictable little sea.

When the moon was big in the sky, I'd sit in the dark so I
could see the surface chop throw back the silver blue frag-
ments of moonbeam. Despite the lack of moon, I decided to

leave the light off, more for the mood than the view. Given the unusually warm weather, I didn't need the woodstove, though I lit it anyway. Eddie lay where he always did, stretched out on the braided rug.

I was going to sit at the battered pine table, but I didn't think I had the strength to stay upright. So I lay on the daybed and recited out loud, like an incantation, my reasons for avoiding any and all confrontations.

"I can't do it again," I said finally to Eddie. "For any reason."

I didn't like to think of myself as a middle-aged guy who sat drinking alone in the dark, talking to his dog about his fears and uncertainties. But I'd been doing that to Eddie since saving him from the pound, so he must have assumed listening to a bunch of worthless crap was part of his daily work product.

"I can't do it," I repeated.

All he did was look at me over the crumbled remains of his biscuit. I let it stand at that and finished my drink, then one or two more to be on the safe side, before letting the encyclopedia of irresolvable quandaries that continually cycled through my consciousness shift into a dream state, thereby maintaining a continuity of torment from wakefulness to sleep.

TWO

A FEW HOURS LATER I awoke to someone pounding on the kitchen door. In the glow from the embers in the woodstove I could see Eddie curled up on the braided rug, his head slightly raised, not bothering to bark, the urgent bashing coming from the kitchen not rising to his standard of alarm. I was still in my clothes, which added to the feeling of squalid disorientation as I swam through a layer of exhaustion, adrenaline poisoning and partially metabolized Absolut.

I hauled myself off the daybed and went into the kitchen. I flicked on the stoop light and saw my friend Joe Sullivan, his face cupped against the window. The wall clock in the kitchen said it was three-thirty in the morning.

"Good, you're dressed. Let's go," he said, shoving past me and filling up the kitchen. Sullivan was about six feet tall but well over two hundred pounds. He'd been a patrolman with a uniform and a car with lights on the top for twenty years, but he'd done well enough recently to get promoted to detective, despite his heartfelt opposition. His wife was the deciding factor, since the new job came with more money and easier hours. At least theoretically.

He was wearing a Yankees cap over his buzz-cut blond hair and a bulky army field jacket. Black Levi's with a pressed-in crease and a pair of alpine hiking boots completed the look. Ostensibly a plainclothesman, one glance and you'd assume cop, unless you took him for a mercenary fresh from an African coup.

"No time for coffee. Too bad," he said, his bright blue eyes darting around the kitchen.

His heavy boots were covered with mud. Eddie was helping him distribute it around the kitchen floor. Sullivan bent over to pet his head.

"Maybe I can make it while you tell me what's going on," I said, splashing water from the kitchen faucet on my face. It woke me up a little but did nothing to improve my equilibrium.

"Your girlfriend's house is burning down. Not next door," he added quickly. "One of the knockdowns."

He walked into the bedroom behind the kitchen, which had a view of Amanda's house.

"No lights're on," he yelled back. "I guess nobody's called her yet. Must be asleep."

"Which knockdown?"

"The one near the tip of the neck. Come on, we gotta tell her. Leave the dog."

We drove the three hundred feet to Amanda's house in Sullivan's busted-up Ford Bronco. He told me he heard about the fire from Will Ervin, the young cop who'd taken over his beat. Sullivan had given Ervin a standing order to report anything that happened in North Sea, supposedly to ease him into his new territory. The transition was now in its seventh month, and Sullivan's interest in everything North Sea was still unflagging. Car accidents, break-ins, bar fights, house fires.

"You can see the glow," he said, pointing to the tree line across the lagoon from Amanda's house.

"What happened?" I asked him.

"I don't know, but the whole thing's involved. Main job now's keeping the fire out of the woods or jumping to another house."

The warm air from earlier in the evening had fled and the stiff northwesterly was back, breaking itself across the tip of the peninsula. I shivered on the hard seat of the old 4x4, an electric itch from the vodka skittering across my nervous system. I lit a cigarette to complete the effect. Before Sullivan could tell me to put it out we were there.

We rang the doorbell and lights flashed on.

"This can't be good," she said, holding the door open with one hand and her silk robe closed with the other.

"You got a fire, Amanda," said Sullivan. "One of your houses on Jacob's Neck. The one near the point."

"You're joking."

"You should get over there," he said.

"Is this for real?" she asked me.

Sullivan brushed past her into the house. We could hear him walking through all the rooms, snapping on lights and opening and shutting doors.

"Why's he doing that? When did you hear about this?" she asked, her face tight with distress.

"Routine precaution," I said, as if I knew what I was talking about. Then I answered her other question: "Just a few minutes ago."

"I got to go now," she said with a shake of her head, reaching for the front door. I slipped my hand around her wrist.

"Not like that. Get dressed. I'll go with you."

She stood up straight and nodded.

"Of course. What am I doing?"

I stood waiting in the foyer until I noticed my legs start to falter. I slid down to the cold hardwood floor and braced myself against the wall. The floor listed to starboard, but I held my ground. My head felt like somebody'd filled it up with lubricating oil. So far my stomach was on the sidelines, relatively calm, but I knew that wouldn't last. I reminded myself that the only way to sleep off a big night was to actually sleep, which had been the plan for tomorrow, a Saturday without cutoff saws or pneumatic nailers, or iced-over job sites at seven o'clock in the morning.

Sullivan stepped over me on his way out the door.

"When you get over there, keep an eye on her. No histrionics. Firemen have enough to do."

"She won't throw herself on the fire. Though I might if this headache gets any worse."

"Now that you mention it, you do look like crap."

"We'll see you there."

A few minutes later Amanda ran past me pulling on a gold barn jacket. I was going to offer to drive, but she beat me to her Audi and had the engine going before I reached the car door. I was glad Sullivan had left ahead of us. He didn't like people speeding through North Sea, even on the way to personal calamity. Amanda's jaw was set and she held the wheel with both hands as she spun the little car through the tight neighborhood turns. I held onto my internal organs.

We approached the flashing red, blue and yellow lights and the hard crackle of VHF radios. Amanda rolled down her window and the acid smell of wood smoke filled the car. The air was soaked with vapor billowing off the gushing fire hoses. Neighbors stood in tight huddles, staring intently and pointing at the burning house, their faces reflecting the strobe lights and diffused glow from the drowning fire. A Town cop stopped our car. It was Will Ervin.

"I'm the owner," said Amanda.

"Joe told me you were coming. Park over there," he said, but Amanda was already underway. She jammed the Audi into a slot in the underbrush and jumped out of the car. I gathered myself up to follow.

There wasn't much to look at. The last time I dropped by, the rough plumbing and electrical work had been completed and the walls recently sheetrocked. The finish carpenters were partway through the baseboards and trim—the job I had over at Joshua Edelstein's.

Now it was a blackened skeleton enshrouded in smoke and haze.

I think we simultaneously remembered that the kitchen cabinets had been delivered and stored in big cardboard boxes in the garage. We moved closer and saw the garage was now a mound of charred timbers, with only the south gable standing like a tombstone. I heard Amanda choke in a breath. I thought she was about to burst into tears, but she burst into something else.

"Motherfucking sonofabitch," she yelled loud enough to provoke a firefighter to spin around.

"What the fuck happened?" she asked him.

"House caught on fire," he yelled, smirking.

"No shit, genius," she yelled back.

I put my hand on her arm, but she shook it off.

"Hey, they're on your side."

She spun around and pushed me with both hands.

"Nobody's on my side," she said through clenched teeth. "Never."

"Christ, Amanda, what's that supposed to mean?" I asked,

but she was stalking off toward the other end of the house. Sullivan's caution was apparently warranted. I wondered how he knew. Prescience instilled by twenty years in a patrol car. I looked for him, but he wasn't in sight. I followed Amanda instead, at a safe distance.

I caught up to her talking to another firefighter, an officer in a yellow slicker and white officer's hat with a black brim and gold emblem. He held a walkie-talkie and nodded while he listened to Amanda. As I approached I could hear him say, "Won't know till we can get the investigators in from the County. But it looks funny to me."

"What's funny?" she asked.

"Too uniform. And too hot. Without furnishings or carpets, fires in new construction don't spread so easily. Tend to be confined to one area. Not involve the whole house. Who are you?" he asked me.

"I'm with her. Nominally."

This close in, the smell of the fire was sweeter, stickier. I assumed because of plastic things like PVC pipes, wiring insulation and vapor barriers. I heard a crash and turned to see Amanda kicking over a stand the carpenters were using to support a cutoff saw. The fire official looked at me like it was my fault.

"Maybe you should get her behind the yellow line," he said to me.

"Sure, just lend me your gun."

"We're not armed."

Amanda was standing over the aluminum stand as if daring it to get back up and fight. I walked behind her and grabbed her around the waist with my right arm. There wasn't a lot of meat on her, but she was surprisingly strong, in a rangy, slippery way. I still hadn't fully mastered my balance, so I had to dig deep to carry her all the way to the yellow tape, where I was grateful to see Sullivan standing with a walkie-talkie up to his face.

I put Amanda back on the ground and held the tape up for her. She ducked under without looking at me.

"The County boys are on their way," Sullivan said to me. "None too happy about it. Dickheads."

"Isn't this what they do?"

"They like it better when the fire's out."

"Oughta strike while the iron's hot," I said.

"That's my thought."

I'd lost track of Amanda again, but then saw her leaning on her car, both hands laid flat on the hood. I walked over to her and wrapped both arms around her waist. I put my lips next to her ear.

"You got insurance," I whispered. "The foundation's still there. Start over tomorrow. Make an even better house."

"Fuck the house," she whispered back. "It's the principle."

"Okay, whatever that means."

"This project was important to me. Something they couldn't take away from me. That's the principle. My life is the principle."

"Who's they?" I asked.

I stepped a few paces back from her face so I could better see her eyes. They were unflinching.

"You said, 'Something they couldn't take away from me.' Who's they? Milhouser?"

She just stared at me, her face now an alien thing.

"That's ridiculous," she said.

"Then what's with all the angst? It's bad, but it's not the end of anything. You buck up and do it again. Get back on the horse."

I tried to hold her, but she wiggled out of my grasp, then came back at me, pushing her chest into mine the way kids used to do on the playground when trying to start a fight. I did the opposite of what I used to do in those situations and dropped my hands to my sides.

"Yeah, like you're the expert on that," she said, an inch from my face. "Nice job of bucking up. I should be taking lessons from you."

She had a valid point. I'd made a pretty spectacular hash of my life, and whatever repair I'd managed was a long time coming. So bucking up wasn't a specialty of mine. I was much better at resignation and denial. And better yet at avoiding emotional conflict.

Amanda and I had built our relationship out of spare parts, and not all of them fit so well together. It's unfashionable to find individual fault for romantic shortfalls, but I knew most of ours were mine. But those places where we'd found common ground were more precious to me than I fully understood before that night under the glow of her burning aspirations. I'd lived most of my life in other places, filled with cruel, demoralizing words. I might not have made much of myself since then, but I wasn't going back there.

"You're right," I said. "I'm the last one to be handing out advice."

I started to visualize my jogging route, which included a stretch from my house through portions of Jacob's Neck, the connection for which was only about a half block from where I was standing. I zipped up my jacket as I turned on my heel and started to jog that way, weaving through the firefighters and onlookers and cops standing by their cars and trucks, hypnotized by the blinking lights.

In a few minutes I was on the sandy road, which I followed by muscle memory down Jacob's Neck to the segment of hardtop that ran in front of the abandoned WB factory, then back on to a sandy path that followed the contours to the tip of Oak Point where my cottage waited for me, equipped with a negligent watchdog, a perfect view of the Little Peconic Bay and the remaining half fifth of Absolut, which fit neatly with a tray of ice cubes into my big aluminum tumbler.

Back within the protection of the screened-in porch I parked myself at the table with the tumbler and a pack of cigarettes. I turned out the light and smoked quietly, looking for signs of something more than indifference from the bay. Some justification for bearing endless witness to the moon-struck water, the black and smoldering sky.

THREE

THE MONDAY AFTER Amanda's house burned down I was at the corner place in the Village buying a large Viennese cinnamon coffee and a customized croissant stuffed with cheese and Virginia ham. After five years of steady seduction I'd finally established a fragile rapport with the tiny Guatemalan woman who ran the pastry counter. This allowed me to wrangle special orders, managed mostly through the lavish use of terms like *bonita, guapa* and *Señorita Lista*.

It was half an hour before I had to show up at Joshua Edelstein's house, so I sat on the teak park bench and pretended the temperature was above freezing. The coffee helped the cause, steaming up in my face and easing down the ham sandwich.

A battleship gray Crown Victoria swung so abruptly into the parking space in front of the bench I almost pulled my feet out of the way. It was Sullivan, resplendent in Yankees cap, tough-cop sunglasses and aftermarket battle wear. He said something into a radio before getting out of the car.

"You like that faggie coffee," he said, standing in front of the bench with his hands in his jacket pockets.

"You're blocking my sun."

"Stay put," he said and went into the shop, returning soon after with a bagel and a tall cup of his own. Looked like a latte. He sat down next to me, taking up more than half the space.

"I got the prelims on the fire from the County," he said. "Wasn't much of a challenge, even for those bozos."

"Arson."

"Oh, yeah. Gasoline siphoned out of a step van the finish carpenters had left on the site. The hose was still sticking out of the tank. Filled up a couple of empty compound buckets. Threw it all over the house, then tossed the buckets in the backyard."

"Didn't put up a sign that said, 'Arsonists at work?'"

"Next-door neighbor heard voices right before noticing the big glow. Heard a truck pull away."

"Heard but didn't see," I said.

"Said he was just lying there in bed, trying to sleep. Understandable. No reason to look. You usually don't know you're a witness to something until some cop shows up at your door."

He took a bite of the bagel. Cream cheese oozed out of the middle and tumbled down the front of his camouflage field jacket.

"Not a professional job," I offered.

"Unless their profession was advertising."

"P.T. Barnum invented advertising. Said there was a sucker born every minute."

"These guys weren't suckers. Smarter than that."

"Smart?"

"Wore gloves and something on their feet that disguised their footprints. Just looked like blobs in the mud. Almost no sole prints."

"Booties," I said, after a moment's thought.

"Booties?"

"Lightweight, disposable shoe covers. Made of Gore-Tex or Tyvek. Used in ultra-sterile, ultra-pure environments. Like clean rooms, where a single piece of dust can louse up a semiconductor. Or in bioresearch, or drug production."

"You know this?" Sullivan asked.

"I know about booties. I don't know if they used them. Just a guess. If they did, you're right. They're smart."

Some more deliberation time passed, which I used to finish off my coffee as a distraction from the envy I was feeling over Sullivan's chocolate-sprinkled latte.

"They wanted to advertise the act, not the actors," said Sullivan.

"A summation both trenchant and poetic," I told him, sincerely.

"I'm gonna assume that wasn't an insult," he said, downing the last of his bagel and cream cheese. "Speaking of which," he said, brushing crumbs off his jacket, "have you talked to Amanda?"

"Had a few insults of her own?"

"After you ran off. She wasn't happy."

"Did she hear the discussion with the County people?" I asked.

"Wasn't supposed to, but yeah. Elbowed her way in. Heard it all."

"Must have been interesting."

"Actually shut her up. I figured exhaustion finally got to her. I had Will Ervin escort her back to her house and told him to keep a tight eye on her and her other place."

"Have any theories?"

"I might ask you the same thing," he said.

"Nothing worth talking about."

"In other words, you're not talking."

"In other words, if I start talking about it to you in your official capacity, I might be jumping the gun."

He savored a gentle pull off the top of the latte, smacking his lips like he'd just dipped into Aunt Tillie's prize-winning apple pie.

"I'm in the mood to try something new this time, Sam. What say you tell me everything you're thinking now, no matter how half-baked, rather than making me guess until I'm ready to start beating you over the head to get it out of you."

"No more beating on the head. Doctor's orders."

"So I hear," he said.

"Yeah? From whom?" I asked.

"I'm not ready to talk about that."

"Christ."

"Though I might've heard a few things one time when I was lifting weights next to a trauma doc. Somebody we both know."

"Fucking Markham."

"He said the same crap about me. You're not the only one who's had his bean used for batting practice."

I'd been through some stuff with Joe Sullivan, and truth is, I probably hadn't been as fair to him as I should have. It was an old habit of mine to keep my lunatic musings to myself until I thought they deserved to be shown the light of day. People misinterpreted that to mean I didn't think they had worthwhile thoughts of their own. That's not what I wanted. I just wasn't done cooking the stew.

"I got into a dumb little dustup with Robbie Milhouser Friday night. Him and a couple of his boys."

"I know. Judy told me."

"Hah," I said. "Who's withholding now?"

"Ross wanted me to ask if you thought there was a connection between that and Amanda's fire. Like I wouldn't have wondered that myself."

Ross Semple was the Southampton Town Chief of Police. The gripe aside, we both knew he held Sullivan in fairly high regard. The only strike against him being his association with me.

"I've got no reason right now to think one way or the other," I told him. "But it's a place to start."

He nodded.

"I'm sure Amanda would get behind that," he said.

"Who the hell knows."

"Still not talking, are we?"

"Not at the moment."

"None of my business," he said, holding up his hands defensively. "It's your love life."

"There's an oxymoron."

"Now who's insulting?"

I stood up and tossed the butt end of the croissant to a skittery flock of chickadees working the sidewalk.

Sullivan looked up at me, squinting behind his tough-cop sunglasses against the sun rising above the storefronts across Main Street. He looked like he wanted to say more, but I left before he had a chance and drove over to Joshua Edelstein's house, where I worked another ten-hour day. I kept my mind focused on cutting miters, coping inside joints and not shooting myself with my pneumatic brad nailer. It was a nice peaceful day, just me, two other finish guys working in other parts of the house, and a pair of electricians installing switches and wall plugs.

In answer to my quiet prayer, nobody turned on the radio, which was invariably set to the most brainless meatball station

Frank's crew could pull in from Up Island. All you heard were the cutoff saws, the pop-pop of nail guns, compressors turning on and off, and the sound of work boots scraping around the plywood subfloor. We even had heat, since the tapers who came through over the weekend had jacked up the thermostat to hasten drying between coats. I never had to say a word to anybody all day, not even to myself.

After work I stopped off at the cottage long enough to wash my face and hands, change my clothes and feed Eddie. He was free to use his secret door to go in and out of the house, but couldn't open a can or pour out his own dry food. At least that's what he wanted me to think. I left him there to chow down and drove over to the Pequot, the crummy little joint next to the marina in Sag Harbor run by Paul Hodges and his daughter Dorothy. It was the only place around where you could avoid the plague of sophistication spreading through the Hamptons, infecting even indigenous dive bars. The clientele was mostly fishermen or mechanics working the marina, so the olfactory ambience alone was enough to frighten off normal people, even if you could stand the smell of Hodges's cooking.

Dorothy was in her mid-twenties and looked like she'd died recently after being trapped inside a dark closet. Based on seeing other young people around the Village, I guessed the sepulchral disposition was intentional. Something I meant to ask my own daughter when I had the chance.

Tonight she was wearing a wifebeater undershirt, over a black bra, with black polyester slacks and mechanics boots. Her hair, also black, had been forced into angry, slickened spikes. Her skin was so pale you could distinguish between veins and arteries. I thought if you looked closely enough you could see the shadows of muscle, ligament and bone. A tattoo on her left shoulder said "Recriminate."

"Hey, Sunshine," I said to her as I pulled up a barstool.

"Vodka on the rocks, no fruit, swizzle stick," she said without looking up from wiping down the bar.

"Make it two swizzle sticks. Feel like changing things up a little."

"You want a menu?"

"Bring me whatever you been pulling out of the water," I told her.

"Not a problem. My father's been serving fresh snorkelers all week."

"I thought it was too cold for snorkeling."

"That's why they're so fresh."

Hodges must have heard me, he came out of the kitchen wiping his hands on the bib of his apron. Somewhere in his sixties, he looked like a guy whose life had shown him some hard treatment. Years of commercial fishing had turned his skin the color and consistency of walrus hide, though the wide shape of his mouth and his bugged-out eyes looked more amphibious than mammalian. He was surely wider around the waist than he'd been as a younger man, but his arms were still thickly muscled and his hands looked capable of squirting clams out of their shells.

"Dotty tell you about the specials?" he asked.

"Dorothy," she said, though mostly to herself.

"She did. Sounds great. Just hold the flippers."

"Flippers are the best part."

He left me alone to drink while he put together my meal. Dorothy talked to me about a story she'd read in the local paper about the rumrunners who used to ply the waters of the South Fork during Prohibition.

"They'd bring the stuff in from big ships that sailed down from Canada and anchored twelve miles off the coast, which was international waters in those days," she told me while she stuffed beer mugs into the dishwasher behind the bar. "They'd use hot-rod boats loaded to the gunwales. Zip around the forks and make stops all up and down the bay shores. Jacob's Neck was famous for it."

"My home waters."

"I know. That's why I'm telling you. I think that old factory was in on it," she said, popping back up and slamming the dishwasher door closed.

"WB Manufacturing. Wouldn't surprise me. Do anything for a buck."

"Why not? Can't stop people from drinking, for Lord's sake."

"No argument here," I said, with conviction.

"Though you could drink less, if you know what I mean."

"And threaten a cornerstone of the Pequot's revenue stream?"

"Good point. Want another?"

"Sure."

The company of the Pequot's owner came with my meal, as it usually did. Hodges had known my father, which made him think of me as a point of continuity with the dead past. A past he remembered as if it were last week, a penchant that caused him comfort and confusion in equal measure.

When I took my first mouthful he looked at me expectantly.

"So, what do you think? Succulent or merely piquant?"

I chewed on the question.

"More abundantly audacious. Exuberant."

"See, Dotty," he yelled to his daughter, "Didn't I tell you?"

She brought him a bourbon so I wouldn't feel bad being the only one with a drink. We talked about nothing for a while, then migrated into the realm of the merely inconsequential.

Then I made the mistake of telling him about Amanda's house.

"No kidding. Wow. There's a pity," he said. "How's she taking it?"

I told him what happened after Sullivan woke us up, including what led to my decision to jog home. He maintained a look of neutrality, which I appreciated. I was less sure how Dorothy, who was nearby pretending not to listen to the conversation, took the news.

"At least she can afford to start over," said Hodges. "Even without insurance, though I guess that's not much of a consolation."

"No. Apparently not."

"That girl's had more than her share of trouble."

"There's something wrong with this drink," I said, holding the empty glass up to the light.

Dorothy plucked it out of my hand and filled it with a handful of fresh ice. Hodges took the cue and launched down a different conversational byway. I don't know how it happened, but something led to something that caused me to mention Robbie Milhouser.

"Knew his father," said Hodges. "Quite an operator."

"That's one way of putting it."

"Okay, sleazebag. But looked good, you know? Handsome. Like that Bouvier guy. Jackie's old man. Slick."

"A dickhead with a pretty face is still a dickhead," I said.

"Easy to say when you got a nose that's always signaling a right-hand turn. No offense."

"Why would I be offended at that?"

The fragrant and boisterous arrival of a pack of fishermen drove Hodges back into the kitchen, giving me a chance to finish off my meal and a few more drinks. Dorothy occasionally slid over to give me an installment of her moonshiner story, trying to persuade me to search Jacob's Neck for evidence of contraband booze. I told her I'd investigated the WB property personally two years ago and found only abandoned machine tools and bowling trophies. And if there was anything in the muck of the lagoon, it could stay there until it turned into fossils.

"Besides," I told her, "who'd drink eighty-year-old booze?"

"You see who comes in this place?" she said, nodding toward the fishermen, now crowded around a pair of tables pulled together in the center of the room, drinking bottled beer and shoving handfuls of fried clams into their mouths.

"If I ever find anything, I'll turn it over to you. For the sake of history or commerce, whatever your mood at the time."

When Hodges came back he still had Robbie Milhouser's old man on his mind.

"You know he was a Town Trustee for a while," he told me, settling in with his second bourbon on the rocks. "Proof that politics is the last refuge of scoundrels."

"I thought that was patriotism."

"The Town had its share of crooks in those days. Not that there was much to steal. Mostly a little skim here and there and a chance to get out of parking tickets. Milhouser still managed to get caught scamming the highway department. I think it was over road salt. I don't remember the details, but he had to quit the board and was lucky to stay out of jail. Still alive, you know. At least as of a month or two ago. Saw him in the hardware store. All grins and handshakes. Good old Jeff Milhouser."

"Jeff. Didn't remember his first name."

"Short for Jefferson. Folks had a lot of money. Or used to. Lost it in the Depression or something. Had the Ivy League airs. Used to see that a lot around here when the place was full of Waspy old money. Not so much anymore."

"You knew this guy?" I said.

"Only for a while. When I was working for him at the Esso station out on County Road 39."

"That's where I worked for him."

"Get out of here. Don't remember you. What was it, early sixties?" Hodges asked.

"I was there a little later. You wouldn't have seen me anyway. Always had my head stuffed in an engine compartment. You're right, though, now that you mention it. Milhouser always wore a pinstriped button-down shirt. And boots from L.L. Bean, back when New England swells were the only ones who thought that stuff was hip."

I listened to him talk while I ate another plate of fish he'd brought out for me, which was nicely seasoned and well cooked, though like all Hodges's preparations, unidentifiable. You could ask him what it was, but it wasn't worth the trouble. You never got a straight answer.

"So we're agreeing Jeff Milhouser was a dickhead," he said in summary.

"We are. Him and his offspring."

"Don't know the kid," said Hodges. "Not that I know of, anyway."

"He's been building houses around Noyac and North Sea. His crew's from Up Island."

"They might be a little too refined for the Pequot."

"Better to stay clear of that bunch. You don't need the trouble," I said.

"Can't be worse than a crew of fishermen after a few weeks at sea. Anyway, we got equipment for that behind the bar."

"They aren't always men," Dorothy interjected from across the room.

"Pardon me, I meant fisherpeople," said Hodges. "She's right, though. Some of those ladies are scarier than the men."

After that we found ourselves diverted along some other long and circuitous conversational paths, which was the norm with Hodges. It was still early, but I was getting heavy with tiredness and iced Absolut, the hard labors of the day catching up with me. I told Hodges I had to call it quits.

"I'll go dig up the check," he said, starting to stand up, and then paused and sat back down.

"Now I remember," he said. "It wasn't the road-salt scam that got Milhouser in all that trouble. It was bank fraud. Damn, I can't believe I'm remembering this." He nodded to himself as he chewed over the memory, his face furrowed with concentration. I was almost too tired to take the bait, but I wasn't getting the check without letting him spill the story.

"Gee, Hodges, what was that fraud all about?" I asked.

"What he did was move a bunch of Town money into one of his own accounts, just long enough to collateralize a loan, then moved it all back out again. This took place inside the same bank, so it must have looked easy to Milhouser, though of course the genius never thought anybody'd notice the transactions. Could have been real trouble, but he got probation on a plea of irreconcilable stupidity."

"Which bank was this?" I asked.

"Right there on Main Street. Don't remember the name."

"Harbor Trust?" I asked him. It was the bank where Amanda used to work and her husband Roy was the manager.

"I think it was some savings and loan. Local deal. They all disappeared a while ago."

Dorothy saved me from more talk about the Milhousers by bringing me the check and gently shooing her father back into the kitchen. I got out of there and headed back to the tip of Oak Point.

I drove past my house and up to Amanda's. The Audi was gone and her house was blacked out, leaving only my post lamp to light our two properties. I walked up to the door anyway and rang the bell. After waiting a minute, I went around to a side window and opened it up. I knew about the missing lock from when the place was owned by an old lady named Regina Broadhurst. I knew about it because she was always on my ass to fix it.

I found my way to Amanda's bedroom and turned on the light. Her suitcase was missing from the closet. The hair dryer and her makeup bag were gone from the bathroom.

The only thing that could nail it down more was a note that said, "I have left for the night."

When I got back to my cottage Eddie was waiting on the little porch off the side door. My plan had been to go right to bed without a last cigarette or nightcap, but now I decided on both. Eddie went with me out to the Adirondack chairs. The surface of the Little Peconic was racing toward Sag Harbor before a stiff westerly pouring in through the slot between Robbins Island and Cow Neck. The air was clear enough to turn the lights on the opposite shore into sharp little pinpricks randomly arrayed along the blackened horizon.

I thought drinking out on the lawn would force me into bed, but it had the opposite effect. So instead I went and put on my running shoes. Eddie looked skeptical, so I stowed him in the house and headed off along Bay Edge Drive. The only car to pass me was a BMW roadster going far too fast for the sandy rutted road surface . It would have hit me if I hadn't jumped out of the way. But I was never in any danger.

I'd been running on that road since time began, and every turn and roll inked into my memory so indelibly I could run it mindless and blind, sure in the embrace of invulnerable night.

FOUR

THE NEXT MORNING I was four stories above the Atlantic Ocean trimming out Joshua Edelstein's widow's walk, toe-nailing the turned spindles and attaching custom molding under the handrails, and occasionally stopping to watch the offshore breeze push the swells up into little cliffs before breaking into clean, tubular curls, throwing off plumes of spray lit up by the sun rising over the eastern horizon.

From that vantage point you could see the estate section of Southampton Village, from Wickapogue to the Gracefield Tennis Club. Since it was the beginning of April most of the big houses were unoccupied, though busy with painters, clea-ners, landscapers and crews working on irrigation systems.

It felt good to be working outside in the early morning sun, even though the breeze was the same northwesterly that had been icing down Long Island for the last four months. If you kept moving you could pretend it wasn't as cold as it really was.

Frank Entwhistle had built Joshua a big house, over 10,000 square feet, so it took a lot of moldings, baseboards, and window and door trim to fill it up. I didn't have to install it all myself; Frank could bring in a whole finish crew for a job this big. I just had to do my part and stay clear of Frank's efforts to promote me to foreman of the crew. I'd already done my bit in management, once running a corporate division of about four thousand people. None of them were finish carpenters, as far as I knew, but the experience had blunted my enthusiasm for management.

I liked Joshua Edelstein, but I didn't know why he wanted a house this big, though maybe I would if I could afford one. I did, however, approve of his widow's walk. I'd definitely have one of those if I could. My cottage on the bay was only a single story. Maybe I could build a separate tower, or a tree house in the Norway maples that lined the back of the property. Achieve a loftier perspective.

Absorbed as I was in the view of the ocean, I didn't immediately notice the police cruiser working its way toward Joshua's house through the bordering neighborhood. My attention was caught by the big white number painted on the car's black roof. Then I realized it was a Southampton Town cop, which surprised me. Southampton Village, a subdivision of the Town, had its own police force.

The cruiser rolled into Joshua's muddy front yard and parked among the fleet of pickups and vans belonging to Frank's crew and subcontractors. Frank was there himself, supervising the final stages of construction of what was the biggest house he'd ever built. Not many of the local builders got a shot at the really big jobs, so Frank saw it as an important demonstration. He walked over to the cruiser and leaned against the driver's side door. He talked for a few minutes, then looked up at me, shading his eyes against the glare off the ocean.

Two men got out of the car and looked toward where Frank was pointing. I waved when I realized one of them was Ross Semple. I didn't recognize the other cop. Ross waved for me to come down.

I unsnapped the compressor hose off the back of my pneumatic nailer so I could bring it with me. Tools like that had a tendency to grow little legs on a big job like this, full of guys from Up Island you may or may not see again. I'd owned it for a while and liked the way it fit my hand.

Ross rarely looked you in the eye when he talked to you, and even when he did it was hard to tell because his glasses were so thick. He had a cigarette going, as he always did, stuck between the fingers of his right hand. He put it in his mouth when we shook hands.

"Sam."

"Ross. You're up early."

"With the roosters, baby. Every day."

Even at ground level I still didn't recognize his escort, a uniformed patrolman. He stood back a few paces with his hand resting easily on the holster holding his service weapon. I didn't introduce myself. He didn't seem to mind.

"Sullivan told me you were working this job," said Ross.

I looked around for Frank, but he'd left before I got down there. A pair of electricians running outdoor cable down a shallow trench for a post light stole curious glances. A cop car on a job site wasn't all that common a sight.

"Sorry I missed him," I said, looking over at the uniformed cop.

"I let him beg off," said Ross. "He didn't want his name on the collar. If that's what this is."

Ross flicked the half-burned cigarette into the mud. He felt all around his shirt and pants for the next one, eventually digging a crumpled pack out of the last possible pocket. It wasn't a very graceful move. Nothing Ross did was very graceful.

"Collar?"

"Arrest."

"I know what a collar is. Who's getting collared?"

"Nobody, if you just follow me back to the station."

I understood now why Frank hadn't hung around. Ross wanted to speak to me in private. The uniformed escort stood still as a centurion. Ross leaned back against the fender of the cruiser and crossed his arms. Then uncrossed them. Then crossed them again. He looked out toward the ocean, squinting his eyes.

"Gonna be a nice day," he said. "'Bout goddamn time."

I pulled out one of my own cigarettes, which Ross lit for me after another prolonged search for his lighter. I'd been trying to hold off until after lunch, but all the smoke coming from the Chief had undermined my resolve.

"Am I allowed to ask why?" I asked.

Ross squeezed together his lips and shook his head.

"Nope. That'd make it harder for me. Better it's like, 'Sam, old buddy, I'd really like to have a chat with you some time.' And you say, 'Why sure, Ross, why don't I come on over to the station right away?'"

I nodded toward my Pontiac.

"Can I drive my own car?"

"Sure. We'll follow you. Bring whatever you want off the job. Don't know how long it'll take."

I unbuckled my tool belt and stuffed it with a Phillips head screwdriver, a pair of pliers and a nail set that had found their way into my back pockets.

"Sullivan told me that big old car's a lot faster than it looks," said Ross.

"Not as fast as your cruiser," I told him. "Maybe off the line, but not the same top end."

"So you won't be tempted to play Smokey and the Bandit."

As if there was any place to run to. Technically the South Fork was an island, with only two bridges crossing the Shinnecock Canal. Your only other getaway was the ferry to Shelter Island. Not an ideal escape strategy.

"No reason for any of that, Ross. I'm just coming in for a chat."

The uniformed cop walked me over to the Grand Prix and watched me stow the tool belt and power nailer in the yawning trunk. He maintained an even distance, outside my reach, but close enough to get his gun out and fully engaged. I'd learned about that procedure years ago, the last time I'd been politely asked to come in for a chat with law enforcement.

It took about half an hour to drive over to the station. It would have been less, but with a patrol car filling my rearview the whole way I felt compelled to stay under the speed limit. Stupid, really. What were they going to do? Pull me over and give me a ticket?

Janet Orlovsky was at the front desk behind a big pane of bulletproof Plexiglas. Before buzzing us in, she studied us carefully, in case people were impersonating the Chief of Police and one of his patrolmen. She glowered at me, which didn't mean anything. She always did. She assumed I'd done something she wouldn't like and she just hadn't discovered yet what it was. My old man used to take the same approach.

The cops and administrative people sitting at desks or standing around file cabinets watched our little parade weave its way to the back of the squad room, where Ross had his office. Somewhere along the way the uniform dropped out.

Ross closed the door behind us and took off his nylon wind-breaker. I sat in one of the two chairs in front of his desk.

"Frank must be getting close to wrapping that place up," said Ross, getting comfortable in his chair, pushing back into the overloaded credenza.

"Getting there."

"We radioed Sullivan on the way in. Still busy over at the crime scene."

"Looks great in his civvies," I said.

"Yeah, sort of like General MacArthur."

"What kind of crime scene we talking about?" I asked him.

He leaned forward again and rolled the chair up tight to the desk.

"Did I forget to ask if you wanted coffee?"

"Coffee'd be great."

He left for a while and came back with two heavy china mugs with the seal of the Town of Southampton stamped on the side. The coffee was good—tasted like the hazelnut/French vanilla blend you got from the corner place in the Village. I was tempted to ask for a croissant, or a cheese Danish.

"So you haven't heard," said Ross, back behind his desk again.

"Something going on? I don't usually listen to the morning news. Gives me a headache."

"Somebody told me you go jogging after work."

"Sometimes. Less recently. I've been getting plenty of exercise on the job. Nice of you to take an interest, though, Ross."

"Lady in your neighborhood said you might've been out running last night. Late."

"Funny time to jog."

"That's what I thought."

He sat back in that abrupt, maladroit way he had and drew heavily on his cigarette. I lit one of my own to keep him company. The windows behind his desk were raised so the sill was just above his head. All you could see were the naked branches of a sycamore tree and a few high clouds dusting the pale blue sky. The wall between the top of his credenza and the bottom of the window was covered with scrap paper in a wide assortment of shapes and colors— some partially crumpled, some half-shredded—stuck to the wall with multicolored pushpins. Typed memos, handwritten notes, grainy Xeroxes of mug sheets and stolen vehicles. Mixed in were kids' drawings of houses, flowers and police cars, probably created a long time ago, judging by the faded paper and the framed photos of teenagers propped up against the wall.

"You know where you put your running shoes, though, I'm bettin'," said Ross.

"I guess."

"Good."

"So is this what we're chatting about? My exercise routine?"

Ross allowed himself a twitchy little smile. I'd known him for about three years, if you can really know someone who's mostly asking you questions and looking at you like he thinks you're lying to him. We went to Southampton High School at about the same time, so I might've known him then, but I didn't think so. I didn't have a lot of friends in those days. Actually only one that I could remember. Wouldn't have been Ross Semple.

"I need your opinion," he said.

"Okay."

"What do you think of Robbie Milhouser?"

"Never seen him jog."

"As a person."

"An asshole."

"How much of an asshole?"

"Significant," I said. "A significant asshole. Though you didn't need me to tell you that."

"I hear the feeling was mutual."

"Like I said, an asshole. Just like his old man."

"You didn't see him last night?" Ross asked.

"Haven't seen him in a while."

"You saw him a few days ago. I guess that's a while."

"At the restaurant," I said, "if that's what you mean."

"That's where you got into it. The two of you."

"That wasn't anything. Just a lot of stupid talk."

"Not how I heard it," said Ross.

"People exaggerate."

"Sullivan told me you're afraid of getting hit. Something wrong with your head."

"You like getting hit?"

"Nobody hits me. I'm the Chief of Police," he said, laughing through his nose. Ross had a good sense of humor, judging by the way he laughed at his own jokes, which was the only way you could judge it.

"So what's with Robbie Milhouser?" I asked. "What'd he do?"

"So you never saw him after that thing at the restaurant?"

"I don't think so, though you seem to know more about it than I do."

Ross twirled his cigarette around in the air, watching the resulting curls of smoke rise toward the ceiling.

"You and Burton Lewis still getting along?" he asked.

"Saw him last week. I remember it. Vividly."

"And the blonde girl. Polack. She's a lawyer, too."

"Jackie Swaitkowski. She's my official lawyer. Burton's

just a pal of mine. Paid her a dollar once to retain her services. For the record, she's Irish. Maiden name's O'Dwyer."

"She keep that dollar?"

Ross didn't have an easy job. The Town of Southampton covered a lot of geography and it wasn't all about big houses on the beach like Joshua Edelstein's. Or drunken group rentals or predators who came out of the City in the summer to feast on the herds of the innocent and overfunded. He had his share of local hard cases and screw-ups to deal with. People like Robbie Milhouser.

"You didn't tell me," I said.

"What?"

"Milhouser. What'd he do?"

"Got his head opened up and his brains mashed into brain puree."

He nodded when he said that, as if holding up both sides of the conversation. Then he threw me one of his awkward grins and drank some more of his coffee.

"Dead?" I asked.

"Oh, yeah. Thoroughly."

"Killed?"

"Yup."

"Who did it?"

The goofy grin he was wearing tightened up across his face. And then disappeared completely.

"If you confess right now it'd save us both a lot of trouble," he said.

He took his cigarette out of his mouth and held it between his thumb and index finger the way Nazi generals would do in old war movies. I don't think he did it for effect. He just never knew what to do with his hands.

"That's funny," I told him. "Seeing if I still have a sense of humor?"

Ross's face softened a little at that.

"No, Sam, we all know you got one of those. The question on the table is whether you have a sense of revenge."

I noticed the sawdust on my jeans. It must have been kicked out of the chop box earlier. It was sprinkling down on the battered industrial carpet in Ross's office. I remembered the piece of molding I was about to install on Joshua Edelstein's widow's walk when Ross pulled me off the job. It was stuck in place with only a single nail. With a stiffening breeze it would likely peel off and go cartwheeling down the beach. A thought more disturbing than warranted by the potential consequences. To calm myself I sat back in my chair and dug another Camel out of my coat pocket.

"You actually want me to say I had nothing to do with this?" I asked him.

He smiled at that, his face softening even further.

"Hell no, Sam. I know you're gonna say that. I want to hear you explain *why* you had nothing to do with it. That'll be worth hearing."

"Didn't know I was that entertaining."

"I wish I was entertaining. Maybe if I had a better sense of humor," said Ross, sitting back himself. "A good joke always cracks me up. But I can't tell a joke to save my life."

"Nothing cracks me up," I said. "Must be a deficiency of character."

"Humor isn't what you say. It's what you leave out."

"*Brevity is the soul of wit.*"

"*And tediousness the limbs and outward flourishes,*" said Ross, using his cigarette to punctuate the emphasis on each syllable, a flourish of his own.

"Didn't know they had Shakespeare at the police academy."

"Master's in lit crit. Cornell. Don't ask me to explain."

"I'm not asking you to do anything, Ross. Except lay off this thing with Robbie Milhouser," I told him.

"The one you called an asshole."

"I might call you an asshole. Doesn't mean I'd kill you. I don't kill people. Even for a good laugh."

Ross's face ignited into another of his oversized, ersatz grins.

"We both know that's not true. The killing part. Not the ha-ha part."

He reached into a drawer and pulled out a pair of photographs. One was a mug shot of a young black man, the other a color portrait of a middle-aged white guy.

"Darrin Eavanston and Robert Sobol. Remember them?"

I leaned over to look, then sat back again.

"I remember they were both shot to death. At different times. Both ruled accidental."

"There's a difference between a ruling and the truth."

"Not to me," I said.

"There is to me. If you killed them."

I didn't see much point in responding to that. Even without the advice of counsel.

"Should I be seeing if Jackie's free for the morning?" I asked.

"Not as long as we're just talking here."

"If that's what we're still doing."

Ross lit another cigarette off the stub of the one he'd half-smoked. Then he nodded.

"That's all we're doing," said Ross. "Shouldn't make you nervous. An innocent man has nothing to be nervous about."

"Lots of things make me nervous. Loud noises, lousy drivers, good intentions. The world's loaded with hazards, even when you have nerves of steel."

"Did you know I did ten years in Homicide in the City?" he asked me, genuinely curious.

"I didn't. I thought you put in your whole time in Southampton."

"While you were living large in Connecticut, rollin' in corporate perks, I was swimming in a proverbial sewer of depravity and despair."

"I'm glad I missed that proverb," I told him.

"Didn't like it. Not one little bit. Scared all the time. Every day dead bodies and nasty killers. They're a type, you know. A subspecies."

"Really."

"Yeah. That's what I decided. Wired different."

"Head full of twisted pairs," I said.

He liked that.

"See, that's the kind of joke I like. I wish I could do that."

"So you did some genetic research. Identified this subspecies."

"Nothing clinical," said Ross. "Just observation. And a little reading." He poked his cigarette at my face. "They tell you it's in the eyes. And the attitude. Confident. But a little paranoid. And a hair-trigger temper that goes off over nothing. All calm and normal and then, bam, in your face."

"Maybe you should've taken abnormal psych. Probably had that at Cornell, too."

"Or maybe mechanical engineering. Like you had at MIT. Pretty fancy training for a carpenter."

"Lot of the same principles. Not as much of a paycheck."

He seemed to like that, too. It began to feel like I was only there to provide entertainment. Some diversion from his daily routine. It occurred to me that he was bored. That his brain was itching for a little engagement, something to put a load on the circuitry.

"Look, Ross," I said, "you're the only one here making any money with all this talk. I can only make it on the job. So you need to either tell me what sort of dance we're dancing, or let me get back to work."

He sat way back and gripped the arms of his chair as if to stop them from wrapping around his chest.

"Sure, Sam. Go," he said, magnanimously. "Sorry to take you away from the job. Which I'm assuming you'll be on for another few weeks."

"Something like that."

"No vacations planned?" he asked.

"No. I never go anywhere. No reason to."

That pleased him.

"Good," he said. "That'll help."

"Help what?"

"To know where you are."

I left him sitting at his desk, watching me leave, his eyeballs fixed on the back of my skull. I'd only made it halfway through the open squad room when Sullivan came in from the other side. He had his sunglasses on, but you could still see the frown underneath. He had a Southampton Town Police baseball cap on his head and his shield hanging around his neck. Under his arm was a plastic bag, stapled shut with an official-looking tag covered in numbers and text scribbled with a magic marker.

"What the hell, Sam," he said to me by way of greeting.

"Ask your boss. He's the one who dragged me in here."

"You give a statement?"

"Why would I have to do that?" I asked him. "You gonna tell me what's going on?"

The men and women distributed around the squad room looked up from their computer screens and over the tops of their cubicles—unabashed curiosity a foible of the professionally vigilant.

Sullivan switched the plastic bag from one armpit to the

other. When he did I could see what he was carrying—a heavy construction stapler, the kind you swung into the work like a hammer. It had an orange handle.

"Look familiar?" he asked me.

"I got one. Used it to install the fiberglass in my addition."

"Somebody used this one to staple Robbie Milhouser's scalp to his brain."

"Not in the design specs, but adaptable to the purpose," I said.

"We found it in the dune grass lining the Peconic. Easy tossing distance from Robbie's body. Lousy with forensics. Hair stuck in the mechanism. Smooth handle. Still has a plastic UPC sticker. Very traceable. We'll know who bought it, where and when. Big Brother, he's watchin', man."

"Then have Big Brother tell Ross to get off my ass."

"Can't do that," he said. "I'm recused."

"You can't be recused if you're investigating the scene, Joe."

"Okay, not fully. I mean from talking about you. Or talking to you, for that matter. I'm only dealing with the facts."

"You're talking to me now."

"Not for long. Veckstrom's the lead guy. Lionel Veckstrom. Ten years in plainclothes. I got, what, ten months? Even if I didn't know you, Veckstrom's the lead guy."

"Give him my congratulations."

"Not one to fuck with, Sam. I'm not joking with you."

"That's good. I never joke."

He held up the plastic bag.

"I'm not gonna find anything to not like on this, am I?"

"Maybe a little rust," I said, trying to see the tool through the plastic bag.

"Right. Laugh all the way to life without parole," he said, then brushed past me, which was good because I really wanted to get out of there and back to the job site to retrieve what was left of the workday. I patted his bulky shoulder as he slid by and headed for the door. Officer Orlovsky watched grimly as she buzzed me back into the outside world.

On the way back to the Edelstein job I stopped for coffee at the corner place and used the pay phone. Jackie Swaitkowski didn't answer, but I left her a message. I was getting used to talking to machines. I didn't have one myself, but I sympathized with the principle. I never liked the imperative of a ringing phone.

On the way back to the car, I saw a heavy-lidded guy with a two-day beard and a young woman park their black Range Rover dangerously close to the Grand Prix. I waited for the woman to get out, which she was only able to do by wedging her door hard against the side panel of my car and squeezing herself through the narrow space. She was wearing a purple leather jacket, skintight blue jeans and spiked heels. She didn't notice me watching until she was at the sidewalk.

"Can you ba-leeve the soize of that stupid thing?" she asked me, looking back at the Grand Prix.

I had noticed that before, but the sheer inertial force of the ten-ton door was brought home to me as I slammed it into the Range Rover a dozen times to make a big enough indentation to allow me to slide onto the driver's seat entirely unimpeded. I don't know why Detroit thought they needed such heavy-gauge sheet metal in those days, but it did come in handy sometimes.

I reckoned all it would take was a little number two steel wool to rub the black paint off the edge of the door to be good as new.

I didn't bother checking in with Frank when I got back on the job. I knew what I had to do, and he didn't care about anything but me getting done in time for the painters.

I took another week to finish the interior and exterior trim. Then all that was left was some custom woodwork on a pair of built-in cabinets and a fancy mantelpiece designed by the architect and therefore impossible to buy from a manufacturer. I had a month to build it, and Frank was more than willing to let me do the whole thing in the shop in my basement. A joyful thing for a guy who never took vacations, and who liked to stay near home to be available for intermittent police interrogations.

FIVE

It was well after normal working hours. I was in my shop about to draw out the mantelpiece on a big piece of birch ply when Jackie Swaitkowski pounded on the basement hatch. The booming sound shot Eddie out of his bed in the corner. He glowered at the hatch with a blended look of annoyance and alarm.

"Oh, you're here," said Jackie when I let her in.

When Jackie trotted down the hatch stairwell the ambience of the shop took a sharp turn toward the chaotic. The way she moved around left contrails, billowing clouds of Jackie.

"Sorry. What do you got to drink? Not vodka. I can't stand vodka. Tastes like rubbing alcohol. You gotta have something else. Wine is fine. Red?"

She squatted down to scratch Eddie's long nose. He'd already forgiven the intrusion. A task light from the workbench along the wall reflected off her huge mane of strawberry-blonde hair and cast a hard light across her face, which looked great. Like a movie star's.

"Geez, Jackie, you look great," I said, involuntarily.

She looked up from Eddie, partly defensive, partly pleased.

"Best face money can buy," she said.

Jackie had been through a lot of reconstructive surgery since losing half her face in an explosion. I was there when the whole thing happened and didn't think you could put it back together again. I hadn't seen her since the last surgery. I was wrong.

"I told Hodges you'd come out looking better than ever."

She stood up from petting Eddie and pointed a finger at me.

"Don't push it."

"You'll have to come upstairs for that wine," I told her. "The shop's off limits to booze."

I escorted her to the stairwell.

"That's a first for you."

"Hard to maintain a respectable drinking habit without fingers or thumbs."

When we got upstairs I helped her out of her bright yellow winter jacket. Underneath was a red and black plaid flannel shirt and baggy jeans that crumpled over the tops of furry off-white snow boots. Appropriate gear for the wild and wooded hills above Bridgehampton where she lived.

I dug an expensive pinot noir out of the liquor cabinet.

"Amanda probably wanted you to save this for a special occasion," she said, rummaging for a corkscrew in the junk drawer. "Though tonight would qualify."

"The only special occasion with Amanda would be seeing her again. Though special for whom, I don't know."

Jackie looked at me with something akin to neutrality.

"Hodges told me you were on the outs. Sorry."

"More to the point, what's so special about tonight?"

"Let's sit," she said, waving me toward the screened-in porch. "I know just the place."

I followed her with my vodka-filled aluminum tumbler and my dog. She waited while I stoked the woodstove and got settled in.

"So?" I asked.

"You're about to be arrested for homicide," she said, then sat back in her chair as if that was the beginning and end of the conversation.

I took a long, deep breath, loosening my shoulders and slackening my jaw. An old trick I taught myself when I was in R&D, following similar shocks to the system.

"What a load of crap," I said.

"Oh, it's a load, all right. Tons and tons of it about to land on your head."

"How do you know?"

"Ross called me to offer a volunteer surrender. No flashing lights, no cuffs, no perp walk. I just bring you in. Out of courtesy to Sullivan, not to you."

"Why now?"

"They have all the forensics back from the labs. It's not good. I am still your lawyer, aren't I? Even though you've only paid me a buck so far and I haven't done anything to earn it."

Jackie held the bowl of her wine glass in two hands as if it was a steaming cup of coffee. I slid the grate on the front of the woodstove further open to stoke the flame.

"That buck was a retainer. Now the real money kicks in."

"I've already talked to Burton," she said. "He wants me to lead and let him work the back channels. And consult, of course."

"It's not going to get that far. I didn't do anything."

61

"Where do you want me to start?" she asked, rhetorically. "It was your stapler, with your fingerprints on it and the bar code still intact. Your footprints out on the beach directly facing where they pulled the stapler out of the dune grass. Your fistfight with Milhouser, witnessed by at least three people. Your physical appearance, as described by the witness who saw the jogger heading toward Robbie's project the night of the homicide. To say nothing of your history of violence, criminal record and antisocial behavior."

"You're wrong there. I can be sociable. Ask Hodges."

"This isn't funny, Sam. This one's serious."

I brought my tumbler over to a spot in front of the big windows where I could stand to look out at the bay. It was too dark to see much of anything. There might have been a moon, but it was overcast. The lights on the other shore were little smudges, diffused by the mists that blew across the water. It was hard to believe that it would ever be warm again. That I'd be able to look out at this time of the evening and see the sun as it set, and watch the wavelets rushing off toward the northeast under the urging of the prevailing summer winds—warm, humid southwesterlies displacing the nasty bite from the north.

"Not according to Ross. Everything I say is funny to him."

I heard her sigh, but she pressed on.

"There's good news. In context, at least. Burton's already agreed to post bail. Could be a million-dollar bond, maybe less if we get lucky with the judge. The prosecutor's likely to try for remand, which your voluntary surrender will undermine. Which is why I worked it out with Ross, who doesn't want a little homicide charge to get in the way of common courtesy. So I think I can keep you out of jail while they prepare the indictment."

I turned toward her.

"I didn't want Burton to do that."

"I know. That's why I worked it out in advance. It's a fait accompli. My advice, as your lawyer, is to shut up and take it, and take a moment to thank God that one of the few people in the world you haven't alienated is Burton Lewis."

I went back to looking at the bay. Jackie kept talking.

"You still have to go in tomorrow to get processed. Early, so there's time for them to check for priors and get your prints up to Albany and back, and still have the arraignment later in the day. If everyone stays with the plan you'll never see any jail time and we'll be able to hunker down on the case."

"I've got stuff to do for Frank."

"And you've got to help me save your damn life. Whether you think it's worth saving or not."

"Christ, Jackie. Quit the theatrics."

She jumped out of her chair and shoved herself into me, her face crammed up next to mine. It was the second time in recent memory that a good-looking woman did that. Jackie didn't smell as nice as Amanda. She did, however, yell as loudly.

"You think you've had trouble in your life, Sam? You don't know trouble. This is trouble. Trouble that can get you locked away for the rest of your life, good as dead. I knew you were going to make this difficult. Like it's all up to you to decide every goddamned thing. You're such a fucking . . ."

I put my hands on her shoulders and gently pushed her back from my face. Then I kissed her on the forehead.

"I'm glad you're my lawyer, Jackie," I said to her. "I knew I'd need you some day. That's why I gave you that buck. A big investment for me. I'm completely in your hands, and I'll do anything you want me to do."

She continued to fume, more out of suspicion than anger. Now that I had her face far enough away to get in focus, I was even more impressed with her plastic surgery. I'd seen that same face seconds after it had been ripped apart, so I felt entitled to savor the outcome. Even when she was yelling at me.

"Okay," she said, slowly, "first tell me you didn't do it."

I heard myself snort.

"Impeach my moral credibility, but don't insult my intelligence."

"Why am I doing that?"

I let her go and dropped back into my reading chair next to the woodstove.

"I could care less about Robbie Milhouser. Of all the people I might want to knock off, he wouldn't even be on the list. And if for some crazy reason that changed, I wouldn't smash him over the head with one of my own tools. And even if that happened, through some inexplicable circumstance, I wouldn't be stupid enough to just heave it out onto the beach. Come on, Jackie, you know that."

"So, you're proposing the intellectual arrogance defense. Excellent. Juries love that. Even more than judges."

"The point isn't arrogance. It's ridiculousness."

"For a smart guy, you don't know much about criminal law. All that matters is the physical evidence, and the witnesses, and whatever past behavior is admissible. And determined cops and prosecutors, which you have aplenty in this case. It's way not enough to just say, 'Hell, if I was going to kill that guy I'd have been a lot smarter about how I did it.'"

"Have some more wine. It's a sin to cork a bottle that good."

She huffed her way into the kitchen, giving me a moment to think without distractions.

"Let's back up," I said, when she came back with a full glass. "Let's assume they prove with the bar code that the stapler was sold to me. It probably was, since I bought one that looked like it when I was doing my addition. That's why it has my fingerprints on it. And why I can't find the one I bought."

"You looked?"

"The day I saw Sullivan carrying it around in an evidence bag. He asked me if it looked familiar, which it did. It wasn't in the toolbox in my trunk, or in my shed, or my shop, the only three places it would normally be."

"All normally locked up?" she asked.

"Normally, but not always. And I don't keep close track of a tool like that. Hardly ever use it. Could have lost it anytime between now and last fall."

"Yours were the only prints on it."

"Really. Interesting."

"Especially to the DA. That and the footprints."

"Of course there were footprints. I was over there. Lots of times."

She made another sound of exasperation, like the deflating of a big balloon. I interrupted whatever she was about to say.

"That big idiot's job was right on my jogging route. I watched the whole sorry spectacle. Occasionally I'd run up there after the crews were gone to get a closer look. Never once did I bring along a hammer stapler."

"We'll mark that down with 'I'm too smart to get caught.'"

"Too smart to do it in the first place. Important distinction."

"What else did you tell Ross?" she asked me, suddenly concerned.

"I didn't tell him anything. He wasn't exactly interrogating me. I don't know what he was doing. Some weird version of cat and mouse."

"Don't underestimate Ross Semple. That wackadoodle act is at least fifty percent that. An act."

"I never underestimate English majors. The allusions alone are enough to bring you to your knees."

She pointed her finger at me, which she'd been doing a lot lately.

"I said this was serious."

"No, it's not. It's kindergarten. It's reductio ad absurdum. None of it matters," I said.

"Don't get all nihilistic on me."

"That's not what I mean. What matters isn't all this ludicrous evidence. It's that it exists at all. And that everything points right at me. That's the staggering significance of the whole thing."

"Why so staggering?"

"Because I didn't do it."

She started to point at me again, then thought better of it.

"I was an English major, too," she said. "But I can't allude for shit."

"*If it live in your memory, begin at this line: let me see, let me see.*"

"New rules. No jokes, no poetry."

After that I avoided the topic at hand so hard I tired her out. The expensive pinot helped. Jackie always was a cheap date. Either way, I got her out of my house without pissing her off or turning her sentimental, always a delicate balance.

She told me it was crucial to get an arraignment in the early afternoon. So I had to be dressed and in a civil mood by six-thirty the next morning so we could go over to Hampton Bays and get me properly entered into the criminal justice system, or in my case, renew an old acquaintance.

So I dressed as promised. In a suit and tie, for good measure. The civility of my mood was the greater question. Especially if you accepted Jackie's rendition of the subsequent proceedings.

SIX

"I CAN'T FUCKING BELIEVE that fucking Veckstrom. And you," said Jackie, swatting my shoulder with the back of her hand. "You do know he's one of the people officially in charge of ruining your life?"

I didn't answer right away, which failed to shut her up, more the pity. I was trying to avoid all conversation until I got a cigarette lit and a decent cup of coffee from the diner down on Montauk Highway. I'd been at the Hampton Bays Police HQ on several occasions, but remembered it to be longer on amenities. This gave weight to the theory that murder suspects receive a different standard of hospitality than casual drop-ins.

When we walked into the squad room that morning, composed in our shroud of surrender, Jackie stopped suddenly, grabbed my arm and pulled me back.

"That's Lionel Veckstrom," she hissed in my ear. "He's assigned to your case. You *do not* talk to him."

Veckstrom was a slender, pretty-faced guy deeper into his forties than the dye in his hair would want you to think. He stood at the door of Ross's office with his shoulders sloped forward, sculpting a shell where his chest should have been. As we approached, I had an urge to grip him by the neck and straighten out his posture, though Ross would have likely shot me before my hand could wrinkle the guy's suit jacket. A very expensive jacket with a perfectly coordinated handkerchief and tie. His glasses were the thinnest horn-rims I'd ever seen. When he talked to Ross he waved a ballpoint pen made of burled wood that he gripped like a pointer. I noticed his nails were more nicely manicured than Amanda's.

"We're here on a voluntary basis," said Jackie as we closed in. "No interrogation. Just the usual print 'em, shoot 'em, plead 'em and release 'em."

"I like the shoot 'em part," said Veckstrom, offering Jackie his hand.

She shook it, I'm sure with a grip Veckstrom felt the next day.

"Ross, we need to move to processing immediately," she said.

"I agree," said Veckstrom. "Shouldn't encourage violent behavior."

"What the hell is that supposed to mean?" Jackie asked.

"Your client is well known to engage in brawls. Like the one with Robbie Milhouser the night of April fifth in front of a restaurant on Main Street in Southampton."

"You're planning to characterize what your own police report describes as a man slipping on a curb, and then accidentally hitting his head on the front of a parked vehicle, as a brawl? Interesting."

"Witnesses claim otherwise."

"After the fact. No mention of it in the report. Revisionist history."

"You want us to believe that a former professional boxer threw not one single punch in the midst of a street fight?"

"If you call that a street fight, better steer clear of the real thing," I said.

"Oh, experienced in that, are we?" asked Veckstrom. Before I could answer back, Jackie kicked me in the shins, right out where everyone could see.

"What did I tell you?" she said.

"He addressed me," said Veckstrom to Ross, obviously for the record.

"Don't address him," Jackie said to me. "Ross, we process right now or we start talking police misconduct."

"Go ahead," said Veckstrom. "It's not going to change the fact that Acquillo had motive, malice and means. Confirmed by forensics and eyewitnesses."

"The witnesses are the victim's asshole buddies at a street fight that didn't happen and one half-blind old lady," said Jackie, warming to the taunt, "who thinks she saw somebody who looks like Sam running at *night*."

"Twenty-twenty with her glasses on. Which in fact doesn't matter. Your client has already admitted to jogging past the murder scene."

"But never at night," said Jackie.

"His memory could be faulty."

"There's nothing wrong with my memory," I told him. "For example, I remember hearing you're an asshole."

Veckstrom smiled at me, but not endearingly.

"We've stipulated that Sam runs on Bay Edge Drive," said Jackie, reaching for my arm again, but missing. "But hadn't been in the vicinity of the Milhouser project for at least a week."

"At least a week?" asked Veckstrom. "Do you mean seven days or five, or twenty? Or do you mean a single day?"

Ross picked that moment to light up the cigarette I wasn't allowed to have. Cheap psychological torture. So I spoke to him.

"Somebody tell this dickhead that a week is seven days. At least a week means seven days, plus a couple more. How many's up for grabs. I'll let you pick a number."

This time Jackie got a good grip on the sleeve of my jacket and yanked me down the hall toward the room where you got photographed and fingerprinted and filled out forms. The administrative cops who handled this stuff were friendly and chatty, not unlike nurses who took your blood pressure or gave you a cup to piss in. We didn't see Veckstrom after that, which I was glad for. Too hard a load on the Zen mantras of patience and forbearance.

—

As the coffee from the diner soaked in I started to hear what Jackie was saying from the Grand Prix's front passenger seat, which to be fair was pretty far away.

Ross was in a patrol car escorting us to the arraignment at the Town courts in Southampton Village. I'd offered to bring out some of the same coffee for them as well, but they demurred. A wise choice.

"My experience in criminal defense amounts to about a half dozen cases, only one of which had any substance," said Jackie, referring to her defense of Roy Battiston, "but even I know sometimes police officers, especially hard-ons like Lionel Veckstrom, use overt antagonism as an investigative technique to provoke idiot suspects into incriminating themselves. Easy to do with a hothead whose lack of self-control likely got him in the situation in the first place. Wouldn't work with everybody. Not your well-educated corporate executive types. Cool as a cucumber, those guys."

"It's hard to be cool with a tie on. Squeezes all the blood out of my brain."

"Then loosen that top button. Because if you pull that shit in front of the judge I swear to God I'll plead you guilty and leave you there and go work for clients who actually deserve to be saved."

"I'll be cool. As well as nattily turned out."

"No. You'll be silent. Neutral. No looks, no noises, not one tiny little peep."

"Okay, but my stomach's been growling all morning. This shitty coffee doesn't help."

I burped to prove my point.

"Unbelievable."

—

The arraignment was an interesting theatrical performance. Jackie's role was righteous defender of civil liberties. Deferential, while exuding confidence that the issue at hand would be easily and promptly resolved as soon as the wise and distinguished judge had a chance to merely glance at the ludicrous proposition the prosecutor was peddling as a pathetic excuse for a case. The Assistant District Attorney equaled Jackie's confidence, but was more sparing in her commentary, as if patiently indulging Jackie's childish flights of fancy.

Any of the third-graders sitting in the back of the courtroom, victims of a civics lesson gone terribly wrong, could see the judge was playing along with various fictions created by people for whom he had little or no professional regard.

The ADA was a tall young woman with translucent skin like Jackie's, though with none of the ruddy blush or seditious fields of freckles. In fact, her flesh tone was so uniform it looked applied with a spray gun. Her blonde hair was thin, longer than it would be ten years from now and securely restrained behind a hedge of hairpins that pulled the edge of her scalp tight against her skull. Her legs, on the other hand, were very nice, and she filled her light blue suit the way fashion magazines wanted every woman to think she could.

The only time she looked over at me I winked at her. She instantly flicked her eyes back to the judge.

My timing probably wasn't all that good because that's when she entered a charge of second-degree murder.

"Your honor," she said, "Mr. Acquillo clearly went to Mr. Milhouser's work site with the intention of causing him bodily harm. Transporting to the scene a construction tool that could be easily adapted to lethal purpose."

Jackie jumped in there with a flurry of counterarguments. The judge listened as if he was trying to read *The Daily News* on a subway while Jackie blared a boom box. All I remember of the exchange was the prosecutor's riposte.

"The People are willing to concede to Ms. Swaitkowski's assertions if she can prove that a hammer stapler is common accoutrement among joggers plying the sand roads of North Sea," she said, the word "accoutrement" spoken in what I fancied to be perfect Parisian French.

After that the judge cut Jackie off mid-sentence and ruled that they could hold me over for trial. Then the discussion shifted to the prosecution claiming I was poised to zip off to Brazil immediately following the proceedings, countered by Jackie's rather poignant description of my voluntary surrender, my reduced financial circumstances, my devotion to my daughter in the City—which I wished Allison was in the audience to hear—and other proofs of my general compliance, incompetence and ineptitude, which rendered flight from prosecution not only unlikely, but sadly impossible.

The kicker to Jackie's argument was that Burton Lewis, a towering figure in the legal profession of New York State, was standing by with his checkbook and personal assurance that I'd show up for all scheduled appointments with the court.

I must have been the ADA's only case that day, because she quickly packed up her stuff and left the courtroom as soon as the judge passed down the weary opinion that he was happy to hold Burton's million bucks in lieu of providing room and board to another worthless miscreant.

Jackie was also eager to get out of there, so we got to follow the leggy blonde up the long aisle. As we walked along, Jackie saw where I was looking and gave me another hard smack on the arm.

"Un-goddamn-*believable*," she said.

—

After we left the parking lot Jackie wanted to talk about the evidence against me, examining in detail the content and style of the prosecutor's delivery. I tried to pay attention, but all I really wanted to do was have a cigarette and feel the wind blasting in through the yawning window of the Grand Prix.

"You're not listening to me, are you?" she said finally.

"I'm listening. I'm also thinking. I can do two things at once."

"I'm glad you're so dismissive of the case against you," she said. "That gives the competing advocates clearly delineated positions."

"They have to tell you about everything they got, right? Not allowed to spring any shit?"

"It's called discovery. We get to see their dirty details, we don't have to show them ours. The only problem is it doesn't take effect until after an indictment is handed up. Before that, it's a confidential police investigation."

"I just want to know the set I'm working with."

"Set of what?"

"Operating conditions. The parameters. Engineering talk. Not on the English curriculum."

"You're already thinking something you're not sharing with me. We can't have that this time, Sam. Don't do that to me."

"Okay. Then you can come along."

"Come along where?"

"To the scene of the crime."

After she was finished giving me all the reasons why we had to clear it with the DA's office, I got Jackie to give up her cell phone so I could call Joe Sullivan. He was also in his car, heading over to Bridgehampton, where a horse farm had reported a break-in.

"Just took riding gear, saddles and stirrups. Not the horses themselves," he said.

"Probably not as easy to fence a horse."

"Don't put it past these bozos."

"Say Joe, any reason why I can't go over to that job site where Robbie got killed?"

"I can't talk to you about the case. You know that."

"So in other words, no problem."

"We're not having this conversation."

"Excellent. Thanks."

I hung up the phone and tossed it back to Jackie.

"He said it was fine."

It was a good day for a drive. The sun was out and making things warmer, both the temperature and color of the light.

Buds were bursting into little flowers on the trees and ornamental shrubs and the pin oaks were finally shedding their leathery brown leaves, yielding to the yellow-green nubs that would be fresh growth by late May. I turned off Montauk Highway at Southampton College and traveled north over the railroad tracks and through the Shinnecock Hills Golf Course, where the PGA occasionally held the U.S. Open. Must be a proud moment for the Indians living south of there on a reservation about the size of the golf course. I passed some of the tiny inlets and harbors that sculpted the bay shore and formed the grassy pools from which the more entrepreneurial of the persistently poor pulled a sizeable share of their daily calories.

I slowed the car considerably when we reached Bay Edge Drive. A '67 Grand Prix isn't much good on sand. I alternately hugged opposite sides of the road to clear ruts and avoid scraping the exhaust system off the undercarriage. I'd installed aftermarket shock absorbers to reduce the car's natural seagoing effect, though the stiffer suspension made for a less-than-creamy ride over the gutted surface. Jackie patted around the door and headliner in search of a handhold, eventually wedging herself into the seat with her feet pushed against the dashboard.

"Let me know when you're going to stop so I can puke out the door," she said.

"Almost there."

Robbie's project was on a narrow two-acre lot that was solid woods until you reached the bayfront. There it opened up to a yard that once comfortably held a single story bungalow not unlike my parents' cottage, but was now filled with Robbie's architectural grotesquerie. It had been a while since I'd seen it up close, and I was surprised at the progress. If it wasn't for all the vans and pickups scattered around you'd think it was ready for the new owners to move in. I stopped the car and let the implications sink in.

"Where's the yellow tape?" I asked Jackie.

"Long gone, Sam. Before you start in on me, it's almost impossible to keep a crime scene frozen in the middle of a construction site, especially after everything's been gone over, photographed and videotaped. As it was, Milhouser bellyached every day until it was released. Claimed financial hardship."

"Milhouser?"

"Jefferson. Robbie's heir. His father."

"So that's that," I said. "We have to trust the cops got everything. That they got it all right."

"Not cops, exactly. Forensics experts. They don't usually miss anything, but yeah. What they got is all we got."

"Interesting."

"I'm sorry, Sam."

"Don't be. It doesn't matter."

"Oh, Christ."

"Let's go look anyway," I said, getting out of the car.

I was halfway to the front door, with Jackie a few steps behind, when Patrick and his sidekick from the other night came out to greet us. They were wearing loaded tool belts and were covered in sheetrock dust. Patrick held a slim tacking hammer.

"You got some kind of balls," he said, slapping the tool on his thigh.

"If it's gonna be hammers, let me get my sledge out of the trunk."

He looked past me at Jackie bringing up the rear.

"Who's the new chick?"

"His attorney, Sport," said Jackie, moving in front of me before I could stop her. "And an officer of the court in an active homicide investigation. You'll want to think very hard about what you're going to say before you say another word," she added, sticking her finger in his face, her new thing, which I preferred looking at from that vantage point.

He started to open his mouth and she moved in a little closer.

"You were saying?" she asked.

A long pause followed.

"I was saying," he took a fake little bow, "what can I do for you folks?"

"We're here to examine what's left of this crime scene," she said, putting her hands on her hips, but holding her ground. "What you can do is move out of the way. Please."

Patrick spread his arms and backed off to the side, shoving the other guy along with him.

"Be my guest," he said.

Jackie strode passed him and I followed, giving Patrick a friendly little nod.

The interior of the house was partially sheetrocked, which explained the dust, but far less finished than the outside. Electricians were still pulling cable and a pair of framing carpenters were ripping out a section of wall. A Vietnamese insulation crew, the only guys I recognized, were sitting in the middle of the room with a stack of woolly pink rolls waiting for instructions. A big Sub-Zero refrigerator was half-uncrated in what would become the kitchen. A cluster of copper plumbing protruded from the middle of the floor, promising a center island that I could tell by eyeball the kitchen was too narrow to accommodate.

Jackie led me to the bay side of the house, anchored by a large glass-enclosed room. Not quite a living room, but more than a porch. No plans I could see for a woodstove, daybed or busted-up pine table.

"This is where they found Robbie," said Jackie. "Right in the middle of the room, which I guess is here."

She stood looking down at the freshly laid hardwood floor.

"They took a lot of photographs," she said hopefully.

"Was it one whack, or a bunch of whacks?" I asked her.

She looked up again.

"More than one. Several. More than necessary."

"Assuming the killer knew the necessary number."

"Right."

"Front of the head, back of the head, side?" I asked.

"Back. All in the back."

"Which way was he lying?"

"I don't remember. It's in the photographs."

I walked over to the window and looked at the Little Peconic. With the sun's arc getting higher with the changing seasons, the water more clearly reflected the blue sky. Seasonal navigational aids—red and green buoys and flags—were back in place outside Hawk and Towd Ponds. Across the bay off the North Fork a sliver of white sail, heeled hard against the persistent northwesterly, moved slowly across a background of gray trees and a blur of waterfront development.

"Let's get some air," I said, walking out a set of French doors onto the muddy plain surrounding the construction site.

"Dog prints in the mud," I said. "I know the culprit."

"Good. They only took casts of the human's."

We walked down to the beach.

"Not much sand," said Jackie.

"Yeah. Only a little up above the waterline. The rest is pebbles. No footprints there."

"The stapler must have been thrown from here," she said.

"But why into the grass? There's only about twenty yards of pebble beach between here and the shoreline. If you're going to ditch a murder weapon, why not just toss it in the water?"

"Doesn't matter," she said. "It's your tool, your finger-prints."

"Now who's being nihilistic?"

Jackie walked up next to me and put her arm through mine. She laid her head on my shoulder.

"I'm sorry, Sam. I'm not up to this. I want to be, but this is so way over my head. We need Burton to get you a lawyer who knows what they're doing."

I used my arm like a nutcracker to give hers a little squeeze.

"If Shakespeare's out, so is self-doubt."

"I want to do it for you, Sam. God knows why. But it's your actual life at issue here, something I can't seem to make you understand."

"I know it's hard to believe, but I used to have a job," I whispered into her ball of frizzy hair. "Before they made me manage everything, I was a troubleshooter. When trying to diagnose a systems failure I'd waste a lot of time with engineers obsessing over current conditions, rehashing what we already knew over and over and over. This would come close to destroying what little sanity I had."

"And your point," said Jackie into my suit jacket.

"You're worrying about the wrong things. I want you to represent me because you already know me. And I know you. And trust you, more than you trust yourself. Burton will look after the technical stuff. He trusts you, too. Neither of us care about your experience in criminal law. We care about your brain. It's a good one."

After a few minutes she nodded. An abrupt, decisive little nod. I let her go and she followed me back through the house.

We maneuvered around various tradesmen, who politely shifted to the side, and Patrick, who didn't. I kept Jackie between us knowing her finger was mightier than a fist. Though she'd been known to bring both into play. Patrick stared at me, transmitting his eagerness to rip me from limb to limb. I'd had a lot of practice with stares like that, professionally and otherwise, so it didn't bother me. I was more concerned about his long reach and ropey arms. Even an amateur can do a lot of damage, any of which I could ill afford.

We made it out alive and I drove her back to my cottage where she'd left her Toyota pickup. The vagaries of the sand road kept her preoccupied and mostly silent, so I was able to send her on her way with a minimum of commentary. I was happy about that. After a while all that white noise gets tiring.

Eddie greeted me with his normal routine—walking up my pant leg so I could scratch his head. After some of that, I took him and my blind allegiance to foolhardy decisions into the cottage to fill up my aluminum tumbler, which I brought out to the screened-in porch, sealed off against encroaching common sense, and drank until absorbed into the black forgiving night.

———

Around three in the morning I got dressed in a fresh set of jogging clothes. It took a while to lace up a new pair of sneakers. My treasured Sauconys, broken-in to the point of disintegration, were in an evidence bag with the rest of the stuff at the Suffolk County police lab. Eddie, cued by the outfit, sat and waited, though none too enthusiastically. He led the way to the side door, where we met the predawn chill of early spring on the Little Peconic.

I led us to the start of the sand road that paralleled the coast. It was still dark, though a pale glow to the east showed the sun threatening to break through the horizon. Most of the houses along the way were still blacked out, but a few had a light on here and there, tradesmen getting ready for the seven-thirty start time or commuters contemplating distant journeys Up Island. Twenty minutes into the run I turned onto Bay Edge Drive and came up to Robbie's project. Without breaking stride, I jogged up to the house. There were two battered step vans parked on the lawn.

I tried the van doors, which were locked. Then I tried the doors to the house, which were also locked, uncharacteristically. So I kicked out a basement window and shimmied inside. The smell of partially cured concrete mingled with that of fresh-sawn fir and composite beams from the first floor structure overhead. I opened the basement hatch and whistled for Eddie, who streaked across the yard and shot down the hole as if pursued by avenging waterfowl. The two of us trotted upstairs.

I'd brought a flashlight, which I used to light my way from room to room. Though a masterpiece of misguided strategies, the house was stumbling toward completion. Tile covered the foyer floor and light fixtures were being installed in ceilings and over kitchen countertops.

I carefully examined every room, then moved back down to the basement, where I shot the little Maglite into all the dark corners. Then I went back up through the basement hatch to where the step vans were parked on the muddy front lawn. I was wearing a pair of cowhide work gloves, which protected my hands when I punched out the glass in the driver's side door of the first van. The back was jammed with crap—chop boxes, collapsible work stands, table saws, battered plastic and metal tool chests, milk cartons stuffed with cans filled with sheetrock screws and random bits of hardware, tool belts and salvaged plumbing and electrical parts—the generic flotsam and jetsam of the average construction site. I looked, but didn't find what I wanted.

That's because it was in the other van under piles of pink fiberglass. A white cardboard box. I stuffed it under my arm and left the van, whistling again for Eddie, who was out on the beach scouring for detritus more to his liking—horseshoe crabs and gobs of putrid seaweed salad.

Under a decent moon and propelled by a lopsided inter-species competition, we made it back to the cottage while it was still dark. I brewed a huge pot of Viennese cinnamon coffee, made with freshly ground beans imported from the corner place in the Village, and a mess of eggs and tasty protein to fortify myself against the upcoming round of peril and deception.

SEVEN

BURTON LEWIS lives a block in from the ocean in a huge house built on the foundation of the one his grandfather built, which was built on the one his great-grandfather built before that. The house has a beautiful white gate you can enter only by getting past Isabella, the middle-aged *Cubana* who runs his personal affairs. There's an intercom stuck out on a curved post so you can call the house without getting out of your car. There is also a closed-circuit TV camera hidden somewhere, as proven by Isabella's ability to start in on me the moment I pulled into the driveway.

"He's not here," she said, before I had the window halfway down.

"But will be here, soon? Or never again?"

"You could call ahead like normal people."

"That's where you're wrong," I said. "Normal people drop in."

"I don't have instructions."

"Goddammit, Isabella."

"He's at the Schooner," she said. "For the afternoon. I don't think he wants to be interrupted."

"From a pool game?"

"He need to concentrate."

"What's he playing for, controlling rights to Morgan Stanley?"

The Schooner was a bar and grill in the woods above Bridgehampton. It was one huge open room encompassing the first floor of a small hotel built by a Hungarian immigrant who'd never been to the Catskills, but imagined his creation as a southern outpost of the Borscht Belt. Surrounding the main building were clusters of bungalows, stone grills with picnic tables, a game room for playing bridge or canasta and a clubhouse with a stage where they used to heckle stand-up comics and dance the bunny-hop. The Schooner was the only commercial survivor in the complex, though even that was difficult to fathom given the persistent scarcity of paying clientele. It did have four rock-solid old pool tables, however, and an authentically dank, retrograde ambience particularly suited to eight-ball and beer. And compared to the Pequot, it was like a night at The Palm.

Burton was a lawyer by trade. He'd started out as a criminal attorney dispensing free representation out of a storefront in the City, but then found himself attracted to the subtle intricacies of corporate tax law, leading him to join, and eventually manage, the law firm his grandfather had formed as a captive guardian of his global banking business. Burton never completely abandoned criminal defense—his caseload was often on par with the two or three full-time associates staffing the storefront operation—but still managed to grow the corporate practice into a small army of lawyers packed into a nineteenth-century building he owned down on Wall Street.

There were about ten people in the Schooner, maybe two percent of capacity. Burton was working the front table, playing a guy in an ochre Oxford-cloth shirt with a polo player on the chest and a pair of wide-wale corduroys decorated with embroidered pheasants. The guy had a tight mat of kinky black hair framing a forehead that towered above a pair of bifocals in slender black frames. He was a lot shorter than Burton, small boned with a little bowling-ball gut. His lips were thin and pale, as if pursing them too tightly had permanently drained away all the blood.

Burton twisted the tip of his cue stick into a little block of blue chalk as he watched me approach.

"Sam," he said. "Just in time to spoil my concentration."

"That's what Isabella said would happen."

"Performance anxiety."

Burton was an ectomorphic somatotype, slender approaching gaunt, with long limbs and loose joints that facilitated graceful, elegant movements. His outfit looked like it came from a vintage clothing store specializing in early-twentieth-century Ivy League toff. He was in his late forties, yet his hair was still thick and naturally brown and cut long enough to fall into his face when he leaned down to take aim at the cue ball.

I scanned the table and saw one eight ball and a single solid nearly camouflaged by a knot of stripes.

"You finish up, I'll freshen the drinks," I said, looking flagrantly at Burton's opponent.

"Oh, sorry," said Burton, standing up again. "This is Hayden Grayson. Budding legal pundit. Hayden, Sam Acquillo."

"Way past punditry myself," I said, putting out my hand.

Hayden's grip was smooth-skinned but firm. A professional handshake.

"Though not beyond puns," said Burton.

"Burton said you might show up anytime," said Hayden. "This is my first trip to the Hamptons. It's very beautiful."

I looked around the inside of the Schooner.

"You oughta see the rest of the place. So what am I buying you guys?"

Burton ordered a Baileys on the rocks and his date an Amstel Light, neither of which I thought the Schooner had ever heard of, but they managed to rustle them up. After my first day in court I felt entitled to a double Absolut, which they didn't have, so I told them to throw a lot of ice and lemon into a tall glass of Smirnoff.

When I got back to the table Hayden was racking up the balls. His movements were spare and exacting. After settling the rack, he pulled it away with a little flourish. Burton handed me a cue.

"Care to break?"

"No, no. Your table."

His break sank a stripe and a solid in the two opposing corner pockets, though most of the balls stayed packed together like a small herd of frightened sheep.

"So who's ahead in this tournament?" I asked them.

"You have to ask?" said Hayden. "Burton, of course."

I was overjoyed to see the bartender light a cigarette. Some genius had apparently outlawed smoking in bars in New York. Fortunately, Schooner management hadn't gotten word, isolated as it was in the northern frontier of Bridge-hampton. I dug out my pack of Camels.

"Hayden writes for and edits *Psychiatric Jurisprudence Quarterly*," said Burton, squinting down the cue at an orange ball cut out from the herd. "You've heard of it, no doubt."

"I don't read anything with words I can't pronounce," I said.

"It sounds much more grand than it is," said Hayden,

taking a tentative sip of his light beer. "Really just the driest of the dry."

"Unless you're a head case in trouble with the law," I said.

"Which is particularly germane to Sam's appearance on the scene," said Burton, standing abruptly, scowling at the orange ball, which stared back, barely threatened much less propelled by his efforts. "If I'm not mistaken."

"I teed that up for you," I told him.

"That's golf, Sam. We're playing eight-ball."

I lucked into sinking three of my stripes before relinquishing the table. Hayden seemed unimpressed, though he felt compelled to say "nice" after each shot. I think anticipating the next "nice" cost me a fourth.

"Ms. Swaitkowski has kept me thoroughly briefed," said Burton, as he studied the disposition of the balls. "And I had a long chat with Ross Semple. He's being uncharacteristically obdurate."

"Blood in the water," I said.

"Something like that."

"Thanks for bailing me out. Jackie thought I'd fight you on that, but I'm really glad you did it."

Burton looked over and smiled at me.

"Good for you, Sam. Genuine appreciation, honestly expressed."

Hayden tried to look like he was happy studying the Schooner's interior decor. It felt like bad form to leave him out of the conversation.

"I got charged with murder," I told him. "Burton's been helping me out. All just a big misunderstanding. How long you guys been hanging together?"

Hayden deferred to Burton by glancing in his direction.

"Oh, off and on for some time now," said Burton. "Hayden's been complaining about the miseries of winter in the City and I thought a recuperative stay in the Hamptons would be just the ticket," he added, right before muffing his next shot.

"None of the pool establishments we've played in town quite rise to the level of the Schooner. That I concede," said Hayden, tilting his beer in a toast to our environs.

I cleared out the rest of my stripes, but was left with an impossible shot on the eight ball. All I could do was avoid dropping the cue ball in the pocket, which I did anyway, leaving Burton in excellent position to even the game.

"So there's a fair amount of physical evidence—shoe prints, lethal staplers, that sort of thing," said Burton.

"So they say."

"I still don't see much of a motive on your part. A brawl at a bar?"

"Hardly a brawl. Milhouser was punching a lot of air and I just settled him down."

"Veckstrom has subpoenaed your medical records from Southampton Hospital, on a theory of Semple's that even the threat of a fight with Robbie Milhouser was a serious matter for you. That you have a legitimate fear of brain damage growing out of your boxing career and various related, extralegal activity," said Burton, before managing to kiss one of his balls into a side pocket, using a gentle, almost silent tap of the cue.

"If I thought Milhouser was a threat I'd really be brain damaged."

Burton looked thoughtful.

"Milhouser was several inches taller and sixty pounds heavier. And about ten years younger. With a reputation for reckless, drunken behavior. And he was supported by two other strong young men. That would sound like a threat to a reasonable jury."

He chose to make his next shot a long trip across the felt

that almost cut the target into a corner pocket, but sank the cue ball instead.

"Damn."

"So they only have to prove I'm both stupid and chicken-shit," I said.

He stood up to chalk the stick, as if that was the cause of the problem.

"When was the last time you went to the boxing gym in Westhampton?" he asked.

"It's been a while. I've been humping on Frank's big job. Don't need to."

"Hm. And when was the last time you got into the ring to spar?" Burt asked me, even though he knew the answer.

"Christ, almost never out here. I don't spar with people who don't know what they're doing. They just get hurt, or pissed, or both. Anyway, I'm fifty-four years old. Why risk some jamoke getting in a lucky shot?"

Burton looked even more thoughtful, as he pursed his lips and nodded.

"I see. So you were afraid of risking . . . what?"

"Jesus Christ."

"Anyway, it's just a theory. I think I'm buying this round," he said, staring into his empty glass of Baileys.

While he was away I sat back to work out a strategy for the eight ball. Hayden's eyes flickered around the table as he sipped his light beer.

"What do you think?" I asked him.

"You should go for a change of venue. These locals are harboring some kind of a grudge," he said, then tore his eyes away from the table to look at me. "Just from what I've been overhearing. Don't mean to interfere."

"No worries. All jurisprudence is welcome. About my case or the next shot on the eight ball."

"I think you should cut into the corner pocket. The side's closer, but too risky. Too much angle," he said. "Add a little bottom spin. Keep you out of the other corner."

"That's what I was thinking."

I was tempted to try for the side pocket anyway, but when Burton got back to the table I sank the ball in the corner, as suggested.

"Well, there goes the trophy," said Burton as he handed out the round of drinks.

"Not until Hayden's up to bat. He insisted," I said, dropping a pair of quarters into the slot to free up the balls. Hayden looked reluctant, but racked up the balls as I threw them out on the table, though not with the same deliberate precision as the time before.

"I'm concerned about this, Sam," said Burton.

"Tell me more about Ross's theories," I said, leaning down to break up the little triangle of balls.

"A person's prior criminal record is usually inadmissible, except all those times when it isn't. I don't know how much the judge will allow, but they'll try to show a pattern of violence, consistent with a vengeful nature. General antisocial behavior, a picture of a man unhinged, out of control."

"Fuck them."

"Ross may or may not actually believe in the theory," said Burton. "He may not even think you killed Robert Milhouser, but he's fairly sure you're guilty of killing someone. In particular that fellow Sobol, who was in on the swindle with Roy Battiston, and an unfortunate drug merchant in Bridgeport, Connecticut named Darrin something. An interesting story. I'd never heard it before."

"Those cases were settled in court. Whatever happened to double jeopardy?" I asked.

"An accidental death can always be retried as a homicide," said Hayden. "Apples and oranges."

"More relevant to you," said Burton, "the police keep their own scorecard. Following the logic of law enforcement, this is the case that'll make everything right."

"A kind of *Psychotic Jurisprudence,*" I said to Hayden.

"That's our sister publication," he said, taking over the table and dropping three ducks in a row. His fourth shot was a delicate combination that sank another of his balls and left the cue ball an inch from the next, perfectly aligned with the corner pocket.

"Nice," I said.

His next shot went wildly wide, giving me back the table.

"Pity," I said.

"Hayden is a symphony of unrealized potential," said Burton.

"I can see that," I said, slamming one of my balls in the corner and scratching an instant later.

"Seems to be a curse today," I said, setting the cue ball back on the table.

Hayden squatted down and peered across the felt to plan his next shot from the cue ball's perspective.

"It's easy to be misled by the way popular culture represents the legal system," said Burton. "Complexities and subtleties make for good entertainment, but the reality is mostly blunt force. A corpse, a suspect with no alibi and a murder weapon that connects the two. A simple formula, custom-made to stir the passions of a prosecutor like Edith Madison."

Hayden thinned out the population of solids while Burton was talking. He had them pared down to a single ball before yielding the table.

"I felt the same way about her ADA."

I put way too much topspin on my next shot, causing the

cue ball to ricochet up off the table and fly straight at Hayden's head. He jerked to the side and snatched it out of the air.

"Sorry, man," I said.

"This isn't tennis," said Burton.

"Must be repressed nerves."

"First sensible thing I've heard from you," said Burton. "Get those nerves out in the open where they belong."

"You sound like Jackie."

"A very bright woman. You should listen."

"She tried to quit my case, but I wouldn't let her. She said she was over her head."

"She is," said Burton, "but I won't let her go under. We'll plan everything together. She'll be fine in the courtroom."

Hayden recovered well enough from his turn at shortstop to put away the game. He sank the eight ball in a corner pocket after banking it off the rail at the opposite end of the table.

"It's a good thing you guys were occupied," he said. "I'd have never made that shot with your eyes on me."

"It's amazing what people can do when nobody's looking," I told him as I invested two more quarters and started stuffing the rack.

"You'll have to try to be cooperative, Sam," said Burton. "I know that runs against the grain."

"Like I told Jackie, all I can say is I didn't do it. You got to take it from there."

"Not even that is necessary," said Burton. "Your break, Hayden," he added, looking down at the freshly racked triangle of balls.

"So you're not even going to ask me?" I said. "Jackie did."

Burton waited until Hayden had the balls scattered around the table, sinking none.

"I never ask," he told me. "What you say one way or the other will have no bearing on how I approach the case. Utterly immaterial."

"Not to me."

He walked over with his cue stick in his left hand and put his right hand on my shoulder.

"Remember, I'd rather you clubbed that man to death than lie to me."

I'd never felt anything but good feelings toward Burton since I met him, and didn't feel any differently then. But I wasn't going to let that one sit where it lay.

"No way, Burt," I told him. "I didn't club him and I'm not lying. My innocence has to be a matter of fact, a firm assumption upon which everything is based."

The gangly introvert smiled at me warmly and gave my shoulder a squeeze.

"Very well, Sam. So it'll be."

He exchanged an uninterpretable look with Hayden before going back to the game, which he won, along with the next two. He declared himself the eight-ball champion and suggested we go to three-way straight pool. By then it was dark outside, and with enough vodka inside me to sharpen my faculties and weaken my better nature, I ran the table my first time up.

Hayden looked at me with a suspicious eye.

"What do you call that?" he asked.

"Killer pool, baby," I told him.

PART TWO

EIGHT

AFTER LEAVING MY WIFE ABBY and my job running a corporate R&D operation I lived in hotel rooms around Connecticut and the northern exurbs of New York. I paid for them with my corporate credit card, which no one at the company, inexplicably, had thought to shut off. Given my mental clarity in those days, this was an important convenience. All I needed to sustain my existence was to reach into the first inside sleeve of my wallet.

I also conserved energy by going from room to room without bothering to bring along my clothes. This resulted in frequent trips to discount stores where I was delighted to find good quality underwear at very reasonable prices. It was at one of these cavernous emporia that I discovered cheap polyester tote bags, an excellent solution to the challenge of transporting my ever-renewed wardrobe of Levi's and cotton T-shirts.

During all my years of marriage to Abby I almost never walked into a retail outlet of any kind, unless you included the deli in White Plains where I bought coffee and a copy of *The New York Times.* Shopping had become an abstraction. Abby purchased all the family's food and furnishings, picked out the restaurants and vacation accommodation, and bought all my clothes. Except for Levi's and T-shirts and workout gear, all of which I ordered through the mail. I had them sent to the company to prevent Abby from throwing out the packages, an unexplainable habit of hers. I got all my books out of the library, and before the company started supplying them, bought my cars from the ad hoc inventory stuck out on lawns with homemade signs taped to the windshields.

For my job I'd spend a fair amount of time in Bombay, Kuala Lumpur, Dubai and the fetid alleys of Cairo, but I never felt more alien than I did walking under the blue-green fluorescent lights of those retail monstrosities.

I eventually misplaced my company car, which they'd also failed to retrieve. It was a silver four-door imported luxury sedan that vanished one night somewhere in Bridgeport, Connecticut. I really liked that car. It was fast and quiet and comfortable. It had a cupholder big enough for a large Diet Coke, which you could fill up partway with bourbon, plus an ashtray and a startlingly loud stereo. I'd occasionally launch the day lying naked on my bed in the hotel room, smoking cigarettes and watching pay-as-you-go movies on the TV, and then suddenly find myself driving the car through the leafy, curvaceous countryside of northern Fairfield County. Usually dressed.

If you head north of Fairfield, past Danbury, you find yourself in Litchfield County, a Manhattanite preserve thick with white Congregational churches and twentieth-century novelists.

One day I managed to wander my way straight through Connecticut and into Massachusetts, where I was met by a big welcome sign at the border. I'd lived a lot of years in Massachusetts, so I took the welcome for what it was worth and drove on anyway. I went as straight north as the twisted two-lane roads would allow, aided by the car's electronic compass with a read-out built into the rearview mirror.

It was a warm, soft summer day following several days of rain. The dominant oaks and maples were laden with billows of dark green leaves. Radio reception filtered out everything but NPR stations playing Mozart or Oscar Peterson or vaguely condescending commentary on issues of the day I regrettably knew nothing about. The roads were filled with pickups and Volvo station wagons plastered with political and social declarations. I envied the unabashed conviction.

Things got a lot hillier when I hit the northwest corner of the Commonwealth. The Berkshires gave way to the foothills of the Green Mountains, which you ascend on narrow switchback roads that follow trout streams and old Indian trails through verdant tunnels made of hemlock and southern pine. Eventually I crested the ridge of a mountain and repeated the experience on a downward plane. Not long after that I was in Vermont.

Somewhere south of Bennington I hit Route 7 and headed north. I was relieved to be driving in a somewhat straight line, going up and over an endless succession of hills, past open fields with huge green mounds in the distance and through strange little villages of eighteenth-century inns, trailer homes and factory outlets.

Nearly hypnotized by the experience, I almost missed the sign for Route 125 East. I spun the front tires of my car over the pitted macadam as I made a hard turn and plunged into another narrow, deep wooded passage. Along the way I stopped for gas at a two-pump station outside Bread Loaf. I talked the sallow young woman behind the greasy glass-topped counter into filling my big paper cup with ice, over which I poured a couple fingers of bourbon and a fresh Coca-Cola.

From there it was an easy run over to Route 100 and then up to Warren where I owned a time-share that I'd never seen. Abby was the one who liked to ski, a pursuit that for me was never more than a theoretical construct. I understood the principle, something about sliding down snow-covered hills in frigid temperatures and periodically breaking your leg. It worked better for me as a vacation from my wife, who for over ten years would spend the bulk of her winter weekends and an occasional full week on the slopes.

I remembered the address from writing countless monthly checks to a place called Fox Run Borders, LLC, which always struck me as inherently contradictory. Even so, it took a lot of asking around town before I found someone to give me directions.

"Oh shoo-wa, that's over thea towa'd the skiin'," a red-nosed old guy in a black T-shirt and Red Sox cap told me. "Near Suga'bush. The place ya're talkin' about is up inna woods. Exclusive. Fulla New Yawkas."

It was easier to find than he led me to believe, probably because of a sign on the road featuring a fox who was neither running, nor looking entirely secure within his borders. More ambivalent, which was how I was feeling.

The development looked like any suburban enclave you'd find down on the flatlands. Little two-story colonial houses with narrow clapboard siding stained a uniform blue-gray, scattered around a simulated town green in the middle of which they were building an octagonal gazebo. Encircling the observable area were tall, mature trees, but the landscape within looked freshly cultivated.

I slowly cruised along the gently curved streets, searching

for number 35G. There was little danger of bumping into Abby. Her lawyer had told me she'd be away for a few weeks, that she'd left some papers for me to sign related to some proceeding he wanted me to attend, all of which as usual I ignored.

After searching most of the neighborhood I found 35G. A woman, probably in her late seventies, wearing oversized canvas gloves and a broad-brimmed hat was out on the lawn fussing with a huge, unruly bottlebrush buckeye.

"Excuse me," I called to her through the open car window, "are you staying here?"

"Not me. I just thought this bush needed some trimming," she said, without looking in my direction. "Of course I'm staying here," she added, punctuating the statement with a deft snip of her pruning shears.

"Do you know Abby Acquillo?" I asked.

She stopped snipping and looked over at me.

"You mean Abigail Vaneer?"

"Vaneer?"

"She doesn't like you to call her Abby. That's what her husband told me in no uncertain terms. Rather grand of her."

She stood next to the bush with one hand on her hip and the other firmly gripping the sharp little tool.

"And I'm talking to?" she asked.

"Friend of Abigail's."

"They're not here. Went to ski in Italy. As if the winter here's not enough for them. After that they'll be at their other unit, I imagine. Not staying here. I'm on for the next two months."

"I don't know the other place. What if I want to leave a note?"

"Nothing to stop you. It's just around the corner. 15A. Right off the common area. Original units. Not as well made, but the trees are bigger. All I've got are these disreputable *Aesculus parviflora*," she said, swatting at one of the branches with her pruning scissors.

I thanked her and went to look for 15A. It was a little hard to drive through the misty, burning haze in front of my eyes. Surprise is always such an affront to the intellectually arrogant.

I tried to picture Abby with Tony Vaneer. I'd met him at a neighborhood party, maybe at our house, maybe someone else's. I rarely cared one way or the other. Abby relished any form of social engagement with the Fairfield County social set, if only to have a go at the other women's fashion sense or interior decor. These events took place on Saturday nights, so I was normally wrung out from an afternoon at the boxing gym and too weak to mount an effective defense. At least there was always plenty of booze and tasty finger food and occasionally a conversation that wouldn't immediately trigger an attack of narcolepsy. Tony was always one of the guys there, with his wife, a washed-out, nervous woman with thin tufts of orangey brown hair who held her cigarette between her fingers like Audrey Hepburn. I remember her calling me a fellow ski orphan. That, like me, she hated the snow.

I don't remember asking her where Tony went to ski, so little did I care. I think her name was Judith. When she talked to you it felt like she was really talking to herself. Distant, absorbed by her inner dialogue. Her husband, on the other hand, was verbose, and had dyed black hair combed straight back and a penchant for white turtlenecks, two things that set me on edge even though I didn't know he was sleeping with my wife.

Number 15A was on a corner lot, with the front of the house perpendicular to the common area. I got out of the car and walked around the house, looking through slits in the drawn blinds. I didn't really need to go inside. I got the gist of the place by the arrangement of the windows and the external dimensions. At least well enough to form a concept.

I got back in my car and drove all the way down to Brattleboro, where I was reasonably sure I'd find the necessary provisions. I spent the next two days securing what I needed, which took me to early Sunday morning, which was part of the plan.

I left the company car in the parking lot of a Holiday Inn and drove a pickup truck I'd stolen from the Brattleboro train station back to Warren. Along the way I stopped to grab a set of license plates off a pickup raised on blocks behind a roadside repair shop. I pulled into a picnic area next to a trout stream to have a late breakfast of bagel and sliced ham, after which I switched the plates. It was approaching midday when I got to Fox Run Borders.

At that time of year few of the units were occupied, the old lady in 35G notwithstanding. It was dead quiet when I pulled in with the pickup and went over to where they were building the gazebo. Through some sort of perverse providence they'd left a big Caterpillar front-end loader on the site, apparently brought in to sculpt the surrounding landscape.

The sunporch off the back of Tony's house had been left open, providing excellent cover for breaking in through the rear door. Tony had equipped the place with an alarm, but hadn't turned it on, another pleasant bit of good luck. I saw a photo of Tony and Abby on the mantelpiece. I resisted the temptation to search the rest of the living area and went down into the basement.

The support structure of the house was what I figured—a pair of central girders supported by a row of lally columns running the length of the building, interrupted in the middle by the basement stairs. Two-by-ten floor joists ran perpendicular from the sill to the tops of the girders.

I went back outside to the pickup and dug an eighteen-inch Stihl chain saw out of the back. I brought along a box of spare chains in case I hit a nail, which would instantly render the chain saw almost useless.

Back in the basement I pulled the start cord, then immediately regretted the lack of ear protection. No matter how hard you try to plan for a weekend project you always forget something. The best I could do was stuff my ears with pieces of paper towel from Tony's washer/dryer area and give myself a reminder about using angry little two-cycle engines in confined, concrete-walled spaces.

I stood on a step stool and quickly cut a pair of holes in the box above the sill plate, about eight feet apart, four feet to either side of the centerline of the house. I shut off the saw and ran upstairs. I looked around the neighborhood and it still looked abandoned. No curtains moving in the windows, no gardeners leaning on rakes looking my way.

I backed the pickup truck across Tony's side yard so I could feed a heavy yellow polypropylene rope coiled in the bed down through the right hole in the sill. I ran back down into the basement and pulled the rope across the length of the basement, around the furthest lally column, then back across and up through the other hole, thus creating a continuous loop circumnavigating the whole row of lally columns holding up the house. I tied the end of the rope to the trailer hitch off the back of the pickup and drove slowly across the lawn, across the street and into the common area, watching in the rearview mirror as the yellow line payed out behind me, subsequently dragging along a lifting-grade industrial chain to which it was attached. In a few minutes I saw the end of the chain emerge from the second hole. I gave it fifteen feet of clearance, then drove back to the street where I parked the truck and retrieved the pull rope.

Back down in the basement, I put on a fresh chain and fired up the saw, which cut through the ends of the joists where they were loaded on the central girders like the proverbial knife through butter. I only bit about eight inches into the nominal ten-inch-wide lumber to avoid nails shot down from the subfloor above me. I still hit a couple, but had the replacement chains to keep production running along smoothly.

I checked my watch when I ran upstairs for the last time and was encouraged to see I'd only been on the job for about forty minutes. This took some pressure off the timetable for the next phase of the process, which was the most difficult to plan for.

I walked over to where the big Cat was parked next to the gazebo project. I assumed it would be tricky to get it started without a key. My father was a mechanic, and I'd literally grown up working on all kinds of cars and trucks, but only gasoline driven, with spark plugs and carburetors. I didn't know much about diesels, except what I learned optimizing a refinery making diesel fuel.

The Cat was a lot bigger up close than it looked from a distance. The engine compartment turned out to be easily accessible and the engine child's play to hot-wire, if your child understood the basic principles of twelve-volt electrical current and internal combustion. The most startling aspect was the noise—even with my chain saw-damaged eardrums the engine was disturbingly loud.

My fears then shifted from whether I could start the freaking thing to whether I could actually drive it.

I found the lever that lifted the bucket off the ground and the one that engaged the transmission. At first the sensation of steering from the articulated rear wheels was a little peculiar, though all I needed to do was drive in a straight line over to Tony Vaneer's colonial ski chalet. I asked forgiveness from the ornamental shrubbery that fell on the way, but otherwise got there in good form. Once in Tony's side yard, I swung the Cat around 180 degrees and gently backed it up until I was about ten feet from the house.

The heavy-grade chain was probably a lot more than I needed for the job, but I thought better safe than sorry. After a few minutes I had it hooked up to the thick pin seated within the massive structure bolted to the Cat's rear end.

The subterranean rumble of the diesel engine finally rousted one of the neighbors, a short, balding guy with an accent that might have been Lebanese, or maybe Palestinian, like a lot of the engineers I worked with in the Saudi Arabian petrochemical plants. He took a friendly interest in what I was doing.

"I didn't know Mr. Vaneer was planning on remodeling. I assume the association's architectural committee approved," he said to me while I was wiping the chain grease off my hands.

"Not my part of the deal, sir," I told him. "I just hope it's okay with his wife."

He smiled broadly, thin laugh lines forming around his eyes and across his forehead.

"Oh yes, me too. That is a hot one Mr. Veneer has on his hands, indeed."

"Well, no worries there," I said. "I know she'll be impressed."

I asked him to get back over to his yard for his own safety before I climbed into the cab of the front-end loader. From there it was a simple matter of engaging the lowest forward gear and opening the throttle up as far as it would go. Given the tonnage and torque loads in play, I hardly felt a tremor as the chain clipped each lally free under the east girder, then it a gave off a slight bump when it scooped up the center stairwell, before clearing the remaining row of lallys. I envisioned the chain sliding up the poles, gaining purchase, and then snapping the flange at the underside of the laminated beam. Looking back at the chain I saw the loop finish the job by tearing a sizeable hole in the sill area as it exited the basement, bringing with it a section of wall, complete with siding, studs and a double-hung window.

The house overall looked pretty much the same, until you noticed a big dimple forming in the middle of the ridge line, the center of the house no longer able to hold as Tony Vaneer's parallel universe slouched inexorably, and irredeemably, back toward the earth.

———

My only audience might have been a retired engineer after all. I saw him waving furiously at me to come back when I jumped out of the cab and trotted over to the pickup truck. I probably would have liked talking to him, but I thought it was better to get out of town and back to Brattleboro, where I returned the truck to the train station with its original plates. I had to put it in a different parking spot, but left five hundred in cash on the front seat as a sop to what I imagined to be my conscience.

I kept the chain saw, which came in handy that week when, inspired by my foray into deconstructionism in Vermont, I hired Walter and Antoine Bick to help make some modifications to the house I'd lived in for ten years in the woods above Stamford—this time focusing on the cosmetic rather than the structural.

You can say all you want about the benefits of regular workouts at the gym, but the Bicks agreed there was nothing quite like crowbars, sledgehammers and chain saws for exercising both body and spirit, temporal and transcendent.

NINE

"Were you planning to tell me, or do I always have to read about it in the newspapers?"

It was the morning after my pool game with Burton and Hayden, and my daughter was on the phone. This was an uncommon event, most of our communication being handled through postcards and the rare glorious time she came out from the City to spend a weekend. She was a graphic artist, and by my reckoning a first-rate talent, a fact too rarely appreciated by the long line of employers she'd already strung together since graduating from Rhode Island School of Design.

"Hi, honey. Nice to hear your voice."

"Tell me it's all a mistake."

"A very big mistake. Definitely. I'm sure the paper had it all wrong. What did you see, *Newsday*?"

"Second-degree murder? Is that part right?"

"Well, somebody definitely killed the guy. It just wasn't me."

The phone went quiet, and my heart went cold. I hated those long empty pauses she bestowed on me when we talked on the phone. I hated the phone, period.

"How's work?" I asked her, for which she rewarded me with another eternal silence.

"You told me you were on a program of self-improvement," she said finally. "I assumed that meant no more fistfights."

"He did all the fighting. I just got him to quit. You can ask Amanda."

I gave her a thorough rundown of the situation as I saw it, pausing once in a while to make sure she was still on the phone, but not giving her much room to respond, even if she wanted to. I wanted to build up some momentum as a defense against the next span of dead air, which I tried to thwart by saying, "Okay, that's where things stand at the moment. I'll stop talking now so you can talk. Go ahead, it's your turn. Say something."

"I thought I was done worrying about you," she said.

"That's my line."

"Burton Lewis won't let anything happen to you."

"He won't. Neither will Jackie."

"Why is it always like this with you?" she asked, not as a rhetorical question, but a matter of fact.

"Your mother taught you to ask unanswerable questions. From me you learned the biggest danger is trying to answer."

"I think elegant evasion was part of the lesson."

"Bob and Weave, two of my closest friends."

There was another pause, but it had a chuckle built into it, which made everything okay.

"You could at least keep me informed of the situation," she said.

"I certainly could."

"Though you probably won't," she said.

"Jackie will. I'll give her explicit instructions."

"You're way too old to be hitting people over the head."

"Don't tell your boyfriends," I said.

"Boyfriend. A compound noun built on an interior contradiction."

"Now who's evasive."

"I'm way too sleepy for this. Just keep me posted, okay? Can you do that?"

"Always."

"Right. Bye, Daddy."

A form of relief akin to joy swept through me after I hung up. I hadn't let myself acknowledge how much I'd been dreading that call. That it happened so abruptly and painlessly sent my heart soaring like a hawk. And I hadn't even had my first cup of coffee. I put two fisted hands in the air and jumped up and down like I'd just scored a goal for Manchester United.

Eddie, picking up on the emotional vibe, barked and spun himself around, his claws clicking on the hardwood kitchen floor.

———

Frank Entwhistle Junior represented the third generation to run the family construction business. His grandfather had started out as a cabinet and molding maker and general woodworker in the service of the wealthy estate builders, who were about the only people building anything out here in those days. He worked out of a cluster of barns and outbuildings that had been a farm in even earlier times, which was subsequently surrounded by development flowing steadily out from Southampton Village. The buildings eventually became a base of operations, storage facility and handy custom shop for his son's and grandson's construction trade. Consequently, the Entwhistles were in a constant state of siege by their neighbors, mostly summer people in renovated shingle-clad Federal-style mansions, who thought the Village should do something about the sounds of table saws and planers, and the flow of pickup trucks and vans going in and out of the compound at all hours of the day. Most egregiously before seven o'clock on Saturday morning, when rational people were doing yoga or warding off hangovers.

My favorite part of the complex was a little white building housing the office where a woman named Glenda Ray Whittle worked for about fifty years as the shop's secretary. These days Frank Junior liked to do his paperwork there, which had more to do with keyboards and liquid-crystal monitors than paper. I liked that he kept the rows of tiny oak drawers against the wall where they used to store file cards and spare parts for the machine tools, and calendars with paintings of hunters blasting pheasants, and airbrushed women in denim short shorts and gingham shirts tied off below their breasts holding half-ton adjustable wrenches like they were feather dusters.

Frank was a short meaty guy with a broad flat nose, round cheeks and a bald head. He was usually preoccupied with managing his business to the point of near obsession, but that never stopped him from having a friendly conversation or taking the time to ask how you were doing.

In defiance of the warming weather he wore a quilted, blue down vest over a heavy chamois shirt. If he'd had the misfortune of marrying my ex-wife, she'd have told him it was a faux pas to accentuate a stocky figure with dark, puffy clothes.

"I'm about eight hours away from finishing the mantel," I

told him over the top of his computer screen. "I'll need somebody to come out with a truck to pick it up."

"That's great, Sam," he said, pleased with my progress. "You're ahead of schedule."

"After I finish the other stuff, I better lay low for a while. Can't make any time commitments."

He looked at me sympathetically.

"Yeah, I guess you got some stuff going on."

"It'll be over soon."

"Sure, Sam. I'll always have something for you. You know that."

"Say, Frank. How well did you know Robbie Milhouser?" I asked him.

He didn't like that I asked the question, but was too polite not to answer.

"Not too well. He's a few years older. Was. Three years ahead of me in school. Never had much to do with him. Even after he started building houses we didn't knock into each other very much. He got his crew from Up Island, don't know much about 'em."

"Your dad and his are about the same age."

Frank snorted at that.

"Jeff Milhouser was one of only two people Dad ever said anything bad about. Probably said something like, 'That fellow is a disappointment.'"

"Who was the other one?"

"Nixon. Had more to say about him."

"Any reason for the grudge?"

He thought about it.

"They served on the Board of Trustees together for a while. I don't think there was anything Milhouser wanted to do that Dad agreed with. And I think he stuck us once on a remodeling job we did at his house. Not enough to make it worth going after, but enough to be irritating. We like to be flexible about everything but our receivables. It's why we're still around."

I was there the day Frank disassembled his scaffolding, reloaded a truck with lumber the yard had just dropped in the driveway, and started to peel a big green tarp off the open second story of a house where he'd just stripped off the roof. The owner stood in the muddy yard and hurled threats of dire retribution while Frank calmly referred back to an unpaid pre-bill, including the cost of the tarp. As a band of thunderstorms gathered over the horizon, the guy relented, handing over a check and tearing off in his Mercedes station wagon. Frank had his crew re-secure the house, cashed the check, deducting the cost of the tarp and the labor to reinstall it, then returned the rest of the money and left the job for good.

"So," I said, "you didn't know Robbie in high school."

"Not really. He was in my brother Joey's class. You'd have to ask him. He's coming over this weekend. I'll tell him to call you."

Joey Entwhistle was a physics professor at Stony Brook. Like Frank, he'd worked for his father every summer through high school and college, then he'd disappeared for about ten years, coming home as the prodigal son, leaving behind a full professorship at Cal Tech and a half dozen published papers on theoretical physics. Another victim of Long Island's gravitational pull.

"He'd be okay with that?"

"Come on, Sam, nobody thinks you had anything to do with that thing."

"Nobody but the Town police, the DA's office, the news media and the entire civilian population of the East End."

"They just don't know what a sweetheart you are," he said, grinning at his deft use of irony.

—

True to his word, Frank delivered his brother Joey to me a few days later. I suggested a lunch meeting at a restaurant on Job's Lane.

"Feed me burgers and I'll tell you anything you want," he said to me over the phone.

Joey was the physical countertype of his brother, slim to the point of scrawny and several inches taller. Yet clearly related, with a more angular version of the same features and hair the same color and composition. He wore a white shirt that had likely never seen a tie and thick, frameless glasses.

"Iced tea's fine with me," he said, sitting down with an eye on my vodka and tonic. He checked his watch. "For the moment, anyway."

"I'm with you. I usually wait till the afternoon to get rid of the tonic."

I have no facility for small talk with people I barely know, but I forced myself to ask about his family and work at Stony Brook so he could get comfortably through his meal. It was easier than I thought. Joey shared the family penchant for social grace.

"So," he finally said, to politely get me started, "you wanted to know about Robbie Milhouser."

"Frank thought you might have known him in high school."

He wiped his mouth with his napkin, then folded it carefully and placed it on the table. His eyes studied me through the heavy plastic lenses.

"Let me make some assumptions that might focus the discussion," he said. "You are accused of killing him, which you say you didn't do. I'm happy to take my family's word for it that you are, in fact, innocent. However, the forces of justice are now entirely focused on prosecuting you and, consequently, no one's out there looking for the real killer. So it's left to you, which if my reading is correct, represents your only hope."

"That's right, Joey, something like that," I said, feeling a little iced over by the stark assessment.

"So what did you think of Robbie Milhouser?" I asked, in the spirit of focusing things.

"An incredible asshole."

"That's established."

"But not without substance or complexity," said Joey.

"About two hundred and forty pounds worth of substance."

"Used effectively to brutalize his fellow students."

"But that's not what you meant."

"Ever see him dance?" he asked.

"Only stagger."

"Danced like Fred Astaire. A natural. What does that tell you?"

"Looks deceive?"

"Indeed. Deception is Nature's masterwork," he said.

"Two minutes into the conversation and you're already pulling a Heisenberg."

"Frank said you went to MIT. Physics?"

"Mechanical engineering. No room for uncertainty," I told him.

"How's your natural history?"

"Took my daughter to the museum to see the dinosaurs."

"Evolutionary biology's always been a hobby of mine," he admitted, sheepishly.

"Never had a hobby. Too busy competing with the fittest."

"If you ever want to study sociobiological dynamics at their apogee, there's no better laboratory than the American public high school."

"Especially if you knew the rats I went to school with."

"Do you remember how kids with above average intelligence were always targeted for persecution? Usually by a few specific bullies, but with the tacit approval of the school population at large. This used to strike me as a perversion of Darwinian principles. Why would the group attack the most gifted individuals, presumably the most able to generate valuable resources for the community, which in turn would contribute to the group's survival?"

"Smart kids aren't necessarily philanthropic?"

"Exactly. Nature considers standouts as much a threat as an asset. Just a theory, of course. Not my field. But as a teenager I instinctively kept my brains to myself, as well as I could. No chess club, no valedictorian addresses. Straight A's in science, so-so in art and literature. Had a secret life from everybody but guess who."

"Milhouser."

"Caught me at a weak moment in the cafeteria. Started grilling me about a lecture on the environment we'd heard during assembly. Got me going on sensitive interrelationships within complex systems, hidden causalities and the law of unforeseen consequences. All the stuff that had my eighteen-year-old brain on fire. I was halfway through an immature dissertation on the paradigm shift of emerging chaos theory before I remembered I was talking to the biggest bully in school. I thought, holy shit, I must be out of my goddamned mind."

"Fred Astaire meets Robert Oppenheimer," I said.

"Not exactly. I think he was just sort of inspired by that lecture. The point is, he knew to talk to me. He sought me out. He had my number, but never did anything about it but have a little chat and scare the crap out of me."

"So you didn't hang with him."

That amused Joey.

"I said I kept my head down, I didn't say I was cool. You could only be cool by wearing a letter sweater, consuming intoxicants or victimizing weaker kids. None of these were appealing to me."

"I think Robbie managed two out of three," I said.

"You mean sports? It was generally assumed he could kick the ass of any starting lineman on the football team, so he didn't have to play ball. Plus, he had the one thing that virtually guaranteed absolute, irrevocable coolness."

"His girlfriend was the hottest babe in school."

"Precisely." He put his hand over his heart. "The only other thing that set my eighteen-year-old brain on fire. Amanda Anselma."

TEN

I DON'T REMEMBER what murky and misguided impulse got me into boxing in the first place, but I stuck with it for the gyms. My favorite was the one in New Rochelle where I met Antoine and Walter Bick and where I could always find the comfort of anonymity and the solace of organized brutality. It had been in operation since well before the war and was appropriately dank and claustrophobic and shopworn, the walls thick with overpainting and the ceilings a tangle of exposed metal rafters. But you went there for the rummy old trainers, ambitious contenders and haunted ghetto kids. And the equipment was as good as anywhere, what there was of it. A row of speed bags, a half dozen heavy bags, jump ropes, medicine balls and a ring. Showers and a ready supply of rigid white towels you could use to either dry yourself or sand down a picnic table.

For almost twenty years it was about all I did other than work. No one at the company ever knew, except Jason Fligh, the only member of my company's board I could say was a friend. The reason was simple enough. Back when we were both trying to raise money for tuition he saw one of my few professional fights. The first up on a triple bill in Chicago. I won, thank God. Which was how Jason remembered it the day I met him, minutes before I had to pitch the board on my division's annual budget. We were pouring coffee at an eighteenth-century serving table they'd rolled into the board-room. Jason described the whole night in rich detail, something people with photographic memories like his are able to do.

I was glad I hadn't asked him to keep it to himself. He just did, knowing I'd rather not have to explain such an alien thing to the lordly, white-haired board members whose notice of boxing barely extended beyond annoyance at Muhammad Ali for changing his name from Cassius Clay.

Jason was an outside director, his regular job being president of the University of Chicago. He was the only outside director who seemed to take the job seriously, and I was the only division head who didn't treat him like an afterthought when I had to speak before the board.

Since moving out to Southampton I'd found a shabbier version of my gym in New Rochelle, if such a thing was possible, up in the scraggly pine barren north of Westhampton. It was called Sonny's, though the name wasn't displayed anywhere. You knew because Ronny, the guy who ran the place, told you that was the name.

When I wasn't killing myself in the construction trades I'd go there on a regular basis to work the bags, mess around with the free weights, sit in a tiny steam room and go comatose in one of two Jacuzzis, the pride of the establishment.

After my lunch with Joey Entwhistle this seemed like the only logical thing to do.

I was a half hour into the speed bag, which was about my limit, when Sullivan appeared a step or two outside my swing. He waited while I finished the pattern. I like the speed bag. It's strenuous work to keep your arms up and moving like that. Unlike the heavy bag, you can hit the thing as hard as you want without hurting your wrists, and it makes a great sound. And I was good at it. Keeping up a steady rhythm on a speed bag is a lot harder than it looks. It impressed the kids who were always crowding into the place, which I hoped dampened any urge to mess with the crazy old white guy.

Sullivan was less impressed, but kept a safe distance until I stopped the bag with my gloves.

"I think it's ready to throw in the towel," he said.

"Not this bag. Always bounces back."

"Haven't seen you here for a while."

"Been pounding on crown molding."

"I hoped you'd be working out this Milhouser thing."

Wearing a simple gray sweatsuit without sunglasses or a sidearm, Sullivan almost looked like a standard-issue, moderately overweight gym rat. Except for the worried look on his face.

"What," I said to him.

"I'm not supposed to talk to you about the case."

"Okay. I know that."

"Did you know there's a special immunity clause that covers steam room discussions? I think I'm gonna go sit in there for a while."

Steam closet might have been a more fitting description. I think Ronny built it that way to conserve on the cost of making steam. The bench slats, however, were real redwood and the walls an unfinished clear cedar, which reinforced the closet sensation. We almost had to share it with a young Shinnecock middleweight, but the thought of being crammed in a hot little room with two sweaty old guys wearing nothing but scratchy towels got him out of there pretty quickly.

"Are you talking to Burton Lewis?" Sullivan asked as soon as the door shut.

"Last night."

"He was at the station after your booking. Spent a couple hours in Ross's office. He didn't look too happy when he left."

"I didn't know about that," I told him. "I knew he wasn't happy."

"I'm not either."

"There's strong evidence of an inverse correlation between happiness and a clear perception of reality."

"That's what I'm unhappy about," he said.

"What?"

"You're not taking this seriously."

"Christ, not you, too."

"What the hell's the matter with you? There's nothing that says you aren't going down for this thing. Nothing. Not a single goddamned thing."

"Except I didn't do it."

He looked straight at me, frowning.

"I'm the one who found the stapler," he said. "I isolated the footprints and directed forensics. I'm the one who put the foundation down on this case. How do you think I felt when the County people told me who owned that damned tool? Whose shoes were all over that site?"

"You got a brain. How can I get you to use it?"

"Careful," he said, sitting back and folding his arms.

"Joe, I can't do this by myself. I can't be the only one in possession of the only two irreducible facts in this whole sorry mess. Somebody killed Robbie Milhouser and that somebody wasn't me."

"I'd be just as happy if you killed the stupid bastard," he said to me, half in jest. I appealed to the better half.

"Tell Ross you want back on the case. Tell him you don't give a crap who killed whom, that you're a cop and this is what you do and if he thinks you won't approach the investigation with perfect objectivity and respect for the rule of law, he doesn't know who you are."

It's very hard to hide what you're thinking when you're only a few feet away in a tiny windowless room, even allowing for the artificial fog. From what I could see, Sullivan was thinking happier thoughts.

"Hard to argue with that," he said.

"Tell Ross that Veckstrom will approach this with an assumption of my guilt. He won't see anything or think anything that would interfere with that mind-set. Somebody besides me has to be open to alternative possibilities. Ross is a good man. He's fair. Even if he wants to fry my ass, he won't fight it."

"He's not big on backing down."

"Neither are you."

He wanted to say I was blowing smoke up his ass, but the sensation was too pleasant to mount an objection.

"Veckstrom's not gonna like having the company," said Sullivan. "He's been in plainclothes for over ten years. Doesn't like to share the big cases."

"You call his clothes plain? Just tell Ross you want the freedom to poke around a little on your own. You won't get in Veckstrom's way."

"Okay, let's just say, theoretically, I'd be able to poke around, what exactly would I be poking into?" he asked.

"I want to know who Patrick is. Him and that crew of Robbie's from Up Island. What's their deal? They seem way too self-possessed."

"What the hell does that mean?"

"Cocky. In command of things. I wonder about his relationship with old Robbie."

"Okay," said Sullivan. "I can tag him."

"And Amanda's house. I'd surely love to know what the County investigators think happened there."

"They think it was arson," said Sullivan.

"Yeah, but who, why and how? What do you think? Any reason it wasn't Robbie and his boys? It makes the most sense."

Sullivan started looking uncomfortable again.

"Proving that will give the ADA another motive," he said. "She already thinks Milhouser humiliated you in front of your girlfriend."

"That's not how it was."

"That's how it'll be when she brings it up in court."

"I still want to know."

"Only if Ross gives me the okay."

"Okay."

"Okay," he said, and got up to leave. And then paused.

"You're right. I liked you for this from the moment I got the call. I never said anything, but it probably showed. Couldn't have helped you with Ross."

"He got there fine on his own."

"I like thinking now that you didn't do it. Cops aren't allowed to fraternize with murderers."

"Could slow career advancement."

"This is a better perspective. Makes me feel more confident. More self-possessed," said Sullivan.

And then he left.

The steam room felt a lot roomier without his pinkish corpulence taking up valuable airspace. Though it wasn't long before I regretted being left alone with my thoughts.

Or more accurately, my fears. Or was it anger?

I remembered reading once that the physiological effects of fear and anger were nearly identical. Evolution had it rigged so while the brain decided between fight or flight, the body was charged up and ready for action either way. All the blood ran into the arms and legs, and engorged the heart and lungs, while draining out of the brain, leaving just enough to fire the reflexes, but little for deliberative, analytical thought. Which is why mortal threats make you stupid. Stupid and dangerous, as the adrenal glands pump your bloodstream full of epinephrine, flushing your cheeks and drying out your mouth.

I don't know if Nature also stirred in a dose of shame to go along with the fear and anger, or if that was an entirely human creation. Though I wasn't ashamed to admit, at least to myself, that Milhouser and his boys, especially Patrick, had frightened me. I knew the type. Once challenged, or worse, embarrassed, they'd never stop. They'd never let it go. I got the drop on Patrick that night, but that wouldn't happen again. Next time he'd own the surprise. Then it's not a matter of who knows how to box, but who's younger, stronger, meaner and as yet, un-brain damaged.

A reminder that we're really only animals after all. Inflicted with the curse of cognition. Capable of moral reasoning, but prone to mindless violence. Mindless in its heedless ferocity, but also in its lunacy. Often begging the question, how could you do such a thing?

What were you thinking?

———

The only sure way to counter the wholesome, cleansing effects of an afternoon at the gym was an evening at the

Pequot. I went home first to check on Eddie, fill his bowls with food and water and make sure he had the cottage under control. I don't know how old he was when I sprang him from the pound, but probably no more than two or three. In those formative years he'd learned to be basically self-sufficient. He was always glad to see me when I showed up, but not so much that you'd think he couldn't live without me. He'd often run up from the beach or bolt out of the wetlands to the west of the property when I drove in the driveway. I never asked what he was doing in there, and he never told.

For some reason, though, he was unusually attentive that night, wagging his broad sweep of a tail and making low, friendly noises. He normally ran around the yard after eating dinner, but this time he trotted over to the Grand Prix and waited by the door.

"In the mood for a little seafood?" I asked him.

He spun around once and looked expectantly at the back door. I let him in and he jumped over the console into the front, where he whined at the closed window. I opened it for him after I started the car.

"Anything else I can do for you?"

There's no more hysterical prohibition than dogs in public eating areas, except in places like the Pequot, where Hodges's Shih Tzus were skilled in squirting out from under the feet of exhausted deep-sea fishermen, and Eddie would routinely curl up under my stool at the bar or one of the little round tables where I read Beckett and Camus under the existential glow of the red-shaded lamps mounted along the wall.

Hodges had already gone home to his boat, part of a plan to keep his work time to something under ten hours a day. This left Dorothy in command of the joint. A tall Croatian with thick jet-black hair named Vinko was cooking in the back and helping serve tables while she held sway at the tattered pine bar. She'd dressed for the occasion, wearing her best black leather corset and matching accessories.

"Love the collar. Do you sharpen those spikes yourself?" I asked her, sitting down to the jumbo Absolut on the rocks she'd poured before I was halfway across the floor.

"My dad calls them hickey deflectors. He doesn't know the guys I date. They actually dig the sharp little points. What's the dog drinking?"

"Same as me. Hold the vodka."

I ordered us both a burger, which Eddie preferred without the bun, and settled in with Immanuel Kant's *Observations on the Feeling of the Beautiful and Sublime,* neither of which I was feeling myself, but I was willing to give it a go.

People must have come in, had some food and drink, and left again while I was sitting there at the bar. I just didn't notice. I was absorbed in Kant, except when attacked by mini explosions of anxiety that would suddenly seize my mind. I promptly stuffed them back down into my lower consciousness, temporarily subdued, but poised to strike again at the next opportunity. This was one reason I liked to read stuff with a little meat on the bones. Better for distracting my brain. Keep it from wandering into dangerous places.

The shrink I was forced to see once told me, attempting an analogy I might understand, that my brain was like a little Briggs & Stratton engine. Would run fine all day under a load, but as soon as you disengaged the clutch it would spin up to unsustainable rpm's, overheat and eventually blow a rod. That's not exactly how he said it, because he didn't know anything about small, air-cooled two-cycle engines. But that's what he was getting at.

I didn't like the guy at all, but he had a point. It probably wasn't a coincidence that I never put in less than a twelve-hour day when I worked for the company. That I sought out the most difficult technical problems and consumed countless hours studying densely detailed engineering texts, seminar papers and quantitative analyses.

I was afraid to stop.

Dorothy came up and leaned over the bar to check on Eddie. He was keeping a low profile, tangled around the legs of the barstool, his head on the brass foot rail, his extravagant tail tucked safely under his butt.

"Should I get him some more water or let sleeping dogs lie?" she said.

"If he wants more he'll ask."

She leaned back and looked at the cover of my book.

"He never left his hometown," she said.

"Who?"

"Kant. Established most of the philosophical fundamentals of his time, back when philosophers were like the only guys thinking about anything, and the dumb sonofabitch never saw London or the Mediterranean Sea. So, is that a work of genius or a con job by a neurotic stay-at-home?"

"I grew up on Long Island and still haven't been to Hicksville. Name scares me."

"Not to confuse Kant with that chick poet who never left her house. That's a clear case of Calvinist gender oppression. Pre-empowerment. You want another one?"

She left me alone to penetrate Kant, which wasn't as hard as I thought until I hit a wall about fifty pages in. I looked around to see if anyone else in the place was studying eighteenth-century European philosophy and was rewarded by the sight of Patrick and two of his oversized friends walking through the door.

They sat on either side of me at the bar. Patrick to my left, the other two guys to my right. I dropped my feet off the brass rail and put one on either side of where Eddie was sleeping. I didn't want any of the lugs to slide into him with their stools.

"So, it's old Vice-Grip," said Patrick, forgetting the name had been forged at his expense.

"Feel free to call me Sam. And be careful with your feet. There's a dog under my stool."

Patrick looked down at Eddie.

"He bite?"

"No, but I do."

"I figured you for all bark," said one of the guys on the right.

"No, no," Patrick answered. "Sam's an old punch-drunk. Professional, right? That's what we're told."

To avoid the problem of looking from one side to the other I just looked straight ahead at the glass shelves behind the bar that held Hodges's modest liquor inventory—all but a few bottles of Absolut he kept for me in the freezer.

"Long time ago. And not much of a career."

"Explains the nose," said Patrick. "Nowadays you can fix those things."

"Yeah, but that won't fix the problems on the inside. Though by the look of you boys, outside ugly is the bigger issue."

"We ought to change your name to Death Wish," said the other right-side guy.

"Somebody already got there. As you can see, not all wishes come true."

Dorothy came out of the kitchen and saw the fresh faces at the bar. She gave them each a menu and a bottle of Budweiser.

"That's a nifty lookin' thing you're wearing there, darlin'," said Patrick when she dropped the beer down in front of him. "You got matching whips and spurs?"

"No, darlin', but I do have a matching black belt and no tolerance for sexist abuse. You gonna read that menu or do you already know what you want?"

After collecting their orders she went back into the kitchen.

"What kind of bitches you hang out with, man?" asked Patrick after the kitchen door stopped swinging.

"Post-empowerment."

While the guys drank their beers I wondered how I was going to get from the Pequot to my car and then home again without the possibility of a situation presenting itself. As I pondered this, I stalled for time.

"How well did you guys know Robbie Milhouser, anyway?" I asked, looking straight ahead at the bottle-filled shelves.

"A couple'a years. Long enough to consider him a major friend," said Patrick.

That set off nods all around.

"What happened to him wasn't right," said one of the right-siders.

"I agree with that," I told them. "I didn't do it, by the way, just to set your minds at ease."

"So they just arrested you for the fuck of it," said Patrick.

"A little misunderstanding. It'll be taken care of."

"Taken care of. That's exactly what it's gonna be," said the other right-sider.

"Did Robbie hire you as a crew, or one at a time?" I asked.

"What's it to you?" Patrick asked.

"He suggested you were a package deal. Just curious."

"You're curious about a lot of things."

"I know most of the builders out here. Thought you might like a reference. That house is almost done and Robbie's not building any more."

"Tell that to his old man," said a right-sider. "It's all his deal now."

I looked at Patrick in time to see him frown at the guy who'd just spoken.

"You're not supposed to inherit shit from your kids," said Patrick. "Supposed to be the other way around. Fucked up."

"Said he's got plenty of work as long as we need it," said the same right-sider, I thought with some defiance. "Makes me want to settle down here, build my own place. Sit on the beach, do a little fishing."

"Go to the discos," said the other right-sider. "Do a little coke. Fuck an heiress."

"The old man's got another project?" I asked the first right-sider.

"At least. More after that. Said he's tappin' a steady supply."

"Hey, bonehead," said Patrick, like he meant it. "That's the man's confidential information."

The other guy didn't seem inclined to escalate. He just shut up and went back to sucking on his beer. I asked him to tell me more about old man Milhouser, just to stir the pot, but before he could answer Dorothy and Vinko came out of the kitchen with their food. This would have made for a good distraction, a little time for me to think, if the aroma hadn't woken up Eddie. He jumped up and was immediately charmed to see we had company. Everyone was introduced and given the opportunity to scratch his head. He sniffed at the air and looked around to see if anyone had thought to get an extra burger for him. With no bun, and two or three fries.

"I didn't think you were allowed to have dogs in restaurants," said the other right-sider.

"It's not a restaurant," said Dorothy. "It's a bar and grill."

That seemed to satisfy him. Everybody quieted down while they worked on their food. I was glad to see Dorothy staying behind the bar. She washed out some glasses, slopped a wet rag over the bar surface and otherwise fiddled around with things. I thought it might be the best time to get out of there, but I wasn't sure. And I didn't like the idea of leaving Patrick and his boys there without Hodges to look after Dorothy and Vinko. I watched her busy herself and tried to send her telepathic messages. It worked so well she disappeared again into the kitchen.

"Come here often?" I asked Patrick.

He was polite enough to finish chewing before answering.

"Nah. First time. Lucky break bumping into you. Give us a chance to renew old acquaintances."

"Can't say it's been an incredible pleasure, but I'm getting ready to shove off," I told him. "Hey Dotty," I yelled at the kitchen door. "I need my check."

"Not a problem. I think we're done here, too," said Patrick. The other guys looked at their half-finished meals. "I heard this was a tough neighborhood. We should escort you to your car."

"Thanks, but I'm all set. It'd be bad for my bodyguard business. Send the wrong signal."

Patrick looked like he was considering that.

"Not when they see you got an armed escort," he said, looking down at his lap. I followed his eyes and saw that he was holding an open five-inch buck knife flat against the top of his thigh. "Much more impressive, huh?"

"Sure. Would get my attention. Already has."

"So, what say we just pay our bills and get on out of here. I could use the air. This place stinks of fish."

Dorothy came out of the kitchen wiping her hands on a dishrag, followed by Vinko carrying a plastic pail, which he filled with dirty glasses stowed below the bar. She stood at the register and printed out my check. Patrick asked for his, too. She nodded without looking over and continued to punch in the bill.

"I want all of you to look at these carefully," she said, slapping little slips of paper down in front of each of us. "I'm not sure I got it right."

Patrick picked his up and looked at it like he'd never seen a check before. When he looked up again he saw Vinko with the business end of Hodges's 12-gauge pump-action shotgun pointing at his chest.

"Hands on the bar everybody," said Dorothy quietly. Vinko racked a shell up into the firing chamber as further inducement. We all complied.

"Not you, Sam."

She stood on a step stool and looked over the bar.

"Say, Vinko, guess what Mr. Personality's got in his lap."

He stepped back a pace, then leaned over to take a look.

"Eez big knive," he said.

"That's what I thought. Sam, see if you can pick it out of there without getting your arm in his line of fire."

First I put my left hand through Eddie's collar. He hadn't moved from the foot of my stool, but I felt better getting a grip on him. Then I reached in and picked up Patrick's knife by the heavy wood and chrome handle. It had the heft and wear of an old weapon. Locking blade notched on the back, razor sharp. I pressed the release, folded it up and stuck it in my pocket.

"I'll mail it to you."

As Vinko watched me extract the knife, the barrel of the shotgun drifted toward the left. I reached up and gently moved it back in Patrick's direction.

"Okay, fellas," said Dorothy, "it's time to move on. Your meal's on the house. Our way of greeting new customers. Sorry about the knife. House rules. If I didn't enforce 'em those fish heads over there would be flashing all kinds of hardware in here, wouldn't you Pierre?"

We all turned around to look at Pierre, who was leaning back in his chair, enjoying the show.

"For sure, Dotty. Filleting all day you forget and slip 'em right in your pocket. Isn't that true?" he asked the half dozen fishermen sitting with him at the table, all of whom nodded enthusiastically.

"Better to listen to Dotty, is what I'm thinkin'," said one of them. "We all seen Vinko handle that thing."

"Shoot the pecker off a mallard at a hundred yards," said Pierre.

Not surprisingly, Patrick saw the wisdom in making an orderly withdrawal. Which is how he did it. Calm and easy, with a grin. His boys looked less sure of themselves, but had the forethought to bring along their uneaten burgers. Before he backed out the door, Patrick gave Dorothy the same little bow I saw him give Jackie at the job site. Both had an air of uncompleted business. Vinko used the end of the shotgun to wave him along and he left.

A ragged round of applause came from the twenty or so men and women sitting around the bar and grill, most of whom I assumed were fishermen or mechanics from the marina. Dorothy gave a bow of her own and took the shotgun from Vinko and stowed it back behind the bar.

"Shit, Dotty, I ain't never bringing this in here again, I swear," said Pierre, holding up a greasy-looking filleting knife. His chorus of fellow fishermen repeated exaggerated denials and waved around their own knives. She told them all to shut up and handed out a free round of beers.

"Once I start giving things away, I can't stop," she said to me as she filled the mugs. "Though it'll keep them in their seats until Will Ervin gets here. Vinko's calling him now."

"Ervin know about the shotgun?"

"Sure. It's not the first time it's been above the bar. I think you should let him follow you home."

"What about you?"

"Pierre's one of my roommates. Half of these other guys live on my street. Not a problem. Here, you get one more on the house, too. Shotgun special."

"Black belt?"

"All my belts are black," she said.

Will Ervin showed up soon after that, and I didn't argue with him when he offered to follow me home. He'd bought the basic story we'd told him at the Pequot, which included everything but Patrick's knife. That'd be too much for the cops to ignore. As much as I hated it, I needed Patrick out on the streets, free to act. I didn't know enough yet. Even if he easily made bail, he'd just go to ground.

So I told Ervin I understood why Robbie's boys would be sore at me, and that I was hoping we could just forget about the whole thing. Ervin shared Sullivan's zeal to protect his North Sea flock, though with a guileless, forthright style of his own. It took some convincing for him to let it go, aided by a promise that I'd report everything to Sullivan in the morning.

He hung in the driveway while I checked the house then took a brisk walk with me to look around Amanda's. It was still dark and empty.

I kept Eddie in the house that night, shutting him off from his secret door. He didn't seem to care. Especially since I let him up on the bed, which I normally didn't do. Mostly because he usually snored, or acted out his dreams with twitches and weird little barks, which would fill my own dreams with phantasms, or wake me up and leave me lying there for an hour or two at the mercy of whatever litany of dreads thrust themselves on my weakened state, suspended between uneasy wakefulness and nightmarish sleep.

ELEVEN

Jackie Swaitkowski never met a piece of 8½-by-11-inch paper she didn't cherish or seek to preserve for all eternity. Sometimes filed in a manila folder or stuffed in a big envelope, or functioning as a structural unit within one of the towering stacks of documentation that rose like volcanic eruptions from every horizontal surface in every room of her house, and even more frighteningly in the glassed-in rear porch she called her office.

Over time, the paper piles began to merge with other classes of printed material—magazines, newspapers, continuing education course descriptions from Southampton College—creating a tangled mass within which lurked material objects of entirely different composition—CDs, Christmas wreaths, used plastic dinner plates, hookahs and bongs, triple-decker skirt hangers, framed watercolors. As these piles coalesced, mountain ranges rose, swallowing up coffee tables and sideboards, engorging spare closets and bedrooms, twisting through the house, the strata folding and contorting in a domestic diastrophism that eventually formed the component parts into an unrecognizable concretion.

All of which escaped Jackie's notice until the day her computer keyboard dropped in her lap, having slid off the desk on the crest of a breaking wave of Victoria's Secret catalogs.

Her solution was to take the computer and move to a rented office above an antique shop on Montauk Highway in Watermill. Looking around the place only a week into her occupancy, and making a rough estimate of available cubic footage, I gave it about a year before she'd be searching for more capacious accommodations. As of now, however, there was an upholstered love seat to sit on, facing a set of leather club chairs, and a coffee table in between to rest your feet.

Eddie claimed one of the club chairs, circling around and scratching at the seat cushion a few times before dropping with a grunt into an alert state of repose.

"Make yourself at home," said Jackie, swiveling around in her chair after a finalizing tap on her keyboard.

The office door had been unlocked, so I'd let myself in, juggling a pair of large Viennese cinnamon coffees.

"That one's yours. Light on the cream, half a pack of chemical sugar."

Jackie dove into the other club chair and snatched up the coffee.

"What a gallant," she said.

"You told me to bring you some."

"I know. I'm just pretending you did it all on your own. Delusion goes good with coffee."

She was wearing a freshly pressed, white Oxford-cloth shirt under a vest made of synthetic fleece and khaki shorts, rushing the season. After reaching over to scrunch around with Eddie's head, she kicked off her flip-flops and, wriggling deeper into the chair, popped the plastic lid off the coffee cup. Her face looked scrubbed, slightly flushed under the freckles, her blue eyes salubrious and radiant.

She'd woken me up that morning with a phone call. It wasn't that early, but I was out cold. I don't set an alarm because I normally wake up on my own, usually an hour or two before I want to, so I can lie there and pretend that being supine with your eyes closed had the same restorative benefits as heavy REM sleep. I was startled by the sound of the phone in the kitchen, and when I got there I couldn't remember what to say when you pick up a receiver.

"Huh?"

"Christ, Sam, it's the middle of the week."

"Jackie."

"Doing anything at the moment?"

"Regaining consciousness. What the hell time is it?"

"Nine something. I think you're drinking too much."

"Or not enough."

"I need you to come over here. There's some stuff we have to talk about."

Eddie walked stiffly into the kitchen, head and tail down. He nosed at his bowl, then looked up at me as he stretched, his forepaws extended and his ass in the air. Then he yawned.

"I know who's got the hangover," I said to him.

"Not me, straight as a judge," said Jackie.

"I'm talking to the dog."

"Oh, great."

"Anyway, judges are sober. They may or may not be straight."

"Speaking of which, I talked to Burton last night. There're things we need to discuss."

"Like what?" I asked her.

"Oh, I don't know. College basketball, lawn care, your murder trial."

"Okay."

"Bring coffee."

"Okay."

Jackie's law practice was a fair reflection of Jackie's personality. Idiosyncratic. Though based principally on real estate, the largest local industry and the center of most legal disputes, public and domestic. Through a series of unconventional circumstances, some my fault, Jackie had found herself working both civil and criminal sides of the real-estate dodge, which put her among a rare breed of attorney, an exemplar of which was my friend Burton Lewis.

"Okay," said Jackie from the club chair in her new office. She took a manila folder off the coffee table and opened it on her lap. On top of the papers inside was a yellow legal pad. She clicked open a ballpoint pen and looked over at me.

"Burton wants me to talk about your alibi. Let's do that, okay?"

"Sure."

"Okay." She wormed down further into the leather club chair. "Milhouser was killed between eight and nine o'clock that night. His crew discovered him at the site the next morning."

"I was eating dinner at the Pequot from about six to seven-thirty. Then I went home and mixed up a tall boy in my aluminum tumbler and went out on the porch where I read a hunk of Freud's *The Ego and the Id*."

"Of course you did. What the hell else would you be reading?

"Not as tough sledding as Kant, I'll tell you that."

"Did you go out of the house after that?"

"Nope. Me and Eddie were on the porch all evening."

"Reading?"

"Just me. Eddie doesn't think much of Freud."

"You read the whole time?" she asked.

"Till I went to bed. Could have been as early as nine-thirty. I was working hard that week. Needed the sleep."

"What about the woman on Bay Edge Drive who said she saw you jogging by at around nine o'clock?"

"What about her? She's got it wrong. I haven't run on that road for weeks. With the cold weather there's been a lot of ice and snow, especially along that rutty part. I'm afraid of twisting my ankle."

"But you told me you were at the job site a week before Robbie was killed."

"Didn't jog. I just walked over there."

"That's not what you told me."

"I usually jog, but the road was too slippery. So I walked."

"Remember to change your story like that a few times for the jury. They love that."

"Not a change. A refinement."

"Not a helpful one."

"Why?" I asked her.

"Why take the trouble to walk all the way over to that site if you weren't jogging? You say you were too tired, that it was cold, that the road surface was unsafe. And yet, you somehow forced yourself to walk all the way over there, almost a half mile, just to look at a construction site?"

"I was going to jog, but I changed my mind."

"Super. Any more refinements?" she asked.

"That's it."

"So nobody saw you that night, or called you on the phone? Amanda?"

"Not likely around that time. We'd been a little on-and-offish."

"I'm getting your phone records from the ADA. In case there're any refinements hiding in there."

"Nobody remembers everything perfectly."

"No. Some people only appear to. People who success-fully defend themselves from murder charges."

"Nobody called me. That I remember."

"And what's the deal with Amanda? You were fighting?"

"Not then. Just taking one of our occasional time-outs. No particular reason."

"Because of that altercation at the restaurant?"

I fought back a surge of frustration.

"It wasn't an altercation on my part. All I did was save the poor jerk from getting hurt or embarrassing himself any more than he already had. Assuming you could embarrass him in the first place."

"Not defending your lady's honor?" she asked.

"Her honor was supposed to stay in the car and out of the way. She's not big on taking direction. So, yeah. I was con-cerned for her safety. Three big threatening drunks, on a poorly lit sidewalk. Easy to get caught up in the action."

"So that's why you pushed Milhouser into the grille of an SUV."

"That's why. To cool him off."

"You claim to have done this to save Robbie from getting hurt. Smashing a man's head into the front of a parked truck doesn't sound exactly benevolent."

"Even at my age, you wouldn't want me to hit you hard enough to drop you to the pavement."

"Then why did you lie to the police?"

"I didn't lie. Robbie told her he fell."

"And you didn't correct a false statement. You lied by omission."

"I guess we all did."

"Including Tommy," she said.

"What do you mean?"

"He didn't tell Judy Rensler anything at the scene. But he told me Robbie fell trying to land a punch. That you just stepped out of his way."

"He might've thought that. He was down the sidewalk. A tree and Robbie's meatballs were between us."

"And he said you decked one of Robbie's friends."

"Didn't deck him. Just settled him down before things got out of hand. He backed off when Judy arrived."

"Doesn't matter. If anyone testifies to what really happened it'll prove you lie to cops, and that there was some version of a fight between you and Milhouser. That's all the ADA needs."

"To do what?"

"To prove there was bad blood between you and the deceased."

"Just a dumb thing that happened one night. There was nothing else there."

"What kind of dumb thing?" she asked.

"I told you already."

"Let's try it again. This time with every detail perfectly recalled."

I took a deep breath and a big gulp of coffee.

"What are the smoking rules in here?" I asked.

"No dope before sundown."

I offered and she accepted one of my Camels. I worked on my recall while I lit both cigarettes and watched her write some notes on the legal pad.

"I admit I was mostly distracted by my date, the best looking woman in the restaurant," I began.

"Sounds more like ego than id."

"Plenty of both," I said.

From there I told her almost everything about that night, except for a few things I didn't feel like throwing into the story. A couple of innocent omissions.

"So Amanda wasn't that upset about Robbie and his friend trying to elbow into your dinner."

"She didn't like it, but she handled it."

"So you're the one who told them to get lost?" she asked.

"Using all my diplomatic skills, which are legion. Ask any-one."

"What did you tell them?"

"To go fuck themselves."

"Excellent. Save that for the jury. It'll spice up the testi-mony. Did it have the desired effect?" she asked.

"Not right away, but they left. And we went back to our dinners, and I thought that would be the end of it."

"So Amanda had no interest in Robbie's business proposi-tion?"

"No reason to. With everything she's sitting on, she could buy and sell Robbie and every other builder in town a few times over. He'd be the last one she'd want to deal with."

"What are you, next to last?"

"I'm just a carpenter, not a builder. And I didn't want to work on her stuff, anyway. Bad for the relationship."

"You didn't, or she didn't want you to?"

"Okay, neither one of us wanted me to," I said.

"So Milhouser wasn't just a rude intruder on your night out. He was a rival of sorts. A potential business partner for your girlfriend, filling a role you either wouldn't, or couldn't, fill yourself."

"She had zero interest in working with Robbie Milhouser."

"But you were the one who told him to get lost."

"That's right."

"Then why did Tommy lie about that, too?"

"He did?"

She lifted up the pad and looked inside a stapled document.

"I have his whole statement. He said Amanda told Robbie and Patrick Getty to get lost."

"Might've been that way. Middle-aged memory and all that. Didn't know Getty was Patrick's last name. Or else I forgot it."

"He also said it was Amanda."

"He's also younger than me. Hit on the head less often."

"Much less. Which is a real worry for you," she said.

"That's what everyone seems to think."

"Which made Robbie a real threat."

"Not Robbie. Patrick Getty and his buds. And they're all still alive, at least as of last night."

I told her about what happened at the Pequot. I kept to the same story I told Will Ervin, for consistency's sake. I didn't want another scolding about sins of omission, or get her any more worked up than she already was.

"When were you planning to tell me?" she asked, leaning half out of her chair.

"As soon as you stopped grilling me."

"You think this is grilling. Just wait," she said. "If you live that long."

"Ervin will tell Sullivan, Sullivan will spread the word around the force. There'll be too many eyes on them to try anything now."

"I thought you said he was a threat?"

"Less now," I told her.

"To you or Amanda?"

"He was never a threat to her."

"Really? Tommy seemed to think so."

"I like Tommy, but that guy oughta stop the speculation."

"He said Patrick never took his eyes off her."

"You could say that about half the guys at the bar. Like I said, she wasn't threatened and she didn't want a business partner."

"Maybe she will now," said Jackie, as she sunk back into the leather club chair and put her feet on the cushion.

"Why's that?"

"She might. Given the circumstances."

"What do you mean?" I asked.

"You don't know?"

"What?"

"The State had the inspector put a stay on her whole development project. Don't know why. I heard about it yesterday when I was over at the Town building. It just came in. I called you, but you weren't home and you don't have an answering machine, which is unbelievable."

"I don't get it."

"The inspector, Glen McDaniel, wouldn't give me any more than that. 'None of your damn business, cutie,' was the elegant way he put it."

"She has all her approvals."

"Better hope it's not environmental. When it's the DEC, you're never free, is what I tell people."

"I think you got that from Yeats," I said.

"Don't start alluding. We had a deal."

"This isn't good."

"She didn't tell you?" she asked me.

"I don't know where she is. I haven't seen her since her house burned down. We're back to offish."

"Which reminds me," said Jackie, looking at her pad again. "The same night you get into a fight with Robbie Milhouser—a builder who wants to horn in on your girlfriend's construction project, but is rejected—that very project is torched. Makes you wonder, doesn't it?"

"Sullivan wonders the same thing."

"So does Ross. And Lionel Veckstrom. Actually, they're not wondering. They're sure that Milhouser, in a drunken rage, burned down her house. And that a few nights later you confronted him and killed him. It hangs together very nicely."

"That didn't come up at the arraignment."

"They don't want to talk about it till they gather all the evidence and build their case."

"Then who told you?" I asked.

"A little birdie."

"You mean a big birdie with a blond crew cut."

She smiled a tight-lipped smile and just looked at me.

"Okay," I said, "so about this DEC thing."

She pointed her pen at me.

"That's not important now," she said.

"You're right. Why should I give a shit."

"I'll see what I can get out of McDaniel when he's not try-ing to impress his homies."

"Thanks, cutie."

I spent another hour playing testimonial ping-pong with her before she had to go to another appointment, for which I was grateful. I don't think what I said made her very happy, but she kept up a good face. I was glad to be back in the Grand Prix heading west with Eddie in the front seat, his head out the window, oblivious to the tempest this caused in the interior of the car. The air was too cool to be completely comfortable, but warm enough to qualify as another harbin-ger of spring. I rolled down my own window and propped my elbow on the door frame.

I felt an impulse to keep on driving until I was off the Island and through the City and on my way to other climes. Until I had a vision of being hunted down, pulled over, dragged at gunpoint from my car and returned to Southampton in chains. I had to accept being imprisoned in my childhood home, the place I'd left to engage the outer world, that I'd crawled back to beaten and deranged.

There had to be some weighty metaphorical significance in all that, I just couldn't figure out what it was. Maybe if I kept reading Kant it would come to me. That might be all my memory-impaired, acuity-disrupted, faculty-degraded brain needed. A little philosophy to postpone the inevitable. The preordained moment when the center of consciousness either shatters or implodes, and like a dying star, shrinks down to a dimensionless point, a singularity where time and space, awareness and love, cease to exist.

TWELVE

I NEVER UNDERSTOOD the sentiment some people felt for their high schools. If you know high school kids, you know they're a breed overwhelmed by anguish, selfishness, delusion and self-doubt. Not their fault, according to Joey Entwhistle, who said they were simply in a developmental stage designed to thoroughly alienate them from their parents, thereby facilitating the transition from dependence to reproductive vitality. To look back on that with wistful longing was evidence of how delusional that phase of life can be.

For my part, I hadn't set foot in Southampton High School since the day I graduated. Only now it wasn't the high school. It was the middle school. I knew they'd built a new high school, but I didn't know where it was. So I went to my alma mater to ask. The woman at a desk inside the lobby told me the new school was over on Narrow Lane, just around the corner. We didn't have a desk inside the lobby when I went there, and definitely not one with a large woman in a blue security blazer with a suspicious look on her face.

"What's your interest?" she asked.

"Sentimental journey," I told her.

"Uh-huh. Check in with security and have a good reason for being there."

The hair piled on the woman's head was the color of richly oiled walnut. It would have been more impressive if paired with a face not covered by half an inch of spackling compound.

"Do you know Rosaline Arnold?" I asked.

"Of course."

Rosaline was the school psychologist. She'd taken a few years off to care for her father. He'd started selling real estate in Southampton during the Truman administration, but after hitting ninety-five was forced to give it up. I'd recently read his obituary, so I guessed Rosaline would be back on the job. I didn't know her well, but she struck me as the type who would return to her professional responsibilities as soon as her father no longer needed her.

"She still at the high school?"

"Yup."

"I'd like to see her."

"For sentimental reasons?"

"After a fashion."

I wondered how Rosaline fared in a high school environment, the type not always distinguished by kindness and tolerance. On first meeting few realized how attractive she was, having trouble seeing past her nose. A big nose. Big enough to challenge the powers of exaggeration.

The security lady leaned back to take a look at my own nose.

"You two related?" she asked me.

"Same species."

"No shame in it."

"Think she's there now?"

She shrugged.

"That's a question for Rosaline. Though don't expect answers. All shrinks do is ask questions."

"That's the Socratic method."

"Well, everybody's got a scam."

The new school apparently wasn't all that new, having been built around 1974. It was made of nicer-looking brick than the high school I went to, though it was not much more of an architectural triumph. More like a standard pre-postmodern, nominally Bauhaus institutional fortress.

They also had a desk in the lobby, this one with two people in blue blazers, both large men appropriately scaled up from the security staff at the middle school. Their hair wasn't as colorful and their blazers barely buttoned over their distended guts. They watched carefully as I approached the desk.

"Is Rosaline Arnold here?" I asked.

They looked at each other, puzzling over the question. The taller one frowned.

"Who?"

"Rosaline Arnold."

"Who's that?"

"The school psychologist. I think she works here."

"Who're you?"

"Sam Acquillo."

"She know you?"

"I think so. Let's ask her."

"You know Rosaline Arnold?" the taller one asked the shorter one.

He stuck out his lower lip like Maurice Chevalier and shook his head.

"Nope. Doesn't ring a bell."

"You have a directory of people who work here? Maybe she's in there."

The taller one thought about that.

"I think they got a directory in the office. But we don't have one here."

He looked like a man who'd just solved a problem.

"If I can go to the office, I can look at the directory. Or maybe Rosaline's working there and that'll be that," I said, brightly.

That made them both unhappy.

"This is the Southampton High School," said the shorter one, as if that explained everything.

"Right. I went here," I said. "Well, not here, at the other school on Leland."

"That's the middle school. This is the high school."

"Right. I went to middle school in the Village. In the building they turned into Town Hall."

I knew I shouldn't have said that, but I couldn't help it. I tried to recoup.

"I got an idea," I said. "One of you stays here to control the entryway. The other escorts me to the office, where we'll either check the directory, or we'll get to see Rosaline Arnold, which I can tell you is worth the experience."

Their unhappiness descended into gloom. Resistance hardened across their faces.

"I got another idea," I said, quickly. "Call the office on your cell phone," I pointed at the phone hanging off the tall one's belt. "Ask them if Rosaline is there and if she'll come out and get Sam Acquillo."

Then I stood back a step and raised my hands, as if to say, problem solved. The tall guy bought it, hoping it would get rid of me. As it turned out Rosaline was there, and willing to escort me into the inner sanctum.

The first thing you'd probably notice as she walked toward you, backlit from a big window at the other end of the hall, is the catwalk posture and pleasant swing of her hips. It caused her full print skirt to wash from side to side, which drew attention to the pleasant curves above her narrow waist and her slender ankles, nicely staged by a pair of fabric wedges. It was only when she drew closer that you'd see the sumptuous aquiline shear of her nose, an extravagance of proboscis sufficient to cause the wary to step back a foot or two when it entered a room.

"Sam Acquillo," she said as she approached. "Still upright and inappropriate."

"Can't have one without the other," I said, accepting her handshake.

"You found me."

"Not hard. You told me where you worked."

"I suppose you want something from me."

"I do, but it's also nice to see you."

"Let's go someplace more comfortable," she said, pivoting lightly on her toe and heading back down the hall. I fell in behind.

"We didn't have comfortable places when I went to high school," I said.

"Let's say relative comfort might be a better description."

The faculty lounge never had the exotic allure for me that it did for the other kids at school. I don't know what they thought was going on in there. Maybe it was the word "lounge," which described types of rooms in restaurants and hotels that you weren't allowed to go into. I figured we were all a lot safer when our teachers were congregated in there, distracted from their official duties, temporarily less of a peril.

My friend Billy Weeds and I broke into the school one night and had a chance to check out what the faculty lounge was really all about. A bunch of couches, some work tables and a refrigerator filled with Coca-Cola, which in those days you'd be as likely to score at school as a whiskey sour. But that was about it.

The place Rosaline took me to wasn't much different. Better furniture, some pretentious-sounding books and nice-looking glossy brochures from the American Federation of Teachers. No Coke.

Rosaline swept toward a cozy seating area and settled like a swan into a dirty leather couch. I dragged over an office chair.

"Once I get into a sofa I have trouble getting up again," I explained.

"I've kept track of you," she said, smoothing her skirt across the tops of her thighs. "You look better than I thought you would, given what I've read."

"Don't believe everything you read."

"I don't. For example, I don't believe you killed Robbie Milhouser."

"Finally."

"Others don't agree?" she asked.

"Only those who want the best for me."

"Typical."

"My condolences on your dad."

"Thanks. But no condolence necessary. He was due," she said. "By the way, he kept track of you, too. In the newspaper. He liked you. I think because you talked to him like he was a regular person, not just a very old man."

"Very old men are just regular people who manage to live a little longer."

"I know Jeff Milhouser, but not his son."

"And you don't think I killed him?"

"Not enough motive."

"So if I had a motive, you think I'd do it," I said.

She sat back in the couch and crossed her legs, in the process managing to pull the hem of the skirt up and over her knee. Her shin looked a mile long.

"Maybe."

"That's helpful."

"Sorry. I wouldn't make the best character reference."

"Actually, you'd be a notch up from what I've gotten so far," I said.

"The prosecutor is quite confident."

"How do you know that?" I asked.

"She told me."

"She did?"

"Edith Madison's a friend of mine. The DA. She used to be in my book club."

"Haven't met her. Only her ADA."

"One of her attack dogs."

"I guess so. Cute pup."

"How's Ross treating you?" she asked.

"Friendly enough. The cop on the case, not so much."

"Lionel Veckstrom?"

"Yeah. How'd you know?" I asked.

"He wants to date me."

"Could be some interesting pillow talk."

She threw her head back and looked at the ceiling, laughing a silent laugh.

"Never happen. Can't bear him."

"Did you tell Madison you knew me?"

"Yes, at great peril to our friendship. She harbors rather a dim view of your mental stability."

"Based on our long association?" I asked.

"Based on the historical record. *Prima facie.* It's not just that you threw away a good career, and a long-term marriage, and reduced yourself to a hand-to-mouth existence."

"If you want to look at it that way."

"But how you did it."

"With style?"

"As I said, a question of mental stability," she said.

I noticed as she tapped the arm of the couch with her long middle finger that she'd grown out her nails and painted them a deep, glossy red. Before now, I'd only seen her in baggy sweat clothes and T-shirts, hair pulled back or unbrushed, no make-up, hands chapped from constantly cleaning and sterilizing her father's house, obsessed with the mortal consequences of infection.

"She can share all this with a friend of the accused?"

"Are you and I friends?"

It's true I hadn't seen her for a while, ever since I took up with Amanda. I hadn't been conscious of it, but I guess I'd steered clear to avoid misinterpretation. Or temptation.

She smiled at me.

"Don't panic," she said. "We're still friends. Of a type."

"I guess I deserved that."

"You didn't come to Dad's funeral, but you sent a note to the rabbi, who slipped it to me. You didn't sign it, but I knew who it was."

"Never try to get one past a psychologist."

"I told Edith about it. Didn't do any good."

"Thanks anyway."

"And to answer your question, she didn't share much with me. Just the vaguest outline. But I could fill in the blanks. I know an awful lot about you."

"Awful waste of time."

"I've had time to waste. Basically lived on the Internet. Doing research, after a fashion. You were one of my favorite subjects."

She looked at me with her soft, sensitive eyes, made more

so by the dominating presence of the mountain ridge in between. They were moist blue, filled with commingled sadness and humor.

"Probably know more than me," I said.

"Definitely," she said with some conviction.

"Puts me at a disadvantage."

She considered that.

"Yes, of course it does. Not a place you like to find yourself."

"See, I didn't know that," I said.

When she smiled, razor-thin crow's-feet flared up from the corners of her eyes.

"What I don't know is why you're here," she said. "Specifically."

"You're good at research. Already been stipulated."

"It bothers you that I've researched you," she said.

"A little."

"Did I ever tell you why I broke up with my husband?"

"No," I said, knowing I'd never ask and would pray she'd never bring it up herself.

"Whenever I pressed him on anything, he'd push back. And the harder he pushed back, the more I pressed. The more you try to protect your secrets, the more curious I get. It's a problem of mine."

"You need a psychologist."

"Or something to research," she said. "A place to put all that curiosity."

"What do you know about Southampton High School? Say about twenty-five years ago."

"Robbie Milhouser was a student," she said.

"I'm curious about what he did. Who he hung out with. His record."

"His confidential record."

"Yeah. The good stuff."

"Which of course I can't reveal."

"Of course not. All you have to do is read it, then we sit around and you tell me what you think."

"Why don't I photocopy the file and bring it over to your house?"

"I don't want the file," I said. "I want to know what you think."

"No one else cares."

"About what you think?"

"About Robbie Milhouser," she said, smiling again. "No one has asked."

"Why would they? High school was a long time ago."

"Then why are you?"

"Curiosity."

She stopped tapping her fingers, but then started twitching her foot. She looked at it and frowned, perturbed by the errant body part.

"I am a very good researcher," she said, looking back up at me. "If modesty will allow. Lucky for you, I'm also open to barter."

"I liked your other business model. I asked you for favors and you did them for nothing."

"My accountants have encouraged me to make adjustments. Anyway, your balance with me is paid in full."

"With what?"

She pointed to her nose.

"This."

Like she said, Rosaline knew me a lot better than I knew her. What I mostly remembered was sitting around her father's living room, drinking tea or rye depending on the hour, and comfortably marking the final ticks of the old man's clock.

"Okay. Now you're out ahead of me."

"The offended always has a clearer recollection than the offender."

"Ah, thoughtlessness. Now I get it."

"You told me I'd been hiding my insecurities behind my nose, so to speak. And if I fixed it, they'd have to live out in the sunlight. Or words to that effect."

"You call that offensive? I can do better than that."

"I took your advice, but did you one better. I kept the nose and shed the insecurities."

From the way she looked, and was looking at me, you could almost believe her. Even if part true, it was all for the good.

"If that's how my personality affects people, I've brought a lot of joy to the world."

"Too bad I'm the only one gracious enough to tell you."

"So, what sort of insult will score some more information?"

She held up her hand and pointed a long, slender index finger at the ceiling.

"Insults have been devalued in today's market. I'm diversifying into historical fact."

"Whose history?"

"Yours," she said, as if disappointed in me for asking.

"I thought you already had that cornered."

"I want to know why you did it."

"You'll have to narrow that. There're a lot of 'its.'"

"Why you punched Mason Thigpen in the jaw."

Thigpen was chief corporate council for the big industrial company I worked for until the last board meeting they mistakenly invited me to, proven by my change of agenda.

"In the nose. I hit him in the nose. Only stupid kids and movie actors hit people in the jaw. The nose is handier and softer and hurts the owner a lot more than it hurts your fist."

Patrick Getty could have verified that.

"I'm sure that's true," she said. "Rather a nasty thought for me personally."

"You read about Thigpen on the Internet?"

She smiled another disappointed little smile.

"A professional researcher never reveals her sources."

"It was no big deal," I said, as I reached in my pocket for a cigarette, then withdrew my hand, remembering the evolved state of the teachers' lounge.

"No. Only that it abruptly truncated the steady rise of a man being groomed for the executive suite. A man universally admired, even by his rivals, as technically brilliant and blissfully unconcerned about corporate politics."

"See where bliss'll get you."

"I don't believe it," she said.

"Me neither. Nothing brilliant about engineering. It's just engineering."

"Not that. The corporate politics. I think you were in them up to your neck."

"So, that's the deal? You tell me about Robbie Milhouser, and I get to mess up your theory?"

She shook her head.

"I'm not that interested in corporations. There's something else I want to know," she said.

If I'd known Rosaline back in those corporate days I'd have tried to hire her. Harness all that obsessive persistence.

"Okay."

"Why did you wreck those houses?"

I'd heard that question before, a long time ago, and didn't love hearing it again. For the cops and prosecutors, and the lawyers on both sides, "I don't know" seemed like a good enough answer. But not for the shrink I'd been forced to see as part of a plea bargain. He wouldn't let up. Though unlike

Rosaline, he had a normal-sized nose and an oversized sense of self-importance. I wouldn't give him an answer if I had one, which I didn't.

I told Rosaline as much.

"I don't believe you," she said sweetly, leavening the bite of the comment.

"You don't think it's possible to not know why you did something?" I asked her. "Doesn't the fact that people hardly ever know why they do anything keep you folks in business?"

Her smile grew.

"There was a time when I'd let you get away with that, Sam. But I got smarter when I shed my insecurities."

I was tempted to ask her if she thought fear and anger made you stupider, but I was in deep enough already.

"Okay, so here's the deal," I said. "You give me what you can on Robbie, and I'll give you an hour of couch time. You can ask me anything you want."

She leaned toward me.

"Couch time it is."

She used her long middle finger to trace the top of her blouse.

"I've already got one of those deals, Rosaline."

"Highly revocable. But I'll take a handshake as a down payment."

The skin of her slender hand was cool and dry, but soft to the touch. Her fingertips slid across my palm when I let go. The door to the lounge opened and a pair of male teachers, delivered by divine forces, barged noisily into the lounge. Rosaline sat back easily into the couch, unruffled.

"Saved by the boors," she said.

"Postponed, anyway," I said, despite my better judgment, which as history proves has never been all that good.

She escorted me back to the centurions at the front desk. As we walked, some sort of electromagnetic effect disturbed the energy field between us. I knew this by the slight spike in my pulse rate. I took a deep breath and let it out slowly.

"Ditto that," she said, handing me off and turning lightly again on her toe, then disappearing down the long institutional corridor, lined with lockers filled with secrets past and present, safe from all but the irresistibly curious mind of Rosaline Arnold.

THIRTEEN

WHEN I FINALLY located Amanda she was covered in soot. She was stationed with another blackened soul next to a large dumpster at the end of a relay line starting inside her burned-out house. Charred chunks of sheetrock, two-by-fours and melted fixtures were traveling down the line to where the pitch team tossed them over the seven-foot dumpster wall.

The day had turned bright, the hard light of the season flooding down through the bare tree cover and revealing the ugliness and wreckage of the destroyed property in stark detail. The air was clear, but thick with the bitter, sickly smell of soaked charcoal.

Amanda used the back of her forearm to clear a wave of hair from her face, exposing a smile for me and Eddie as we approached.

"Welcome to the glamorous world of real-estate development," she said.

"Thanks. I think I'll observe from here," I said, standing clear of the ash and dust. Eddie didn't like the smell and feel of the place, and was happy to stay close to my side.

"I hope we can talk," she said as she took one end of a shredded piece of half-inch plyscore to help hoist it up and into the dumpster.

"That's why I'm here," I said.

Amanda stepped out of the human chain, which reconfigured itself without interrupting the flow of debris.

"I want to plead temporary insanity," she said as she wiped her hands.

"You had a rough night."

"I've had rougher. I've been storing up a little too much lately," she said, moving out of earshot of the crew. "I wasn't even aware. Not consciously. The fire triggered something. I took it out on you. I want to say I'm sorry, but I don't think that's adequate."

Like Rosaline Arnold, an excess of curiosity was one of my greater failings. But there were a lot of things I didn't want to know about, that I preferred to leave unexamined. How I felt about Amanda was one of them. Maybe because of that I never tried very hard to understand her. As if I was afraid of what that understanding would reveal.

One thing I did know was she'd absorbed a disproportionate amount of sorrow in her life, probably more than you could withstand without some adverse consequences taking root. More than I could take, that was certain.

My wife Abby's life was one of uninterrupted good fortune, if you discounted her choice of husbands. She honored that providence by filling nearly every waking moment with expressions of disgruntlement and complaint. I realized over time that she really didn't care if I agreed with her or not, as long as I said something that sounded like I was listening, which I did less and less. Eventually all conversation, acerbic or otherwise, dwindled to nothing and a permafrost of silence and disappointment settled into the structure of our relationship.

Long before I'd ever imagined I'd be sleeping with Amanda, I loved to talk to her. I used to go see her at Roy's bank, pretend I was a worthwhile customer, which I wasn't. It was the only pleasure I knew in those days. She didn't know it, but she was the last and only tether I had to the world, more like a gossamer thread, barely holding on.

Standing there next to her burned-out house, I remembered what it was like to see her at her desk. To bathe in the glory of a welcome look. I didn't trust it, but I loved it. I didn't know there could be such a thing.

I'd said to Sullivan that it couldn't be worth it. But it was.

"I won't fight with you. I wouldn't know how," I said.

"I know. It'll never happen again," she said. "I don't expect you to believe me. Just give it a little while, and you'll see."

Her voice was tired, but the words were clear and unstudied.

She reached up and took my face in both hands and kissed me on the forehead.

"There. Now we look almost the same," she said.

"Hardly. You look like the inside of my hibachi."

"I went to see my friends in the City. I hadn't heard about Robbie until I read the paper this morning. They don't really think you had anything to do with it, do they?"

"They have all this damning evidence and no other suspects. I'm new to this, but I think that emboldens the prosecution."

"It was that dreadful scene at the restaurant," she said.

"Didn't help. Jackie's going to want you to back me up on that one."

"So ridiculous," she said.

"That's what I kept saying until they were sticking my fingers on pads of ink and asking me if I had a passport."

She wrapped her arms around me and held on for about a minute.

"What a nightmare," she said into my shirt.

"So you never wondered about it," I said.

She looked up at me like she didn't understand what I meant.

"About what?"

"The fire. Robbie."

She looked at me carefully for a second, then shook her head.

"At first, of course," she said. "But I've known Robbie Milhouser my entire life. He was all show. You saw that. Even if he was capable of the thought, he didn't have, you know . . ."

"The courage?"

"That's right. All bluster, no balls," she said.

"He took a swing at me. Imprecise, but enthusiastic."

"He didn't know you. Misinterpreted the gray hair."

Even under the grime, I could see that Amanda's olive skin was approaching its palest state—which on her showed more as a spectrum shift from the deep reddish brown of summer to a slightly yellow cast that a few bright days in May would quickly dissolve.

"How long had he wanted to team up with you?" I asked.

She shook her head and shrugged.

"I don't remember exactly. He came by the job here and tried to get me into a conversation. It took a while for him to come out and say he wanted to form a partnership. I tried to be polite, but all I could think was, how ludicrous. Then he left and I forgot all about it. Until he spotted me in the restaurant."

Holding her, I thought she felt thinner than I'd remembered, more fragile.

"And what do you mean by damning evidence?" she asked.

"He was killed with my hammer stapler. I bought it last year to install the insulation in my addition."

The worry on her face that had been competing with other emotions took over. Worry and disbelief.

"That's just nuts," she said. "How can they be sure?"

"Fingerprints. And it still had the bar code from the store. It's mine."

I explained what else they had on me. Including my footprints all over the scene.

"Of course your footprints were there. We went there together so you could show me all the wrong things they were doing. A lesson in crappy carpentry, I think is what you said."

"You'll need to say that, too," I said. "About being there. You can hold on the construction critique."

"Burton won't let this get too far," she said. "I'm sure of that."

"Jackie's my lawyer. Burt's consulting."

"You can't ask for more than that," she said, her voice pitched for ambiguity.

Jackie had defended Amanda's husband after he'd tried to defraud her. There wasn't much Jackie could do to save him from the foregone conclusion, but she mounted a spirited defense. Everything she did was spirited. But you couldn't blame Amanda for having a few mixed feelings.

I cast about for a change of subject.

"Any more trouble with the houses?" I asked.

"Can't do much more with this one. So I had a security company concentrate on the other site," she said. "All quiet so far. The only thing worth reporting was a guy in an old Pontiac who drove by every day, slowing down when he passed the house. I told them if he made a move to shoot first and ask questions later."

"Better safe than sorry."

"Is that your philosophy?" she asked. "Always play it safe?"

"Yes. In principle. More honored in the breach."

"I think it's safe enough to take a walk, what do you say?"

She took my hand and led me toward the street, then north toward the bay.

Eddie took the lead and we followed him through the neighborhood of plain but cared-for single-story houses that Amanda owned along the lagoon to the east. For years they'd been occupied by long-term, year-round renters, but most of those people had died, or retired to Florida, or wised up in time to buy a place of their own before real-estate prices in the Hamptons wiped out its own middle class. Now they were mostly seasonal rentals, though at least one had emerged as a full-time group home for an illegally large number of immigrant laborers.

I asked her about it.

"I can't have the place teeming with people, but I'm not going to throw them out," she said. "Everybody wants them to cut the lawns and clean the toilets, then just disappear at night like vampires in reverse."

"You got bigger issues than that," I said. "Like the DEC?"

She looked up at me.

"You heard? That was quick."

"Jackie caught word of something down at Town Hall. I just guessed it was environmental."

Several houses down from the group rental, right before a swath of wetlands that fronted the Little Peconic, was the house Amanda had grown up in. It was the freshest-looking place in the neighborhood. She'd had the exterior completely refurbished and the grounds professionally landscaped.

Nobody lived there, but housecleaners and gardeners came and went to maintain the property in its pristine, revitalized condition.

She squeezed my arm as we walked by, but whatever associations the sight of the house had stirred were left unspoken.

Eddie caught the smell of the wetlands and hurtled ahead, ears up and tail fully raised. The breeze picked up as we moved closer to the water, a sturdy northwesterly bearing the aroma of the saline, mildly putrescent tidal marsh tucked in behind the narrow pebble beach. Various species of seabird took flight in a burst of fluttery panic, flushed out of the tall grass by Eddie's unwelcome arrival.

The road ran over a narrow causeway across the wetlands and stopped at the beach, which you entered by squeezing through a white-painted barrier intended to prevent SUVs from trampling the wildlife preserve. Amanda led the way to a dry strip just shy of the tidal line, where she dropped to the ground and lay flat on her back, arms out and feet crossed. I joined her, noticing the deepening blue sky for the first time, etched as always by the leisurely flight paths of gliding gulls and hulking terns.

"I'm screwed," she said, after a few minutes.

"Put that in layman's terms."

"I'm thoroughly screwed."

"Oh," I said.

"The DEC has shut me down pending a further investigation into why they should or shouldn't ruin my life."

"I thought you had all that stuff worked out."

"I had a full phase-one environmental study completed and approved."

"I remember. I was there for the celebration. Party of two, as I recall."

"I recall being issued building permits for a half dozen houses. One of which I'd be installing carpets in right now if it hadn't been for the pyrotechnics."

"The DEC trumps the local boys. Even I know that," I said.

"The DEC were the ones who passed on phase one in the first place. I had a whole testing crew on the WB site for a week. I took them into every nook and cranny and fed them coffee and expensive pastries—even offered to launder their gaudy orange jumpsuits."

"Must have changed their minds."

She was quiet again for a minute.

"I guess. I don't know. Who knows?" she said, finally.

"Are you allowed to clean up the burn site?"

"Probably not, technically. But I'm not losing that crew. Too hard to replace."

"So you don't know what caused the change of heart."

"Nothing they're willing to share. All I have is some bureaucratic gobbledygook about new information and my options for redress. That's a laugh."

"They might just want to double-check. Sniff around a little, write a report, hit the town and go back with tales of drunkenness and cruelty."

She scooped up a handful of smooth rounded pebbles and tossed them at the water. I heard two or three plunks.

"That's an uncharacteristically optimistic thing to say," she noted.

"Always been a fan of a half-full glass."

Some more time went by, which Amanda filled by tossing pebbles into the bay. Eddie checked in on us, licking our faces to make sure we weren't dead. His breath was perfumed with the dross that collected along the bay shore.

"I've always just done what I'm supposed to do," said Amanda. "I bought all the bullshit about how to be a person, and all that's ever come of it is crap. I used to have nothing and life was crap, and now I have so much, and it's still crap. Tell me why I should keep trying to make something worthwhile out of all of this . . ."

"Crap?"

Amanda was a person I always had a hard time getting into focus. That was my fault, not hers. Even when she was right in front of me, or like now in profile, something about her or me made it impossible to know if I was really seeing her at all.

"I've been getting into Kant," I added. "Maybe he knows."

"Who else reads all the books the rest of us tried to avoid in college?"

"You need to meet more retired fighters. The heavyweights are a bunch of crazy existentialists. Just love *Being and Nothingness*."

"That's sounds more up my alley."

"Not if you ask me. If somebody said, 'What's up with that chick Amanda Anselma?' would I say, 'Oh, you mean Ms. Abject Fatalist? Ms. Existential Despair?' No, probably not."

"I can't believe it. You're actually trying to cheer me up."

"That's what I do. Spread cheer wherever I go. A mission from God."

She laughed a not entirely cynical little laugh.

"Weren't you the one who said God had a lousy sense of humor?" she asked.

"No. I said God wanted to be a practical joker, but had trouble coming up with jokes that were actually funny."

"Maybe only to Him."

"Another question for Sartre."

"Maybe he knows why God doesn't want me to develop Jacob's Neck."

"With all due respect, I think the Almighty's got other things to do. The answer to that is entirely within our ability to grasp."

"So you think there is something going on?" she asked. "Not just rotten coincidence?"

"Rotten, yeah. Not sure about anything else."

"Meaning you're only partly sure, but you're not going to talk to me about it."

"Engineers keep half-baked hypotheses to themselves."

"Oh, now we're engineers. Do they read Kant?"

"Only the empiricists. In between crossword puzzles."

"Let me know when one of those hypotheses is ready to come out of the oven."

"Only if we get to celebrate."

"Half-full glasses all around."

Eddie and I escorted her back to her burned-out house. I opened the door to the Grand Prix so Eddie had a place out of the way to curl up, which he was more than happy to do.

I spent the rest of the day helping Amanda and her crew pick through the charred remains and assess what might be saved. She was expecting experts to come by the next day, which is why she wanted to clear out as much of the clutter and destruction as possible.

It looked to me like the first-floor joist system and a big part of the northwest corner were salvageable. As were all the mechanicals in the basement. I pointed that out, which I pretended cheered her up a little.

It was dusk when we made it back to Oak Point. I'd dragged my homemade Adirondacks out to the edge of the lawn facing the Little Peconic at the first hint of warming weather. It was too cool for rational people to sit outside and drink, but that's what we did anyway, which speaks to the prevailing state of our rationality. Amanda even had a special concoction her friends in the City had stuffed into her suitcase, a customized cosmopolitan mix featuring Absolut Citron and pomegranate juice.

"What a thing to do to an innocent vodka," I complained.

"Vodka's never innocent, and even empiricists need to try something different once in a while."

It wasn't bad if chilled properly, especially after the second or third glass. And the air wasn't as cold as it should have been, or maybe we were warmed by seasonal expectations, reflected back upon us by the iridescence of a moonlit Little Peconic Bay.

"I think I'm getting hungry," said Amanda eventually.

"It's all the pomegranate juice. Whets the appetite."

"I'm too loopy to cook. But I bought lots of cold edibles that're in the fridge."

"After I wash this crud off of me."

"Agreed."

I went down the basement hatch and turned on the water to the outdoor shower. The faucets were already open, so the water would be warmed up by the time I stripped off my clothes. There was still a slight danger of freezing temperatures, so I was pushing the timing a little, but next to sleeping out on the uncomfortably chilly screened-in porch in early spring there was nothing like a stupidly frigid outdoor shower.

It was too dark to see the cloud of vapor, but I could feel it when I stepped into the enclosed shower stall. I stood motionless under the scorching stream for a few minutes, lost in the feeling of the water as it steamed away the day's accretion of stress, effort and avoidance.

I kept soap and shampoo in a little cedar cabinet mounted to the wall. I think I was about to reach over to pop it open when a tiny click, like the snap of a very thin glass straw, went off somewhere deep inside my head. A shrill ring followed the click, which would have drawn more of my attention if my throat hadn't choked on the air and my heart rate hadn't suddenly ripped into a thudding staccato. The floor of the shower stall began rocking like a washtub caught in a ship's wake, sloshing up and down at random forty-five degree angles. And then all the way to ninety degrees and over I went, my left shoulder absorbing most of the fall.

The phrase "my heart beat right out of my chest" ran across my mind as I felt the pounding heartbeats interrupt every shallow breath. The shower stall by now was rotating like a carnival ride, and all sense of up and down, side to side vanished. The ring in my ears was escalating into a siren. I somehow made it to my hands and knees, feeling the slippery redwood slats that formed the floor.

The world continued to turn and spin, but I stopped caring about that and concentrated on slowing my heart. I wondered, how much can it take? Can a heart actually beat itself to death? I sat on the floor and wedged myself against the wall, steadily slowing my breathing, cupping my hands over my mouth to retrieve CO_2.

Then I suddenly couldn't breathe. My throat clamped shut and the siren in my head began to crackle, and then decayed into a wet scream. A scream no one could hear because it wasn't audible to the world. It was all inside my head.

Another voice was in there, too, questioning, is this it? Is this what we've all been waiting for? Is this how the end feels—hot, wet and naked, screaming silently into your hands as you wait for the final ball of incandescence to burn it all away?

I didn't get the answers, but I was still producing questions when I heard another click, or more like a dull thud, that instantly caused everything to go black as time, as consciousness and further interrogatives flicked into oblivion.

—

I lay frozen in the cold rain. I could see a grass hut just a few yards away. It was crowded with people huddled under the dubious shelter. I wanted to join them, but all I could move was my eyes, which I had to blink frequently to keep them from filling with water. I wanted to shift positions to take pressure off my sore shoulder, but I couldn't. A vast weariness clung to my limbs, drawing me down to the earth, my jaw slack and my tongue lolling, an uncontrollable wad in my mouth.

The gang under the hut stood looking impassively at the rain. I knew they'd be no help to me. But the harder I tried to move, the less possible it seemed to be. It was like this for so long I almost started getting used to it when Eddie suddenly trotted into the area between me and the hut. His tail was wagging, slowly, the way it does when he wants to say hello, usually out of the blue, just for the hell of it. He looked over at me and barked, something he rarely did. I liked that about him, that he dispensed his barks sparingly, strategically.

I wanted to say to him what I usually said, something like, "Yeah, yeah, easy for you to say," or "Frame that argument a little more clearly and maybe we'll have something to debate." But I couldn't, because I couldn't move my mouth or activate my vocal chords.

So, naturally, he kept barking. More and more insistently. I started worrying about the neighbors. I didn't know them, except for Amanda, and I didn't much care what they thought of me, but I always thought a barking dog was sort of rude.

"Knock it off, will ya?" I demanded, in my mind.

But he kept barking, and waving his long feathered tail.

"Sam, Holy Christ," said Amanda.

Then the rain abruptly stopped. Eddie was still barking.

"Eddie, shut the hell up," said Amanda, which he did, more or less.

The hut evaporated before my eyes, and the cedar walls of the shower enclosure emerged. That and Amanda's wet hair, which fell from her forehead and smelled like tropical flowers, covering her face as she felt around my body.

"What the hell happened?" she asked.

She had a flashlight. When I opened my eyes she pointed it away from my face. She kept asking me urgent questions, but she didn't know I couldn't speak. Or move. On the other hand, maybe I could.

"Uh," I said.

"Uh?"

"Fell."

"You fell?"

Now I had Eddie's wet nose poking around my face, his warm, prickly fur scraping over my wet body.

"Eddie!" Amanda yelled. "Get the hell out of here. He's all right."

"I am?"

I picked my left hand up off the floor and wiggled my fingers. I located my right hand and used it to push myself up so I was sitting with my back against the wall of the shower enclosure.

"What the hell was that?" I asked.

"You tell me."

I looked at my legs sticking out in front of me. In the cold dark it was hard to see my toes, but I knew they were wiggling. I drew my knees up to my chest and flexed my leg muscles. Everything operational.

"Fucking hell, I'm cold. I got to dry off."

"I'm calling an ambulance."

"No you're not. You're going to help me stand up. Then you're going to hand me that towel."

"What happened? Talk to me."

"I am. I'm talking to you now. I'm telling you to help me stand up."

I gripped her arm and together we stood. The floor of the shower enclosure had been reattached to the earth. I snatched the towel off the hook and wrapped it around me.

"That was interesting," I said.

"Let me drive you to the hospital," said Amanda.

"You want to help me?" I asked.

"I do."

"Follow me into the cottage. If I pass out along the way, leave me where I fall."

"Okay. Sure."

My equilibrium seemed as good as it ought to be after a few tumblers of Absolut and pomegranate cosmopolitans. My head was clear—no more little clicks—but I thought I heard a distant ring. Before we reached the side porch I gently shook off her grasp and walked on my own. The ground held and my heart stayed calm in my chest.

Eddie had stayed welded to my side. When I reached the side porch I squatted down and scratched his ears, letting him look me over.

"I'm okay, man. Everything's okay."

"You have to let me get you to the hospital," said Amanda, almost knocking me down as she shoved her way into the kitchen.

"I don't want to go to the hospital."

"That's not up to you."

When I stood up the world tipped a little, but then righted itself. The ringing in my ears was gone. My mouth was dry and my hands and feet tingled, but otherwise, no major upheavals. I walked into the house.

"It has to be up to me, beautiful," I said to her. She and Eddie followed me into the bedroom where I dug out some clean clothes. After slipping on my jeans I sat on the bed and took stock again. All faculties seemed nearly intact. Acuities an open question.

"You're afraid to go," she said.

"I am."

"I thought you weren't afraid of anything."

"I'm afraid of hospitals. People die in those places."

"You still haven't told me what happened."

"Just had a little vertigo. Slipped and hit my head."

"You should have seen your face when I found you. It was awful."

"I've heard that before," I said.

"Eddie was going berserk. It didn't sound normal. I knew something was wrong."

"Worried about getting his dinner."

I went into the kitchen and poured another drink. Amanda scowled at me, but didn't say anything. The three of us went out to the screened-in porch where I sat at the pine table. Eddie and Amanda secured the floor. As I settled down, I noticed tiny pinpricks were sticking at my fingertips where I held the chilled glass. I worked on regulating my breathing and slowing my pulse rate. Amanda worked on her scowl.

"What happened to all the edibles?" I asked.

"You actually want to eat?"

"And drink and be merry."

I let her talk me into staying put while she went to get the food. I was glad to be alone on my porch for a little while. I took off one of the storm windows so I could look through the screen at the water and hear the sounds of the birds and bay waves. The air was cool but calm, and the porch would stay warm enough as long as I stoked the woodstove.

My hand had a slight tremor when I took a drink. I switched the glass to my left hand, which was steadier. An unwanted recollection of the punchy old guys who hung around the gym in New Rochelle forced its way into my mind. Their lumpy faces and hands swollen into balloons, the flesh pink and smooth, stretched taut with edema. Hands that shook so badly they couldn't hold a full cup of coffee. Their heads bobbing uncontrollably, involuntarily agreeing with everything you said.

You'd think the owners of the gym would shoo them away, afraid the ravages of the trade would deter young fighters. But every gym had the same old guys. A standard feature of the ambiance. Nobody saw them as a cautionary tale, the blindness of youth and commerce being what it is.

The next time I took a drink my right hand was steady. Along with my resolve. As of that moment I was alive and as fully functional as I had a right to expect. Until that status changed, I wasn't living in anticipation of the moment it would. Thoughts like that are dangerous. Inhibiting. Make you think you might actually have something to lose.

"Fear and anger make you stupid," I told Amanda when she showed up with a wicker basket full of comestibles.

"Some manage it with a light and cheerful heart," she said.

She had the good sense and generosity to keep our dinner conversation superficial. I bored her with tales of my days as a troubleshooter for the hydrocarbon-processing business. Drinking coffee under a tent with guys in white robes after spending the afternoon scaling a cracking tower that soared above the desert sand. The sweetness and gentility of the maintenance teams, desperate for knowledge and thrilled by my company's technological prowess.

I taught them what I could, though I doubt those young engineers, or the people back at our office in White Plains, ever understood what the enterprise truly meant to me—the ideal undertaking for a brain never safe on its own, undistracted and free to wander, malevolent, into dark and lethal domains. Places where things could happen that were incomprehensible, unexplainable in the cold light of day, even to myself.

—

Southampton Hospital was only a few city blocks from the high school. It was also made of red brick, the Village standard. Unlike the school buildings it was tucked inside an established neighborhood of Victorians and early shingle-style homes, mature Norway maples and copper beech festooned with building permits, or notices of an upcoming hearing before the architectural review board. Likewise, the streets were lined with pickups and vans, and the syncopated rhythm of construction filled the air. Fresh framing lumber and reddish brown cedar shakes strained against zoning setbacks and height restrictions, casting shadows over the occasional bungalow or modest two-story colonial, bearing uneasy witness to the neighborhood's original intent.

I found the guy I was looking for in the hospital canteen. This was easily done, since the canteen was so small and Markham Fairchild was so big. He was working on a bacon, lettuce and tomato sandwich from one of the vending machines, nodding his head to a compelling beat coming through a pair of white earphones. I imagined something along the lines of Bob Marley, a stupid stereotyping of Markham's Jamaican origins, since it turned out to be Dwight Yoakam.

"I like all those country guitars," he said, peeling off the earphones. "And the lyrics. Little stories."

I sat down across from him with a cup of astringent vending machine coffee.

"If they have to plug it in to play, Doc, I'm not interested," I told him.

He wiped his hand with a napkin and reached across the table. I saw mine disappear briefly into his handshake.

"You bleeding out from somewhere or just come to call?" he asked.

"No blood, no buddies in the ER."

"Capital."

"I'm just looking for some free information."

"That's fine for you, Mr. Ah-cquillo, but I pay a lot of money to Georgetown University for the information up here," he said, tapping his temple.

Markham's specialty was trauma care, often fielding patients fresh out of the OR. I'd first met him while regaining consciousness. The hallucinatory sensation that I'd been transported to a land of brilliant and affable giants had never quite left me.

"I'm a carpenter," I said. "What'll you take in trade?"

"I could use a new house. Somet'ing with a little elbow room for a change."

"Big order."

"Big doctor."

"I've only got a couple questions. How about a bookcase?"

He took a bite of his sandwich and nodded.

"A deal," he said, letting me off a lot easier than Rosaline Arnold.

"You remember the first time I was in here, after getting beaned by Buddy Florin?"

"Didn't know the name of the perpetrator, but I remember the hole in your head."

"They stuck me for about an hour in a tube that made a noise like a four-cylinder engine with a couple of burned valves."

"That's the MRI. How dey examine your brain, or whatever you got left in der."

"That's my question. Do you remember what it said?"

"I had an attending in those days. He told me what it said. Now I'm an attending, so I got to look again to see if he was right."

"But you remember what he said."

Markham's mouth stretched into a smile wide enough to catch a sparrow.

"That's one of the t'ings you learn at Georgetown. How to remember everyt'ing. How technical you want it?"

"Just looking for headlines."

He looked at me the same way he did back when my scalp was full of stitches.

"Funny you ask about this now."

"Just curious."

He paused, scrutinizing me. Then his face relaxed, as if an internal debate had been resolved.

"Okay, if you really want to know, you're a classic right prefrontal cortex."

He reached across the table, and without having to lean forward, tapped the middle of my forehead.

"Lot of action there, according to the MRI. Lots of bangs and bruises."

I felt my heart cinch up inside my chest. This wasn't the first time I'd heard about frontal lobes.

"What's that mean?" I asked.

"You know, the most complicated t'ing in the universe, that we know about, is that three pounds of pinky gray cauliflower inside your skull. That goes for everybody, even the dumbest Homo sapien on the planet."

"Or the smartest chimp."

He shook his head.

"Not quite. His brain is wired up different from the one you've been using for a battering ram. Especially in the prefrontal cortex. That's where you get to be human and he don'."

"So it's too complicated to know."

He shrugged.

"They researching these t'ings all de time. Got lots of ways of chasin' down traumatic brain injury. I can show you the diagnostic guide. Bigger than the phone book." He tapped his head again with his index finger. "Though I got most of it up here. No damage."

"Okay, what about vertigo?"

"Sure. See that more with the cerebellum, but sure."

"Same as memory loss?"

"That's your frontal lobes, for sure. And big time over in the temporal. Different neighborhood, but I remember you had some flare-ups there, too."

"Flare-ups?"

"On the MRI. Very colorful t'ings."

"Amnesia?"

"That's a nice myth for Hollywood to make movies about. You can destroy the short term. Strokes and Alzheimer's do that. Not usually the long term. Though you can have a gap that doesn't come back. That's pretty common with the head trauma. Or lots of blood loss. Like your blond friend the cop. He got plenty of each in a big fight and don't remember anyt'ing."

"Do you see progression over time?"

"Sure. Come in for another MRI, throw in some other tests, we know for certain what sort of trouble we looking at. I'll know better den because I have my hands on the wheel. Much better than lookin' at other people's tests."

He sat back in his chair and rested his hands on the tops of his thighs, elbows akimbo.

"But, like I say, Mr. Ah-cquillo," he said, "we only know about one percent of what actually happens in the brain, or why. There are more possible connections in der than there are molecules in the universe. Too much to know. We can see patterns, but almost anyt'ing is possible with the traumatic brain injury. Especially multiple injuries over time. But we do the best we can.

"Sorry," he said, "but I can't give any more discount information. They're waiting upstairs for the attending to finish his snack."

"Sure, of course."

He'd been looking hard at me while we talked. Even with his abiding grin, it wasn't a particularly happy look. But now his face hardened even more.

"One more t'ing. You don't always see a damaged prefrontal right away. The symptoms sneak up on you."

"Why's that?"

"'Cause, like I say, that's where you keep your personality, the trickiest part of the brain function. The effects can be subtle, almost invisible, even to the patient himself. It's a clinical consequence, but sometimes you need a good head shrink to spot the signs. And den, trust me, you might not want to be meeting up with these people."

"You don't?"

"Most common indication is a change in social behavior. Empathy, judgment, awareness of risk, rejection of authority and a whole collection of personality disorders the head shrinks call pseudopsychopathic, though it don' seem so pseudo to me. Anyway, that's what I didn't tell the boss of that cop friend of yours and this other guy lookin' like he's straight from IBM when they come to see me, just like you, asking for free information, which I tell them to go find somewhere else. And that's who's got those MRIs of yours. I tell dem, don't go flashing subpoenas at me. Take it down the hall to the people who care about all that."

With that he stood up to leave. I almost sprained my neck looking up at him. He reached over the table again and took all of my shoulder along with a fair amount of the rest of me in his huge paw.

"Jus' do me a favor and stop by my nurses' station. Give dem some of your blood and make an appointment to come back and we take some more snapshots. I write the order."

"I think you're the one doing me the favor."

"It doesn't have to be a big bookcase," he said. "And no tropical hardwoods. Remind me too much of home."

And then he left me in the hospital canteen, alone again with my mental powers, however suspect and capricious. I'd spent most of my life devoted to logic and reason. Whatever the value of intuition in solving engineering problems, everything was ultimately based on trust of hard fact. Quantifiable, testable, empirically sound truth.

But old Kant would tell you, reality is only as sure as the mind perceiving it. I wished I could get him to take Markham's seat across from me in the hospital canteen so I could put it to him straight:

Can a man be outsmarted by his own brain?

PART THREE

FOURTEEN

ABOUT A MONTH after I'd modified Tony Vaneer's Vermont ski hideaway, I woke up on the floor of a sweltering room in Bridgeport, Connecticut. For most of that month I'd been drinking Jack Daniels on the rocks, when rocks were available, or straight up in a plastic cup when they weren't. I'm not sure if I got through a whole bottle each day. I'd buy the stuff by the case and by the end of the day any form of arithmetic was way beyond the possible. Recollection was also a challenge—degraded further by waking up in a lot of different places, few involving a bed.

This time it was a floor, a solid hardwood floor painted dark red, which is how I interpreted my first waking sight. As I gained an addled, blurry form of consciousness, I went to sit up. That's when I noticed the broken ribs, which felt like a sharp knife being slipped into my lungs. A startled little squawk came out of my mouth, and I fell back on the floor.

The room wasn't entirely fixed in place. It tilted and turned with nauseating bumps and jolts. I forced my mind to calm down and took slow, deep breaths, testing the limits.

I felt around for wounds or blood, locating the center of the pain, but nothing else. The blood was all on the floor; it wasn't paint. Some of it was mine, I concluded from the stinging clot on my lip and the reddish brown spray down the front of my shirt. The rest belonged to the dead man propped up against the wall directly across the room from where I lay. Everything between the bottom of his sternum and above his belt was rust-colored spongy looking slop. A river of blood had traveled down his left side and fanned out across the floor.

I sat up against the wall, imitating the other man's position. There wasn't much else in the room. An overstuffed sofa decorated with swatches of half-completed needlepoint, a couple of rolling office chairs, an upended coffee table and a floor covered in cans, bottles, titty magazines and buckets of take-out chicken, the bones strewn everywhere—some afloat in the sea of blood—plus a rusty old Frigidaire and a gigantic TV balanced precariously on a pair of milk cartons. Two windows, one door. No pictures on the walls, no written explanation of how I got there or why my blood was mingling with a dead man's.

I gathered myself together for about a half hour before trying to stand. By then it was almost easy. I leaned against the wall and felt for my wallet. It was still there, stocked with cash. I opened and shut my hands, breaking open scabs across the knuckles, getting the circulation flowing and loosening the jammed-up joints.

I'd been in a half dozen full-out fistfights in various bars, clubs and street corners that month, that I remembered. But I couldn't recall where I got the fat lip. It was too fresh. Must have come along with the ribs.

On the other side of the door was another room. Nobody was there, dead or alive. I went from there into the kitchen where I washed out the gash with dish soap. I took a Salem out of a crushed pack on the drainboard and lit it with the gas stove. The menthol fumes went great with the hangover and the coppery taste of my busted lip. I caught sight of myself in a mirror. Along with the split lip I had a black and purple bruise over my right eye. My beard was about a week old, grayer than my hair. I was grateful that my eyes were too bleary to see much else.

I found my silk baseball jacket hanging behind the front door. It had been a dusty taupe color when Abby had given it to me. Now it was hard to tell. I zipped it up over the filthy shirt and went down two flights of stairs and out to the sidewalk in search of a drink. I recognized the neighborhood. Crossing the street to get a better perspective on the apartment building, more of my memory trickled back in.

I'd gone to the building with my friend Antoine Bick and his cousin Walter, the guys I'd hired to help me gut Abby's house. It actually took us the whole day and most of the night to get the stuff into a pair of semis, including extras like hardwood floors, ceramic tile and the custom kitchen she'd just finished installing. Abby was still in Europe with Tony Vaneer, so we had the leeway to execute a thorough and professional job. Whatever the team didn't want for themselves we took down to New Jersey and dumped in a landfill.

Antoine was gracious enough to let me stick around after that, or thought it too much trouble to tell me to get lost. I'd been hanging with him and Walter and two or three other associates, whose social life entailed a zesty mixture of sugary alcohol, exasperated but hopelessly charmed young women, illegal drugs and gang warfare. They mostly let me settle my own disputes, usually the result of being a middle-aged white guy in traditional Levi's, button-down dress shirt and silk jacket, smoking filtered Camels in clubs and apartments that hadn't seen a white face since the death of Martin Luther King had brought out the riot squad.

Things leveled out after they started calling me CB, which I later learned was short for Charles Bronson, growing out of my original moniker, Death Wish.

"Don't go dissin' the old ghost, dog," Antoine would tell the occasional challenger. "He got a mental situation. And hits like a motherfucker."

As I got my bearings, I knew where to go from there. I started to walk down the street, but then yielded to the perverse urge to jog. My ribs lit up with every stride, but I could still get enough air in my lungs to allow a slow but steady pace, which is how I usually ran anyway.

People on the sidewalk moved cautiously out of the way. They didn't know what I was about, but assumed it couldn't be anything good.

There was a breakfast joint on a corner a few blocks away that served heart-choking mounds of colorful local cuisine and fat doughy hard rolls with bottomless cups of charred coffee. Antoine loved the place because it was owned by his late mother's best friend, a woman named Éclair, the appropriateness of which nobody had the courage to point out when she was within earshot.

"Hey, CB," yelled Walter, seeing me come in, "you ain't dead."

Antoine looked genuinely glad about it. The others were perplexed.

"Éclair, get this man a coffee," said Antoine. "Can't live without the shit. If you please, ma'am," he added when she shot him a baleful look over the Formica counter.

I sat in the booth, squeezing a wiry little speedball named Franklin Leghorn into the corner, and lit a Camel.

"You might've checked my pulse," I said to Antoine.

"Sorry, man. The way Darrin was goin' at you with the butt of that gun, I figured you for white meat tartar."

"Who's Darrin?" I gripped my midsection as a jolt of pain streaked across my ribs. "What happened back there?"

"You're messin' with me."

"No. I can't remember. Not quite," I said, after thanking Éclair for the chewable coffee, which she'd learned to give me as a double in a tall Styrofoam cup.

"Fuck, man," said Antoine. "Darrin got aberrant with this evil little shotgun. I don't know what set him off."

"You fed him enough crack to get all'a Bridgeport high, then tole him his bitch been fuckin' some Chinaman sellin' fruit outta the back of his Expedition," said Walter.

"I did? That was inauspicious."

"CB save our ass," said Walter to Antoine.

Antoine looked embarrassed.

"I sincerely thought you was dead," he said to me. "Darrin come out with this sawed-off, lookin' like he's plannin' to ventilate the room. Then you're in his face, screamin' shit, grabbin' at the barrel of that gun. We's all tryin' to find cover in Darrin's fucked-up little crib, while you and my boy're beatin' on each other like psycho versus psycho. Old Darrin was givin' me the look of hate when he wasn't workin' on shootin' your ass. You really don't remember this shit?"

In truth, some of it was coming back. I'd actually had most of the outline when I woke up, but I thought it was a dream. Or some execrable phantasm courtesy of all the bourbon I'd been drinking.

"Yeah," I told him. "I think I remember. I shouldn't be drinking so much. Degrades the mental acuity."

Everybody smiled at that.

"If that's the case, CB, your acuity be turnin' into some sorry shit," said Franklin, earnestly.

"So who shot Darrin?" I asked the table. The smiles disappeared and everybody but Antoine started looking around the room.

"Not entirely certain about that, CB," he said. "With all the screamin' and commotion, you tryin' to get the gun from Darrin and him beatin' on you and swingin' around that ugly little barrel, it just went off."

"Went off?"

Walter sighed a loud sigh.

"Here's the way it went down," he said, waiting quietly to get full command of the floor. "Darrin come bustin' in yellin' he gonna smoke Antoine, throwin' in some derogatory nonsense we don't have to dwell on here."

"That's right," said Antoine.

"That's when CB does the kamikaze thing with the screamin' and grabbin' at the sawed-off. The point is, Darrin can't get the muzzle pointin' where he wants to, so he's smackin' CB with the barrel like this," he demonstrated a vigorous two-handed thrust that caused Jared, the guy next to him, to lean out of the way.

"Damn, Walter, not so realistic."

"And then jammin' the butt of the gun in CB's guts like this," said Walter, pantomiming the action.

"He'd'a shot you dead if it weren't for us jumpin' on the barrel of that gun," said Franklin to me. "Darrin had some kind of supernatural strength in him, that's for certain."

Walter shot a withering look at Franklin, who raised his hands, then did the zipper-my-mouth move across his lips. Walter sighed again and pressed on.

"Like the man said, we all jump in on things, but then

Darrin got clear of everybody for a moment, and had that piece leveled at my chest, which I personally assumed was the moment of truth for yours truly, but for some reason he decide to use that golden opportunity to jam the butt end one more time straight into CB's face, which I agree with Antoine should've been the curtain call for your ass. CB goes flyin', and Franklin here, wriggly little fucker that he is, gets back in Darrin's face before he can swing the sawed-off back into the game."

"See, Antoine. I tole you that," said Franklin. "You gotta start believin' me when I tell you shit."

Antoine looked conciliatory.

"Sorry, man. You're right about that," said Antoine.

"So, basically," said Walter to me, "you was out cold when that gun went off. So cold we figure you was dead or about to be. I'm not sure why you ain't dead, like you oughta be, but that's a question for modern science, which ain't at our immediate disposal."

"We shot the motherfucker, is what he's sayin'," said Jared.

"Shot him with his own piece," Franklin added.

"And was gonna say it was you that done it, since you was dead anyway and past the point of arguing," said Walter. "And before you get all indignant about it, you gotta admit, it was a natural decision."

"Or tell the truth. Simple self-defense," I said.

They all looked at me piteously.

"We all gonna pretend that's sheer naivety on your part," said Antoine.

"Okay," I said. "Sorry. Being dead, even temporarily, slows your mental faculties."

"You got that right," said Franklin.

"What's the difference between faculties and acuities?" asked Jared.

"Only one of 'em got tenure," said Antoine, grinning at me, the only one in the room likely to get the joke.

"Where's the shotgun?" I asked, eliciting more patient, knowing looks.

"Where nobody ever gonna see it again. Maybe in a million years when some archeologists be excavating Bridgeport," said Antoine.

"Not much reason to be doin' that," said Walter, "'less they studyin' lifestyles of the beaten down and fucked up."

"So nobody called the cops," I said.

"We was still debatin' the options," said Antoine. "And now you throw a wrench in the only plan we all liked."

I had to admit I wasn't going to be much strategic help. I was a little preoccupied trying to separate the alcohol poisoning from the broken ribs, smashed-in mouth and emerging headache. It wasn't getting any easier to breathe, and the possibility of internal injuries was haunting the fringes of my ground-up consciousness. I might have considered driving to a hospital if I still had my car, the slick import I was getting around to returning to the company when it disappeared at some time from some place, neither of which I could quite remember. Instead, I grappled with the decision of what to have for breakfast, checking out the half-eaten meals around the table for inspiration.

I'd picked well, judging from the first half of the meal, though the ultimate outcome was undecided after a small army of Bridgeport city cops arrived.

The criminal justice system seems to operate in several different dimensions at once. There's the one we all want to believe in, the one described by officials invited to address a sixth grade civics class. There are the various versions seen on television and at the movies. There's the cynic's dimension, where criminal justice is all venality and corruption, a cruel oxymoron. Then there's a dimension no one outside the system itself really knows or understands, guided by precedents and protocols both ancient and improvised, where there's plenty of justice in the true sense meted out every day, though the process defies common wisdom and experience.

It was in this context that I found myself sitting at a large, beat-up wooden table in a precinct house somewhere in Bridgeport chatting with investigators from two different judicial districts. One Fairfield, which included Bridgeport, and one Stamford, my former hometown.

My legal status at that point was cloudy at best. They'd brought me in on a warrant from Stamford in connection with a massive act of vandalism. It was committed at a house in the leafy section of town known for its stone-walled colonialism and pre-postmodern cubes.

"That's my house. You can't arrest me for gutting my own house," I told the guy from Stamford, who was frowning into a manila folder full of paperwork.

"The complaint was signed by an Abigail Acquillo."

"That's my wife. Until she divorces me. Then she'll likely get what's left of the house. On a very nice lot, she'll tell you."

"It says here you two're divorced."

"Not until I sign something. And I haven't signed anything."

The guy looked unconvinced.

"You can't just tear apart a woman's house."

"You can if you're properly motivated."

"While you're here," said the cop from Bridgeport, impatient with his colleague from Stamford, "we thought you might tell us what you know about Darrin Eavenston."

"He's dead."

"We know that. We told you that."

"Not me. You told Antoine when you arrested him and his crew."

"You weren't on the list. We didn't know about you," said the Bridgeport cop.

"Pays to keep a low profile," I told him.

"Not low enough," said the cop from Stamford.

"Besides the vandalism thing, you're apparently a missing person," said the Bridgeport cop. "Your wife is seriously looking for you."

"Wants me to sign something."

"So what about Darrin?" he asked.

Then I realized what was going on.

"You want me to tell you about the shooting in return for help on this Stamford thing?" I asked.

"We're not saying that. You're saying that. We're just asking you if you know anything about Darrin Eavenston, right Cliff?" he asked the Stamford cop.

"Yeah," said Cliff. "Before I haul you back home."

I still wasn't feeling all that great, having had only a little of Éclair's cooking and coffee and a few hours to move from partial intoxication to an all-out hangover. I wondered what the precinct policy was on serving cocktails to vandalism suspects.

"You guys have any coffee?" I asked. "Black's fine. Espresso's even better, if you have it."

"You want that in a demitasse?"

"Go ahead, Bernie," said Cliff. "I'll watch him."

Bernie shrugged and left us.

"There's a bit of a flaw in your strategy here," I told Cliff.

"What's that?"

"You're trying to threaten me with something I'm not

afraid of, to coerce me into talking about something I'd talk about for free."

Cliff's confidence might have wavered at that point, but it didn't show. What he knew was that he had a warrant in his pocket. Anything else he heard was for somebody else to sort out.

My admiration for the Bridgeport police went up considerably when Bernie came back with an excellent cup of French vanilla.

"Okay Bernie," said Cliff, "we had a little talk while you were out. He's ready to give it up." And then he winked at me.

"Excellent," I said, toasting the air between me and the cops.

Bernie pulled out a small pad and a pen.

"You talk, I write."

I spent the next hour describing the scene in the apartment the way I thought it probably unfolded. I didn't know how well any of it would be corroborated by the other guys, but I had some faith that the Bicks would stick to the story Walter had laid out at Éclair's, knowing it was the only one I had to work with and, if believed, sympathetic to their cause. As it turned out, my narrative, designed to flow seamlessly into an unimpeachable case of self-defense, turned out to fit neatly with the cousins' testimony.

That it came from me, a white, heretofore law-abiding corporate executive, albeit recently degraded, was probably the deciding factor in ultimately absolving the whole crew. None of which I knew at the time, or even cared about as the world inside the interrogation room blurred around the edges and the two cops started to sound like they were talking inside an echo chamber.

I tried to point this out to them, but they didn't seem to notice until I threw up Éclair's breakfast and Bernie's cup of French vanilla and passed out face down in the result.

—

So I got my hospital stay anyway, which settled the question of internal injuries, which I didn't have, and raised the issue of a concussion, which I did.

I was surprised to learn from Cliff McCloskey, the Stamford cop, that I hadn't signed the divorce papers, but I had signed over the house in a quit-claim transaction weeks before. With all the frivolity this had slipped my mind. Not that remembering would have changed what I did.

Cliff was there to greet me back into reasonable consciousness. He escorted me over to Stamford, where I was scheduled to consult with the Stamford DA. She'd just had a meeting with her counterpart in Bridgeport, who'd asked for her help in brokering my ongoing cooperation in the Darrin Eavenston thing.

So I spent a few agreeable hours with Cliff and the DA, a young woman aging before her time under the stress of her job. We hit it off for a bunch of reasons, including some shared marital difficulties. The upshot was she offered me a deal. Cliff told me most people would recommend I get a lawyer, but if it was up to him, he'd just take the deal and thank his lucky stars. I told them I'd used up my lucky stars, but her deal sounded fine—a little time in detox, a fat check to Abby and a year's probation, which included some time on the couch after the drying-out phase.

I took Cliff's advice.

The abrupt end to my bottle-a-day medicinal program wasn't the worst of it. It was the regular visit of the staff psychiatrist for whom I developed a thorough and abiding hatred, which eventually he came to devoutly return. A corruption of his professional standards over which I still feel a certain pride.

On the day they let me out another doc came to visit, this one a neurologist. He told me to try to avoid getting bashed in the head for at least the next few years.

"Nobody knows for sure, but concussions like this could lead to Parkinson's, or worse," he told me. "You won't be the first boxer to be mumbling in his beer before you're out of middle age. Though judging from your blood alcohol at admittance, booze'll probably get there first."

"That's the competitive spirit for you."

"It's your life. Though you might think about the people who love you before you throw it all away."

"Too late for that, doc," I told him. "Nobody does and it's already gone."

—

I did manage to live long enough to get another concussion about four years later when a thug named Buddy Florin sucker punched me while I was standing at a urinal. The doc that time said it had to be my last one if I had hopes of keeping my faculties, acuities or any other mental function reasonably intact.

So Ross Semple was at least right about one thing.

There was something wrong with my head that getting hit wouldn't likely improve. And it frightened me, to a depth and degree I didn't like thinking about. Probably because there was something else wrong with my head, this related to multiple beatings of an entirely different kind.

FIFTEEN

THE MORNING AFTER my consultation with Markham Fairchild I woke to a slightly chilled, smooth-skinned naked body sliding under the covers of the daybed where I slept on the screened-in porch. Before I fully reached consciousness, or even opened my eyes, all sorts of pleasant things occurred.

"That was your wake-up call," Amanda whispered, her lips brushing my left ear.

I held her and burrowed deeper into the covers. I'd taken off the storm windows, perhaps prematurely, since you could see your breath if you were brave enough to look.

"What happens if I reset the alarm?"

"We send in Helga with a bullhorn and riding crop. Not nearly so agreeable."

"I'll be the judge of that."

"In the kitchen there's espresso to be made and eggs to scramble. Ham to fry and dogs to greet."

"Dogs?"

"Okay, one dog. Multiple personalities."

"You have no idea."

While Amanda worked up breakfast, I took a shower in the outdoor stall. All frigid and steamy glory, no vertigo or weird little clicks. The morning light was pale, but deepening with the season.

When I got back to the porch, in clean blue jeans, work shirt and threadbare wool sweater, Amanda had a fire going in the woodstove and mounds of steaming delectables arrayed on the pine table. She wore one of my flannel work shirts, which must have been warm enough since that was all she had on.

"Before you thank me," she said, using her fingers to explore the back of my head, "which I flatter myself to think you'd do, I need to ask you a favor."

"I'm not sure I can take another quid pro quo."

"More like tit for tat."

"Fair enough."

"I'm meeting with the DEC today. I'm feeling out of my depth," she said, rocking me back and forth.

"Okay."

"But I need the reasonable Sam. The engineer. I want the prizefighter to stay home."

"With Eddie. The other schizoid in the house."

"That's right," she said. "I need your brain."

"The reliability of which is up for debate."

"I don't care. I'll take it as it is."

"Your money."

—

The meeting was held in a tiny claustrophobic conference room on the ground floor of Southampton Town Hall. The two DEC guys who sat at the end of the table were wearing light-blue polyester shirts and sporting oily complexions and do-it-yourself haircuts. They both had stacks of paper pouring from manila folders in the style of Jackie Swaitkowski and an assortment of hand-held electronic devices, the purposes of which were as obscure to me as the monuments of Stonehenge.

Amanda had a file of her own, stuffed with site drawings, correspondence and official approvals to move forward with construction. I had a ballpoint pen, a pad of paper and the determination to get out of there without a lawsuit or related catastrophe.

When we walked in the door the DEC guys fumbled awkwardly to their feet and offered to shake hands.

The older one, Dan, had convinced himself that a goatee would make him look youthful. It was mostly gray, like his hair, though the part that would have been a moustache created a muddy brown outline around his mouth. He bought his glasses from the same catalog as Ross Semple. He was taller than the other guy, and only slightly paunchy, where the other guy was unambiguously fat. His name was Ned. His hair was still its original color, and looking at his boss every day had probably spared him from a goatee. His features were inversely proportionate to his girth. Tiny nose, mouth and close-set eyes clustered in the middle of his fleshy face. He wore a permanent expression of curiosity and expectation reinforced by the way the whites of his eyes encircled his pupils.

"I'm Amanda Anselma. This is Sam Acquillo. He's the engineering consultant on the project," she said as she dropped her leather briefcase on the table with a commanding thud.

Dan dropped back into his chair as Ned offered us coffee. This left Dan alone with us in a dead silence that Amanda allowed to hang until Ned came back in the room.

"Beautiful town, Southampton," said Dan, as Ned handed out the coffees. "This is our favorite duty, right Ned?"

"Only way we can afford to stay around here," said Ned with a misplaced claim on our empathy.

"My mother was supposed to inherit her uncle's place in Montauk," said Dan, "but he surprised everybody by giving it to the Catholic church and moving to Florida. Then my mother died and where does that leave me?"

"Staying with me in a motel on Montauk Highway," said Ned.

"Not the same room," Dan made clear.

"So," said Amanda, calmly, "what can we do to resolve this?"

The two of them straightened up in their chairs.

"Right," said Dan. "Let me introduce ourselves. Ned and I are the field investigators for DEC Region One."

"Nine regions. Figures the Hamptons would be in number one," said Ned.

"Regional offices dispense service licenses, enforce regulations, monitor local conditions, but policy directives come out of Albany. We're the feet on the ground."

"My certification from Albany says I've passed the required phase-one environmental impact study," said Amanda. "No one said it could be arbitrarily revoked."

Dan anchored his elbow on the table and pointed at her.

"Suspended, ma'am. Important distinction."

"Arbitrarily suspended. And you can call me Amanda. Dan."

"I can understand your concern, Amanda, but this action has been executed through full due process."

I suddenly regretted not having Jackie Swaitkowski along. This was her home turf. Murder trials were just a fun hobby. Burton Lewis had guided Amanda through her father's estate settlement, but even he would have deferred to Jackie on matters of local real estate. But that was an impossibility. Amanda never spoke ill of Jackie for defending Roy Battiston, but there was a bigger problem—Jackie was still his lawyer, an insurmountable conflict of interest.

"What due process?" Amanda asked. "All I received was notice of the suspension."

"Right," said Dan, "here's the way it works. In order for the DEC to overrule certification we have to go to the State's Attorney General and show just cause. If he agrees, then he takes it to a State judge, who issues a temporary restraining order. If he agrees. The judge. Or she. Whichever."

Amanda looked over at me and I shrugged.

"Let's reel it back to the just cause part," I suggested.

"Right," said Dan again. "That's when something significant comes to our attention, something heretofore unknown, that might, if proven, represent a noteworthy threat to the environment, then that would constitute just cause. That's how I understand it. Right, Ned?"

Ned didn't look like he'd been listening, but he quickly agreed.

"That's right. A significant threat."

The two of them nodded in unison.

"So what sort of significant thing came to your attention?" Amanda asked.

"That's what we're here to investigate."

I was starting to like Dan. He reminded me of the government liaison people I used to deal with offshore. Usually all the serious stuff had been negotiated, the bribes paid and backs scratched by the time I got involved. People who communicate officially all day only know the elliptical and oblique. Suggestive, just shy of insinuation. Sometimes quite elegant and lyrical, a triumph of nuance over substance. A form of bureaucratic poetry.

"What she meant, I think, is who brought what to your attention?" I said.

I knew that was a good question because Dan looked over to Ned before answering. Ned pursed his lips and shrugged, as if to say, can't help you there, boss.

"We received confidential information. Which came into Albany, not our office at Stony Brook. "

"You're joking," said Amanda.

I wished again we had Jackie along.

"What do you mean confidential?" I asked "You don't know who it was?"

"Or you're not telling us?" said Amanda.

Dan looked uneasy.

"I guess you'd call it an anonymous tip," he said, then added quickly, "But very credible."

"How the hell do you know that?" asked Amanda.

"That I can't tell you," said Dan.

"Why not?"

"Not in the loop," he said, "and glad for it. I'm a site investigator. My job is to investigate the site, not the source. But," he said, looking at Ned.

"But, you have a few options," said Ned, who shuffled around inside his manila folder until he came up with an envelope with an elaborate-looking return address in the upper-left corner.

He slapped it down on the table.

"The temporary restraining order is only good for ten days. It's our responsibility to get on the site and look around and confirm or deny there's an issue within that designated time frame. If we don't hit the deadline, we go back to the judge, who could give us another ten days or say, 'Sorry boys, you had your chance. Apologize to the lady and toddle on back to Stony Brook.'"

"Or," said Dan.

"Or, you could bar us from the property. That's your right. You could fight the inspection, fight the judge, fight the DEC, fight the State's Attorney, and figure out a way to explain to the reporters we contact why you're afraid of an inspection. This is one of your options."

Amanda had started out in the publishing trade, copy-editing magazine articles, answering the phone, schlepping coffee for the editors, until she became an editor herself, after which a very bad thing drove her back to Southampton, where she ended up in a bank, where she worked her way up to personal banker. Along the way she married the bank manager, Roy Battiston, who tried to hijack her inheritance, the proceeds from which threw her into the world of real-estate development. None of which prepared her for this meeting we were having with the DEC.

"When do you want to start?" I asked. "We have the schematic of the site plan. You could be ass deep in test procedures in less than an hour."

"Just give the word," said Amanda.

Dan sat back in his chair and waved his hands in the air.

"Whoa, what's the hurry? Let's talk about the focus of the investigation."

"If it'll get this resolved and Amanda back on schedule," I said.

Ned waddled over to a large file box with a pull-out drawer, inside of which were rolled-up drawings looking like ancient Roman scrolls. When he spread one of them out on the table, I felt a little jolt. It was the original tax map of Jacob's Neck and Oak Point, drawn around the time my father built our cottage. I'd seen it before in a variety of iterations in support of a massive redevelopment plan, the one that eventually landed Roy Battiston in jail and Amanda in the house next-door to mine. I shook off the associations and tried to concentrate on what Dan was saying.

"The issue is here," he said, tapping his pencil on the abandoned WB plant. "Ned, give me the old architecturals."

Ned heaved himself up again and this time dragged over the whole box. He dug out a roll of brittle, brownish yellow drawings. I'd seen similar examples before: hand-drawn copies of the original blueprints. Beautifully, painstakingly rendered.

Dan lifted the corner of each drawing until he came to the one he wanted. Then he yanked it roughly out of the roll. I heard myself admonishing my junior engineers to be gentle and respectful of architectural antiquities.

"See here," he pointed to a sub-elevation titled "Subterranean storage." The drawing had been in the roll, but creases showed that it had been folded once as well. The title of the drawing in the identification box said something like "Typical of holding cellars constructed at considered locations serving the industrial establishment."

"The facility goes back over a hundred years so we don't know their original purpose," said Dan. "But the information we have indicates there's a potential for at least some of these subterranean storage units to be containing what's best described as toxic waste."

I wasn't looking at her, but I could imagine Amanda's face turning white. It was almost quiet enough in the room to hear the blood drain away. I studied the elevations.

"Looks like laid-up stone and mortar," I said.

"That's right," said Dan. "Nothing fancy. About as porous as you can get."

"The site study found zero contamination in the soil or the water. In the ground or the lagoon," said Amanda.

"No such thing as zero, ma'am," said Ned. "You probably

mean within allowable limits."

Amanda graced the room with a brittle smile.

"I'll leave the nuance to you," she told him, without looking his way.

"Point taken," said Dan. "It's a good sign. But we won't know for sure until we find and examine every one of these units and determine the adjacent soil composition."

"Splendid. When do we begin?" she asked. "As Sam said, we're ready anytime. You only have ten days."

"Nine," said Ned. "Today's the first day."

"Tomorrow morning will do fine," said Dan. "We just need to get onto the factory site."

"When you're talking to people in Town, don't feel obliged to throw around words like 'toxic waste,'" I said.

Dan nodded readily.

"Absolutely. We're just doing the State's work. No need to elaborate."

"An informant's work," said Amanda. "An anonymous informant."

"Like I said, Amanda," said Dan, "that's not my part of the house."

Watching another person struggle to preserve composure as a surge of wrath tried to hijack her better judgment was informative. So, I thought, this is what it looks like. Easier on the observer than the forbearer. Amanda's olivey tan had in fact tilted toward the green, which nicely set off the bright red spots glowing from her cheeks.

"Very well," she said quietly. "What time shall we meet at the front gate?"

"Early's better," said Dan. "Seven-thirty?"

"Fine."

"We can be done sooner if we get full cooperation," he said, with an attempt at a warm smile.

"What do you think you've been getting so far?" Amanda asked.

"Well," said Dan, moving along, "we'll be spending the bulk of our time finding those chambers. And if we don't get 'em all, we'll just have to call Albany and get that judge to extend the terms of the TRO. Which he'll do without a doubt if the State's Attorney wants him to, 'cause he always does. So, you could save us all a heap of time right now," he tapped again on the site map, "by showing me where they all are."

One of the ways I solved engineering puzzles was to start with an unbiased look at the operating conditions, the set parameters within which the system was malfunctioning. More often than not it was an assumption at the sub-process level that assured failure at the end game. Most people resist the notion that a petty piece of established information could possibly be incorrect. A flaw not of analysis but in human nature.

Scientists call this getting stuck in a paradigm, something the more rebellious of whom are famously eager to shift.

Amanda, meanwhile, only looked like she wanted to slaughter the guys from the DEC.

"I don't know what you're talking about," she said.

"You know," said Dan, as if disappointed in himself. "I haven't done a very good job explaining the information we're working with. What got the State's Attorney's interest was the possibility that the owners of this property, and I guess that would be you, Amanda, might have, how do I put this, had some foreknowledge of this potential hazard. Who might be, you know, hoping nobody'd find out, given the concealed nature of the situation and the fact that a phase-one study had already given you a clean bill of health. Understandable, considering the money at risk, but you can also understand why the DEC would want to have a little look-see ourselves."

I reached over and took one of Amanda's hands in both of mine. Her skin was dry and cool to the touch.

"Say fellas," I said to Dan and Ned, "I just realized we got another appointment." I checked my watch. "And damn, we're already late."

I let go of her hand and gathered up her papers, shoving them back into the briefcase.

"We're gonna have to catch up with you later," I told them, standing and pulling Amanda to her feet. "Where'd you say you were staying?"

Dan stayed deadpan.

"The Breezewater, out on Montauk Highway. Nice view of the Shinnecock."

He handed me a card from the motel.

"I'm in twenty-three. Unless we're out painting the town. So what about tomorrow morning?"

"We'll get back to you."

"Here," he said, pointing to the card, "let me write down my cell number. If I don't pick up leave a message."

"Okay. "

"I'm going to say you're working out logistics. So we can have full access. If anybody asks," said Dan, at once more and less inscrutable.

"Thanks."

"Until I hear from you tomorrow. Say by noon. After that, everything escalates."

"Okay," I said again, then slipped my arm though Amanda's and escorted her out of the room, down the hall and back outside into the cool daylight of early spring.

"What the hell was that all about?" Amanda asked, once safely in the front seat of the Grand Prix.

"Deep water."

"I don't understand."

"That, beautiful, was a set-up."

"What on earth for?"

"I don't know. I can guess, maybe, but I'm done with assumptions."

"Don't we have to let them in?" she asked.

"That's a question for Burton. You're paying that damn lawyer, you oughta get your money's worth."

"I've never paid him a cent."

"All the more reason."

———

When we got to Burton's I called Isabella from the gate. I could tell by her pleasure in reporting Burton was back in the City that she was telling the truth.

"Did Hayden go with him?"

"No. But you can't talk to him. He's swimming in the pool."

"Little chilly for that."

"That's what I tell him, but he's like you. All polite talk and no convincing of anything."

I drove from there to one of the last pay phones in Suffolk County, next to the men's room in the basement of a restaurant on Job's Lane. They probably forgot it was down there and it just lived on, a ghost in the machinery of modern telecommunications.

I had a secret phone number for Burton when I really needed him. It wasn't a direct line, but his executive assistant would usually pick up, which was the next best thing.

"Sorry, Sam," she told me. "He's out of reach until later today. I think he's playing chess in Central Park. If it's really an emergency, I can send out a runner."

"That's okay. If you could give him a message and have him call me or Amanda as soon as he can. With my apologies. We're on a bit of a deadline," I said, then tried to make a long story short.

I'd left Amanda in the car. When I returned she was lying back in her seat with her eyes closed. It reminded me of how she looked on the way home from the incident with Robbie Milhouser. Either bitterly dejected or simply gathering strength for the next round. Composing herself. At rest, but on the verge.

When I told her we'd have to wait for Burton to call she asked me to take her home. She was quiet on the way back to North Sea. Just as well, since there were lots of questions floating randomly around the inside of the old Pontiac, most of which I wouldn't be able to answer.

Then she surprised me by sliding over and wrapping two strong arms around my shoulders. She squeezed hard, her face pressed into the crook of my neck.

"You try to be a good person," she said. "Most of the time."

"Ah, come on."

"You want to think that isn't true. It makes it easier for you, which I suppose makes sense. It's much harder to accept that even good people can do evil things."

I waited until she made it all the way to her house and disappeared inside before letting Eddie take her place in the front seat of the car. I headed south again, through the Village and all the way to the parking lot at the end of Little Plains Road where you could pull up and look at the ocean. When I was a kid I lived with the delusion that looking out on that vast and irritable body of water would inspire answers to any question. What I know now is that the questions you're likely to ask while looking at the ocean are impossible to answer. So instead, I took the experience for what it was worth. A chance to allow the solemn sea to remind me of how little Nature cares that human beings want their existence to make sense.

A chance for a respite from the ceaseless and untenable struggle to prove Her wrong.

SIXTEEN

AFTER THE MONTAUK HIGHWAY flows like an ancient
tributary across the western border of Southampton Village,
it disperses into a confusion of side streets, storefronts and
neighborhoods, losing all distinction until it reaches the
other side of town, where its identity is restored and volume
engorged by merging with County Road 39, itself a descen-
dant of Sunrise Highway, the other main artery connecting
the South Fork with the rest of Long Island.

In an open area overlooking the confluence of traffic is a
wooden building, not much more than a swayback row of
storefronts welded into a single edifice, exhausted and forlorn.

This is where Jefferson Milhouser had his office, if that
described the miserable little closet he'd stuffed with a heavy
mahogany desk, a pair of file cabinets and a leather easy
chair serving the dual purpose of guest seating and storage
repository that would make Jackie Swaitkowski feel right
at home.

My original plan for the day, delayed by meeting with Amanda and the DEC, was to pay Milhouser a visit. It was late morning when I dropped Amanda off at her house, so there was still plenty of time.

I thought I'd break the ice with a phone call, but his number was unlisted. Robbie's number was still active, so I tried that and got to listen to a dead guy tell me he was unable to come to the phone, but if I wanted to leave a message, he'd call back as soon as he could. I fought the urge to see if he was as good as his word and called Frank Entwhistle instead.

Frank didn't have Jeff Milhouser's number either, but he knew where I could find him.

"I'd tell you to give him my regards, but I don't think I have any," he told me.

Then I placed another call, to Jackie Swaitkowski.

"Are you nuts?"

"People keep asserting that," I told her.

"Sometimes I think you're working for the prosecution."

"Then come with me."

"No."

"I'm going anyway."

"Not without me."

"Great."

"What are you trying to prove?" she asked.

"My innocence."

"By talking to the victim's father?"

"I just want to ask a couple of questions."

"This ought to be a treat."

I had her meet me at the corner coffee place in the Village so we could drive together over to Milhouser's.

She was wearing her stable-girl outfit, complete with barn jacket and cowboy boots. It must have been the influence of the big horse show they had in Bridgehampton every year, because that was the closest she'd ever been to an actual horse.

Her massive ball of strawberry-blonde hair struggled against a pair of black plastic barrettes. Her lips were the color of a freshly waxed fire engine

"Hey, Annie Oakley. Where's Trigger?"

"You're thinking of Roy Rogers."

"Not in that lipstick."

"Get your coffee and let's go," she said. "I want to get this over with."

As we drove she asked me why I wanted to talk to Jeff Milhouser.

"Robbie's crew told me they're now working for the old man. I just want to know if he realizes who he's dealing with."

"That's all?"

"Until I think of something else."

When we got to Milhouser's office I was glad I brought Jackie along. It wasn't hard to imagine what kind of reception I was going to get. I just hadn't let myself think about it until I saw his name on the sign: "Jefferson Milhouser, Construction Management, Floors Refinished and Installed, Real Estate, Fine Arts."

I went ahead and knocked.

I heard a yell from inside telling me to come in. Jackie glowered at me as I opened the door.

"Hello Mr. Milhouser. I'm Sam Acquillo."

"Sammy Acquillo," said Milhouser, looking at me over the top of his *Newsday*.

You could probably trace the roots of my boxing career to elementary school when some jerk thought he could call me Sammy and get away with it. But I figured hearing it from an old man who thought I'd killed his son was worth a pass.

"What the hell do you think you're doing?" he asked me.

"That's my question," I heard Jackie murmur.

"This is Jackie Swaitkowski. She's my attorney. We tried to call but the line was busy."

"So that gave you the idea you could just drop by?"

"People call me Sam, Mr. Milhouser. And I didn't do it."

I hadn't offered my hand and he hadn't moved from his desk. He looked better than I thought he would. I guessed his age to be around seventy, but he was still slim and reasonably good looking, with a full head of wavy white hair and delicate, Anglo features that made him look a lot more like Burton's father than Robbie's.

"They call me Jeff. And why should I believe you?"

"Because I want to talk to you. And I can't see you talking to somebody you think is capable of such a thing."

"That was a poor choice of words. Capable is exactly what you are."

His eyes were light blue, like the color of a robin's egg. A random sprinkling of age spots spread across his pale skin.

"He just wants to talk with you," said Jackie. "If you're uncomfortable with that we'll leave immediately."

"That's a switch. Hardly heard a word out of him when he was a kid. Surly little bastard, is how I remember it. Big chip on his shoulder."

Jackie arched an eyebrow at me, but didn't say what I knew she was about to say. Milhouser took the moment to surprise us both.

"You like iced tea?"

"Not especially," I said.

"I love it," said Jackie.

"I do, too. They got an excellent iced tea at the pizza place next door. I was about to go get some and sit out in the sun. It's too nice to be cooped up in here."

"Can we join you?" Jackie asked.

"It's a free country." He looked at me. "At least if you're not about to rot in jail for the rest of your life."

When he stood and grabbed a jacket I was surprised again, this time by his height, which was a lot less than I remembered.

I got a cup of coffee and followed Milhouser and Jackie with their iced teas around to the back of the building where there was a round plastic table with folding chairs and evidence of recent meals and cigarette breaks. Milhouser moved quickly, with a straight posture and his son's bearing.

The coming spring was apparent in the cool sea breeze and light green fuzz on the boxwoods that lined the back of the building. Despite the breeze the sun was warm enough to heat up your face and throw a glare off the lawn furniture. Jackie and I put on our sunglasses. Milhouser just squinted.

"You're probably wondering why I haven't called the cops or thrown you out on your asses," he said after we sat down.

He looked from me to Jackie and back again while he stirred a packet of artificial sweetener into his tea.

"A little," I admitted

"You want to talk to me. Maybe I want to talk to you."

"About what?" asked Jackie.

"I want to know why he did it."

"I didn't," I told him. "No reason to."

"Not according to Ross Semple."

"You talked to Ross?" Jackie asked.

"Hell no. I read it in the paper. I'm no fan of Semple's, but he can't be wrong all the time."

"He usually isn't. He's just wrong this time."

"My wife's dead, did you know that?"

"No," said Jackie, quicker to catch the implication.

"Too bad. Might've made Acquillo here think twice before taking the only other thing that mattered to me."

"I've got a daughter. I couldn't imagine losing her," I told him.

He watched me carefully as he took a sip of tea. In the bright sunlight he looked more his age, his pale eyes nearly bleached white, the age spots on his cheeks and forehead more noticeable, drawing attention to a pattern of broken capillaries at the tip of his nose.

"So this is why I can talk to you," he said. "You can't do me any more harm. Even if you came here to kill me."

"Honestly, Mr. Milhouser," said Jackie.

I just let the comment sit where it fell.

"So you're taking over Robbie's project," I said.

"Projects. You wouldn't believe all the things that kid had going on."

"I was thinking about the place over on Bay Edge Drive," I said.

"Beautiful house. Just beautiful. It's Robbie's monument."

"I hear when it's finished you're moving the crew on to another job."

He looked down into his iced tea and grinned.

"So that's what this is all about. You want to steal Robbie's crew. You got some kind of gall."

Jackie rose to object, but I put up my hand to stop her.

"Why would I want to do that?"

"To give them to the Battiston woman. Who else?"

"Not a chance. I just want to know how they hooked up with Robbie."

"I don't know. They're from Up Island. Seem like good men to me. I put that tall one Patrick in charge. A natural leader. Already been doing some floors for me. Loyal to my boy, that's for sure. Honest, too. I checked all the books, nothing funny going on. All on the up and up."

"Did you have a reason to doubt that?"

He grinned again and looked at Jackie.

"I always knew he was a smart one, even though he never said much of anything. The only kid at the station who could fix anything. It didn't surprise me when the Fourniers snatched him away from me."

What I remembered was going to work for Rudy and John Fournier because Milhouser didn't like me hanging out in the repair shop. He wanted me manning the pumps and cleaning windshields.

"Do you remember a guy named Paul Hodges? He worked at the station a few years before me."

Milhouser frowned as he tried to remember. Then it came to him.

"Now, that was a mechanic. Knew his boats. Took care of all the outboards. I used to send him to the marinas. Wasn't our main trade, but with Hodges I thought it might turn into something. You could always charge an extra forty percent for marine work. More mystery in it, which equals more money."

"Why'd he leave?"

"Typical Vietnam vet." He twirled an index finger around his ear. "Prone to moods. Couldn't control him."

"Still can't."

"That's how I thought of you. Like a moody jarhead without the medals. Hodges a friend of yours?"

"I guess so."

"Figures."

"I never gave you any trouble," I said.

"I knew your old man. Apples don't fall too far from the tree."

Jackie suddenly had a coughing fit noisy enough to make me start thinking Heimlich.

"I'm okay," she croaked out. "Sorry. I think I swallowed a lemon seed."

"I've told them about that," said Milhouser.

He sat quietly with me as we waited for Jackie to catch her breath. When she got there she took up another thread of the conversation.

"So why did you check the books?" Jackie asked.

"You're back on that?" he asked.

"Just curious."

He shook his head in disgust.

"Wouldn't you? What kind of a businessman would I be if I didn't check the books?"

I knew what kind of businessman he was, but he still had a point.

"So Robbie ran a tight ship."

"The tightest. Could teach his old man a thing or two."

"Your crew said he left plenty of work for them."

"He left some. I had some. Now it's all in the same pot. Though I don't know what that means to you. What do you care?"

He was still squinting, either because of the sun or to improve his concentration, it was hard to tell.

"I'm just curious about those guys."

"You still haven't told me," he said.

"What?"

"Why you killed him. God knows I can't figure it out. They said you had a fight at a bar someplace. Everybody drunk. Making assholes of yourselves. No reason to kill a man."

"That's right. No reason. That's what I've been saying."

"That was your tool that had Robbie's blood all over it. You can't explain that away."

"Those matters will be thoroughly dealt with when we get into a court of law," said Jackie.

He looked at me this time.

"She's a heck of a mouthpiece, I can see that," he said. "Didn't used to be so many lady lawyers. I like it."

"You ought to see her break a horse," I said.

"I'd like that."

"So," said Jackie, slapping the tops of her thighs. "I think we've covered everything we wanted to cover today. We should let you get back to your work."

"I'm just gonna get back to enjoying this glass of iced tea, if you want the truth."

"We do, actually, Jeff," I said. "The truth is exactly what we want."

"Thanks for talking to us," said Jackie, standing and pulling me up on my feet. "I know it's hard hearing it from us, but we're sorry for your loss. And we hope eventually justice will be served."

"In a pig's eye," he said, almost cheerfully. "But thanks anyway."

We'd almost gone beyond earshot when we heard him call us back. Jackie sighed, but let me retrace our steps. He still sat at the table, but now more relaxed, with his legs crossed.

"Do me a favor when you see that Battiston woman," he said to me.

"Amanda Anselma. She's divorced from Roy Battiston."

"Whatever. Just tell her the offer's still open. It's not too late."

"What offer?" I asked.

"She'll know."

"I want to know. Tell me."

That made him smile. A smile without humor, all teeth and no eyes.

"You don't matter, Sammy. Just tell the girl the offer's still sittin', but the clock she's a-tickin'."

I heard Jackie take in a big breath through her nose. She stuck her hand through my arm and got a grip on my bicep, then pulled me around and drove me out from the back of building and into the Grand Prix. We rode in silence to the coffee place where she'd left her Toyota pickup. Before she got out of the car I asked her.

"Thoughts?"

"I'm over my head again, Sam. Where I always am when I get within ten blocks of you, feeling like people are laughing at all these punch lines and I'm just sitting there thinking, 'What the hell's so funny about that?'"

"What did you think of Jeff Milhouser?"

"It's not him I'm worried about."

"What do you mean?"

"It's you. You're no different than any other dumb lunk all tangled up with a smart woman. Let me rephrase that, a very smart man, made dumb in the presence of a very smart woman."

She snapped open the door and started to step out when I grabbed a wad of her jacket and pulled her back into the car.

"What does that mean?"

She kissed the tips of her fingers, then used them to tap the hand that held her. I let her go.

"Ask your girlfriend," she said, then sped across the seat, opened the door and disappeared into the crowds of preseason pedestrians out testing the weather and searching for paradise.

I drove back to Little Plains Road so I could look at the ocean again and mete out a few more unanswerable questions.

Like why my father had asked Milhouser if he needed a kid to work at the station during the busy summer months, a fact I'd forgotten until Milhouser dredged up the recollection. And how well they knew each other. There were only a few gas stations in town in those days, all of which did repairs, a necessity of the times. Milhouser's was at the intersection of County Road 39 and a connector leading up to North Sea, a logical stop for my father on the way home.

I never saw them speak to each other. I only remembered the day my father told me to go over there and apply for a job. That was when Milhouser told me my father said I was handy with cars. Last year Ross Semple told me my father bragged to his father that I was a tough fighter. He hadn't said these things to me, and never would. In fact, he never said anything to me I could remotely construe as a compliment, or even a criticism, right up to the day he died, beaten to death by a couple of punks in a men's room at the back of a bar in the Bronx.

Consequently, I never really knew what he thought of me. Maybe now that he'd been dead for a few decades I'd start to get new information. I just had to keep my ears open and listen for echoes from across the divide.

SEVENTEEN

THE NEXT MORNING Burton called me on his cell phone. It was early enough to catch me en route to the outdoor shower with a big mug of cinnamon hazelnut in my shower-safe New York Yankees mug. Eddie had been asleep on the braided rug, but the phone startled him into action. Which amounted to a stiff, yawning stagger into the kitchen. He looked at the coffee like he'd consider giving it a shot.

"Forget it, you'd be up all day."

Then I picked up the phone.

"Yeah."

"What an eloquent salutation," said Burton.

"Social niceties don't start around here until after nine."

"Niceties being a relative concept."

"I guess you got the message."

"Yes. Very interesting. I'm on the Long Island Expressway and expect to be at the house in less than an hour. What say we meet there? Isabella will arrange for breakfast."

"Fine with me. Just tell her to keep the vitriol out of my eggs."

"Certainly. Niceties are standard at the Lewis residence."

The weather looked eager to repeat the performance of the day before. Most of the morning mist had burned off and the bay was etched with wavelets that were barely ripples. The breeze was decidedly south-southwest, mild and kindly. The maples along the back of the property were freshly regaled in light-green baby leaves, and the lawn—a refined blend of native grasses and invasive flora—expressed an exuberance that it seemed uncivil to restrain with anything as pitiless as a lawn mower. At least not this early in the season.

Eddie followed me out on the lawn, where he stopped and shook himself out. Then he trotted on, crossing the end of Oak Point Road and disappearing into the wetlands where he usually went in the mornings for purposes unknown. It might have been a way to vary his diet, or maybe it was just a dog's version of the morning paper. Catching up on events of the night before.

I saw something move out of the corner of my eye and turned to see Amanda waving from her side door. I held up my mug and motioned her to join me, which she did, resplendent in a terry-cloth bathrobe, a headband holding back her unbrushed hair.

"Burton called from the highway," I said, handing her a filled mug and leading her to the Adirondacks at the edge of the breakwater. "He wants us to come see him when he gets here, in about an hour."

The rising sun warmed our necks and threw our shadows down over the breakwater and across the pebble beach. Even with the light air there were two or three sailboats plying the shallows off the south shore of the North Fork. Serious sailors impatient for a change of season, happy just to be out there feeling the glare of the sun off the water and sniffing at the nascent south-southwesterly. Hodges might have been one of them, having endured the battering winter firmly tied to the dock aboard his old Gulf Star. He'd been known to take an occasional winter sail, feeling his way past the unmarked shoals just to demonstrate to himself that it was smarter to stay hunkered down in the teak-lined warmth of the cabin and wait for spring like everybody else.

Amanda cupped her coffee with two hands, her long slender fingers, with freshly polished nails, linking gracefully as if in prayer.

"I have to apologize again," she said.

"Oh, hell."

"I know you hate apologies."

"They're a waste of breath," I told her.

"I feel like I can't continue with you unless I can have recurring and ongoing forgiveness."

"You do. Glad that's settled."

"It's not only what I've done. It's how I've been."

"You got reasons to be a little edgy."

"You think I'm edgy?"

I laughed.

"Don't try that trap on me, Miss Anselma. I used to be married. Learned all the tricks."

"Edgy would be nice. I was thinking I've been hysterical and neurotic."

"Yeah. With an edge."

"And paranoid. I'm definitely getting paranoid."

"What, just because somebody burns down your house and your development project's sounding like a Superfund site?"

"Not funny."

"No, the funny part is the anonymous tipster whose information was convincing enough to get the DEC to get a TRO out of a sympathetic judge. PDQ."

"So you're saying I should be paranoid?"

"No. Paranoia's delusional. You should be suspicious."

"Big downgrade from paranoia."

"Burton will ask you how much you knew, if anything, about those cellars," I said. "Don't get offended. He has to ask."

"What do you think? About how much I knew?"

"You didn't know anything. Otherwise, you'd have checked them out well before the phase-one inspection. To do otherwise would be both foolish and immoral."

"Qualities I could tack on to edgy and paranoid."

"Don't forget," I said, "I didn't know they were there, either. And we've been over that place pretty thoroughly."

"Thank you. I'd forgotten that."

"But if it'll help, I'll cop to it. What's a little environmental racket on top of a murder charge?"

"That's so sweet."

"My first nicety of the day."

I'd seen the original drawings of the WB facility, but never a cellar elevation. They had the same identification box in the lower-left corner as the ones Ned showed us. I didn't remember the exact date they were drawn, but it was sometime in the early twentieth century. I'd never forget such a thing, even with my degraded frontal lobes. If nothing else, I'd remember they were built with stone and not the prevailing brick of the complex. Stone wasn't used much on sandy Long Island, and certainly not for large industrial construction. As far as I knew, all the WB buildings were built on thick, raised slabs, better to stand up to heavy equipment and avoid water infiltration. They were, after all, adjacent to a lagoon.

"Have you accepted my apology yet?" she asked. "I've lost the thread."

"I accept whatever it is you want me to accept. Unconditionally, and in perpetuity, so we don't have to keep going through this."

"Does that preclude occasional pleas for reassurance?"

"Yup. You're all set, for life. Imagine the time saving."

With bold concepts like this, you wonder why my relationships with women were often less than entirely successful.

For the sake of efficiency I convinced her to take her shower with me in the outdoor stall, which turned out to be a fun idea for everybody. It meant that we were an hour later than I'd promised Burton, but he assured us Isabella didn't mind watching her homemade Belgian waffles and cheese omelets cooling on the serving trolley. Our guilt was soothed by the fact that Burton and Hayden had already downed two platefuls, along with a bowl of fresh fruit and half a carafe of café noir.

They were sitting on a slate patio beneath a pergola laden with emerging clematis and wisteria. Hayden was in a white-and-blue-striped tennis outfit last worn by Jay Gatsby and Burton was in a state of exhaustion. Since he could never talk specifically about his work, the only polite thing to say was, "So, workin' hard?"

"Indeed," he said, telling us he'd been up all night preparing a bankruptcy filing that was big enough to affect global financial markets when it was announced later that day. "You won't be surprised to know there are weighty tax implications surrounding the implosion of a large corporation—rather like a pack of jackals feeding on a staggering herbivore. Get it while you can."

"I feel that way about the waffles," I told him.

Amanda and I did our best to catch up with the breakfast

routine while Burton and Hayden picked their teeth and debated the merits, or even the technical feasibility, of a fixed tax code versus our current system of intricate variability. A system Burton admitted was beautifully designed to enrich those capable of navigating and optimizing ambiguities and approximations. People like Burton himself.

"Or you could take my approach," I said. "Maintain a tax status well south of the poverty line."

"Ingenious," said Hayden.

"Only if his friends keep feeding him breakfast," said Amanda.

"I'm sorry I wasn't able to speak with you straight away, Amanda," said Burton. "I think I have the gist, but let's hear the details. I hope you don't mind if Hayden sits in. He's quite the legal scholar."

"I knew nothing about underground cellars or anything like that until those two guys from the DEC pulled out their maps," said Amanda.

"I told her to say that so you didn't have to ask," I said.

"This is what they're accusing you of?" he asked.

"Not directly. By implication."

We told him everything we could think of about the DEC guys as well as Amanda's successful phase-one environmental study.

"You were wise to conclude that meeting," said Burton. "These sorts of administrative actions have very few built-in protections."

"Kafka lives on," said Hayden.

"I'm telling the truth," said Amanda. "I swear to God."

"We'll draw up a letter to the commissioner expressing your eagerness to cooperate fully in the field investigation," said Burton. "Not as good for the soul as swearing to God, but more legally persuasive."

"Anything," she said.

"At least it undermines any claim that you resisted their investigation," said Hayden. "Should they charge you with anything."

"Kafka would do the same thing," I said.

"We shouldn't delay further," said Burton. "Hayden, if you would, bring Amanda to the office and write something up for her. Isabella can notarize it. She loves to get out the stamp," he said to me.

"Really."

"Anything you need to tell me?" Burton asked, once Hayden and Amanda were beyond earshot.

"There's something fucked up going on."

"Put that in layman's terms."

"I don't know exactly," I said.

"Is Amanda telling the truth?" he asked.

"Define truth."

"So you're not sure."

"I'm not sure of anything," I admitted.

"But you have theories."

"None that make any sense."

"The DEC doesn't pursue these things without cause. Deterrence depends on credibility."

"I want a closer look at that drawing."

"Right now Amanda needs to cooperate as fully as possible," said Burton.

"Can I borrow your cell phone?" I asked.

"Certainly. Phone service comes with breakfast."

I fished Dan's number out of my wallet. He didn't answer at the motel so I called his cell.

"Mr. Acquillo, nice to hear from you."

"I'm calling to tell you we're eager to cooperate as fully as possible."

"Good decision."

"We just wanted to make that intention official."

"We'll be faxing a letter to the commissioner's office to that effect," said Burton.

"We'll be faxing a letter to the commissioner's office to that effect," I told Dan.

"That is official."

"We just don't want any misunderstanding about Amanda's willingness to give the DEC total access and cooperation."

"Sounds good to me," said Dan. "Tell your lawyer I said hello."

I cupped the phone.

"He said to say hello."

"So when can we get on the site?" Dan asked.

"As soon as you want if you have a pair of bolt cutters."

"We'll call if we need anything. I've got all the drawings."

"More than we do, obviously. Do you mind if I get another look at that cellar elevation?" I asked him.

"Long as I'm there when you do it."

"Fair enough. I think I know where to find you."

"You betcha," said Dan.

I signaled to Burton that I was ready to end the call and he nodded his okay.

"How was that for full cooperation?" I asked him.

"And you with so little experience."

After that we caught up on my own legal matters. I told him of my visit with Jeff Milhouser, leaving out any mention of Amanda. I didn't want to be talking about her when she got back with Hayden. She could smell a sudden change in conversation a mile away. I also told him about Rosaline Arnold and my sentimental trip to Southampton High.

"What do you expect that to achieve?" he asked me.

"I don't know. But it was worth it just to see Rosaline again."

I was about to tell him more, but seeing Amanda and Hayden walking down the path, I took my own advice and asked him about the NBA playoffs instead.

"Yes, that's a yearly contest the New York Knicks seem committed to boycott."

"Despite the gentle encouragement of their fan base."

"We do our part. We're talking about the Knicks," he said to Hayden as he drew near.

"I'm only there for moral support," said Hayden. "Unless the Sixers are in town. Then we get to watch a game with a little meat on it."

"Hayden's from Philadelphia," said Burton, "where every sport is a variation on the theme of thuggery."

"Home of Smokin' Joe Frazier and the Italian Stallion," said Hayden.

"One of whom was an actual person," I said.

"Sam used to be an actual thug himself," said Amanda as she settled back into her chair.

"Me and Smokin' Joe prefer fighter."

"Retired fighter sounds even better," she said.

"I think for Sam 'recovering' is closer to it," said Burton.

"Not me, Burt. I'm done with it for good. Doctor's advice."

"Smart doctor."

"Big doctor."

I managed to steer the talk back into professional sports and away from further commentary on my personal circumstances, legal or pugilistic. When it looked like Burton was starting to nod off, we made a graceful exit. As we walked through the house, I looked back through a window to see Hayden combing his hand through Burton's hair. Since I'd known him, Burton had resisted getting into a steady commitment. We never talked about it, but I guessed the reasons were economic as well as romantic. He never seemed to suffer for it, though I always wondered if that was just his well-bred self-discipline.

Watching the roll of Amanda's hips as she walked ahead of me—almost gliding through a series of opulent rooms—I thought, fear and anger aren't the only things that make you stupid. Something else, also buried deep in the medulla oblongata, the part Markham would call the lizard brain, was even more likely to interfere with judgment and overthrow the rule of common sense. Something neither Burton nor I, despite our arrogant faith in the intellect, would ever be able to control.

—

When we got back to the cottage there was a unmarked patrol car in my driveway. The driver was sitting out in one of the Adirondacks throwing tennis balls into the bay so Eddie would have an excuse to leap like Rin Tin Tin off the breakwater. Amanda wanted to get back to salvaging her demolished house, so I got to take the other chair.

"He ever get tired of this?" Sullivan asked, giving the tennis ball another throw.

"Only when you stop being impressed."

"I had a long talk with Ross Semple about your case."

"What's his mood?"

"Optimistic. But I convinced him to let me back in. You told me he would. You were right."

"Great."

"Took a while, so I only just started doing anything."

"Like cozying up to the suspect's dog?"

"Like having a little chat with Patrick Getty."

Eddie ran up to the chairs, dropped the tennis ball and shook out his fur, spraying us with sand and salty bay water.

"Nice," said Sullivan.

"All part of the experience."

Sullivan threw the ball into the bay again and Eddie looked at him like, what did you do that for?

"Go get it," I told him. "Go on."

Now on a practical mission, he trotted across the lawn to the beach access, skipping the heroics off the breakwater.

"Ever wonder what goes on in their brains?" Sullivan asked.

"Not that one. You don't want to know."

"Did you know your boy Patrick has a record?"

"No."

"A few B and E's early on, worked his way up to larceny. Did five years. Mostly clean after that, though there was one assault charge the accuser later dropped."

"Too bad. Be good to know who won the fight."

"Ervin's been keeping an eye on him as best he can. Can't exactly afford surveillance."

"What about his posse?"

"Need to look at their IDs, but I'm guessing the same deal. Have that feel about them."

"What did you and Patrick chat about?"

"I told him I wanted to get to know each other a little. Got the usual bullshit about a paid-off debt to society, not looking for trouble, yadda yadda. He said you were the one I should keep my eye on. You and your crazy bitches."

"He's safe from me. The bitches will have to speak for themselves."

"Not your kind," he said to Eddie as he approached with the tennis ball in his mouth.

"So what does this tell us?" I asked him. "Patrick's an ex-con. Should have figured that out ourselves."

"Jail time is the difference between big talkers and the genuine product," said Sullivan. "Much more serious cats. I want them out of my town."

"Do you think Robbie knew they were cons?" I asked him.

"Makes you wonder, doesn't it?"

"All I do is wonder, Joe," I told him.

I left him in the Adirondacks and went back to the cottage to grab a couple of beers. Besides needing the drink I needed a few minutes alone with my brain, hoping something useful would shake loose and drop out on the lawn. But all I got was more confusing mental clutter. So I decided to concentrate on the beer instead. Something simple I could understand.

"Veckstrom doesn't want to be my mentor anymore," said Sullivan when I got back to the breakwater.

"I didn't know he was."

"He told me when I first got promoted where to put my files and how to get calling cards printed with my name and the official Southampton Police emblem."

"Really knows the ropes."

"He's actually younger than me, but he's got a college degree. In criminology, plus two years of law school."

"That explains the tie."

"Don't ask me why he decided to be a cop. Ross thinks he's smart. I think he's smart."

"I think he's a dickhead."

"So I hear."

He hung around long enough to down another beer and give me some inside information on the case without seeming to do so. I appreciated the effort, though there wasn't much new or alarming. Except the ADA's prediction that the grand jury would hand up an indictment within the next three weeks.

"If you were planning to share one of those alternatives you were talking about, I wouldn't wait too much longer," said Sullivan.

"Say Joe," I said, struck with a sudden thought, "do you remember when Jeff Milhouser got in trouble for some scam on the Town?'

He was standing. He looked down at me, took off his black baseball hat and scratched the top of his head with the same hand.

"Vaguely," he said. "It wasn't anything that concerned me as a beat cop. Too downtown."

"I'd like to get some of the details."

"Ross would know. He's always kept it cozy with the Town board. Why the interest?"

"No particular reason. Probably a waste of time."

He put his cap back on and nodded.

"Probably is," he said, and left me there with Eddie and my deepening sense of anxious disorientation. It was a familiar sensation, one I'd often felt on the job when an analysis of a wayward system would start producing strange data, tangles of nonsensical conclusions, incongruities intertwined with further incongruity. I'd actually become nauseated as I tried to force an explanation out of the jumble, knowing it was a doomed strategy, that the failure wasn't in the analysis, but in the validity of the data itself. The underlying assumptions looked so reliable, yet were somehow hopelessly corrupt.

I remembered a young Swiss process engineer named Edouard Baton weeping into his computer keyboard after the two of us had spent twenty-eight straight hours fruitlessly trying to restart his company's hydrogen plant.

"How can it be that we always get the wrong answer?" he sobbed.

"There's nothing wrong with our answers," I told him as the truth, and the solution, dawned on me. "The problem's in the question."

EIGHTEEN

A COUPLE OF HOURS LATER I was standing naked in my kitchen talking to Rosaline Arnold. It was well into cocktail hour, and I was about to fill the aluminum tumbler I usually brought with me into the outdoor shower when she called me on the phone.

"Don't you have to give me a credit card number if you're going to talk to me in the nude?" she asked.

"I got rid of those things. I'll have to send you a check."

"Just bring it over when you come tonight."

"Tonight?"

"I have some research findings to share. We have a deal, and I have an assortment of hors d'oeuvres, a patio and a full liter of that industrial solvent you drink on the rocks."

"Okay."

"Come as you are."

The evening was warm enough to keep the windows down in the Grand Prix on the way over to Rosaline's condominium on the east side of the Village. The sky was mostly deep blue with a bank of charcoal-gray clouds along the eastern horizon. It made for a theatrical backdrop behind the oak trees, whose fresh, light green leaves were lit up by the low angle of the sun. As I passed Hawk Pond, I could see the flags at Hodges's marina hard out behind a stiffer easterly than the movement of the oak leaves would suggest. The surface of the water in the shallow harbor was filled with miniature blue-gray, chrome-tipped waves on which a small flock of seagulls bobbed in place as if tethered to tiny moorings.

The fresh spring air reminded me I was out of cigarettes, so I stopped at the convenience store on County Road 39. The Asian guys who ran the place had two registers going serving a steady crowd of lawn cutters, group renters and plutocrats out picking up toothpaste, six-packs of beer and quarts of half-and-half.

Back when I used to visit the Arnolds, I got in the habit of bringing the old man a magazine or a newspaper—a different one every time. I visited enough that it got difficult to be original. That's why I had my head buried in the magazine racks until I came up with a copy of the *Daily Racing Form*. Which is probably why Hayden Grayson didn't see me when I stepped behind him in the line at the cash register.

He had a large cup of coffee and a gigantic sugared confection. Looked like road food, but before I could wish him a good trip back to the City, he was engaged with the guy at the register. He put the coffee cup and heart-choking cinnamon roll on the counter and then dropped a twenty-dollar bill on top of the cup's plastic lid. After the guy at the register starting ringing him up, Hayden interrupted him and asked if he could throw in a roll of Tums. When the guy turned around to pluck the Tums out of a small display behind the counter, Hayden slid the twenty off the coffee lid and replaced it with a ten. The guy put the roll of Tums down on the counter and punched at the register.

"Out of twenty," he said, palming the ten without looking at it and pulling another ten and a few small bills out of the drawer.

Hayden busied himself collecting his booty and making a quick break for the door, so he still didn't know I was there until I caught up to him climbing into one of those weird little SUVs that remind me of a Reebok sneaker.

Before he could snap on his seat belt, I jumped into the passenger seat and shut the door.

"Did I ever tell you about my mother's theory on littering?" I asked him, reaching over and sliding his keys out of the ignition.

"Whoa, Sam," he said. "You startled me. And no, never a word about your mother. And what's with the keys?"

"Her theory was that anyone who litters is an incipient murderer. Killers in training. She thought if a person had so little concern for common civility that he'd throw a piece of trash on the ground, that he's on the path to sociopathic disregard for the consequences of his behavior. And the trip from common thoughtlessness to depravity is little more than a short hop."

"Interesting," he said, still eyeing his keys in my hand. "I think there've been studies along those lines. None of which would support your mother's hypothesis."

"Yeah, well that's the kind of shit they used to say about Sigmund Freud, and look at him now."

"Disgraced?"

"He agreed with my mother that people could represent themselves as one thing, even to themselves, while actually being something entirely different."

"You seem to have given this a lot of thought," said Hayden.

"Just in the last couple minutes. People used to tell me that I'd never make it to the top if I didn't play golf. Even though I never had time to learn, I always liked the idea of the game. Nice landscaping, not a lot of sweat, nobody trying to knock your block off like they did in the sport I was more familiar with. Plus it involved hitting a ball into a hole, something I'd learned as a kid hanging around pool halls. A little different, but maybe there were some transferable skills."

"I've played golf. Nothing like pool. Sorry."

"Then you're probably a scratch golfer. A lot of pool hustlers are."

"I didn't think that cue ball aimed at my head was an accident."

"Reflexes never lie."

"No harm in letting my lover win a few games of pool."

"Don't make the mistake of thinking he doesn't know," I told him.

"What the hell does that mean?"

"Just what I said. Give me that ten in your pocket so I can bring it back to the guys in the convenience store. Then I'll give you back your keys."

"I don't know what the hell you're talking about," he said, rearing back in affront.

I gestured to him to fork over the bill, which he did, despite the look on his face.

"This doesn't mean that things won't work out for you," I told him as I climbed out of his ridiculous vehicle. "Just don't forget, I'm watching."

"Until they send you to prison for the rest of your life," he called to me as I walked across the parking lot.

I turned and walked backwards, tossing him his keys which he caught with his left hand.

"That's right," I told him. "Nothing to lose."

———

Rosaline's condo was in a complex they'd built in the late seventies not far from the high school. The landscaping had matured nicely, but the exterior trim looked dated and ground up by the corrosive air blowing off the ocean a half mile to the south. The cars in the lot were a mix—Volvos, Mercedes and BMWs along side pickups and sloppy Chrysler four-doors from the late eighties. Testimony to the skyward trend of real-estate values, inexorably displacing the kind of people these condos were originally built for.

She answered the door in an oversized work shirt with the MIT seal embroidered over the heart. And nothing else, unless you counted her glimmering earrings, which hung almost to her shoulders.

I handed her the *Daily Racing Form*.

"Oh, goodie, now I'm all set for the track," she said.

"It was either that or *The Wall Street Journal*. I think the odds're better with the ponies."

"What do you think?" she asked about her shirt, doing a single spin, which challenged what remained of the outfit's mystery. "I thought it would make you feel at home."

"Always ready to give one for the team."

"Not yet. Have a drink first."

Her apartment was like a favorite shoe. Worn, out of fashion and form fitting. There was a fireplace with a stack of fully engaged hardwoods, the wood smoke mingling subtly with scented candles burning on the mantelpiece and strategically arrayed on side tables and built-in bookshelves. It was clean, in the way places can be clean when scoured by someone who takes the term seriously. The decor spare and balanced, eternal. Duke Ellington was on a stereo that came out of nowhere, filling the room like the aroma from the candles. Pervasive, unobtrusive, enveloping.

One wall of the living room was covered in photographs, some in the self-conscious formality of the turn of the century, a few sepia tones going further back, others from the mid-twentieth century, with oversaturated colors and shaggy haircuts. All more or less predictable and homey, but for the recording of nose types, staggering size and angularity being common elements.

"No fruits," I called to her retreating form.

"I know, I know," she yelled back. "My memory's not that bad."

The temperature outside was a crisp mid-sixties, but in Rosaline's apartment it was ten degrees warmer. I peeled down to my shirt and rolled up my sleeves.

"Mind if we hang out on the patio?" I hollered at the kitchen.

"That's the plan," she hollered back. "I'll meet you there."

The patio was more like a slate-covered landing, with a pair of outdoor chairs and a coffee table in between. But it was completely enclosed, private and secure from the prying eyes of neighbors on either side. The common area beyond was heavy with bright green growth, freshly planted spring flowers and perennials, the obvious passion of one or more condo denizens.

I settled into one of Rosaline's wicker lounge chairs and lit a cigarette. She appeared with my vodka and a rye on the rocks for herself. She dropped an ashtray down on the coffee table the moment a cylinder of ash at the end of my cigarette was about to slough off.

"Daddy's drink," she said, as we clinked glasses.

"One a day'll get you to ninety-five."

"Two a day. And he was ninety-seven."

Her dark brown hair looked recently done up, with loose, heavy curls tumbling down over her shoulders. Her liquid blue eyes were, as always, distantly entertained, as if partly engaged by her own internal monologue. Her legs, now generously on view, were still the alabaster white I'd remembered from prior get-togethers involving vodka and rye on the rocks.

"I talked to an old friend of yours the other day," she said. "You'll never guess, so I won't make you try."

"Lou Panella?"

"Jason Fligh."

"Really," I said, as taken by surprise as she hoped I'd be. "What was the occasion?"

"I called him."

"How's he doing?" I asked.

"He said when you left, the board stopped being fun."

"Fun for whom?"

"He asked me how you were doing and wondered if he should get in touch with you. I said sure."

She studied me as if to test my reaction. I shrugged.

"Jason's okay with me. It's you I'm wondering about."

"You interest me," she said.

"I don't make a very happy lab rat."

"Oh, I'm certain of that. You're private to the point of misanthropic."

"People aren't that bad. If you don't have to talk to them," I said.

"You're only enduring this because I have something you need."

"No, I'm enduring this because I like you. It's more fun to get things I need from people I like."

"Not very misanthropic of you."

"Another theory shattered," I said.

"You don't have much regard for psychologists, do you?"

"If I dispute that you'll say I'm dissembling. If I agree, you'll say I'm projecting hostility. There's no good way to answer that question. Reminds me of conversations I used to have with my ex-wife."

"Not the best association."

"Markham Fairchild told me there's nothing more complicated than the human brain. I don't think that means you shouldn't try to find explanations for human behavior, but people need a better perspective on the magnitude of the task."

"Psychologist people," she said.

"Psychologists, philosophers, district attorneys."

"Edith Madison thinks your defense will be based on diminished mental capacity."

I laughed. I couldn't help it.

"Why not?" I said. "That seems to be everybody's favorite theory. I don't give a shit. As long as Frank Entwhistle thinks I'm smart enough to install trim and build bookcases, I can be Sam the Idiot."

"Not if you're in prison."

"Some have wood shops."

"You told me once you learned evasion from a boxer named Rene Ruiz."

"Yeah, the day I failed to evade and he broke my nose. That kind of thing only has to happen once to make a big impression. I think you shrinks call it intermittent positive reinforcement."

She laughed this time.

"I have no intention of shrinking you, Sam. I know when I'm competing over my weight class."

"Not with me all diminished."

She took a long sip of her drink, her eyes holding to mine over the lip of her glass.

"So, about Robbie Milhouser," she said.

"Oh, Robbie. I'd forgotten about him."

"I had to send to deep storage to get his file. That'll be on the record, so I've already jeopardized my career as a school psychologist."

"I didn't want you to do that."

"I know. No reason for anyone to know unless you need to reveal the information for your defense. Then we have a problem."

"I won't let that happen."

"Anyway, it's a thick file. He had a busy time in high school."

"It's not easy to be an accomplished fuckup."

"Fuckup doesn't jive with the record," she said. "He graduated with a three-point-eight average, with commentary from people who thought he was brilliant. Some of whom I know and aren't the type to dispense unwarranted praise."

"Joey Entwhistle had similar intimations."

"The physicist."

"Didn't dissuade him from thinking Milhouser was a dangerous thug," I told her.

"Brains and brutality are anything but mutually exclusive. As proven by Robbie's impressive string of suspensions."

My only friend in high school, Billy Weeds, had an official profile like Robbie Milhouser's. He spent nearly as much time in detention or suspended from school as he did going to class. It made being his friend an interesting challenge, though it didn't stop me from going along with every nutty caper he proposed. I was just better at not getting caught.

"Amanda told me he flunked out of college," I said.

"You'll have to sweet talk the school psychologist at Hofstra if you want that inside information."

"What if the psychologist is a grimy old man?" I asked her.

"Depends on how badly you want the information. Can I pour you another drink?"

"I'm persuadable."

I had to endure her running her fingertips down my forearm as she left the patio on her way into the condominium. Whatever aroma she was featuring lingered with the sensation on my arm, which activated some circuitry connected to other parts of my physiology.

I lit another cigarette and tried to concentrate on the condo association's profligate daffodil garden.

She came back with my drink and a new outfit, a sprayed-on top so poorly fitting it stopped an inch or two above her navel and a full-out sloppy-looking pleated skirt. She'd replaced the shoulder-duster earrings with shorter danglers covered in a profusion of silver and semi-precious stones.

She also had a white pad of paper, from which she withdrew a sheet tucked inside.

"I was afraid to hold the file for more than a few days. But I took notes."

"That much information?"

"I told you Robbie had a fat file. Everyone wanted to write an opinion. Even more interesting was the consistency. They all said basically the same thing."

"Not as much of a dope as you'd think?" I asked, reluctantly.

"A classic underachiever. Great scores on aptitude tests. High IQ, if you believe in that test, which I don't, though it tells you something. He'd tend to sprint along getting good, or excellent, marks and then suddenly take a dive, mess up so badly it would shock his teachers. Usually accompanied by other behavioral problems. Acting out. Fights, vandalism, general obstreperousness."

"Why do you think?" I asked her.

"I don't know."

"You don't?"

"Not without speaking with him, for which I'd need a time machine. Or a séance."

"But you have a guess."

"That's all it would be," she said.

"Good enough for me."

"He was profoundly disturbed."

"There's a news flash."

"Something was troubling him beyond the turmoil of adolescence."

"Maybe he knew he'd grow up to be a dickhead," I offered.

"I know it's not popular with some people to say so, but really bad teenage behavior is often a means of communication," said Rosaline.

"Telling the world they need a kick in the ass."

"Sometimes. Depends on how bad the behavior."

"I remember a lot of high school hardballs. How bad was Robbie anyway?"

"I'll let you decide. But you can't blame me for telling you."

"Why would I do that?"

She handed me a yellowed piece of Southampton High School letterhead. On it was a single paragraph titled "Incident on away-game bus." The names of the two principals were blacked out. It took me a few minutes to read it and a few more to have it sink in.

"The boy is Robbie Milhouser," I said.

"That's right. And the girl?"

"Amanda?"

Rosaline nodded.

"The guidance counselor had her own notes in a private file. It wasn't hard to cross-check. I think she wanted the whole story recorded somewhere. I'd do the same."

"It doesn't say what kind of sexual things happened."

"Only that they were uninvited."

"Joey Entwhistle said she was his girlfriend."

"She might have been at some point. There was nothing about that in the file. And before you ask, no. No charges were brought against Robbie Milhouser, not even a suspension. The whole thing was dropped after Amanda disavowed the report, which by the way was given by one of her friends, and corroborated by a few others. But without the victim's testimony, you got nothing. Especially in those days."

I stood up and walked out to the condo garden. At closer proximity I could see the density of the plantings, some in bloom, others budded up, others barely emerging, all timed to maintain a constantly evolving profusion throughout the warm months. I admired the care and forethought and wondered if I'd ever want to do something like that on Oak Point.

Rosaline came up next to me and took my arm.

"You're not mad," she said.

"Of course not. I never shoot the researcher."

"If you're not mad, what are you?"

"Curious," I said.

"Me, too."

"About what?"

"Amanda didn't seem like much of a quitter, if you read her file. The report itself made it sound like she gave Robbie quite a fight. Why stop there?"

"Not her style," I said.

"I'm not sure what that means."

"I'm not sure either. It's just what came into my head."

Rosaline put her head on my shoulder.

"I didn't want to drop a mood wrecker at the start of an intimate dinner party," she said. "But if I told you later I'd feel dishonest."

"Not at all," I said. "Disturbing revelation always whets the appetite. And speaking of wet," I held up my empty glass.

"I never know what you're thinking," she said, taking my glass and pulling me by the arm back into the house.

Me neither most of the time, is what I wanted to say to her.

She'd put bowls filled with colorful stuff on the coffee table and a small plate of celery and carrots to dig it out of there. I chewed on that while I chewed on what she was telling me.

"I can hear the wheels going from over here," said Rosaline, sitting across from me.

"Sorry," I said, dipping another stalk into the green stuff, which I liked a little better than the maroon, black and yellow-speckled stuff.

"As much as I'd like to say we had a deal, I don't think it'd be fair to make you honor it tonight," she said.

I sat back and killed a few more seconds chewing the hors d'oeuvres.

"The truth is, Rosaline," I said, "I really try not to think about what happened to me with Abby and my job. Do I know why I did what I did? No. I just did it. And then I looked back and said to myself, geez, man, what did you do?"

She listened to me very carefully, studying my face.

"Maybe your conscious mind doesn't know. But what about the subconscious?"

"Oh, Christ, Rosaline. Let me get my five-pound sledge out of the car and you can beat me with it. That'd be a better way to spend the next hour than trying to psychoanalyze me."

She smiled that smile of hers conveyed entirely through the eyes.

"I know that, Sam. What I mean is, you *do* know. That's why you don't want to think about it, and why you don't want to talk about it. You know the truth about yourself. You've been through some things, and you've grown more introspective, but you're still essentially the same person who manned the helm of an incredibly complex and far-reaching organization. You are still the man who invested everything you had, your heart, your soul, your time and deeply held faith in the value of your work, and the idealization of your marriage, even as both were disintegrating before your eyes."

There are people who actually pay to hear that kind of shit, I wanted to say, but couldn't. It wouldn't have been fair to Rosaline, who I knew thought she was trying to do a good thing. That's the problem with the brilliant and well-intended. It's hard to stop them when they think they're on to something.

"Okay, Doc. I'll cop to it," I said instead, hoping a quick surrender would satisfy her.

"For all your combative and cynical behavior, I think you're fundamentally tolerant of others. You endure their foibles and foolishness."

"And alliteration."

"But there's something you cannot abide, something that reaches into a dark place, releasing another essential component of Sam Acquillo. The one you know is there, but refuse to acknowledge."

"A something?"

She thought about that. Then shook her head.

"No. More an act."

I knew she'd get to it somehow anyway, so I just asked.

"Yeah? What?"

"Betrayal."

NINETEEN

THE NEXT MORNING Eddie and I headed out on our easterly jogging route, which took us down around the lagoon and by the WB plant. As expected, the cyclone fence was open and a white DEC van was parked near the entrance with its side door and back hatch wide open revealing racks of expensive-looking analytical equipment.

Eddie flushed Dan out from behind a small outbuilding. He was wearing earphones and holding what looked like a boom mike supported by a thick nylon harness. He pulled off the phones when he saw me approach.

"This yours?" he asked, pointing at Eddie.

"In theory."

"Scared the crap out of me."

"Sorry. How's the study going?"

"It's going."

"You can't tell me?"

"Nothing to tell." He pulled the boom out of a holster

CHRIS KNOPF

sewn into the harness webbing and gently laid it on the ground, then moved his torso around, stretching his back muscles. "You'd think they could make that thing lighter."

"Field guys always bitch about something."

He sat down on a windowsill that protruded from the outbuilding.

"We went through the original phase-one study and everything checked out, not surprisingly," said Dan. "I know the guys who did the work. Pretty thorough. But we've only now had a chance to look for those cellars, the crux of the matter. You sure you don't know where they are?"

I sat on the ground so he wouldn't have to look up at me while I briefed him on my background, that I'd been on hundreds of industrial sites all over the world that were engaged in processing all manner of toxic and explosive chemical compounds. I hated that kind of talk, because you mostly heard it from people needing to assert their importance in the world. But I needed Dan to know my bona fides so I didn't have to get into technical debates, or have to listen to the third-grade version of things I knew better than he did. He took it like I hoped he would.

"If you can think of any way to avoid bringing backhoes in here and digging up the place, I'd like to hear it," he said. "The State pays me either way, but Amanda pays for the holes."

"I need a closer look at the drawings," I told him. "Like I said, I'd never seen them before."

"Fair enough."

He hauled himself up and walked back to the van, where Ned, also wearing headphones, was glued to a bank of CRTs examining oscillating waveforms and scrolling tables of data. Dan tapped him on the shoulder and he jumped.

"Sorry, Ned. We've got company."

258

Ned pulled off his headphones and shook his head.

"No, my fault. You shouldn't be listening to Pink Floyd and radar pings at the same time."

"Sam wants to get another look at the cellar elevations. I said it was okay."

He retrieved them from the box and we all went over to the main building where we could spread out on a dusty conference table.

I'd spent a lot of time with the original drawings and their subsequent iterations. Running through the scrolled sheets refreshed my memory and stirred up some odd and slightly unwanted associations. But there was nothing there I hadn't seen before beyond the cellar elevations.

I used an Agfa lupe I'd brought in the pocket of my running shorts to compare the paper and drawing style, especially the lettering and flourishes that were common to the day. Without a document expert it was hard to know for sure, but the cellar elevations looked like they belonged with the first set drawn in the twentieth century. There are a million little details you could compare on a hand-drafted architectural drawing. A forgery would be an impressive achievement.

"You think they're real?" I asked Dan, looking up from the lupe.

"Forensics could nail it, of course, but the people in the State's Attorney's office thought they were legit, and so do I."

"Me too. Can you say the same about the other information?"

"They do. Said it's as clean as it gets."

"The term toxic waste covers a lot of territory. Anything more specific?"

Ned rummaged around in the box and came up with a report from the DEC lab, basically a laundry list of possible feedstocks, compounds and component chemicals used in the manufacture of rubber rafts beginning around the Second World War and into the fifties and sixties after vinyl was introduced. I once lived in a sea of these technical papers, plans and reports. It was like looking at the faces of your old football team in the high school yearbook. Familiar and strangely distant at the same time. I forced myself to concentrate until I saw it. The bad thing.

"Ah, shit," I said, despite myself.

"What?" he asked, trying to look over my shoulder.

"Buna-N. I didn't think they used it for rafts."

"WB mixed up a lot of it," said Dan. "That's all we know."

"A copolymer. Part acrylonitrile."

"Right. An IARC Group 2B carcinogen. Could've been in a lot of things these guys made. Can you say acrylics?"

I looked out the window at the rusty, overgrown plant site. Then back down at the cellar elevations.

"But why?" I asked.

"Nobody cared about toxic waste back then. You wouldn't believe the shit we uncover."

"No, why the missing drawings, why the anonymous tip, and why now?"

"Not my turf, like I told you," said Dan.

"I know. I'm just talking. Don't know what else to do."

I walked outside leaving the DEC guys to pack up the drawings. Eddie was lying in the grass waiting for me. He'd been to the site plenty of times and knew there was nothing interesting there for him anymore. Just as well. I didn't like him sniffing around the place anyway. God knows what could be in the air, in the soil. Actually, I could guess. So could Dan. Which would be easily confirmed by any junior chem engineer with a simple test kit.

Everything made sense and everything didn't.

Dan came up behind me.

"I need two more days with this gizmo," he pointed to the instrument mounted on the end of the boom lying in the grass nearby, "and then we can move to drilling test holes. Give that a few days before we start bringing in the heavy equipment. After that it'll get harder to keep this thing under wraps. But I'll do the best I can. I'm not in the business of destroying people's investments."

I thanked him and told him to take all the time he needed.

"Nothing's happening to Amanda's project till this gets resolved, one way or the other," I told him.

"You got that right."

I thanked him again and jogged off with Eddie. We completed our usual westerly route, which included a run though a bird sanctuary, a favorite of Eddie's, and a stop at a roadside deli for Gatorade and dog biscuits served from behind the counter by the leathery Frenchman and his chubby Cambodian wife who ran the place.

"He like zee *petit gâteau*, no?"

"Mostly the presentation," I told him. "Don't give him too many. We still gotta run back."

Which we did. We passed by the WB plant on the return trip and saw the DEC van still there and Dan walking slowly through the weeds, boom in the air and face creased with concentration. Questions hung like a sickening vapor over the whole scene, and all I could do was jog on by, focus on my breathing and not spraining an ankle on the rutty road that led back up to the tip of Oak Point.

———

I wanted to bring Eddie with me into the Village but assumed where I was going they'd frown on dogs. Made no sense to me. In Europe you bring dogs everywhere, including restaurants and bars, and never once have I heard of a dog-borne pandemic. If I had the money, I'd bring him to Paris. Stuff his face full of *petit gâteau*.

The *Southampton Chronicle* building sat on a hill that over-looked the backside of the Village center, which made it look both watchful and appropriately aloof. It was on the way to the big new library—my next stop if the foray into local jour-nalism proved unfruitful.

I didn't know what to expect and had only the roughest plan of attack, knowing nothing about the inner workings of a newspaper. I was surprised to see a reception desk inside the front door, just like any old office anywhere.

"I'm here to see a reporter," I told the pert, round-faced receptionist.

"Certainly," she said brightly. "Any one in particular?"

"How about an old one?"

She pulled out a plastic-covered list of names.

"Let's see. I don't know everybody perfectly well, but I can think of a few gray heads. I don't mean that in a bad way," she added, looking at the gray head standing before her.

"I didn't think you did."

"Some people think gray hair means wisdom. I do."

"Wise decision. So what do you think?"

"Roberta is like my mother's age. Or there's Kyle who's like been here forever. Not sure if he's here now. We're a weekly," she added, as if that explained everything.

"But you're sure about Roberta?"

"She gave me half her bagel this morning on the way in. I didn't eat it, though. It had cream cheese. Bad for the tummy tone."

She put both hands flat across her midriff to illustrate the value of restraint.

"Let's give Roberta a call," I suggested.

"Sure. And who may I say is calling?"

"My name's Sam Acquillo, but she won't know me. Just see if she'll give me a few minutes to ask some questions."

"Okay."

While she called I had a chance to admire the blank opacity of the reception area. There were no clues it belonged to a newspaper. If I'd been transported there in a blindfold I'd think I was in a machine-tool factory. I expected to walk directly into a buzzy newsroom filled with hard-charging cynics who looked like Edward R. Murrow and spoke like Cary Grant. What I got was Roberta Camacho, a late-middle-aged woman shaped like a red delicious apple on a pair of sticks. She had a head of hair you'd call mousey, but only if the mouse had been dead for a while. She was, however, hard-charging, coming through the access door with hand thrust forward and eyes staring intently over a pair of cat's-eye reading glasses.

"Roberta Camacho, and I know exactly who the hell you are," she said to me as I shook her hand.

"You do?"

"You're the guy from North Sea accused of murdering Robbie Milhouser with a hammer stapler. You here to confess? Give me the scoop? What a prince."

"I'm just looking for some information," I said, as the heartsickening realization hit me.

"Sure. I tell you, then you tell me."

"I'm an idiot," I told her. "Of course you'd want to ask me a bunch of questions. And here I am delivering myself to you.

"That's brave of you to say. Most guys wouldn't admit that in public," she said, pulling a small steno pad out from under her ample arm and flipping it open.

I sat down on one of the innocuous leather and chrome chairs in the waiting area. She sat in the other one.

"What I know so far is the police have fingered you as their only suspect, but the grand jury has yet to hand up an indictment. Though people close to the case feel that's forthcoming. They're just dotting i's and crossing t's. What's your opinion on that?"

"My opinion is that the clarity of my thinking has eroded somewhat recently, for a variety of reasons."

She didn't write that down.

"What about off the record? You have something to tell me? Is that what you're here for?"

As punishment for my stupidity, I made myself listen to what Jackie Swaitkowski would have said if I'd told her I was going to the *Southampton Chronicle* to do a little digging around. I played it as a lot of loud words ending with "what the hell were you thinking?"

"No. I honestly just wanted to get some information. I guess I never thought beyond that."

She flipped her steno book closed and sat back in her chair.

"Are those cigarettes in your shirt pocket?"

"Camels."

"If you let me have one I'll let you use our special smoking area on the side of the building."

"As long as we don't have to talk," I said, following her through the access door, down a dreary connecting hallway to a side door, and out to a picnic table around which clung the bitter residue of banished smokers. We sat down and shared an ashtray.

"Tell you what," she said. "Let's really just talk off the record. I have no problem with that."

I remember back at the company being warned in the sternest terms to never speak to anyone from the press under any circumstances without our PR people's prior approval and involvement in the interview. It was one of the few direct commands I submitted to with unqualified obedience. So much so that the head of corporate affairs complained I was undermining our credibility by stonewalling the media.

"You told me not to talk to them," I'd said to the PR guy.

"Not not talk. Just not talk without our involvement."

"So I don't talk about the wrong things?"

"I don't like the characterization, but I accept the gist of it. We need to control our message."

"You do, I know," I said sincerely. "And you're good at it. I'm a lot better at controlling product quality. Let's stick to our strengths, what do you say?"

We eventually reached a compromise where the PR people would send over questions or requests for information from the media—which usually meant industry magazines, but sometimes the general press—and I'd write back an answer. I never saw anything in print attributed to me that resembled anything I ever wrote down, which proved the wisdom of our strategy.

Roberta and I stared at each other and smoked in silence for a few minutes. Then my curiosity got the best of me.

"What's that mean, exactly, off the record?" I asked her.

"You tell me anything you want and I promise not to print any of it. Except those things that will win me a Pulitzer Prize or get me fired for letting some other paper get a scoop on something I should've had."

"Pretty airtight deal."

We quietly smoked some more, then I put out my cigarette and tossed her an extra from my pack.

"Sorry to bother you," I told her, standing up. "You don't have to escort me through the building. I can walk around."

Which I started to do when she called me back.

"What if I answer your questions first and then you decide if you'll answer some of mine."

I walked back to her.

"I can't afford to mess up here," I said to her. "It's not my life being at stake. It's the crap I'll have to take from my lawyer."

Her face, heavily jowled and marred with the antique vestiges of acne, looked amused.

"I spent almost twenty years as a reporter at the *Boston Globe* before marrying a guy I didn't know at the time was about to inherit a place on Gin Lane. You want to check out if my word is good, call anybody there who knew me. I have no reason to break a trust with you. I don't care that much about your story, and I don't need the money or the job."

I sat down and took the cigarette I'd given her off the table and lit it. Then I gave her a fresh one.

"You wanna talk about messing up," she said, waving it at me.

"I was looking for a way to research a news story that's about ten, maybe fifteen years old. I thought it might be quicker to ask a reporter who was around at the time."

"That was early on for me, but I was here. What story?"

"Jeff Milhouser and some sort of bank fraud."

"The victim's father," said Roberta.

"He was a Town Trustee back then. I was told he used Town money to collateralize personal loans."

"Can you wait here?" she asked, then lumbered back inside the building, leaving me alone with my self-recrimination.

She came back ten minutes later with a handful of loose paper.

"Pulled this off the archives," she said. "Piece of cake. Ain't computers grand?"

"So they tell me."

Roberta leafed through the stack till she found something she liked, which she read, then handed over to me. It was a report on Milhouser's plea bargain, in which he gave up his seat as a Trustee, paid a hundred grand fine and got five years' probation. The charge was the way Hodges remembered it. Milhouser was trying to start a retail nursery business on County Road 39, but was having trouble raising the capital with his house fully mortgaged and his credit rating in the toilet from a prior bankruptcy. He'd told East End Savings and Loan that the money he used to buy a six-month CD, which collateralized the loan, had come from an inheritance, when in fact it was Town funds. It was a simple plan, in every sense of the word, that came a cropper when accounts payable at Town Hall started bouncing checks before the CD term came due and Milhouser could jockey the funds back where they belonged.

The Town Treasurer at the time, a guy named Zack Horowitz, had authorized the withdrawals based on Milhouser's suggestion that the Town take advantage of new investment vehicles being offered through some big commercial banks. What made Horowitz think this was a good idea, or why he let one of the Town Trustees handle the theoretical transactions, wasn't clear from the news story, but the report of the Treasurer's resignation, shortly after Milhouser's scheme was uncovered, explained how he probably stayed clear of criminal court himself.

The bank's position on the matter was more curious. Since the nursery deal fell through before he could close, Milhouser was able to return the loan, so technically, from the bank's point of view, no harm was done except for some slight misrepresentation on the loan application. Milhouser's legal trouble was then solely with the Town.

"You remember this?" I asked her.

"Sorry. Vaguely at best. Is it okay to ask you something now?"

"I guess."

"Why are you interested in this?"

I didn't know what was worse. Feeling endangered by a boneheaded move or being asked to examine motives I always preferred to leave unexamined.

"I don't know."

"No fair."

"It's the truth. I don't know. It just seems interesting to me. A little ripple in the continuum."

"Of course. One of those."

I found myself imagining I had an understanding with Roberta Camacho. That was probably what she wanted me to think.

"I'll tell you when I know myself," I told her.

"You'll tell me everything—me and nobody else. When you're ready. I'll wait. I'm patient. No deadline pressure. We're a weekly."

"So I hear."

I stood up again, this time like I really meant it.

"Thanks for your help," I said.

"Don't thank me till I ask my other question."

"Yeah?" I asked, unhappily.

"It's all about jealousy, isn't it?"

"What do you mean?"

"Where I come from a fistfight in front of a beautiful woman is always about the beautiful woman."

"It wasn't a fistfight. And it was about her real-estate development, not her," I said.

"So not an old boyfriend."

"Not since high school, if you believe what you hear."

"Do you?"

She wasn't taunting me. It was more of a challenge to my reserve. A prod. I wish I could say that it didn't work, but it did.

"It's irrelevant."

"Why do you think that, if you really do?"

"No such luck. But thanks," I said, and walked away with as clear an intent as I could express without looking like a bigger idiot than I felt.

"For what?"

I could have said "for the serving of humble pie" but she wouldn't have known what I meant, and she'd still be calling after me. But I would have meant it. For those who live inside their minds the greatest hazard is hubris, an assumed immunity to false perception, an unflinching loyalty to cold logic. It's the arrogance of reductionism—that every problem can be dissected into its irreducible parts and then reassembled into an entirely coherent solution, its mysteries laid bare. I'd always known this was delusional, a lazy habit of the mind. I'd scolded myself on the matter before, and now had a chance to do it again.

I was consoled, however, by a new line of thinking, a new arrangement of the random information I'd begun to gather up, reshuffle and reconfigure into a freshly conceived potential.

Interesting, I said to myself, with all due humility.

PART FOUR

TWENTY

THE DETOX FACILITY I'd been confined to was in Westport, one of the tonier tanks in the area, courtesy of my ex-wife, who couldn't bear any ex-husband of hers writhing with the DTs in so sordid a town as Bridgeport.

The first thing I did when I got out was find the nearest bar. I knew just the place, a fern bar on Boston Post Road that had worn into an approximation of a local joint, frequented by a jovial blend of barflies, retired stockbrokers and narcissistic Peter Pans working as underpaid golf pros and crewing on racing yachts up and down the Gold Coast. Better yet, the place was within walking distance of the detox facility, important for a newly released patient without a car.

It was early fall so the weather was okay for a walk. Over the last two weeks I'd been able to work out at the over-equipped, under-utilized gym several hours a day. I thought that was the main reason my headaches had subsided and my reflexes were returning to nearly normal. I still had a

little money left over from the conflagration of the divorce
and a fresh new debit card to get it when needed. Other than
that, all I had were the clothes I was wearing when they
admitted me and a cottage out on Long Island that I hadn't
seen in a while.

I was halfway to the bar when a dark blue Mercedes
brushed by me and pulled on to the shoulder. I kept walking,
hands in my pockets, head down.

The driver's side door opened and Jason Fligh flowed out
in a three-piece pinstriped suit and black silk duster.
Big, but still evenly proportioned in middle age, he would
have filled all the space in front of me even without the
Mercedes.

"Sorry I'm late," he said.

"Late for what?"

"To pick you up when you were released."

"No kidding."

"I told them I'd do it. Obviously they didn't tell you. Get in."

I had mixed feelings about seeing him. I'd been dedicat-
ing myself to the pursuit of amnesia, trying to rewire my
memory reflexes so the sight of certain human faces or
everyday objects wouldn't instantly trigger a flood of
remorse. The last month had been particularly challenging
to the program, given the facility's curious insistence on
complete sobriety.

It was vaguely comforting, though, watching him cast concerned sidelong glances at me as we drove along in silence.

"Where you staying?" he finally asked me.

"Haven't worked that out yet."

"I'd say you could stay with me till you figure it out, but
you'd have to come to Chicago."

"I like Chicago, but you're right. I'm bound to New York
and its hallowed environs."

"So where am I driving you?"

"Adelaide's. Take a right here. It's down there on the right."

"Great, I'm hungry, too," said Jason. "I'm buying."

I didn't want to correct him on my intent, especially since he was buying. We made it halfway through the first round of cocktails before it dawned on him.

"Are you allowed to be drinking that stuff?" he asked.

"They told me to lay off the bourbon. This is vodka."

"And here I am aiding and abetting."

For his sake I paced myself, which was probably smart given my reduced capacity. We talked about baseball and his wife's law practice and the manifold achievements of his children, who were spread around the country at top-tier universities. I told him what I could about my daughter, though at the time she wasn't talking to me or returning my letters or answering her phone without a machine to intercept my calls. I didn't tell him that part so as not to cast a pall over the joy he took in kid talk. He avoided talking about the University of Chicago probably for similar reasons. That would make it even harder for me to hold up my end of the conversational quid pro quo. I dragged him into it anyway because I knew he enjoyed his work almost as much as his kids. And I liked listening to him, since he actually had a pretty interesting job. This went on straight through dinner, making it easier for both of us to avoid discussing me. Though when the check arrived it became unavoidable.

"So, Sam, what's your plan?" he asked.

I didn't have one. I didn't have a plan for when I'd start planning. All I had was the fuzzy outline of a concept, the centerpiece of which was a preliminary decision to breathe and take in food. I didn't want to tell him that, so I said I was working on some temporary things that would keep me busy and maybe after that figure out something permanent. The way I said it sounded really convincing to me, but Jason didn't buy it exactly.

"Baloney. Now, tell me what you're gonna do," he said.

I didn't have an answer.

"You don't care, do you?" he said. "I can see it. You're planning to drift back into never-never land where you'll be until some other desperate foolishness puts you back into the system, which you may or may not survive next time. You'll continue this cycle until me and your daughter, who's told me she's done with you forever, which I don't believe by the way, are standing there holding hands at some cemetery while the Catholic clergy struggles to find a redemptive lesson in the whole sorry mess."

I thought he was a little optimistic about my daughter and the priesthood bothering to show up, but the rest of the storyline had a credible ring. Though it put me in a quandary. I knew he wanted to buck me up, but I actually liked the sound of it. Everything but the funeral bit at the end, which if I played my cards right could be dispensed with.

The only problem was I found self-destruction sort of tedious to be around, even my own. I really didn't want to inflict any of that on people like Jason Fligh, good people whose true hearts deserved greater respect. People it's immoral to drive away just so you can disassemble yourself in private. So I took the only path that was left open to me. I lied.

"I hear you, Jason. You're right. I got to get myself together."

It was nice to see him light up as he sat back in his seat and flashed an atta-boy gesture.

"That's right. So tell me, what's your plan? I'm waiting."

My plan, I thought. Hm. I'm already fed. It's still warm enough outside to sleep under a bush without coming down with hypothermia. I've only had two watery drinks in the last two hours after a very long dry spell. That's it. Another drink.

"How about one more round and I'll tell you," I said.

He bought the ploy and I bought the drinks. Thus energized I started to weave a story about how during the day and in the evening while getting ready for insomnia, I'd think about my parents' cottage on the Little Peconic Bay in Southampton. How it was standing there empty and forlorn, bearing dumb witness to the passing seasons and infinite variation of wind and weather playing across the sky and resonant inland sea. As I went on from there I became lost in my own narrative. When I stopped, Jason was leaning over the table looking mesmerized.

"Lord. If you're not going there, I am," he said, after a short silence.

"I thought you were an Upper Peninsula guy."

"I'm reconsidering."

Then I said the thing I only meant as a bit of a throwaway. Halfway through I realized that was a mistake.

"So you oughta come see for yourself. Make up your mind."

He looked at his watch.

"How long's it take to get there from here? I have an eight o'clock flight out of La Guardia, but I can move it to tomorrow morning."

"I don't know. Two, three hours. Not sure what kind of shape the place is in. It's been sitting empty a couple of years."

He reached across the table and swatted my shoulder.

"I grew up on the South Side, Sam. Trust me, I'm flexible."

He jumped up and palmed the check off the table and went to pay it. I polished off the rest of my drink and shrugged off my reservations. What the hell difference does it make? A comfortable car ride, an uncomfortable night in a dusty, damp old cottage, and go from there.

I slid down in my seat and let it happen.

———

He asked me on the way if I wanted to hear about the company and I said no, which he seemed glad about. Instead he updated me on the baseball season and current events I'd missed while in the tank. He let me smoke, giving himself an excuse to light one of his cigars, so we drove along the highway for some time drowned in wind and noise. The Mercedes was so quiet with the windows up the contrast was startling, but not unwelcome. It was getting harder and harder for me to think of things to say so Jason didn't have to do all the talking.

In a little more than two hours we were on North Sea Road heading up from Route 27. I hadn't stayed there since my mother died in a nursing home in Riverhead almost two years earlier. My sister flew in from Wisconsin to handle all the paperwork and formalities. She liked doing that kind of thing so I didn't interfere. But she couldn't bring herself to stay at the cottage. So that was my part, to check out the mechanical systems and make sure there was no water or wildlife leaking in. Even though my mother hadn't been in the house for a while, in my mind it was still the place where she lived. Her presence was woven into all the furniture and decorations, saturating the walls and filling up the open spaces in between.

I felt it all the moment I opened the door. The narrative of her life expressed in texture, smells and dead silence. I told Jason to hang by the back door while I went into the basement to throw on the power. The lightbulb above the panel popped on, and the well pump chugged to life. The smell of mold was pronounced, but everything looked the way I'd left it. No damage there.

Jason had prudently stopped at a deli on Route 27 to buy coffee and pastries for the next day. And some ice for that night to take advantage of the quart of Dewar's my mother left under the sink. I turned on the fridge to store Jason's cream and preserve the ice. Then I went out to the front porch and took down most of the storm windows to let the cooling breeze from the Little Peconic cleanse some of the must out of the air. I got us both ashtrays and we settled into the hard wicker chairs my mother kept out there to hold stacks of magazines and shopping bags filled with other shopping bags, all of which I'd tossed out at the first opportunity. I turned on a lamp that threw off a meager light. We could still see the moon hanging fat and orange just above the horizon, casting a wedge-shaped wash of light across the Little Peconic Bay.

"Can I ask you something?" said Jason. "You don't have to answer."

Though you always have to answer, don't you.

"What?"

"Why'd you do it? What happened?"

Jason grew up with almost nothing but a set of parents who mandated he stay at the top of his class from kindergarten through the doctoral program in economics at Stanford, which he did, helped along the way by football scholarships and a hundred part-time jobs. Jason was the type of man who worked at remembering his whole life, and kept that perspective within view every day. To him, the thought of destroying a career, and consequently a marriage, and rounding it out by a swirling descent into drunken oblivion, fell below anathema to the depths of abomination.

"It was all gone long before it was over," I told him.

He drew in the last tolerable mouthful of cigar smoke and shot it above his head at the ceiling.

"Why didn't you start fixing things before it got to that point?" he asked.

I didn't have much of an answer for him, even after I tried for a few minutes to dredge one up.

"I was too busy doing the work to look after my job," I said.

He looked unsatisfied but didn't press it. We drew down the Dewar's a little more in comfortable silence. Then, before Jason went to bed I tried to thank him, suddenly feeling the enormity of his kindness bearing down. He waved it away with an easy grin.

"So, this is your plan?" he asked me.

"It wasn't before you asked me, but I guess it is now. This is the whole plan. Good through tomorrow morning when we eat the cinnamon buns."

"Good enough for me," he said, leaving me alone on the porch where I fell asleep and stayed well into the middle of the next morning, when I woke up to find him gone. A sturdy bodhisattva in a dark blue Mercedes, delivering me unto the Little Peconic Bay, a novitiate in the ways of bewildered anguish.

TWENTY-ONE

AFTER MY VISIT with Roberta Camacho I had an escort on the way back to North Sea. It was a plain-wrapper Crown Victoria just like Sullivan's, only it wasn't Sullivan. Similar sunglasses, but beyond that Lionel Veckstrom was a whole different kind of cat.

The day had turned surly, with a low cloud cover turning the sky a gray mud. A thin mist covered the pitted windshield of the Grand Prix, slowing me down, mindful of how the big car handled over a slick road surface. Veckstrom slowed with me, maintaining his distance.

I let him tail me as far as Towd Pond, where there was a restaurant I rarely went to, but figured I'd get coffee at the bar. I knew what was coming and I didn't want the guy at my house. No particular reason, I just didn't have the hospitality in me. Must have been the crummy weather.

I had a cup of hazelnut in a thick china mug in front of me by the time he made it to the next seat over. It reminded me of my last encounter with Patrick Getty. Maybe I should call him and his boys and we could all have a little get-together.

"Workin' off another hangover?" he asked me as he sat down.

"Ask my lawyer. Jackie Swaitkowski. But don't stand too close when you do."

"Tough broad."

"Especially when you call her a broad. Listen, hero," I turned and said to him. "I've already done one stupid thing today. I may have more in me, but I'll pass on talking to you. Provoked or otherwise."

He shrugged.

"It's a free country. At least for me. I can sit here and talk to myself and nobody can say much about it. I might even talk a little about how your case is going, if I was feeling like it."

"It's going great. Thanks anyway."

"Bernie Gelman told me you had a mouth. When it wasn't full of booze."

"Especially then. Who's Bernie Gelman?"

"Bridgeport, Connecticut investigator. We worked together in Duchess County in the day."

I remembered. A short greasy little guy with bad skin and rapidly receding crown of curly black hair. Looked very unhappy at Antoine and Walter Bick's trial. I could see why, given how he wanted it to turn out.

"That surprises me," I said, honestly. "I'd expect you to attract a bigger thinker."

"I said I worked with him. I didn't say I liked him. I didn't even know he was in Bridgeport till I started looking into you. I learned a lot of things."

"I'm a big proponent of life-long learning. Been trying to get through Immanuel Kant. You're a smart guy, maybe you could help me figure him out."

"Don't know Kant. Too busy studying Enrico Ferri and James Q. Wilson. They both have a lot to say about people like you."

I swiveled around in my stool and faced him, even as the little Jackie Swaitkowski inside my head told me not to.

"Excellent. More free psychoanalysis. Can't have too much of that."

Veckstrom was still well-dressed in a white shirt, club tie and raw silk sport coat. His face had a scrubbed and close-shaven look. No blemishes, no hairs sticking out of the wrong places. Not hard to interpret the psychology there. It said: I might have chosen to be a cop because the profession interests me, but don't think I'm one of them. I live on a higher plane, and there's no room here for you.

"They never found the punks who killed your father. Hardly tried, is how I heard it. No point. Hard to tell the good guys from the bad guys in those days. Piss you off, did it?"

I pointed my finger at him.

"Come on, Veckstrom. You gotta do better than that. The trauma of a murdered father, his killers gone free, instilling in the young man antisocial tendencies. Manifest in a variety of ways—affiliations with lowlifes, violent and self-destructive behaviors, a wicked bad temper and a pro-nounced disinterest in regular church attendance."

"You forgot the repressed lust for revenge. Unfocused, free-floating and easily attached to any person who might represent, symbolically, the unpunished killers. Big guys with big mouths. Nasty arrogant buggers. Swaggering around threatening old men and pretty girls."

"Criminals," I said, warming to the topic. "People who'd proven in the past they were also willing and able to break a few social conventions."

"Very good."

"Only I didn't know that about Patrick and his boys at the time. I thought they were just a bunch of drunken builders coming off a hard winter, just like we were. Maybe not with the same style, but the same idea."

Veckstrom looked like he'd lost track, but tried not to show it.

"You know Patrick Getty had done time," I said. "You'd have to know that."

"Of course," he said, recovering. "Exactly my point."

"Right. So you know where."

"Yeah. Hungerford. Medium security. Should have been harder time, in my opinion, but that's your typical prosecution. Rather cut a deal than deal with the paperwork."

"Hungerford. Really."

"Yeah. Pussy time," he said.

"Pussy prosecutors. Piss you off, don't they?" I asked him. "Makes you just want to kill somebody, doesn't it?"

He smiled a humorless smile and waved the bartender over to order his own cup of coffee. I knew the tactic. Buying time.

"Doesn't it make you wonder," I asked, "why an ex-con like Getty isn't getting looked at? Why am I a better pick than a known felon? Prosecution just going the easy route? More fun to bag an ex-corporate man, better story for papers? Come on, you're the learned one. No theories?"

"Getty's prints weren't all over that stapler."

"That's because it didn't belong to him. It belonged to me. I can show you where I used it to install insulation. Forensics can match the staples. Shoot a few into a barrel of water."

"Your prints and nobody else's," he almost growled at me.

"On the handle? I heard about clear prints on the chrome. What about the orange handle? If you'd spent more time getting your hands dirty you'd know which end of a hammer stapler you swing."

A breath of doubt tried to gain purchase on his expression, but he held tough.

"The physical evidence is as good as it gets," he said. "Don't start putting your hopes there. Never works."

"I don't have hopes," I said. "Gave them up a while ago."

"Smart decision."

I stood up and put enough money on the bar to cover both our coffees.

"You're right. They get in the way. A hope is like an assumption, a theoretical construct. A paradigm. You get too loyal to any of those things and your IQ falls about fifty points," I said before leaving him there and getting back into the Grand Prix.

I was glad to be close to home. I wanted to pick up Eddie so I could run a few things by him in the car on the way over to Jackie Swaitkowski's. That always helped me work through my assumptions. Even my theories. And despite what I'd said to Veckstrom, maybe a hope or two.

———

I was irritated to find Jackie with another client. I was forced to pace around the sidewalk and occupy myself looking at artwork and tchotchkes in the shop windows that lined Montauk Highway. Worse for Eddie was succumbing to a leash, but I had to keep a grip on him in case he ran into a Lhasa apso out to prove something.

I tried to interest him in a flock of collectible hunting decoys but only insulted his intelligence. We were both happy to hear Jackie call to us from her second-story window.

"Some people actually make appointments," she said as we walked up her staircase.

"I've tried that. Not as sure as just showing up."

"You think it's made all better by bringing the dog?"

"No, but he does."

I was gratified to see her new office space filling up on schedule. I had to shovel a stack of papers off the couch so Eddie and I would both have room to sit.

"Before you get too comfortable, tell me why you're here," she said, dropping into one of the opposing chairs.

"I'm supposed to be communicative and here I am communicating and what do I get?"

"Oh, please."

"I just had a cup of coffee with Lionel Veckstrom."

She sat up a little in her chair.

"You didn't tell him anything did you? Or provoke him?"

"He did all the telling and provoking. I just bought the coffee."

"So what did he tell you?" she asked.

"Something I should have asked about a long time ago, and didn't. Like a dope."

"So tell me."

"You need to take a trip with me."

"That's what he told you?"

"I always love your company, Jackie, but this time I really need it or they won't let me leave the Island."

"That's a cinch. Where're we going?"

"I'll tell you on the way. How's tomorrow?"

She leaned forward so quickly she almost propelled herself out of her chair.

"Oh, no. Not this time. You have to talk to me. Or no trip."

This is the problem with being communicative. People actually expect you to tell them things.

"We need to go visit another one of your clients. One who didn't do as well as I'm hoping to in court."

"You're kidding."

"Roy Battiston. Hungerford Correctional Facility. All the more reason to have you there, assuming he still likes you."

She ran her fingers up into her disorderly ball of hair and shook her head.

"If he does, that's good, though I don't like him. I do like you, Sam, God knows why, but I'm not even going to discuss this with you until you tell me what you're thinking."

So I told her what I'd learned about Jeff Milhouser's unsuccessful gambit with the Town funds, though I spared her the means I used to get the information. I'd maybe save that for the ride when we were moving too fast for her to jump out of the car.

"That's fascinating, Sam, but I still don't know what the hell it has to do with your case."

"East End Savings and Loan. The bank where Milhouser tried the fiddle. Something Amanda told me a long time ago."

"They were bought up by Harbor Trust," said Jackie. "Moved into their building there on Main Street."

"See? Everybody knows this but me."

"Roy was the manager?"

"Not at that point, but he was there, working his way up. Opening accounts, building relationships, loaning money."

Jackie fell back and pulled up her legs like she was riding the chair sidesaddle.

"What makes you think Roy will talk to us? Assuming I even agree to do this."

"He'll talk if we want him to."

She knew what I meant. Roy was in prison for defrauding Amanda. But he could be in there for a lot worse. Jackie and I were the only two people in the world who knew that. Worse for Roy, we could also prove it.

"I can get a message to him," said Jackie, halfheartedly.

"No, no. Surprise visit. Can't have him forewarned. For that matter, same goes for Veckstrom and Ross, or Edith Madison. None of them can know."

"That'll be a neat trick."

"You got to meet me part way on this, Jackie. It's got to be done like this. You can do it."

"I still have to get the prison people to cooperate."

I scoffed.

"You've done harder things than that."

She looked at me quietly for a few moments, then shook her head.

"If I'd known what it would be like having you as the guy who saved my life, I'd have jumped right in front of that explosion."

Eddie stood up and stretched when he saw me make moves toward leaving. He put his head in her lap so she could say goodbye. I just patted her shoulder.

"Bring a sweater. It can still be cool in Upstate New York."

"Unbelievable."

—

There was enough time left in the day to make one more stop. I peeled off Montauk Highway and took Cobb and Wickapogue Roads southwest toward the estate section of Southampton. The weather was still lousy, casting a drab shadowless light on the giant naked frames of a half dozen mansions going up on what used to be a small farm specializing in flowering bushes. If it weren't for the staggering size of the houses, it would look like any other suburban development. That and what you couldn't see from the road, that they were all paid for with cash, just a slice off last year's bonus. A field filled with the ripening blooms of Wall Street, seeded by a relentless wind out of the west.

Burton's place was even bigger, but it was harder to tell, snuggled inside the sweeping boughs of ancient sycamore and copper beech. Assuming you could get past the gate.

"You don't like me to say this, but you really should call ahead," Isabella squawked at me over the intercom.

"I'd need a cell phone for that. Can't afford it."

"People living in huts in the rain forest have cell phones. You just don't like to call anybody."

"So, is he there?"

"No, I'm trying to tell you. He's at the club for the Wednesday cocktail hour. You can't go there."

She was certainly right about that. Besides the lack of portfolio or pedigree, I'd never be seen at a cocktail hour. Not when there were so many more hours available for drinking cocktails.

I drove into the Village to use the last lonely pay phone in Southampton. People coming in and out of the restrooms looked at me like the curiosity I was. At least on the other end was a cell phone. Burton's.

"Yes, they have these every Wednesday," said Burton. "First I've been to this year. Trying to get my money's worth."

"That'd take a lot of cocktails."

"Why don't you join me. As my guest."

I looked down at the khakis and blue Oxford-cloth shirt I'd worn to the *Southampton Chronicle*. They were both well worn around the edges, but likely no worse than Burton's.

"I think I'm actually suitably dressed," I told him. "I just need a jacket at the door. A medium long. Something with gold buttons, but no embroidery unless they have the Acquillo crest."

"I'll check with the staff."

Back at the Grand Prix I realized I had another impediment. Eddie, who always came as he was.

"Talk about a lack of pedigree," I said to him on the way over there.

Burton probably could have cleared the way for Eddie to come inside, but having me as a guest was enough blemish on Burton's good standing. So I left Eddie in the car with the windows open where he was just as happy spread out across the huge back seat.

A thin, nicely groomed guy in a traditional suit greeted me at the front desk with a blue blazer draped over his arm. I thought about introducing him to Lionel Veckstrom. They could compare haberdashers.

"Mr. Lewis has retired to the billiards room," he said to me.

"That's where I want to retire. Only I'm more into eight-ball."

"All we have is a pair of pool tables. Billiards sounds more sophisticated," the guy explained with commendable honesty.

They weren't just pool tables. More like massive empire furniture made of carved mahogany and topped with almost silken green felt.

I was glad to see Burton was alone.

"I wonder why I'd want to play with you after that last demonstration," he said, twisting the tip of his cue into a cube of green chalk.

"Everybody gets a lucky game."

"I suppose I'll have to let you break."

I dropped a pair of solids but did little to scatter the pack. So I took care of that with my second shot. I never liked picking balls out of a crowd, even if it meant losing my turn.

"No word from the grand jury, I suppose," he said, leaning down for his first shot at a duck in the corner. The cue ball came back nicely, putting him in good position to sink two more before rushing the third with ill effect.

"Not yet. Probably dotting i's and crossing t's," I said.

"I've had several lively meetings with Ms. Swaitkowski. I think she's doing all she can before we get the indictment. It's hard to mount a defense when you don't know the particulars of the prosecution."

"It's liable to be particularly imaginative," I said, sinking number three and number four, each in a side pocket, after which I told him about my conversation with Lionel Veckstrom.

"Imaginative indeed," said Burton when I was finished. "But tricky to make work in a courtroom. Subjective argument can always be neutralized by subjective argument, with the advantage going to the defense who only has to establish reasonable doubt. If I were them, I'd emphasize the tangible evidence. Murder weapons and footprints at the scene."

"The murder weapon was mine and I was at the scene. That doesn't mean I killed him."

"That's where the prosecution portrays your character."

"I thought that was a subjective argument," I said, feeling genuinely at sea.

I thoroughly muffed my next shot.

"Combined with the physical evidence, enough to tip the scales," said Burton, reassuming control of the table.

I watched him clean up his share of the balls using his gentle, precise touch. Every ball dropping on its last roll. I waited until I had the next game in the rack before I brought it up.

"So Hayden told you about our fun at the 7-Eleven."

"He did," said Burton, giving nothing away by his inflection.

"I thought he would. Get out ahead of it."

Burton's break dropped a solid and a stripe. He tried for another solid and missed.

"I'm getting older, Sam. A little constancy would be welcome at this point. Something you ought to consider yourself. Since you're older than me."

"How much are you willing to pay for constancy?" I asked him.

"How much are you?"

I'd heard a similar question, phrased a different way, at a party in New Canaan back when I was married to Abby. The interrogator was a woman at least ten years younger than me. She was married to a tall twitchy scarecrow of a guy who was in the process of making a half billion dollars in the technology infrastructure. Oblivious as I usually am about these things, her proposition was pretty clear. I told her I was all set, but thanks anyway. That's when she asked me if it was worth the cost of my life.

I let two more rounds go by before attempting to answer Burton's question.

"I'm sorry I asked you that, Burt. It's none of my business."

He stood up straight and chalked his cue.

"I'm not sorry," he said. "Tell me your answer first."

It felt like candor was more important than usual.

"I don't know.'"

He leaned over and sighted down the pool cue.

"Exactly," he said.

I let him play for a while, then said, "Of course, I have a little less to lose than you do."

"How do you value the human heart? By the net worth of the owner?"

"I love debating with lawyers."

"Not a debate. An inquiry into an important subject."

"I meant it when I said it's none of my business. I'm just trying to look after you. You've certainly done enough of that for me."

"I didn't know," he said.

"Didn't know what?"

"You said to Hayden, 'don't think he doesn't know,' which is what compelled him to confess to me."

"You'd have gotten there."

"Maybe. Did you know it's possible to be a successful legal writer and a cheap hustler? Or a mechanical engineer and a prizefighter. Dual personas within a single person is not uncommon."

"We've known a few of those."

Burton stood holding his pool cue out at an angle from his body like a lance.

"I want to give this one a try," he said quietly, "not in spite of the confusion in his mind, because of it. Now that I know it's there. Thanks to you."

I nodded and tried to look happy about it.

"You're a good man, Burton," a truthful thing that was easy for me to say. "Just watch your back."

"That's a task I'd rather delegate to you. Since you'll be doing it anyway," he said, before winning the game, and the next two after that.

Vulnerability wasn't a quality I ever associated with him, but that's what it sounded like, on more than one level. I liked thinking of him as invincible, by temperament and circumstance. I hadn't been the easiest friend. Yet Burton never showed anything but unflinching faith and generosity. Which is maybe why I was such a pain in the ass. I knew I'd never be able to reciprocate.

Probably all he ever wanted was what I gave him that night. The right to do something stupid with your eyes open, without condemnation. And the reassurance that no matter how stupid the thing you did, you didn't have to do it alone.

TWENTY-TWO

JACKIE ALWAYS LOOKED reluctant to climb into the Grand Prix for anything longer than a trip into Southampton Village. Not that we had another option. Her Toyota pickup was half the age and twice the wreck, with oversized tires and amped-up shocks that made the thing ride like a slab of granite.

She did get to the cottage almost on time, which was a first. I had matching travel mugs of coffee ready for the two of us, and a box of Big Dog biscuits for Eddie.

"You're bringing the dog?"

"I can't leave him alone that long."

"I thought you had it rigged so he goes in and out by himself and gets his own food and drives himself to the vet."

"Not for his sake. For mine."

Eddie never gave me an argument about a ride in the car. In fact, there was hardly anything that gave him more joy. Long rides, short rides, they were all occasions for unrestrained delight.

The car itself was a bit of a question mark. My father only got a few years out of it before he was killed. He kept it in pristine condition, which helps explain why I could bring it back to life after a million years sitting in a shed. I think my mother forgot it was there.

Even an alleged performance tank like the Grand Prix wasn't all that complicated back in 1967. And I had little else to do after Jason dropped me off at the cottage. I replaced the battery, points, plugs, and wiring harness, pulled and cleaned up the carburetor, changed the oil and used a bicycle pump to inflate the tires. It started on the third try. There were a few thousand more things to fix and replace after that, but at least I had transportation.

I loaded up the trunk with tools and whatever spare parts I had in reserve and left the rest to providence. And positive thinking.

"This baby loves the open highway," I said to Jackie, patting the steering wheel. "Gets the oil flowing, lubes the joints, burns up carbon deposits . . ."

"That must be what I'm smelling. Couldn't be oil."

I had both windows down so Eddie could run back and forth and stick his nose out. Jackie looked back at him, looked at me and shook her head while trying to get control of her hair.

"If we're doing this the whole way you can let me out here."

"You want a hat? I've got one in the trunk."

We took Route 27 all the way to the Southern State, and from there up the Cross Island to the big bridges, and onto the Cross Bronx, which was running at its usual five miles an hour, filled to bursting with irritated, impatient drivers. Acting like this had never happened before. The Grand Prix kept its cool, according to the temperature gauge. As did its driver, who unlike his passenger was philosophical about the lack of air-conditioning.

"It's a mind-set," I told her. "You realize you have no air-conditioning, you start getting hot. Just imagine you're out on the tundra, or having lunch with your mother-in-law."

Eddie kept his head out the window while we were stuck in traffic, barking at any vehicle suspected of carrying another dog. As always, I wondered, to what end? But at least it kept him occupied.

Once we made it to the George Washington Bridge, things opened up and we sailed up the Palisades with the wind at our back. An hour and a piss stop later, we were approaching Hungerford, New York, a small rural town whose largest contributor to the tax base was a massive medium-security prison. You could see it from the highway, following the contour of the hills over which it sprawled. The original complex dated back to the late nineteenth century. It was made of red brick and unnecessarily adorned with architectural detail, especially given the aesthetic sensibilities of the residents.

Flowing out from the old buildings were plainer modern additions, built of red-stained concrete block to match the design vernacular. All of which was contained within two rings of twenty-foot-high cyclone fence topped with curls of jagged-bladed bands of razor-sharp steel.

To get inside you had to go through two checkpoints. The first had a friendly young man in a little hut who looked at our IDs and crossed our names off his list, made a joke about checking Eddie's dog tags, then directed us to the parking lot where I left Eddie in the car. From there we passed through another cyclone-fenced entrance. The gate slid open, then closed behind us, leaving us in an enclosure. The next guy was a lot less friendly and asked what seemed like random, meaningless questions, but I knew why. He was seeing how we responded, looking for nerves or indecision.

We played it straight down the middle. On Jackie's advice I'd brought along a sports jacket and tie, and she almost looked like a lawyer in her gray suit and sensible closed-toe pumps.

He buzzed us through the second gate and then a solid door that led to a narrow hallway, at the end of which was a large desk occupied by two prison guards, a man and a woman. They also checked our IDs and asked a few questions. Then they came around and ran metal detectors over us and patted around our nooks and crannies. The female guard asked Jackie if she preferred that done in private. Jackie said this was the closest I'd ever get to copping a feel, so go ahead.

After that they brought us into a windowless room with a table and a half dozen chairs. I was expecting to be in a little divided glass-walled booth where we'd have to talk to Roy over a telephone. This was much better.

The guards told us there was a routine cell check in progress that would keep Roy occupied for about half an hour, but he'd be in shortly after that. So we sat and waited. To kill some time I got around to asking Jackie how she pulled this meeting off.

"Pleaded, whined, lied, cashed in favors. All the things I usually do."

"Roy doesn't know we're coming?"

"No, but we can't make him see us if he doesn't want to."

"Any chance of that?" I asked.

She thought about it.

"I don't think so."

Soon after that he showed. A far thinner, balder, paler version of the Roy Battiston I'd last seen in a courtroom in

Southampton. He used to be one of those overweight guys who seemed to sweat at room temperature, but now his skin looked chalky dry. The blue prison jumpsuit was big on him and folds of skin hung off his jowls and throat. In his early forties, his remaining hair was a gray-flecked, indistinct brown. He held a knit beanie in both hands, which he worried and twisted into a ball, then flattened out again. He looked slightly curious, but contained. Not wary, but guarded. What I remembered—that open, expectant, just-here-to-help-any-way-I-can bank manager look—had been replaced by a furtive energy, hidden behind an ashen haze that clung to his face.

No one tried to shake hands before he sat down across from us.

"This is a surprise," he said.

"We appreciate you seeing us," said Jackie.

"You're my lawyer. I have to see you. I guess this guy sometimes comes with the deal," he said, gesturing at me.

"How're you doing?" asked Jackie. "How're you holding up?"

He thought over his answer.

"In the beginning it's a nightmare you can't wake up from," he said, looking at me, the guy who put him there, "but it gets better. I've always been a good learner. I've learned how to play the game."

He pointed at my chest.

"If I know you there's a pack of cigarettes in there," he said. "They're worth a lot more in here than out there."

I took out an almost full pack and tossed it to him. He put it in his pants pocket with no further comment.

"So, you here to get me sprung?" he asked.

"The parole hearing's only six months away," said Jackie. "I'm very optimistic."

"I'd rather hear you're dead certain."

"There's nothing I know of that could get in your way," she said in a flat voice.

"I'm a model inmate. From day one. All the white-collar guys are. The guards treat you better. But don't buy that stuff about country club prisons. If this is a country club, the club rules were written in hell."

"Then I'm sure we'll do fine."

"So, what's up? If you're looking for a loan, I'm probably not in the best position to help," he said with an empty smile.

"I think we have a mutual acquaintance," I said to him.

"We probably have a number of those," he said.

"Patrick Getty. Where'd you meet him? Doing laundry, having lunch? Selling cigarettes?"

The brown eyes behind his prison-issue glasses showed little reaction.

"We don't get many oil millionaires in here."

"Different branch of the family. This one's into larceny and assault."

He shrugged.

"Doesn't ring a bell," he said.

"Jackie, how closely do they monitor associations people make inside prison?"

"Every move, every wink, every nod," she said.

Roy looked down at the table where he was kneading the beanie like a hunk of dough.

"I know a lot of people in here," he said. "I can't remember all their names."

Roy had grown up when you could be poor and still have a Southampton address. He'd lived with his extended alcoholic family in what used to be called a beach colony, a romantic term for a cluster of shacks built on pilings, barely heated and rotting at the edges, a mile or two from the beach. Roy was the only one of the clan to make it out of there alive. A college education and a career in banking providing the wherewithal to put a thousand miles between him and the drag of his past, until he tried to add a few light years.

"Do you remember Robbie Milhouser?"

He looked up again, the left side of his mouth forming half a grin.

"Sure. Big man on campus. Let you know it every chance he got. Every class has one. Stupid intimidator. You were one of those in your day, right Sam?" he asked.

"No. I kept to myself. Like you. Had bigger plans."

"Too bad they didn't work out. For either of us."

We let that hang in the air for a moment. Then Jackie spoke.

"Did you know he was dead?" she asked.

He looked at her with faint surprise.

"Really? No kidding. I didn't know that. I guess if you make enough enemies one'll finally get you."

"I didn't say he was killed. Just that he was dead."

His little half grin formed into a smile.

"If he wasn't killed you wouldn't be here asking me about it," he said. "Is that other fella dead, too? The oil guy?"

"Patrick Getty," I said. "He worked as a carpenter for Robbie's building business."

"You think he killed Milhouser?"

"Do you?" I asked.

He raised his hands, briefly releasing the tortured beanie.

"I don't know about any of that stuff. How would I know that?" he asked Jackie.

"It's just an interesting coincidence. That you knew a guy in here who'd end up out in Southampton working for another guy you knew," I said.

"So it's a national secret that carpenters can find work in the Hamptons?"

"You knew his father, too, didn't you?" Jackie asked.

"Long-time Southampton people all know each other," he said. "You'd know that if you hadn't grown up with the potato farmers in Bridgehampton."

"I grew up in Bridgehampton with the professors of civil engineering," she said dryly.

"She meant back in the old East End Savings days," I said. "Didn't Jeff Milhouser have a little deal with a wrinkle or two?"

He sat back in his chair, but still left one hand in contact with the beanie.

"Oh yeah, that was sweet," he said. "My boss was the one who signed off on that loan. Fantastic. They had to can him to keep the banking commission from lowering the boom. Guess who got his job?" he asked, pointing at his chest.

Rosaline Arnold said I'd been up to my neck in corporate politics back at my old company. I don't know why she thought that. I understand that politics is a word applied to mass behavior, whether the mass is two people or ten thousand. It's what people do when operating within an organization, rigid or chaotic. The really good corporate politicians know how to manage up, focusing their energies on deceiving or pleasing their superiors as a means of advancement, often but not always at the cost of the people alongside or in lower layers. I knew from the beginning I didn't have that kind of temperament.

My mind was drawn to the technical core, the processes and machines, the tangibles that formed the basis of the company's reason for being. So the only people I cared about were those in my immediate vicinity. Men and women who were my peers and later I had to manage. I held many of them in high regard, though few were anything like me. But we had plenty of common ground on which to operate, and a culture that suited me, one dedicated entirely to the work. Some liked to socialize with each other, but mostly they all went home at the end of the day to their spouses and children and the presumption of a simple life.

I knew those privates lives were actually brimming with anxieties and troubles, dysfunctions and heartbreak, as well as occasional contentment and prosperity. But that was out of view, and when I led the group, that's where I wanted it to stay. If someone came to me for help, I gave it eagerly, but you'd never catch me asking how things were going at home with the wife and kids.

That same myopia extended to office politics. I didn't want to know about it, and my colleagues were glad to keep me in the dark. I was often surprised by the outbreak of hostilities between individuals or groups, learning that the conflict had been festering for months or years.

So I had little training in divining the motives of the human heart when I ran the company's R&D. That's why I was an easy mark for a guy like Roy Battiston, with the warm and convincing manner of a congenial salesman, cloaking rapacious venality and aching ambition.

But like Roy, I could be a pretty fast learner.

"Lucky for you," I said. "Must have been a good job."

"Luck is the intersection of opportunity and preparation," said Roy, something the old can-do Roy would have said, only now it sounded more like Jack Nicholson than Dale Carnegie.

"Jeff Milhouser's taken over Robbie's building business. So now Getty's working for him," said Jackie.

"I used to tell people it was impossible to lose money in Hamptons real estate. Maybe Jeff will prove me wrong," said Roy.

"Don't think much of him, huh?" I asked.

"Don't think of him at all. Don't care."

"He just lost his son," said Jackie.

"Don't care about that either. I lost my life, only I had to keep breathing. If you think the world's worse off without Robbie Milhouser you're a bigger hophead than I thought."

"Careful," I said.

"Hophead, boozehound. You two are made for each other. Oh, that's right, you aren't exactly a couple. Sam's fucking my wife. Nice little bonus for you. I got to have her when she didn't have a pot to piss in. Helped support her mother and her brain-dead kid. Now they're both dead, and I'm in this shit hole and she's richer than stink. But that's okay, the boozehound who put me here is banging her. And now he wants to swoop in and get a little information. Maybe wants me to help with a little problem he's got. But gee whiz," he said, and then stood straight up, leaned out across the table and screamed in my face, "what would be my motivation?"

The door to the room snapped open. A short, stocky Latin-looking guard pointed the end of a nightstick at Roy.

"Sit down, man," the guard said.

Roy sat.

The guard looked at us.

"You want I should stay?"

"No, we're fine," said Jackie, in a steady, clear voice.

"You sure?"

"We're okay," I said.

He left us to look at Roy slumped in his chair, back to bunching and reforming his hat.

"So you're sure that parole hearing's going to be a walk in the park?" I asked Jackie.

"That's what it's looking like," she said.

Roy looked at her then back at me as we talked.

"I wonder what could mess it up," I said.

"Roy would have to somehow fall out of favor with the prison authorities."

"By doing something in here?" I asked.

"Or causing something out there," said Jackie.

"Or maybe something from the past might re-emerge, " I said. "Maybe just enough to put a crimp in the proceedings."

If Roy was turning pale you couldn't tell under the prison pallor. In fact, you couldn't tell what he was thinking or feeling at all. He just looked at me in silence, crumpling his hat. Then his face lit up with a grotesque simulation of a smile.

"Wouldn't that just be a kick in the ass, huh Sam? Golly, what a mess that would be."

I looked over at Jackie. She was the one turning pale.

"But none of that's going to happen, Roy," she said, calmly. "So there's nothing to worry about."

"I'm not worried," he said quietly. "I have every confidence in you. Everything will go according to plan."

"Well, then, that's that," he added, his half grin planted back on his face. "Sorry I can't help with this Milhouser thing. I didn't know he was a friend of yours," he said to me. "When they catch the guy who did it, he won't be coming here. Rap like that is strictly maximum security. You don't even want to think about that kind of time. I have lots of new friends who've been there. And they have friends, too. They'll be sure to give Robbie's killer a fine reception."

Then he stood up abruptly.

"You'll have to alert the guard I'm ready," he said. "If I touch that door I'm liable to get a stick up my ass."

Jackie did as he asked, and he left after a goodbye handshake. His hand was dry as a bone, his grip surprisingly strong. Roy had apparently been seeing a lot of the gym, probably for the first time in his life.

Jackie was silent as we worked our way back through the security gauntlet on the way to the car. She waited while I let Eddie pee and sniff-search the parking lot. She was staring out the window when we got back.

It wasn't until we were on the highway that either of us felt like talking.

"Holy crap, Sam," she said. "What have we wrought?"

It was generous of her to say 'we' when I was the one who engineered Roy's downfall. I was the one who forced him into the fraud rap and spared him prosecution for the murder of a couple little old ladies.

I don't know what I expected, but it wasn't what I found. The fleshy, terrified and remorseful Roy Battiston disappeared into the penal system and was replaced by something else. A vindication of the old canard—that which doesn't kill you makes you stronger.

Or was that the real Roy Battiston, his outer layer of obsequiousness stripped away with the fat, revealing the true nature beneath?

He knew what we could do to him, and he didn't care. Or worse, might even welcome it, counting on the collateral damage.

There was no more threatening Roy Battiston. No more leverage.

I recognized what it was. There's nothing you can do to a man who has nothing to lose.

—

"Somebody named Dan Ned is looking for you," said Jackie, looking up from her cell phone.

"That's Dan *and* Ned. Heroes of the DEC."

"They left a number. Do you want to call?"

"Sure."

She dialed the number and handed me the phone. Dan picked up.

"This is Sam Acquillo," I said. "Calling from the Throgs Neck Bridge."

"Did you know Ned's a genius?" Dan asked.

"I wouldn't dispute it."

"We poked holes in that site all the way from the south gate to the north fence."

"The one facing the lagoon," I said.

"Yeah. There's a stretch of ground that runs between the fence and the water. About thirty feet wide and three hundred feet long, curved like a crescent. It's so overgrown you'd think it's at the same elevation, but it's not. There're no topographicals on the site map, but on a hunch Ned pulled one off the Web. The crown is about fifteen feet above sea level."

"No kidding. It must have been a defense against high water, storm surges."

"Probably, since it's made out of stone," said Dan.

"Really."

"Yeah, but here's the kicker."

"It's hollow."

"Oh yeah. Honeycombed more like it. We used the radar to find the cavities. We counted three in symmetrical succession running east to west. My guess the pattern holds the whole length of the embankment. It's old, probably from the earliest days of operation. Ned thinks it supported the docks and served as a holding area for cargo going in and out. That close to the lagoon it would have to be raised. The water table's barely eight feet down."

It was getting hard to hear what he was saying with Jackie chirping at me from the other side of the Grand Prix.

"Hold it a second," I said to Dan.

"What is it?" she asked again.

"They found the cellars at the WB plant."

"Wow. What's in them?"

"I bet if I can hear him speak I'll find that out."

"So why are you talking to me?" she said.

I went back to Dan.

"So, what's in them?"

"That's why I'm calling you. I think you and Ms. Anselma and her attorney ought to be there when we open them up. Call it half courtesy, half cover our asses."

"Okay. Where are you now?"

"I'm at our office in Stony Brook. We came up here to download our data into the central servers and make some sketch maps out of the radar images. Gives us a rough guide to dig the holes."

"I'd like to see them."

"You're actually not that far away," he said. "We'll be here for a while. Come on over."

He gave me directions to the office, located at the Stony Brook SUNY campus. Jackie reminded me to check in with Ross before nightfall to confirm I was back where I was supposed to be.

"You don't want to know about the cellars?" I asked.

"I do. Even though it's none of my business."

"Okay. We'll get back in time."

Ten minutes down the LIE Eddie requested we stop. We got on the service road and found a weedy lot. I kept an eye out for broken glass while Eddie hand-picked the ideal spot. Jackie came along to bug me about Roy Battiston.

"Do you think he really didn't know Robbie was dead?" she asked.

"If he knew Patrick Getty, he knew for sure. Even if he didn't, somebody from home would have told him. For all I know he subscribes to *The Southampton Chronicle*."

"Why pretend otherwise?" she asked.

"I don't know."

"So he also has to know you're the accused."

"Sure."

"So if he's not talking, what did we learn by going up there?" she asked.

All I knew was that Roy had told us a lot, we just didn't know yet what it was. Jackie hated when I said stuff like that, but it was the truth. It was forcing me to re-examine the whole bag of assumptions I'd been gathering and coalescing in my mind. I never liked hashing these thing out in public, at least until I was ready. In short, I needed time to think. So I told her a convenient half-truth.

"I don't know."

I think she half-believed me.

The trip to Stony Brook took less than an hour. It was a big campus, more like a park with large buildings. The DEC office fit right in.

Like Hungerford, they had our names on a list. I hadn't felt so official in years.

"I called Dan. He'll come out to get you," said the guard.

We were blessed with Dan and Ned, both of whom were happy to make Jackie's acquaintance.

"Jackie's my lawyer," I told them.

"You gonna be there for the big opening?" asked Dan.

"No, I'm helping Sam on a slightly different matter," she said. "I'm just along for the ride."

"Nice for us," said Dan, ushering us through the warren of

DEC offices, laboratories and tech rooms filled with colorful cartography and brilliant displays on liquid-crystal monitors, manned by wholesome-looking people wearing T-shirts and athletic sandals, the men mostly bearded, the women indifferent to decoration aside from a discreet pearl in the lip or diamond on the nostril.

Dan's office looked like it used to be a conference room, with a big oak-veneer table laden with stacks of papers and drawings encircling a small work surface. I liked the feel of it, almost enough to feel a slight pull of envy, which I quickly repressed.

"So, here's what we made up," said Dan, spreading a black-and-white printout about the size of an average blueprint on the table. It was a simple tracing of the original site plan with the cellars sketched in along the northern side, just as Dan had described. They'd used a drawing program to fill in some detail on the first three cellars at the east end, indicating stonework and possible entryways based on the old elevations.

"If the pattern holds there's room for up to eight of these storage cellars," said Ned. "There's evidence that they're interconnected, so I suggest we start at the east end and go from there. X marks the spot." He pointed to a box labeled "likely entryway."

"Whatever you say, Ned. You've been right so far," I said. His circular face formed a professional smile.

"We'll bring lights and cameras along with some test kits. You can bring your own cameras if you want. We'll also have spare protective boots. I don't think there's a call for hazmat. As you point out, there's no evidence of contamination in the lagoon, which is hard up against these enclosures."

We spent time going over the planned approach, what they would do and what they wanted me and Amanda to take care of. It was good to focus on logistics—a good distraction from the greater implications. Throughout, Jackie maintained a studied reticence, occasionally clearing her throat or tapping the table. The only thing left was to schedule the day.

"I've left messages for Amanda and Burton Lewis, her lawyer," I told them as we retraced our steps back through the building. "I'll likely know by tomorrow."

"As soon as you can," said Dan. "Be another check in the cooperation column."

Ned and Jackie were leading the way, actively engaged in social chatter. Dan was giving me a traveling description of the various offices and working rooms. We were near the entrance when he said, "Here's where the Regional Director lives. And next door is the Assistant Regional Director. I don't know if he's got an assistant, but it wouldn't surprise me."

On cue, the Assistant Regional Director opened his door, pausing for us to pass by. I looked over at him standing there next to his nameplate on the wall. Dan almost ran into me when I stopped and put out my hand.

"Zack," I said. "Zack Horowitz."

Zack looked taken aback, but shook my hand.

"I'm Sam Acquillo. You obviously don't remember me."

"Sorry, can't say that I do."

"I'm from Southampton," I said.

He still looked at me blankly.

"I used to work there, but it's been a long time."

"Yes it has. It's really great to see you."

He smiled at me good-naturedly.

"I'm glad to hear it, but I still don't remember seeing you."

"That's okay. I forget everything, too. Don't worry about it."

By this time Jackie noticed we'd dropped out of the parade and had come back with Ned in tow.

"Sam?"

"It's nothing," I said, getting underway again. "I just bothered some guy I thought I recognized

"The Assistant Regional Director," said Dan. "Good guy. I like him a lot better than you-know-who."

"Does he drive a giant SUV? All black and chrome?"

"That wouldn't be too environmentally PC, would it? Nah, he's got a Beemer Z3. Quite the sport."

"Definitely not the same guy. Kind of embarrassing."

Dan and Ned walked us all the way back to the car, so Eddie had a chance to say hello before committing a bit of himself to the environment of the Department of Environmental Conservation.

"Nice," said Jackie.

I spent the rest of the ride back to Southampton deciphering for Jackie everything she'd witnessed at the DEC office. It was payback for keeping her mouth shut and her nose out of the conversations.

When we crossed the Town line I headed back up to Sag Harbor, where we had dinner with Hodges and Dorothy at the Pequot.

For them it was a simple meal, for me a type of last supper. Or maybe just a welcome distraction, depending on how the next few days would turn out, which version of the truth would emerge from the tangle of potentials, the competing sets of assumptions, all paradigms—shifting and otherwise—up for grabs.

TWENTY-THREE

"How DID I GET STUCK coordinating this ground-opening ceremony?" Jackie complained over the phone, which rang as I was on my way to the outdoor shower. "I've got nothing to do with this thing."

"You're the one with the modern communications capability."

"Modern last century. How can a former head of R&D be such a Luddite? Or maybe the answer's in the question."

"The real question is when are we getting together."

"Twelve noon. Bring a sandwich."

I was happy with the timing. It gave me a chance to call Joe Sullivan to see if he could meet me before that. He suggested the diner in Hampton Bays, a chance to stock up on a year's worth of trans fats and triglycerides. The day was bright and clear, making the trip south a good opportunity to take in the fresh growth on the oaks and maples and catch the occasional ornamental bush looking like a pink cotton ball or lavender sachet.

The white narcissus were reaching their peak, rising proudly above beds of viny groundcover lapping at their feet. Passing Hawk Pond the water was a blue steel, pestered by the cool northwesterly that had been with us all spring.

The diner was full of tradesmen diverted from the exodus that flowed in every morning from the west. There were a lot of older guys there, more Anglo than Spanish, foremen and contractors who could afford to get on the job later in the morning. Guys with swollen hands and bellies pushing through suspenders, with swordfish embroidered on their baseball caps and cell phones on their belts instead of hammer holsters.

Sullivan both fit in and stood out in black T-shirt and baseball cap, fatigue pants and belt-mounted two-way radio. Softer hands but bigger shoulders, nonchalant, but more alert to his surroundings. He was already halfway through a greased aggregation of starchy breakfast food, lubricated with maple syrup, color added by the ham steak on a separate plate. I pointed to the ham as the waitress came over.

"Just one of those and some wheat toast," I said. "Hold the cardiac arrest."

"So you're still here," said Sullivan.

"Where else would I be?"

"Ross said he let you leave town. He asked me if you were a flight risk. I said only if you bring the dog."

"I also brought Jackie. The deciding factor."

"Did we learn anything useful?"

I slid a sheet of paper under the edge of his plate.

"I'll know after you pull these records."

He looked at me skeptically before looking down at the paper.

"Records?"

"Phone records. Between these people on these dates."

He picked up the paper and held it at arm's length, the inaugural sign of middle age.

"As usual, you're not asking for much. Just the highly difficult, career-threatening and time-consuming."

"Can't take too much time. I've got the sword of Damocles hanging over my head."

"Don't know him. Sounds like an Arab."

"Greek. Same basic neighborhood."

"You gonna tell me what all this means?" he said, looking more closely at the paper.

"It's a theory," I said. "I just need a little corroboration. You can see how I've written it up, so if I'm right, you should see calls at certain times between certain people. You can do this, right? Find this stuff out?"

I never knew what cops could do and what they couldn't. I was always surprised either way.

"Technically, yeah. Falls within the parameters of a routine investigation. Now that I'm on the case, I don't have to clear it with Ross, unless you want me to."

"Not yet," I said. "Let's see what we come up with."

He slid the paper back to me.

"Some of these dates are a little general. Get as specific as you can," he said.

I'd just finished doing what he asked when my ham steak showed up. We ate in silence for a while, then Sullivan said, "I heard about your chat with Veckstrom. He's lovin' you more every day."

"That's good. There's not enough love in the world these days."

"He asked me about the prints on that hammer stapler. He wanted to know why I told you there weren't any on the handle. I said, 'There aren't?' We looked at the file and sono-fabitch, there aren't."

"That's what I was hoping."

"You didn't know?" he asked.

"If I used that stapler to club Milhouser over the head, why aren't my prints all over the handle? And if I wiped them off, why didn't I wipe off the whole thing?"

He shoveled a few pounds of home fries into his mouth to help him concentrate.

"It's a little insulting that the State's case relies heavily on me being either stupid or crazy," I said. "Jackie keeps telling me intelligence is a lousy defense, but for Pete's sake, give me a little credit."

Sullivan looked sympathetic.

"I think you'd be a much smarter killer than they do, Sam," he said. "Sincerely. I wouldn't want you killing me."

"Thank you, Joe. Very good of you to say."

Sullivan picked up the paper again and took more of it in.

"There're some interesting names on here," he said. "One in particular."

"Are you going to make me explain?" I asked.

He dropped the paper back down on the table and shook his head.

"Nope. If I do that, you'll tell me you don't want to, then I'll get all pissed off and say you have to, and then you'll tell me some sort of bullshit to get me to back off, and that'll be that. So why don't we skip the dance and let me just pull the phone records."

"Thanks," I said.

"It's your ass."

"That's what people keep telling me."

—

I got to the WB plant ahead of schedule, but Amanda was already at the front gate. She had peg-legged khaki jeans stuffed into boots with laces that started at the toe and went most of the way up her calves. She had a lightweight leather jacket on top and a white shirt with the collar pulled up. I looked around to see where she'd landed the Sopwith Camel.

"Should I be paranoid that I haven't heard from you for a while?" she asked when I got out of the Grand Prix.

"If I said no, would you still be paranoid?"

"Of course."

"You're a great-looking paranoid."

"Mother always said to dress for disaster."

"Or celebration."

"I'm trying to get used to the new optimistic you," she said.

"The realistic me. The odds are there's nothing toxic down there. Otherwise it would have shown up by now."

"I was up to my armpits in soot again all morning," she said, leaning against the Grand Prix's sturdy left front fender. "But we're officially done with the gutting. The building inspector told us we could keep most of what we wanted to. I had to start before dawn to be ready to see him, then get cleaned up and over here in time for this."

"Good work ethic."

"Always had one of those, Sam. You can't fault me there."

"Me, too. To a fault."

"What are you working on so hard these days?"

"Saving my ass," I said.

"I like your ass. I'm just not always sure you want to save it."

"Me neither," I admitted. "But I want it to be my decision."

By this time Dan and Ned's DEC adventure van arrived pulling a trailer with a tiny backhoe. We watched them pull up next to the Grand Prix and roll out of the vehicle in down vests and white hard hats.

"Hey, folks," said Dan. "Who're we missing?"

"Burton Lewis. The lawyer." I checked my watch. "Just give it a few minutes. He'll be here."

Ned took the opportunity to hand out Styrofoam cups, which he filled from a huge thermos, much to my joy. As we drank the coffee, he briefed us on how we were going to approach the operation and the probable sequence of events. He'd just started to hand out neoprene boots and flashlights when Burton thundered up in his yellow and fake-wood paneled Ford Country Squire.

"Sorry I'm late," he said, stepping out of the Ford, looking like he'd answered the same casting call as Amanda, wearing khakis over a pair of L.L. Bean Maine Hunting Shoes, red flannel shirt and a herringbone marksman's jacket. He reached into an inside pocket of the jacket and pulled out a silver case.

"It's my new digital camera," he said. "Can't hurt, right?"

"Tally-ho."

Dan reviewed everything again for Burton while we put on the boots and hard hats and played around with the industrial-strength flashlights. Then Burton, Amanda and I followed the van on foot as it plowed its way over the undergrowth that had filled in the path running along the cyclone fence, heading down the east side to where it took a sharp turn and paralleled the strip of territory next to the lagoon where the storage cellars were located.

Driving like a dauntless field guy, Ned got the van within twenty feet of our destination. Then, with ill-disguised enthusiasm, stuffed himself into the caged cockpit of the backhoe and drove it off the trailer the moment Dan had him unhitched.

The noise and fumes coming from the little beast were unsettling after the subdued tone of our preparations. Amanda held my arm as we watched Ned use a handheld GPS to zero in on his point of penetration.

In about five minutes we were looking into a slanted black hole in the side of a bank of tangled foliage.

"Fascinating," said Burton. "It's like bloody archeology."

"How bloody depends on what we find," I said, edging up to the hole with my flashlight.

Dan cleared his throat and gently moved me out of the way. Then he stuck his own flashlight in the hole, immediately followed by his head.

After an intolerable wait, we heard him speak.

"Cool."

He sat on the ground with his feet in the hole, then popped out of sight,

"Come on in," he called from the darkness. "Just watch your step."

I let go of Amanda's hand and followed. The hole was in a stone wall that curved up to a concrete ceiling. You only had to step down about two feet to reach the floor, which was also concrete. As the beam of my flashlight flicked around with Dan's, I saw a room lined with stone and filled with exactly nothing.

"So far, so good," I yelled out the hole. "Come see."

The space had a heavy, choking smell, like fetid vegetation. The air was damp, but the floor was dry to the touch, as was the laid-up stone wall.

"Look over here," said Dan.

He'd been in front of me, blocking the view of an arched doorway at the far end of the room.

"Let's wait a second so Ned can take some samples," he said, using his flashlight to guide Ned's less graceful entrance through the hole. We watched him kneel and swab the floor, open and wave around little canisters, open others and set them on the floor, shoot his flashlight at the face of a hand-held device and do all those other things chem engineering people delight in doing.

As he worked, we listened to Burton reminisce about trips into the Pyramids and catacombs, the sewers of Paris, the caves in the cliffs of Monte Carlo and a coal mine in West Virginia. The closest I'd come to that experience was crawling inside a giant pressure vessel to grab a sample of a contaminated catalyst. I didn't like this environment a whole lot better, so I was glad when Ned said we could move on.

Dan made us wait until he checked out the next cellar, which proved to be an exact duplicate of the one before. We had to endure another round of test sampling and travelogues before we moved on. This time, however, things were a little different.

"Barrels," Dan called out from the darkness.

Amanda grabbed my hand again.

"Ned first," said Dan, although Ned was already on the way.

"Damn," said Burton, quietly.

"Let's just see," I said.

So the three of us stood in the semi-dark for about ten minutes, listening to the rumble of their conversation on the other side of the wall.

"It doesn't mean you can't have remediation," I heard Burton saying. "It's done all the time."

"He's right," I said to Amanda. "I worked a lot of these sites at the company. Every time we closed a plant something like this happened."

"Any in the Hamptons?" she asked.

"We need Sam," Dan called.

I asked Burton to take Amanda's hand, then went through the passage. It took me a few seconds to locate them in the bigger room and I was confused by the frenzied criss-cross of flashlights. I followed the sound of their voices.

"Check it out, Sam," said Dan. "What's your opinion?"

They cast their flashlights on a wall of containers, stacked three high. The bright, colorless light of the flashlights made it hard to focus at first, but as I got closer detail began to emerge. And then I was close enough to reach out and stroke the side of one of the containers.

"Wood," I said. "They're old wooden barrels."

"Right," said Dan. "Not good. Porous."

I squatted down and felt the dry floor. Then I stood again and took a few paces back.

I don't know if I started laughing before or after the thought struck me.

I went to the end of the wall where the barrel that began the first row was almost clear of the one above. I muscled it out away from the wall.

"Hey, careful," said Ned, flashing his light at the floor under where the barrel had been standing. While he was doing that I slipped the little geologist's hammer out of his utility belt and swung it down hard on the top of the barrel. Both Ned and Dan literally jumped back in horror.

"Hey!"

I hit it again and then a third time, finally loosening a slat on the top so I could get my hands around and pull it upward.

"Jesus, man, we need special equipment if we're gonna do that kind of stuff," said Dan.

"You're right," I said. "I've got it back at the house. I just didn't think to bring along ten-ounce glasses and a couple trays of ice cubes."

I dipped my hand in the barrel and held the liquid up to my nose, then touched it with my tongue.

"What the hell are you doing?"

"Sampling a little Scotch. Could be bourbon. It's been sitting here a long time. Anyone bring peanuts?"

TWENTY-FOUR

I LEFT AMANDA AND BURTON with Ned to guard the inventory while he took test samples and went with Dan to check the rest of the cellars. Unfortunately, no more booze appeared. The last cellar had a door to the outside, a table and chairs and what were probably canvas cots, now just piles of musty disintegration.

We tried to push open the door but only managed a thin slice of daylight. We could see the tangle of flora through the crack. It would be easy enough to find from the outside.

"Let's go rejoin the party," I said to Dan.

Ned, wearing official DEC goggles and gloves, was filling and corking the last of his glass cylinders. Amanda was standing with her arms around Burton and her head on his shoulder. She looked up hopefully when I shot her in the face with my flashlight.

"All clear," I said. "Nothing down there but a rumrunner's dormitory."

I got the next hug. It was nice, especially with the buttery soft leather jacket in between.

"We'll go through the whole place and take samples at regular intervals," said Dan. "You'd want us to do that."

"Yes we would," I told him.

"I'll get a generator and some can lights and see if we have enough sample kits. Ned, you can start prescreening the hooch so we can help Sam's internist work up an antidote."

After showing Amanda and Burton around the rest of the place, we went back outside to the bright daylight and renewed circumstances. Burton gave us a history lesson on liquor trafficking on the East End during Prohibition that was more thorough and no less enthusiastic than Dorothy Hodges's. I stuck in a joke where I could, but Amanda was too stunned with relief to absorb wisecracks.

I drove her back to her house where she said she wanted to curl up in a ball and sleep for a few weeks. She asked me to come by later in the evening to watch over her, if I wanted to.

"Leave the vodka at home," she said. "I've got some Glenfiddich stashed somewhere. More appropriate to the occasion. Why are you looking at me?" she added.

"I like looking at you."

"Not usually like that."

"Sorry. It's not you. I'm just thinking."

"Okay. I'm too wasted to think. Offer's still open," she said, and then disappeared into her house. I kept looking at the space she'd just left behind until I was distracted by Eddie with his paws on the car door, looking in the window. I let him ride the hundred feet back down our common driveway. They say dogs have no sense of time, so I told him we were driving to Maine and back. It made him happy.

The phone was ringing as I unlocked the door. It was Rosaline Arnold, only this time I was dressed for it.

"I think I know what was wrong with Robbie Milhouser," she said when I answered.

"You've been thinking?" I asked.

"I've been researching. I went back to storage and pulled everything they had on him all the way back to grade school."

"Wow."

"Then I cross-referenced everything with data pulled off the Internet. Just to get a little corroboration."

"And?"

"Come on, Sam, I'm not doing this over the phone. Plus I have visual aids."

"You're in luck. My afternoon schedule just opened up. How do you feel about dogs?"

———

I fed myself out of Tupperware containers while changing into sneakers and a silk baseball jacket. Eddie hung around the whole time, knowing as he always did that he was coming along.

The nice weather seemed determined to persist. Now late afternoon, the sun's angle was deepening the color of the trees, and the sky was working on a design for the upcoming sunset. It was cool. Too cool with the window down for a lightweight jacket, but I was committed.

For no good reason, I took a slightly different route over to Rosaline's. I wanted to see how the day was treating the potato fields just north of County Road 39 and wasn't disappointed. The sun's clear light through the cloudless sky turned the bare, freshly tilled earth a supple gold. The trees and bushes planted around the new houses forming along the fringes between fields had begun to fill out and a few years of wear had settled them into the landscape. With spring's emergence the traffic on County Road 39 had also begun to bloom, so I waited awhile to cross and head south to Rosaline's condo complex.

"No newspaper?" she asked when she answered the door, genuinely disappointed.

"I took the high road. No newsstands."

"You did, however, bring a dog. As promised."

Her hair was piled on top of her head, held precariously with bobby pins and stuck with a yellow pencil. She wore a men's dress shirt and melon-colored shorts. I guessed her father's, since they were several sizes too big. Eddie expressed his social grace by jumping all over her.

"Is it too early for cocktails?" she asked in a gross display of the rhetorical.

"Out on the patio. I want to see the latest perennials."

Eddie started sniffing the corners of her apartment while I went straight to my favorite wicker chair. She followed soon with glasses, bottles and several fat old manila folders. I helped her unload.

"Sit, sit. I'll pour."

"I didn't expect you to keep digging," I said.

"I'm compulsive, what can I say. It's the Internet's fault. It's an amazing research tool, but can only take you so far. Eventually you have to get your hands on some good old-fashioned paper and ink. Cheers."

She pulled up her legs so her heels were hooked on the edge of her seat, using her thighs to support the files as she leafed through. Eddie gave a sharp little bark from the other side of the French doors and I went to let him out. I walked him around the garden area for a few minutes so he could sample the local scents and piss on a few flowers, then bought him back with me to lie on the patio.

"Anyway," said Rosaline, picking up where the conversation

left off, "I already had my name all over requests for Robbie's high school file, so why not go for broke. I still haven't figured out what to say if I'm questioned. Maybe you can come up with something."

"How about the truth?"

"Illegally sharing a student's confidential information?"

"I'll keep thinking."

"The good news is what I uncovered is in the public domain."

"Like what?"

She handed me a photocopy of a page from a church ledger. St. John's Episcopal Church, Southampton. It listed marriages performed from January through April, 1966.

"Find Milhouser."

I followed the columns till I came to "Emilia Silverio and Jefferson Milhouser."

"Nice Italian girl," I said. "Must have felt funny in that bastion of Waspdom."

"You see the date?" she asked.

"Yeah. 1966."

"Here," she said, handing me another piece of paper.

It was a printout from the birth registry at Mt. Vernon Hospital, Mt. Vernon, New York. I traced down the columns until I found "Robert, to Emilia and Marco Silverio."

"And the date?"

"1961. Son of a bitch."

"Son of Italians. Very unlucky ones. Let's move to the obits."

The first was a scanned clipping from *Newsday*. An obit with a little American flag, indicating a veteran. Marco had owned a shipping and storage business out of Long Island City until a sizeable hunk of something to be shipped or stored fell on his head. He left a wife and a one-year-old son.

Rosaline waited until I finished reading so I could look up at her face and see another piece of paper held in her hand.

"I'm enjoying this, Sam," she said. "Rummaging around in archives, on and off the Internet, especially those involving vital statistics, gives me an intense voyeuristic delight. In fact, at certain times it actually makes me a little wet. Does that sound perverse?"

"Not at all. What else you got?"

She handed me another scanned clipping, this one from *The Southampton Chronicle*.

Emilia had been spared the violent death of her first husband, but she was just as dead, this time from multiple myeloma, a less immediate but far more painful way to go. She left a husband, Jefferson Milhouser, and an eight-year-old son, Robert.

"Jeff's not his father," I said.

"Nope. It's amazing how you see a family resemblance that's not actually there. Think about it. They don't look anything like each other."

She put Robbie's high school yearbook picture down on the table next to a headshot of Jeff from his days as a Town Trustee. Broad, burly Mediterranean next to lean, lanky Anglo.

"What kind of a teenager do you think you'd be if Jeff Milhouser was your only parent, your principal mentor?" she asked. "You don't need a degree in psychology to figure that one out. I have one, by the way, and I did figure it out," she added.

I picked up a picture in each hand and looked at the faces.

"Can I use your phone?" I asked her.

She looked disappointed.

"You're brilliant, Rosaline," I said when I realized why. "But you know that. You did an amazing thing. And you didn't even have to."

Her face lightened up again.

She stood up and ran her fingers down my cheek. Then went inside to get the portable phone. Eddie jumped up, too, but I told him to relax. I finished off my drink and poured a fresh one over the dwindling ice and stared some more at the Milhousers.

I couldn't remember Sullivan's direct line, so after Rosaline brought me the phone I went through the cumbersome process with the switchboard. I paced around the garden to help speed things up. He eventually came on the line.

"Got me just in time, Sam. Ready to head home."

"How'd you do with those phone records?"

"Not sure. They might be in the fax bin. When do you need them?"

It was one of the things I missed about a hyperproductive, anxiety-fueled corporate environment. Everyone knew you wanted everything immediately all the time. Even when you didn't. I took a breath.

"Sooner better than later, Joe. I'm sort of snuggin' up to an indictment here."

"Yeah, Veckstrom said it could be any minute. Who told you?"

I felt a sharp tug in my chest.

"Nobody told me, Joe, I hadn't heard. But you can see why I'd be feeling a little urgency."

"Let me go check."

A hundred years later he came back on the line.

"Yep, I think it's all here. Expedited, by the way. Don't think I just was sitting on my hands."

"I'll be right there."

"Nah, I'm here with Will Ervin. He'll drop 'em off at your house. Courtesy of the Town of Southampton, Department of Public Safety. To schlep and protect."

I thanked him in a way I hoped he'd know was genuine.

"Do you have your computer turned on?" I asked Rosaline.

"No, but it doesn't take long. What do you want to know?"

"If you can pry around in my personal life, I'm assuming you can do that with anybody," I said.

"Depends on the person."

"Show me."

Eddie peeled off to explore more of the condo while she took me to her office in the second bedroom. Like the rest of the place it expressed a comfortable, cheerful wear.

She brought a kitchen chair with her to set next to her office chair so I could watch the action. I'd spent a large part of my working life staring at computer screens, though the displays looked nothing like you see today. Just a lot of data stacked in rows against white or dark green backgrounds. I was aware of the Web in the last years of my career, but I was too involved in other things to pay much attention. It was now a few years into the twenty-first century and I was about to get my first close-up look.

"Okay," she said, her hand poised on the mouse. "Who's the target?"

"Zack Horowitz."

"Can you narrow that? Dates, places?"

"Long Island. Fifteen years back to today."

The whole world knows now how this stuff works, but it was a shock to me how fast things came up on the screen, and how nice everything looked. And how much information there was. All of this amused Rosaline.

"Did you know that TV is now in color?" she said.

The path was a little jagged, but we could follow Zack's life backwards from his current role as Assistant Regional

Director of the New York State DEC through a stint as Head of Environmental Affairs for a tech company in Bethpage, several years as a staff consultant and then as a specialist in governmental contract compliance with the Long Island office of a Big Five accounting firm, a period of private practice, and finally arrived at his gig as Treasurer for the Town of Southampton.

Buried in the middle of a brief profile of Zack was a piece of biographical chaff that appeared nowhere else, which Rosaline insisted was pure chance.

"Everyone commands the Web. No one has control."

That didn't matter to me. Just that it was there: "While serving as Director of Lending at the Southampton branch of East End Savings and Loan, Zack was elected Town Treasurer, beginning a long, successful career bridging the professional worlds of private enterprise and community-based public service . . ." And from there it blathered into self-serving corporate propaganda, which surprisingly made no mention of Zack's intimate involvement in Jeff Milhouser's attempts to bridge public service with commercial fraud.

As interesting as this was, it didn't distract me from Rosaline's hand resting on my thigh, slowly sliding toward the inside. I put my hand on top of hers to halt the progress.

"Sorry, Sam," she said. "It's the proximity."

I knew what she meant. This close in you can easily get caught in a cloud of scent-borne pheromones.

"It's a nice thought," I said.

"But."

"But I don't know. There's some sort of life at the tip of Oak Point. Can't see past it right now."

"I know. I'll print this stuff out while you go back to the patio. Unless you want to try a cold shower for two."

I opted for another vodka instead. By now the sun was hugging the horizon and cooler air was riding in on lengthening shadows. I settled into my wicker chair, in no hurry to leave. It wasn't just Rosaline's comfy aromatic apartment. I wanted to wait for the cover of darkness, an ambiance more conducive to both love and ruin.

Reflecting the mood on the patio, she came out in a linen dress and sandals, carrying a platter of munchies and a handful of printouts. She asked if Eddie could have some cheese.

"If you can stand all the adoration."

"So what's with Zack Horowitz?" she asked as she tossed hunks of cheddar in the air for Eddie to catch. "If you want to tell me, which you probably don't."

"You know as much as I do," I said. "Except that he was Roy Battiston's boss back at East End Savings when Jeff Milhouser was caught mishandling Town assets. The Town's treasure, you could say. And, as you know, Zack was also the Town Treasurer."

"Lovely," she said, popping a chunk of peppercorn cheese in her mouth.

I could have said the same thing about her. She'd never believe me, but I liked the nose. A clever joke on God's part. Build a softly sensual, brainy woman with a nearly perfect physique, then throw in a prominent irregularity and see what happens. For me, it just made the rest of the package that much more appealing. A handy point of contrast, always in evidence.

I had a habit of seeing the same divine sense of humor manifest in lots of people's lives, in those random intersections where luck not only meets opportunity and preparation but other forms of luck, both good and bad.

Even as I rode the waves of destruction, I couldn't think of myself as unlucky. I had experiences and warehouses filled with memory. I didn't have the grace to attribute that to good luck. I held those achievements as mine alone. Along with all the responsibility for what followed. I wouldn't allow fate a role in any of it. Fate was a disinterested bystander, preoccupied with the work of elevating and devastating other people's lives. But never mine.

That was the arrogance of defeat. That it was all my fault.

I wondered if that same habit of thought plagued the mind of Zack Horowitz. Or if he'd tried to banish history through selective amnesia, concentrating on a life of service, built on atonement and rationalization. Either way, none of it amounts to a hill of beans when fate comes to call.

I spent another hour watching night fall with Rosaline. She let me move the conversation onto other things, so the time spent was even more agreeable than it had been, making it harder to pull away.

"I know it doesn't seem like it, Sam, but I don't want to add to your burdens," she said. "I know it wouldn't do any good, and might even scare you away, and then I'd really feel like crap."

"We're fine," I said. "Better than fine. Let's leave it at that."

"Okay," she said, and softly shut the door, floating back into her world of comfort and order, sparked by the mutually sustaining forces of lust and curiosity.

TWENTY-FIVE

AMANDA'S LIGHTS WERE ON when I got back from Rosaline's. I turned off my headlights, parked on the road and walked down our common driveway. I felt like a jerk sneaking into my house, but I wanted a chance to look at those phone records before Amanda knew I was home. As promised, Will Ervin had left them wrapped in a plastic bag and stuck partway under the doormat on the side porch.

I made a cup of coffee to dilute the effects of Rosaline's vodka and took the phone records and some notes out to the pine table on the screened-in porch. I brought along a yellow legal pad on which to draw boxes and arrows like engineers used to do before we drew them with keyboards and liquid-crystal monitors.

I liked this kind of work, making flow schemes and process diagrams. Not as a tool for analysis but as a way to graphically represent a conclusion I'd already drawn.

I'd expected to search through pages and methodically pull numbers out of long columns, then cross-check those numbers with another set. But that work had already been done. I now knew why Sullivan said to be as specific as possible with what I was looking for. What I held weren't the records themselves, but the answer to a query. A report developed by a type of analytical software. Of course.

So it didn't take very long to fill in my boxes and draw my arrows. It was mostly a pro forma exercise. But rather than a petrochemical product at the end of the process it was the consummation of entirely human motivations and behavior. A schematic of pathological cause and effect.

I went into the bathroom and splashed cold water on my face and ran some though my hair. I caught myself looking in the mirror. That was something I rarely did, because I never liked what I saw. It wasn't all vanity, though I admit I'd turn my head a little to get a better angle on my busted nose. I saw things when I looked into my own eyes that seemed to betray thoughts or feelings I was unaware of. It was unsettling.

I pulled myself away and went to put on a clean shirt. Then I called Amanda to tell her I was on my way.

"Right now?" she asked.

"Yeah."

"Don't laugh," she said, and hung up the phone.

She answered the door with a towel wrapped around her head.

"I just got out of the shower."

"No kidding."

"I need a few minutes."

"Take all you want. I know where the Scotch is."

"Bring it out to the terrace. I'll meet you there."

The terrace was actually a patch of lawn on the side of the house facing the channel to the lagoon where she kept a set of white plastic recliners and a small glass table. It wasn't long before she was out there with me, dressed in a silk kimono, her wet hair brushed smooth, a glass of wine in one hand and the bottle in the other.

"Did you sleep?" I asked her.

"Like a dead person. I knew I would. Lately I'd be just about asleep when I'd think of those two men from the DEC with their maps and charts and official-looking papers. A jolt would run through me and I'd be wide awake for hours. This time all I had to do was remember your voice saying the cellar was all clear. And I blissfully fell into the abyss."

"I've fallen in a few of those. Weren't so blissful."

She frowned at me.

"One was in your shower, as I recall," she said. "Any word on that?"

"Nothing official. Had a little chat with Markham Fairchild."

"And?" she asked.

"He's worried about my right prefrontal cortex."

"Me, too, even if I don't know what it is."

"A part of the brain. Apparently controls social behavior."

"Then I'm not so worried," she said.

"You're not?"

"You've been very social to me. And always well behaved."

"That's because I love you," I said.

"You love a lot of people, Sam. You can't help it. You try not to, but it happens anyway. And they love you back. Whether you like it or not."

"Geez."

"I know, you hate this kind of talk. But it means what happens to you is no longer your concern alone. It affects other people. That wasn't true when I first met you, but it is now. You're a full citizen in the land of the living. And some of us here care about the condition of your brain, by reputation a pretty good one."

I didn't know what to say to all that, but I had brains enough not to argue. I wouldn't have put it the way she did, but she had a point. It was a realization I'd come to late in life. People will grow on you if you let them. They'll work their way right through the prefrontal cortex and down into your vital organs, lodging themselves around your heart. They might even save your life, even if you don't realize they're doing it. What I'd learned was you didn't have to fear any of it. Even if sometimes it meant you had to feel the pain of loss. The occasional charges were worth the investment. In fact, it was the only investment worth making.

"I don't know how good it is, but my brain's been getting a workout lately," I said.

"I can imagine. How are things progressing?"

"Word is the indictment could show up any minute," I said.

"Oh dear."

"But I've been able to put a few thoughts together."

"Promising thoughts?"

"Depends on how you look at it. I'm still curious about some stuff. I need to talk it out."

"I'm glad to help if I can," she said.

"Actually, you're the only one who can."

"Really."

"Yeah. Like for starters, when did he approach you?"

"And that would be?"

"Milhouser."

She took a long pull of her wine and let her head fall back, showing off her long lean neck, to which the hard year of stress and striving had added new lines and bands of sinew.

"He approached me when I said he did," she said.

"At the restaurant."

"No, Mr. Inquisitor. I'd spoken to Robbie Milhouser at the project on Jacob's Neck. If you don't believe me, get Joe Sullivan to give me a lie detector test."

I stood up from my plastic chair and walked halfway across the lawn toward the lagoon. The houses lined up along the northwest shore were all lit up and you could hear voices bouncing across the water, though you couldn't hear what they were saying. Words without meaning. Sound without comprehension.

I went back to Amanda, who was pouring another glass.

I sat on the edge of the chair and leaned toward her, my elbows on my knees.

"It was a Milhouser. But it wasn't Robbie."

The look on her face betrayed a chorus of conflicting impulses.

"Oh God, Sam, do we have to?"

I tried to make it as easy as I could.

"I think we do."

"And if I say I'd rather not you'll just persist. That's your way."

"Sometimes."

"Dammit, I hate this."

"It was Robbie's father Jeff," I said. "He's the one who approached you. On Robbie's behalf."

She pushed her seat into recline and wrapped the kimono around her knees.

"All my life people have been trying to tell me I can't do things I think I'm able to do," she said.

"Is that what he did?"

"In effect. Someone on the architectural review board told him about my master development plan. He said it was too big a project for a person of my experience, meaning none, to handle on my own. I needed a construction manager and another crew. Robbie's."

"Okay. So you told him to get lost. Like you told Robbie at the restaurant."

She looked like she wanted to be absorbed into her recliner, but answered me anyway.

"This is the part I knew you wouldn't understand. I actually told him I'd think about it. I was so tired. We were just finishing up the north house. I don't know what felt worse, my nerves or my back. I was having self-doubt, okay? I'm making him sound worse than he was. He was a pretty slick old guy. Fatherly," she added, as her voice trailed away.

"Nothing would have come of it," she said, her voice coming back. "Even if I thought I needed help, I wouldn't have chosen Jeff Milhouser. And certainly not Robbie. I know I should have told you, but I was ashamed of the thoughts going through my head. And then after the restaurant thing I was embarrassed that I hadn't said anything."

"I'd've helped you if you'd asked," I said.

"It happened during one of those funny times when neither of us was trying very hard to see the other."

"I still would've helped."

She looked up into the night sky.

"I know. I wanted you to think I was strong enough to do this on my own."

"You are. Strong enough and doing it on your own."

I liked the vantage point on the lagoon from Amanda's terrace. In front of the houses on the other side of the channel you could see the outlines of Boston Whalers and shoal-draft sailboats tethered to moorings throughout the little body of water. It was hard to imagine that over a hundred years ago it was crammed with steamboats and fast-passage schooners trading with the bustling industrial plant.

"What about the other time?" I asked her.

"Sorry?"

"The other time Jeff Milhouser came to see you. There has to be another time."

"What difference does it make how many times he came to see me?"

"Every difference in the world," I said.

"I don't know why you're so interested in this."

"Tell me."

"You're not letting this go are you?" she said.

"What did he say to you?"

She sank even further into her chair, collapsing into herself.

"It was the day after the house fire. I was staring at the ruins and suddenly there he was, like he appeared out of thin air, like Beelzebub or something. He said this was the kind of thing that happened when you lacked professional construction management. He said I'd been rude to Robbie, but he was still willing to help. That he was only trying to protect me. I didn't know what to do, so I did the brave thing and ran away. Just like I did when I ran from Southampton the first time. And then when I ran back again. I ran in fear. Then Robbie's killed, and I think, oh God. And then they arrest you. What am I to do? Tell everything that happened and hand them a motive? I hid in the City, but after a while I thought, Burton will never let this get too far. They couldn't possibly win a case against an innocent man. And I wanted to come back. I wanted to see you. I wanted everything back to the way it was before. But that old bastard was right. It just keeps getting worse."

"I can see why you wouldn't tell the cops, but how come you didn't tell me?" I asked.

She turned her face away from me as she talked, so it was hard to hear what she was saying.

"When he told me he wanted to protect me I told him I had all the protection I needed. And then he said, 'Yeah, but who'll protect the protector?' It took me a second to figure out what he meant. Then it all became clear."

"Misplaced concern," I told her. "I'm still here."

"That night of the fire, I was so angry, confused and afraid. I didn't know what to do. I was on the verge of driving back to Oak Point to beg forgiveness when Milhouser showed up with his offers and not-so-hidden threats. I was afraid everything was about to turn ugly. I didn't know what he could do to you. I didn't know what you would do if threatened. I thought if I just left for a while so we couldn't talk about it all the trouble would just blow away."

"Never does."

"I know. I was just afraid. Didn't you tell me fear makes you stupid?"

"Yeah. Fear and anger. And I think there's a third thing."

"Scotch?" she asked, holding up the bottle. I took it from her and poured another one.

"Okay," I said, "a fourth. You already brought it up."

"Love?"

"Worse than all that other stuff combined, because it's with you twenty-four hours a day. Makes you deaf, dumb and blind."

"You're just discovering this?" she asked.

"Yeah. I should alert the world."

"When did this revelation come to you?"

"It crept up on me. I've been thinking a lot about not thinking clearly. You get out of practice when you're working with your hands all day. Not that it's stupid work, but there's a routine to it that doesn't stimulate the brain cells the same way. We were both up to our ass in construction for months on end, as you recall."

"Hope to be again."

"That's the other thing that crept up on me. Letting work interfere with living some sort of normal life. I thought I'd done that once and learned my lesson. But there we were, passing each other in the driveway, not talking for days at a time. And when we did it was all shop talk."

"I suppose you're right," she said.

"One of those conversations sticks in my head. It was out in the driveway, as usual. It wasn't that long ago. You were really busting ass getting that north property finished. Things had gotten a little out of sequence, you remember? Like you had the kitchen cabinets already delivered but there was a piece of wall between the kitchen and garage that hadn't been closed in yet, and you couldn't get the insulation sub back on the job. As it turned out, I had a couple rolls of insulation left over from my addition stashed in the shed. I went and got it for you. I said I'd put it in for you to keep things moving, but you never wanted me to do that kind of thing. You said, 'Come on, Sam. Even I can install insulation.' So I said, 'Okay, let me give you the necessary equipment,' and I went back to the shed and got my insulation installation kit. It was a little white cardboard box. Everything you need for the job. Staples, a little cat's paw and needle-nose pliers to pull out misplaced staples. A special tape that'll adhere to the vapor barrier in case it rips. And of course, the main attraction, my hammer stapler with the orange handle. We stuffed the rolls of insulation in the trunk of your car and I dropped the box in the back seat. And that's the last I saw of the hammer stapler until that day at Southampton Town police headquarters when Sullivan held it up in a plastic evidence bag."

There's no such thing as utter silence. I learned that years ago sitting at night in my Adirondacks at the edge of the breakwater. The water itself always made little lapping, gurgling noises. And there were always bugs in the wetlands to the west and planes flying in and out of the City, gaining and losing altitude. Motorcycles or cars with bad tailpipes out on Noyac Road.

"When we were talking about fear and anger, we forgot to mention hate," she said finally. "Robbie Milhouser was all three of those to me. You can't imagine."

"I can get a start. I know something happened in high school."

Her hand was shaking, but she managed to get the wine glass up to her lips.

"Of course you do. That's when the fear started. I was trapped. It wasn't that anything actually happened. It's that it could have and I would have been helpless. And it wasn't even Robbie, it was all the jerks who hung around him who were egging him on. The whole school thought we were secret lovers, but I'd never had anything to do with him. He wanted people to think that. So when those boys caught me at the back of the bus, he thought he had to do something to prove we were together. I could see what was coming. I was terrified. If two of my girlfriends hadn't been there, who knows what would have happened."

She was quiet again. I didn't know if she was finished, so I lit a cigarette to fill the dead air. She did have one more thing to say.

"There was never a time when I didn't wish him dead. And now this evil old bastard trying to force him on me. Threatening me. Threatening you. What could I do?"

The bugs were out in full, though the bay was quieter than usual. I was glad to have the cigarette to occupy my hands. I took a puff and let the smoke drift on its own out of my mouth.

"You could make a calculation," I said to her softly. "Of the two Milhousers, Robbie was the bigger threat. Literally and emotionally. The old man was spooky, but without his son, less able to intimidate. Or maybe it was Robbie's turn to put the pressure on. Call you the day after the fire and ask you over to his project. 'Come on, Amanda,' he'd say. 'Think how easy this can all be.' Wouldn't be hard to convince him to come alone. Could be just you and him in the big, dark, empty house."

This time her whole body shook, as if a little tremor had started at her shoulders and run down to her feet. She put the wine glass on the table.

"Dear God," she said.

"Before you leave, you pop the trunk of the Audi and look around for a little protection. Maybe in the heat of moment you forget the stapler was mine, maybe you remember but don't think about things like fingerprints or UPC codes. The stapler was too convenient. Heavy and hard edged, but slim enough to slip into the back waistband of your jeans.

"You get there and Robbie's alone as promised. He's on his best behavior, trying to win you over with his boyish charm. All this does is convince you that his interest is both commercial and romantic. This is beyond intolerable. It can't go on anymore. It has to end there.

"It's easy to say, 'Okay, handsome, show me around the place.' Which puts him in front of you as you walk about, so when you get out to the sunroom there's plenty of room to get in a good swing. The first one drops him. But he's pretty big, so it takes a couple more to finish him off.

"But now what? You hadn't planned for this, exactly. In a slight panic, you run outside and throw the stapler into the beach grass. Then you do the only thing you can do at that point. Run. You need time to recover. And until you recover your self control, stay clear of the cops and other suspicious types. Like me.

"As it turns out, you don't have much to worry about. All the attention is immediately drawn to me. Since you know I didn't do it, you have all the confidence in the world they won't be able to prove it, especially with Burton looking after me. But I'm such an obvious suspect nobody even thinks of looking anywhere else. And certainly not at you. The only one who could do that was me."

"You really think I'm capable of such a thing?" she asked.

I nodded.

"I do. I saw you the night of the fire. I recognize the condition. Blind, crazy fury, fueled by bitterness, disappointment and fear. So yes, I think you are capable of such a thing, under those circumstances. That was the most obvious assumption as I stood there with Sullivan in the squad room, even without all the other evidence popping up. In particular, the so-called incident on the bus."

She looked like she was about to say something, but I raised my hand to cut her off.

"My brain had all the answers, but my heart wasn't in it," I said. "I wanted to believe there was a different truth out there. Only now I've got an interesting little problem. I had to find a way to track down this alternate truth without making things worse for me, or drawing attention to you. Especially among the people I usually count on to help me figure things out."

Especially them. Beloved people who had enough worry on their minds. Some of whom, like Burton, loved Amanda, too. The isolation I felt, with my greatest fears locked out of sight, had been another lesson. There was a time when I locked my whole self away. I didn't want to go back there.

"What do you believe now?" she asked, when I gave her a chance to speak.

"What should I believe?"

"That I wanted to kill Robbie Milhouser. And you're right. I could have. But I didn't. And now you want me to say that. It's important to hear the words."

"It is," I said. "And I believe you."

She took in a long breath.

"I never got to use your insulation kit," she said. "The subs showed up the next day. I don't even know where it is."

"That's 'cause you left the box at the house, didn't you. You don't know by now what happens to your tools when you leave them on the job?"

I tossed my watered-down Scotch, uncharacteristically neglected, out on the lawn. Then went to get a fresh one.

I stayed at her house that night and watched her sleep, overcome with relief and exhaustion. But no chance of rest for me. I had a head full of calculations and probabilities which were enough to keep me awake most of the night. That was fine. I now only had one theory to concentrate on. And I admit it, the favored of the two, once not much more than a matter of faith and hope.

My alternate truth.

I worked in her bedroom on a yellow legal pad, a soft reading light over my shoulder. It wasn't an easy workspace, but what the heck. There are worse ways to spend your time than looking at Amanda doing anything, awake or not.

TWENTY-SIX

THE NEXT DAY I was in Jackie's office going over my plan. She fell in love with her part right away. Especially when I wouldn't share all the other parts.

"You've *got* to be fucking kidding me," she said from between the stacks of paper on top of her desk.

I stopped her before she had a chance to launch the usual barrage.

"Jackie, I need you to do this for me."

"What if he won't play along?" she asked.

"I think he'll have to. But I won't know till I try."

"Dammit, Sam. I told you not to hide things from me."

"I have to for a little while. Not just for my sake. Other people could be affected. And if it all blows up, you've got deniability. Come on, Jackie. I've been a pain in the ass, but I've never let you down."

She wasn't used to personal appeals. It shut her up more effectively than I would have thought. I didn't sell past the close, getting out of there as fast as I could. I made it down to the sidewalk before she called from her second-story window.

"Catch," she yelled.

It was a cell phone with a twelve-volt charger trailing behind like the tail of a kite. It's a good thing I have quick reflexes or I'd have been sweeping microcircuits up off the concrete.

"It's an extra," she said, giving me the number. "If anything screws up during the day and you want to abort, call me immediately. I'll do the same."

The cell phone was such a good idea my first call was to Amanda with similar instructions. It was fun talking to people while I was driving the Grand Prix. I hadn't done that since I lost the company car somewhere in Bridgeport, with the phone still in it. A bonus for the car thieves.

The first big hole in the plan was slipping out of town, technically jumping bail, in a 1967 Grand Prix. I held to the back roads as far as I could before hopping on Route 27 heading west. After passing Quogue and clearing Southampton jurisdiction, I breathed a little easier, even though I was now officially in serious trouble with the law.

Timing was important. My object was to be sitting in the parking lot of the regional DEC office in Stony Brook at four in the afternoon. This was another big hole in the plan, another uncontrollable variable. I'd considered calling Dan or Ned to see if Zack Horowitz would be in the office that day, but that seemed even riskier. So instead I kept the cell phone charged and at the ready.

At four-thirty the place started emptying out. I tucked into a parking spot where I was shielded, but could still see the faces of people coming down the front path. I didn't see Dan or Ned, to my relief. But I did see Zack at about quarter to five. He had a briefcase and a sports coat draped over his arm. I waited as long as I dared, then got out of the car and walked up to him. He stopped cold.

"You know who I am now, don't you," I said to him.

Zack was a trim, good-looking guy. He was maybe a few years older than me, but staying out of the ring had done a lot to preserve his face. He had light eyes, thinning but adequate dark gray hair and angular features. I liked his voice. It was a soft tenor, articulate, though graced with Long Island inflections.

"I knew then," he said. "I have a good memory for names."

"So you knew I'd be back."

"I hoped you wouldn't," he said.

"I need you to come with me," I said, which caused the first look of alarm to cross his face. "Right now."

"I don't understand," he said.

"I don't have everything, but I've got enough to send your life into hell starting from the moment you walk away from me," I told him, holding up Jackie's cell phone.

"How do I know that?"

I handed him a copy of the phone records. As he studied them, little pink clouds formed on his cheeks.

"This will effectively destroy my life," he said calmly.

"It has to happen eventually. I can do it with you or without you. The latter could be worse, but I have no guarantees. If you come with me now I promise to do what I can to help you through it." I looked at my watch. "You can take the next thirty seconds to decide."

"You're asking an awful lot of a person who doesn't know you."

"Okay," I said. "Think about the ones you do know. How's that been going for you? Do you think helping me is gonna be worse?"

He studied me.

"My wife will wonder where I am," he said.

"Call her and tell her you'll be late. Very late."

I pointed to the Grand Prix and told him to lead the way. All the way he looked poised to make a run for it. But he got in the car and let me drive him out of there. I told Eddie to leave him alone, but Zack said it was okay, that Eddie probably smelled his golden retriever. Then he called his wife and gave her what sounded like a believable excuse for not coming home right away. I didn't know if it was or not, but now that this plane was off the ground there was no going back.

"Should I be afraid for my life?" he asked quietly.

"Not from me," I said. "This isn't a kidnapping."

"More of an extortion," he said.

"Okay, I guess, technically. I'd like to think of it as leveraged persuasion."

He seemed to relax a little at that. He was obviously alarmed, but he did a good job of containing it. Zack was a very controlled guy. I wondered if it was a skill acquired over years of staring into menacing shadows.

"Whose idea was the bank scam? Yours or Roy's?" I asked him.

He still had his jacket draped over his arm. He slid it off and put it in his lap.

"Wonder Boy's," he said. "Though I planted the seed by showing him how to make decent returns on extremely short-term investments, even with puny interest rates. All you needed was a wad of stagnant cash, which was ever-present in the institutional accounts. We used to go out to lunch and talk about it. I liked being this guy's mentor. He was so anxious to learn. And in those days I liked showing off. Like a jackass.

"I got him involved in the routine sweeps we had going with a few companies, the teacher's union, some other stuff.

All pretty small potatoes. And then he comes to me and asks that question you can never even think about when you're a banker. 'What if we borrow some of the Town's money and do our own little twelve-hour sweep? You're the Town Treasurer. Who's going to stop you?' I thought he was kidding, but he was serious. I don't know, bravado, boredom, who knows. I thought, yeah. Just once. So we did it. It was exhilarating. We didn't take any of the money. The Town was the sole beneficiary. It was just to do it. So we did it again, until it became routine. We set up a small ledger account to take in the proceeds. I was actually thinking I'd spring it on the Board of Trustees some day, hand them a nice hunk of dough, smooth over the fact that we were sending the municipality's entire working capital to God knows where every night."

"Enter Jeff Milhouser."

"He'd gone to Roy first, thinking a junior loan officer would be an easier touch. He thought I'd be the stone wall, if I'd even talk to him. He was already skating on thin ice with the board after some goofy deal with road salt. The guy was always working some angle, but he had friends all over town, including on the board, and frankly things weren't very well monitored in those days."

"Roy cooked up the scheme."

"Sure. He was ready to go to another level, way beyond anything I ever thought of. For me it was just a game. Roy had much greater ambition than that."

"So I hear," I said.

"I didn't know they were doing it until it was underway. Roy swept one of the big Town accounts, but instead of sending it out to the investment houses it went right into Milhouser's account and from there into a six-month CD. Just long enough to produce the paperwork that would satisfy the underwriters that he was good for a big loan. I know this because my signature was on Milhouser's loan application. Roy stuck it under my nose, told me what they'd been doing, and essentially said either I sign it or he'd blow the whistle on the sweeps game. I couldn't believe my ears. I told him he'd go down with me, but he pointed out that I was the head of lending. He was just a junior guy following instructions. And by the way, he'd kept meticulous accounting of every unauthorized transaction, none of which carried his name, all of which carried mine.

"For the next few months I did everything I could to cover the Town's reduced working capital, but it was impossible. I hardly said another word to Roy Battiston, or Milhouser. The fools assumed I'd be able to keep a lid on everything, that I'd have to because my career and reputation were at stake. But I couldn't."

"So you cut a deal," I said.

"It wasn't easy. Milhouser was furious. But I got him to understand that while he had hooks in me, I had hooks in him. If we cooperated we'd get through it with minimum damage. If we fought, it'd be mutually assured destruction."

"So," I said, "the deal was you'd guarantee the bank wouldn't press charges. You'd take the hit with the Town for sweeping the Town accounts, but he'd have to cop to borrowing the funds to collateralize his loan. Since they were stuck in a CD there was no way around that. You'd also threatened the bank's board with a public relations nightmare if they made too big a deal over it. It was in everyone's interest that the whole matter die out quickly and quietly. That included, of course, both you and Milhouser leaving Town government."

"Very good, Sam," said Zack. "You must know something about small-town politics."

"Nah. But I'm a quick learner. Speaking of which, I think I also know what Roy got out of the deal."

"My job," said Zack, with a bitter laugh. "That was his goal all along. All he wanted was to trap me in something he could use to pry me out of there. I'd already put my neck in the noose the first time I made an unauthorized investment. Milhouser, a skunk of the same stripe, just facilitated the execution. I had to leave anyway. The bank manager worked out a resolution, which he agreed to do for the same PR reasons as the Town. But he needed my head as part of the bargain. I was happy to give it to him and get the hell away from Southampton. And Roy Battiston."

"Not far enough, apparently," I said.

"The second stupidest thing I ever did was not moving to Montana or Costa Rica. I tried, but my wife wouldn't leave Long Island, and I couldn't tell her why we should. As long as I was nearby, and in government, that noose was wrapped around my neck. I knew one day I'd feel the tug."

He would have probably told me more, but Jackie's cell phone rang. Or rather, played the first few bars of "I Wanna Be Sedated" by the Ramones. It took me a few minutes to figure out what was going on and once I did, how to answer the phone. It was Jackie.

"How's it going?" she asked.

"Fine here. Why?"

"How close are you?"

"Half hour, give or take," I said.

"Are you sure about the timing?"

"Do whatever you want to do, Jackie. I trust you."

"Oh great. More pressure."

Zack looked interested in my side of the conversation. When I ended the call he asked me, "So, are you going to tell me where we're going? It's only fair. I've told you a lot."

"You have," I said. "I appreciate it. We're going to North Sea."

As we drove he caressed his sports coat where it draped across his lap, his long slender fingers absentmindedly picking at the fabric and folding it along the seams.

"It was a good day when I heard Roy was going to jail for some real-estate scam," he said. "I thought, there's karma for you."

"It must have been a big disappointment to hear from him again."

Zack looked up from his sports coat.

"It was devastating. It was just an envelope with an old blueprint and a note telling me to hold on to it and wait for further instruction. I felt like those fellas in the movies who ask the Mob for a favor, and then twenty years later get the call. Payback time. It's Faustian."

It was getting close to dusk by the time we reached the outskirts of Southampton, marked by the narrowing of Route 27 from four lanes to two. Zack Horowitz had been quiet during the last leg of the trip, and I hadn't pushed him to do any more talking. I needed to concentrate on the plan, if so grand a name could be applied to what I had in mind.

I turned left off Route 27 and after that merged onto North Sea Road. I wanted to feel more confidence, but couldn't muster it. Too many variables. Too little leverage. But it was all I had.

Zack withstood the fun-house ride over Bay Edge Drive with less complaint than Jackie. When we got to Robbie's project there were two pickups parked out front.

"Look familiar?" I asked him.

He nodded.

I had him walk in front of me as we went around to the back of the house, carefully stepping over the last of the construction debris, some of which I scooped up and tossed to the side as we approached the French doors.

They were open to the bay, letting a soft breeze into the room, along with me and Zack.

"Look, guys," I said to Patrick and Milhouser. "I brought a friend."

Patrick had a big smirk on his face and shook his head in disbelief. Confusion and anger competed for possession of Jeff Milhouser.

"Where's the Battiston woman?" he demanded.

"Her name's Anselma," I said. "She's anything but a Battiston woman."

"Hello, Jeff," said Zack, stepping out from behind me.

"She called and said to meet her here," said Milhouser, looking at Zack.

Patrick moved closer, staring at me. Milhouser touched his arm and he stopped.

"We've changed the agenda for the meeting," I said. "But hang tight. We don't have a quorum yet."

"That mean she's coming? And what's he doing here?" Milhouser asked, pointing at Zack.

"Consulting on environmental issues," I said.

Milhouser's confusion deepened.

"You want some answers from this asshole, let me beat it out of him," said Patrick, looking at me.

I pulled Zack across the room and planted him next to Milhouser.

"Do me a favor, and keep Jeff company while I take care of this," I said, gesturing to Patrick to follow me outside.

The only light out there came from the room behind us. I turned and walked backwards, being very careful to keep my footing as I watched Patrick come at me, backlit. Before he got too close I rotated to the left, and I was glad to see him rotate with me, so that in a few steps I had my back to the house and he was in the pale light.

I reached down and picked up a three-foot-long piece of two-by-four that I'd tossed there on the way in. Patrick looked surprised.

"You got to be kidding me," he said.

I showed him I wasn't by cracking him across the top of the head. He went down on his knees with his hands covering his head.

"Fuck," he yelled.

I'd used a similar approach one time before on a thug named Buddy Florin, the last guy who thought being bigger, younger and stronger were the only deciding factors.

When Patrick tried to stand up I hit him on the right shoulder as hard as I could, knocking him into the mud where he rolled over and tried again to get back on his feet. I hit him again on the other arm, and as he fell back down, I kicked him in the face.

He pitched backwards, holding his face with his left hand, his right hanging uselessly at his side. I dropped down and stuck my knee in his chest. I gripped his shirt with one hand and held the two-by-four above his head with the other.

"Like I told you before, it only gets worse."

"Some fucking boxer," he said.

"Not allowed to box anymore, sorry. Doctor's orders."

I dragged him to his feet and held him by the back of his shirt. I shoved him through the French doors and told him to lie face down on the floor.

"You broke my fucking arm," he said. "I need a doctor."

"Good Lord," said Zack.

Milhouser just snorted.

"We'll take care of that after we have a little chat," I said, checking my watch. "If Jackie's on time for once in her life, it won't take that long."

Milhouser had been holding his white golf jacket in his hand. He put it on and zipped up, looking ready to bolt.

"I don't know what the hell this is about, Acquillo, but it's not what I came here to do, so if you'd kindly . . ."

He was interrupted by the sound of Jackie calling from the front of the house. To my everlasting wonderment, she was actually ahead of schedule.

"Hi, fellas," she said, as she walked in the sunroom. "What's up?"

I introduced her to Zack Horowitz, while keeping an eye on Milhouser, whose confusion had moved through anger and now looked more like indecision. Patrick mumbled something into the floor.

"Zack," I said, like I was kicking off a weekly staff meeting, "why don't you outline for Jackie the statement you're planning to give the Assistant District Attorney. Just the highlights for now."

"I'm here to act as your attorney until you can pick one of your own," she said to Zack, holding up a steno pad. "I'll be taking notes."

Zack nodded.

"I've been aware of a campaign by Mr. Milhouser to gain control through extortion of a large real-estate development in this area," he said to Jackie in his softly modulated voice.

"You idiot," said Milhouser.

Jackie looked up from her pad.

"If you don't mind, sir. I don't want to miss anything," she said.

Zack started talking.

"A little over two years ago I received a document in the mail from Roy Battiston. It was an old drawing of a series of storage cellars located on the site of a factory sitting at the center of this planned development. With it was a note from Battiston saying the cellars were full of toxic waste, heretofore undetected. With the drawing was a note from Battiston telling me to keep this information confidential until notified."

Jackie held up her hand to stop him while she caught up. Then she nodded.

"One might ask," Zack went on, "why the Assistant Regional Director of the New York State DEC would meekly comply with such an outrageous demand. One that would put him in direct violation of the duties of his office. As I said in the beginning, Mr. Milhouser was engaged in a campaign of extortion, and I was one of those on the receiving end."

"Jesus, mercy in heaven, what a load of bull," said Milhouser.

"So you sat on this thing like you were told," I said.

"Yes. Until this gentleman paid me a visit," he said, pointing down at Patrick.

"The gentleman Sam Acquillo is currently standing over with a two-by-four," said Jackie. "Got it."

"He said he was there to deliver a message from Roy Battiston. That I was to give the drawing of the cellars to Robbie and Jeff Milhouser. That the Milhousers would know what to do with it. He was clear that my personal safety, as well as my professional career, relied on following these directions to the letter."

Patrick chimed in from the floor.

"More bullshit," he said.

"After taking a day to recover from fear and self-loathing, I tried to reach Roy at the state penitentiary. I called several times, working my way through their system, and finally got him on the phone. The first thing he did was warn me that the line wasn't secure. But by this time I was so emotionally overwrought, I spoke freely. He said, 'Just do what I asked you to do, then get out of the way. Or go eat a gun or something. I could care less.' And then he hung up on me."

Jackie was writing furiously in her steno book.

"So you did what he asked you to do?" she asked.

"Almost. I called Robbie, the thought of speaking to his father being unbearable. As I talked, it became clear the whole thing was news to him. So I explained, again quite freely, the situation. He cursed a little, and told me to come see him right away and bring the drawing." Zack looked around the room. "He said to come here, so that's what I did."

"I'm not listening to any more of this garbage," said Jeff Milhouser, unzipping then re-zipping his jacket to emphasize the point.

Jackie walked over to him.

"He wants you to stay put, Mr. Milhouser," she said, jerking her head in my direction. "I would. Go ahead, Mr. Horowitz."

Zack moved to the center of the room, closer to where Jackie now stood.

"I guess I was encouraged by Robbie's confusion. I realized the drawing was the only leverage I had, so I didn't dare bring it. I left it where it was, locked in a drawer in my office. When I got here it was well after dark. Robbie was here, and so was he."

He pointed at Patrick again.

"They didn't look happy with each other," said Zack, "Robbie was very agitated. I think he'd been drinking. You could smell it. Robbie asked me what would happen if there really was toxic waste on the site. I said it could be anything from a simple disposal, to a massive cleanup, to a permanent condemnation of the property. While we were talking Getty was on a cell phone in the corner. I didn't think much about it until this one shows up."

He pointed at Milhouser.

"I think it dawned on me and Robbie at the same time that Getty had called him. Robbie started yelling at both of them, saying things like, 'What the fuck is going on here?' and 'Who're you working for?' directed at Getty, who didn't say much. But Jeff Milhouser was talking plenty. He spoke with this belittling, condescending tone, telling Robbie to grow up and stop being a big dope. That they had a golden opportunity to take Battiston's old project away from his wife, and if she resisted, they just had to wave the drawing at her. One whiff of 'toxic waste' and the whole deal would go down the tubes, he told his son. That just made Robbie angrier. He said they didn't need to do anything that mean, that he was going to win her over honestly, that they were old friends. Jeff just sneered at him. He was pretty angry now himself. I admit, I was terrified. For some reason I picked that moment to blurt out that I hadn't brought the drawing."

Jeff Milhouser sat down on a pair of stacked sawhorses, his hands resting on his knees. His face was intent, calculations running freely behind his eyes.

"Robbie starting yelling at me, 'You destroy that thing,'" said Zack. "And Getty walked over and grabbed me by the throat." Zack's hand involuntarily mimicked the attack. "He said we were going back to Stony Brook to get it. Jeff Milhouser stood next to him and called me a variety of names, though none as cruel and demeaning as what he called his son. That's when Robbie grabbed Getty by the hair and pulled him off of me. I'd never seen two grown men, big men, actually fight before. I never imagined."

"You better think about what you're doing, Horowitz," said Milhouser.

"It's all I *can* think about."

"Then you're stupid."

Zack ignored him.

"They were punching at each other and trying to grab each other's clothing. Getty was also kicking at Robbie's legs. Robbie was trying to wrestle him. He was bigger, but Getty was hitting him very hard. I'm making it sound like a long drawn-out thing, but I think it only lasted a few seconds. Almost before I knew it, Robbie was on the floor. Dead."

Patrick picked his head off the floor and tried to twist around to look at Zack.

"Wait a minute. Uh-uh," he said.

Milhouser stood up again.

"Shut up," he said to Patrick.

"No, you shut the fuck up," he said back.

Patrick looked like he was trying to stand. I put my foot on his back and shoved him back down, but kept my eyes glued on Zack, trying to keep him and the universe motionless for just another moment.

"Tell him," Patrick yelled at Zack.

Zack looked at me. I shook my head.

"Tell him," Patrick yelled at Milhouser. Milhouser also shook his head and looked down at the floor.

"You fuck," Patrick said into the floor. "I had the situation under control. But this fuck," he strained to look at Milhouser, "has to get in the act. With a fucking hammer sta-pler. Hits the guy right on the head. I can still hear it."

I nodded to Zack.

"That's correct," he said to Jackie. "I witnessed it. Jeff Milhouser came up behind Robbie and struck hard once. Robbie leaned down and tried to cover his head, and Jeff hit him again. And again, and even after he'd fallen to the floor, he hit him again. His own son. His own flesh and blood."

Milhouser still stared at the floor.

"No flesh and blood of mine," he said. "Just a big, stupid greaseball. I should have known he'd get stuck on another greaseball. Must be the inferior genes."

Then as if suddenly alert to the situation, he looked at Jackie.

"I'm not admitting a thing."

He pointed at me.

"It was his stapler," he yelled.

"But you didn't know that at the time," I said to him. "It was in a box Getty took from the insulation subs. Amanda used the same guys. She borrowed my stapler and they walked off with it. Just happened to be the first thing that came to hand. Jeff here had the sense to wipe down the handle. Dumb luck for both of us, my prints were on the rest of it.

"By the way," I added, "the box is now in the trunk of my car. I'm guessing Jeff had to paw through it to get at that stapler."

Jackie asked me to toss her the cell phone.

"Can I call him now?" she asked.

"Sure," I said.

"Who's 'him'?" Milhouser demanded.

"Joe Sullivan. Southampton Town detective," said Jackie, punching in the number. "He'll want to get these statements while they're nice and fresh."

"Aw, Christ," said Milhouser, like he'd just spilled a cup of coffee in his lap.

We all listened to Jackie talk to Sullivan. Milhouser made a few attempts to stride out of there, but Jackie just snapped her fingers at him without looking up from the phone and he went back to sitting on the sawhorses.

In the subsequent silence, I remembered one more thing to ask Zack.

"How'd you get the drawing to the DEC?"

He smiled a tired smile.

"While the two of them were yelling at each other over Robbie's body. I ran like hell. Getty even chased after me, but I have a sports car and he has a big pickup truck. Milhouser had a threatening message at my office waiting for me. But that was unnecessary. We were back where we were at East End Savings. Everybody had hooks in everybody else. Mutually assured destruction."

Of course I knew about the BMW. Zack had roared by me on Bay Edge Drive that night while I was jogging. He was on his way to Robbie's house. When I got there his car was in the driveway parked next to a pair of pickups. I'd gone that way on a hunch that somebody'd be there. Maybe I could prove they'd torched Amanda's house while the act was still fresh. But seeing all the cars, I didn't like the odds. I was afraid to get into it. Afraid for my head. So I ran on by, and headed south up to Noyac Road.

If I'd stopped maybe I'd be the one dead and Robbie would have had the murder charge. Or maybe I could have saved him and myself in the bargain. I'm not big on that kind of speculation, but it was something I thought I'd have to live with for a while before I'd know how I felt about it.

I felt a little bad about lying to everybody about being there, and worse about the old lady who ID'd me, but I hadn't seen any good in admitting the truth, and probably never would.

"So as soon as I could, I drove the drawing up to Albany," said Zack, "and after extracting a promise of anonymity, ostensibly to protect my 'source,' I handed it over to the State's

Attorney. At least I got one thing off my conscience. I'm glad
they didn't find anything. It makes it that much better."

I wanted to say his conscience seemed okay with letting
me hang for something I didn't do, but I had to keep him on
my side. There was still a long legal road ahead.

———

While we waited for Sullivan, Jackie advised them all on
what she'd do if she were them, free of charge. By the time
the big cop walked into the sunroom with Will Ervin and
another uniform, Patrick was on his feet and the incriminating two-by-four back outside.

Milhouser still looked indignant, even bewildered. I wondered if he'd convinced himself of his own innocence, the
same brain that had reacted with murderous rage now settling into a soothing state of denial.

I'd have to ask Rosaline.

Sullivan decided the best thing was to bring everybody to
the hospital so they could check out Patrick's arm, then take
statements there or head over to the HQ in Hampton Bays.
He called ahead to Ross while Ervin and the other cops led
Zack, Patrick and Milhouser out to their cruisers.

Jackie said we'd be right behind. But when I got outside I
plopped down on the muddy ground, then lay back, spread
my arms and legs, and looked up at the starry sky through
the spring leaves. Jackie squatted next to me.

"You all right?"

"I think so," I said. I took a deep gulp of air into my lungs
and closed my eyes.

"Don't ever do that to me again," said Jackie.

"What?"

"Put me in a state of abject terror for weeks, thinking I'm

going to make a mistake that puts my friend in jail for the rest of his life, then hide information from me, which I explicitly asked you not to do, goddammit."

"I wasn't sure. Honestly. There was another thread I had to tie off."

"How long have you known it was Milhouser?"

"About fifteen minutes," I said.

"Get out of here."

I sat up and looked at her.

"It was obvious one of them had burned down Amanda's project. But I never believed it was Robbie. Not given the way he was looking at Amanda that night at the restaurant. Despite all the bluster, there was something different in his eyes. The hope of forgiveness."

"For what?"

"Robbie had a lot of natural bully in him, but his stepfather's ridicule and brutality fueled the flames. The only parent he had and all he ever got was contempt. I knew that old bastard was the pivot point the day we went to see him. He said all the right things about his boy, but his eyes, like Robbie's, said something different. It wasn't grief, it was triumph. That and the booties."

"Huh?"

"He has a floor-finishing business. Between coats of urethane floor guys'll wear booties so they don't mar the fresh finish. Same thing the arsonists wore when they torched Amanda's house. A job in every way intended to send a signal. That takes the mind of a planner, a schemer, and someone unburdened by conscience. People have written Jeff Milhouser off as a basic screw-up, but he's worse than that. He's a basic sociopath. I thought his history might give up something I could use to trace back to Robbie's death. And it did, in the form of Zack Horowitz."

"How the hell did Roy get in the act?"

"I never understood why he put the brakes on developing Amanda's property after the Town ordered an extensive environmental study. He said it was because of the notification requirements, which was legitimate enough, since all that attention could have blown the scam. But those cellars made the study itself the real worry. He didn't even share the information with his partner Bob Sobol, who was an engineer. He'd have known they could be filled with hazardous waste. Roy's another all-star schemer. He had the presence of mind to keep that drawing to himself, and then put it someplace safe—with Zack Horowitz—where it could be deployed at some future date."

"I still don't get it."

I leaned up on my elbow.

"That's because you're a good person. You don't think like they do. Roy has had plenty of time to nurse his bitterness. Jeff Milhouser was the perfect outside partner. Roy's natural ally. And Patrick the ideal go-between. Roy thought he could manipulate his way back into Amanda's project, sort of a silent partner, pick up a piece of the action. Wouldn't that be a kick. But if all he managed was to wreak a little havoc and revenge on me and Amanda, that'd be fine."

Jackie was quiet for a moment.

"Don't get mad at me," she said.

"What do you mean?"

"When I ask you something."

"Okay," I said, lying flat on the ground again.

"You don't ever wonder about Amanda?"

"All the time."

"And?"

"A priest once told me faith was believing in something

even when—especially when—all the evidence pointed in the opposite direction."

"You know what that makes you?"

"A recovering empiricist?"

"I could list a few more things," she said, standing and holding out her hand so she could pull me to my feet. Then we put Robbie's monument at our backs and followed Sullivan over to the hospital, where Markham determined Patrick's arm was just badly bruised. But he wanted to keep him there overnight for observation.

"Anyt'ing of yours you want to get X-rayed while you're here?" Markham asked me and Sullivan.

A desk sergeant Ross sent over from headquarters was there to record everybody's statements, helped along by Jackie's notes and testimony. I was glad to hear all the stories come out like I wanted them to.

After that they let me head back to the tip of Oak Point where I had a case of wine, a bottle of vodka and a dog waiting for me, along with a life filled with equal measures of hope, faith and exasperation.

TWENTY-SEVEN

YOU'D THINK A FACE as big as Markham's would be easier
to read, especially when you're sitting just across a desk from
him. On top of the desk were open files and huge envelopes
out of which he slipped X-rays and other gray-scale images.
He had a phone up to his ear, held there with his shoulder so
he could use both hands to hold the images up to the light.

On the other end of the line was the neurologist who took
all the pictures. I don't know what his side of the conversation sounded like, but Markham wasn't saying anything that
made any sense to me at all. If it hadn't been for the occasional verb or preposition linking the technical terms, I'd
think he was speaking Greek.

I'd already sat through two other calls he'd made to spe-
cialists who'd also reviewed the data. None of that made any
sense to me either.

"Well, Mr. Ah-quillo," he said after ending the call and jot-
ting down a few notes in one of the files, "you got all dat, right?"

"Sure. Clear as a bell."

He gathered the stuff off the desk and led me over to a row of light boxes mounted to the wall, where he took me through a tour of my skull, moving from angle to angle, from MRI to X-ray and back again. He also used anatomical drawings, cutaways also rendered from several different angles. It was pretty interesting, and would have been more so if it hadn't been my brain at the center of the discussion.

When he finished the lecture he said, "Dis is usually when we ask the patient if he has anybody he can talk to about the situation."

"I actually do, believe it or not."

"Since dat's about all you can do, I suggest you do it the next chance you get. Don't go keepin' dis to yourself."

"That's the plan. Honest, Doc. What do I owe you?"

He put out his giant paw to shake hands.

"My new bookcase is already filled up," he said. "Got space for another just like it."

It was hardly a fair trade, but that's what he wanted to do and I couldn't talk him out of it. I got him to agree to tell me if he ever needed help with anything. He shook my hand again and strode away, heading back to his trauma ward, eager to sort through other matters of life and death.

I called Amanda from the nurses' station and told her to meet me at Hodges's boat where it was docked at Hawks Pond. I'd asked him the day before if he'd loan it to me for the afternoon. I knew I'd have something to talk to Amanda about and wanted to be somewhere other than Oak Point. The occasion called for a different setting, equally sublime, but distinctive.

She arrived as I finished preparing to launch, dock lines untied, engine warming up, fenders stowed. She wore a broad-rimmed straw hat, yellow shorts, white top and high-heeled sandals like any sailor would. The beach basket in her hand was filled with wine and tasty things wrapped in tissue and foil.

We followed the channel markers across the pond and then out into the Little Peconic. The breeze was out of the southwest, where it would mostly stay until late August. It warmed the air and rustled the trees, and provided just enough gusto to move Hodges's heavy cruiser at a stately pace. I was glad for that, not wanting to wrestle with anything more challenging than a corkscrew.

Amanda leaned back against the coaming and dabbed suntan lotion on her face and knees and gave me an update on her projects. We debated over which property to tackle next, deciding on a house between the current rehabs on Jacob's Neck with a lease about to run out.

I had a fresh backlog of architectural details to make for Frank—gates, benches, built-ins and custom trim that would keep me busy in my shop well into the summer.

After clearing the last set of buoys, I pulled the ties off the mainsail and clipped the halyard to the head of the sail. Then I had Amanda hold us in the wind so I could raise it up the mast.

"Not as easy to steer as the Audi," she said.

We managed it anyway, and I took the wheel from her, killed the engine and we heeled to starboard as I let the wind grip the sail and shove us back toward the north. Once the jib was out, we were fully underway at a gentle five knots. There were a few open fishing boats bobbing around the buoys, but otherwise we had the bay to ourselves.

"I spent the morning with Markham Fairchild," I told her once we were comfortably settled into a stable port tack.

"Really."

"I already gave him his bookcase, so he had to give me all the test results."

"What did he say?"

"He said he had just the right spot for the bookcase and ordered another one."

"If you aren't going to tell me you shouldn't bring it up."

"I want to tell you. That's why I wanted to get out on the water today. To talk about it."

She looked ready to do that, but I suggested we wait for wine and cheese, having missed breakfast. She busied herself with that while I flicked on the ancient Autohelm and set a course we could hold for at least an hour.

"Okay," she said after we clinked glasses. "Spill it."

"Markham got the MRIs from when I got slugged by Buddy Florin back from the Town evidence room. Then he had me do it again, and took another set of X-rays. They also ran a bunch of blood and urine tests to compare with others in the past, including what I gave them the day after conking out in the shower."

She tensed.

"You're leading up to something."

"I am."

She set her wine glass on the cockpit table and sat back, folding her hands in her lap.

"Before you say anything," she said, "I want you to know that I'll be there for you no matter what. I know I haven't always been. I've sent you all kinds of foolish mixed messages. I think I'm over that. I think you're over doing the same thing to me. I've been through too much with you now to have it any other way. So whatever's ahead, I'm seeing you through it whether you like it or not."

"That's fine with me, as long as you skip the cosmopolitans."

"Sorry?"

"Yeah, keep your poisonous concoctions to yourself."

I stood up and leaned over her with as much grace as the sea motion of the boat would allow and kissed her forehead.

"Now I'm confused," she said.

"My mother told me I was allergic to eggs when I was a little kid, but I grew out of it. As far as I know she never fed me pomegranate."

Amanda put her hand over her mouth.

"Oh my God."

"Markham said my blood was still chock-full of histamines and leukotrienes the day after I passed out. So they ran allergen screens, including one for the component parts of pomegranate, which I told them I had the night before. Markham said it was pretty rare, but something in me really hates pomegranates. Enough to bring on anaphylactic shock. He said, 'Don be t'inkin' dis is all good news. Anaphylaxis do in more people every year den lightnin'.'"

"What about the MRIs? What did they say?"

"He still thinks I should give up my boxing career, which I already have. But he said the latest stuff looked pretty good, that the neurologist saw little lasting damage from the last concussion. Doesn't mean some evil crap couldn't sneak up on me over time, but right now, all clear."

She got up this time and wedged herself next to me behind the helm. She put her arms around my middle and her head on my shoulder and stayed like that for a long time as we reached across the Little Peconic Bay, holding hard to the prospect of peace and serenity that the sacred waters promised to bestow.

ACKNOWLEDGMENTS

Thanks again to Mary Jack Wald, my literary agent and guardian angel, and to Martin and Judy Shepard of the Permanent Press.

Special thanks to John Acquino of Southampton for the lesson in deconstructionism.

Other special thanks to Norman Bloch of Thompson Hine for his tour of the New York criminal justice system, and his colleague Rich Orr for making that possible.

For medical advice, my sincere thanks to the Docatola of Rock and Rolla, Peter King, MD. And for that connection, Dave Newell, native guide of the Vermont countryside.

Any inaccuracies or hanky-panky with facts supplied are mine alone.

For editorial wisdom and syntactical tough love, my thanks to Anne Collins of Random House Canada.

On the visual side of the house, thanks to Patrick Kiniry for cover artistry, and Dan Lorenz of Lithographics for pre-pro generosity, and Susan Alhquist for tireless devotion to production quality.

As always, deepest thanks to valued readers and advisers—in particular, Randy Costello, Sean Cronin and Mary Farrell. And Anne-Marie Regish, who keeps the whole machine running in the midst of startling chaos.